- The Children's Eye Unit at Moorfields Eye Hospital, London
- The Ulverscroft Children's Eye Unit at Great Ormond Street Hospital for Sick Children
- Funding research into eye diseases and treatment at the Department of Ophthalmology, University of Leicester
- The Ulverscroft Vision Research Group, Institute of Child Health
- Twin operating theatres at the Western Ophthalmic Hospital, London
- The Chair of Ophthalmology at the Royal Australian College of Ophthalmologists

You can help further the work of the Foundation by making a donation or leaving a legacy. Every contribution is gratefully received. If you would like to help support the Foundation or require further information, please contact:

THE ULVERSCROFT FOUNDATION
The Green, Bradgate Road, Anstey
Leicester LE7 7FU, England
Tel: (0116) 236 4325

website: www.ulverscroft-foundation.org.uk

ROSELAND

The summers spent at Roseland, the sprawling ancestral home of her best friend, Eloise, were among the happiest of Cathy's life. Tucked away on the Cornish coastline and brimming with history, Roseland seemed to belong to another century.

Cathy has barely been back since Eloise's death a decade ago. So she is shocked when Jack, the love of Eloise's life and father of her children, announces that he is getting married, and that the wedding will take place at Roseland.

As Cathy and Eloise's family gather at the house for the first time in years, long buried secrets and resentments come to the surface. Nobody likes Jack's new bride, but is she really the imposter everybody claims, or are they haunted by memories of Eloise? And how can Cathy look to the future, when the past refuses to let go?

JUDY FINNIGAN

ROSELAND

Complete and Unabridged

CHARNWOOD
Leicester

First published in Great Britain in 2023 by
Sphere
an imprint of Little, Brown Book Group
London

First Charnwood Edition
published 2024
by arrangement with
Little, Brown Book Group
London

All characters and events in this publication,
other than those clearly in the public domain,
are fictitious and any resemblance to real persons,
living or dead, is purely coincidental.

*A catalogue record for this book is available
from the British Library.*

ISBN 978–1–4448–5248–6

For Richard
And my gorgeous grandchildren:
Ivy, Edith, Kit and Bobo.
And for the others already on the way!
God bless.

Prologue

A blistering sun hung low over the horizon, gilding Roseland's castle-like façade with a deceptive warmth. Built by the early forebears of the Trelawney dynasty, the Jacobean manor had imperiously dominated the surrounding acres of lush farmland for centuries, its dark leaded windows seeming to keep a commanding, somewhat supercilious watch over the valley of the River Fowey. It was magnificent; some might say intimidating. Today, though, it was dressed to impress . . . to *beguile*.

Trees were laced with colourful fairy lights, and the long, undulating gravel drive was edged with storm lanterns, luring visitors towards the grand entrance. The flanking porticoes were strung with yet more lights, like a jewelled necklace worn to soften the contours of an austere face. The nearby lake, silvered by spotlights, caught its glittering reflection. For even on the brink of destruction, Roseland dazzled.

It would have been easy to miss the crow, spiralling silently above one of Roseland's many protruding chimney tops. Its ragged wings barely moved, only the tips of its dark feathers rippling on a light breeze now. It picked up as the sky darkened, clouds as grey as the granite walls of Roseland starting to swirl upwards, billowing higher.

For a moment, it seemed the wedding party was taking place, after all. Roseland's windows sparkled with light, while raised voices drifted across the rose garden, accompanied by loud pops and the tinkle of glass, as though the bride and groom had just arrived triumphantly in the great hall. Except there was no champagne; no toasts, either to the prodigal groom, or his imposter bride.

There was only the infinitesimal fracture of brittle glass, as flames took hold in earnest and the temperature inside the manor house soared, the ancient bones of Roseland straining to breaking point. Hairline cracks quickly began to spread, until at last the stained-glass panes exploded outwards in a cloudburst of gem-like shards.

The house seemed to let out a sigh of surrender, thick smoke surging out of every blackened crevasse, leaving gaping holes like rotten cavities in a once-luminous smile. Far above it, the crow continued circling.

1

One week before

A vintage black cab chugged up the steep lane from the beach towards the church, gears grinding as it stopped in a lay-by tucked against the clifftop opposite the lychgate. Its sole passenger emerged equally slowly. A willowy, genteel-looking woman dressed in a flowing grey silk dress, her silver hair swept up in an elegant chignon, she seemed to belong to another age. Indeed, suffused in shimmering sunlight that turned her papery skin translucent, she appeared almost ghostlike: an ancient Trelawney apparition.

Then she moved, unexpectedly brisk and decisive, instructing the taxi driver to wait for her, before she hurried across the empty road, a bouquet of roses clutched in her arms. Another pause as she contemplated the way ahead: narrow steps leading from the pretty gateway up a stony hill to Talland Church. The woman sighed, lifted her chin and set off.

As she reached the Celtic chapel, the land flattened slightly, offering a reprieve. But Juliana Trelawney's destination lay some thirty metres beyond, up a twisting, overgrown path bordered by ancient tombstones. No balustrade to help her had survived up here, and her frail body bent almost double as she battled against the keen salt breeze.

Finally, she reached the very top of the hill to find the elegant headstone that seemed to be waiting for her, its honey-coloured stone illumined not by sunshine, she thought fancifully, but by joy at her arrival. Sinking down onto the bench nearby, her fingers trembled as they traced the familiar inscription on its back. Her breath came slowly, her heart racing after the arduous climb. It got harder each time, but she would never forgo it.

For ten years, Juliana had made this weekly pilgrimage. She didn't know how many more would be granted to her, and each one was precious. Placing the roses beside her, she gazed at the breathtaking view. Endless sea glinted silver and gold in the sunlight, blending seamlessly with the summer sky to create a vaulted, cathedral-like dome over the bay.

After a few moments, she stooped to kneel by the grave, removing her last bouquet from a crystal urn and replacing it with the fresh roses she'd brought — white, always, whatever the season. For her daughter's birthdays, she brought armfuls of pink peonies, but she was always glad to revert to the purity of white. Pink seemed too jolly, as if the birthday were a celebration, when in fact there was only sadness and regret. Guilt that never eased.

As she fussed with the stems, Juliana murmured: 'Such a gorgeous day, Eloise. The beach is absolutely crawling with children, all having a wonderful time. Do you remember when we used to take the twins down there? Of course you do. Paddling and sandcastles. The girls never wanted to go home. *Five more minutes*, they always begged. They loved the beach so. I wonder if Isabella did, too, when she was a little girl. I expect so, don't you?'

Roses arranged to her satisfaction, Juliana grabbed the arm of the bench and pulled herself slowly to her feet. 'I have to go now. But I'll be back next week. Rest, my dear. You're safe. Your girls are safe.' Her throat felt choked with emotion. 'Sleep tight, darling.'

She hesitated a moment longer, before walking away. When she reached the church, she paused, wondering if she should go inside. But no. She preferred to save her prayers for Eloise's graveside. Besides, she disliked the sympathy of well-meaning locals, their chirpy good wishes barely masking their curiosity. *Nosy parkers*, she always thought.

Determined to avoid any chance encounters, Juliana gripped the handrail tighter and attempted to hurry down the remaining treacherous steps.

'Here. Let me help you. Take my hand.'

The voice was familiar, and yet not. Warily, Juliana eyed the tall, blond-haired, middled-aged stranger waiting beneath the lychgate, one hand confidently outstretched. He was smiling, his manner informal, as though he knew her. Usually, villagers approached her with cautious deference. She trawled her memory until recognition clicked into place. 'Oh. Jack Merchant.'

'Hello, Juliana.' His blue eyes crinkled at the corners; he looked pleased to see her.

'What are you doing here?' Frustration with herself for being slow to recognise him made her terse and irritable. She felt at a disadvantage, and she hated that.

'I've come to see you, of course.' He captured her hand, his grasp strong but gentle.

'Not Eloise?' Juliana tugged her hand away.

A furrow between his straight, thick brows. 'Not today. But I guessed I might find you here. I have something for you.' He reached into the breast pocket of his navy linen jacket, then held out a square white envelope. 'There you go. Hand delivered, as promised.'

'What's that?' Juliana eyed it suspiciously. Letters rarely signified anything good.

'An invitation. To my wedding.' Jack squinted, registering her confusion. 'I brought my fiancée to see you, the other day, remember? The three of us had tea and talked about it.'

'Talked about what?'

'The wedding,' Jack repeated patiently. 'I'm getting married, Juliana. In a week's time.' He nodded, urging her to take the envelope. 'At Roseland.'

Juliana gasped, seizing the envelope and crumpling it between her frail hands, before tossing it to the ground. Dignity prevented her from stamping on it, but she would have liked to. 'No. Never. I won't allow it.'

Brushing past the man who had been her daughter's first, great love, and was the father of Eloise's three daughters — therefore maintaining an irritating, unwelcome connection with Juliana's family — she headed for the taxi waiting dutifully on the other side of the road.

Jack followed. 'Juliana, please. Let's talk.' He knew she couldn't stop him getting married at Roseland; he'd already sought and been granted permission by the National Trust, who had managed it since Juliana signed the Grade 1 listed money pit over to them after the death of her husband, Sir Charles. But while Jack didn't need Juliana's permission, he still hoped for her blessing.

'Don't you have patients to see? Cancer waits for no man. Or woman,' Juliana said hoarsely. 'Or have you forgotten that, along with my daughter?'

Jack bit back the response that rose to his lips. He still mourned Eloise's death from breast cancer ten years ago, frequently wondering if, as an oncologist, he might have done more to help her, had he not been in Australia at the time — banished there by Juliana's own husband. 'I've taken a day off to play postman,' he quipped lightly.

Juliana glared at him, deliberately stepping on the crumpled envelope as she stalked towards the taxi, allowing the driver to help her into the back. 'Thank you, Bob.' He nodded, returning to his own seat as she waved away his offer to shut the door. 'Goodbye, Jack.'

'Juliana . . .'

'There will be no wedding at Roseland. I might not live there, but I'm still its mistress. It belongs to me, and it always will.'

Tactfully deciding not to correct her, Jack said quietly: 'No one wants to take Roseland from you. As I believe I told you the other day. But your granddaughters —'

'Shall inherit everything, in the fullness of time. I may be eighty-five, but I'm not dead yet.' Juliana nodded at the driver, watching her now in his rear-view mirror. 'We're done here, Bob. Home, please.' A sideways glance at Jack. 'To Roseland.'

Bob fired the ignition. 'Of course, Lady Trelawney.'

'Isabella's coming.' It wasn't a lie, exactly. His eldest daughter — Juliana's first granddaughter — hadn't yet *declined* the invitation. As Juliana reached for the car door, Jack flicked out a hand to rest on it. 'Izzy will be at Roseland for the wedding,' he said coaxingly.

Juliana hid her rush of hope beneath a haughty

frown. 'I don't believe you. Izzy . . . Isabella hates me. She would never come here. And you should never have come back to Cornwall, either. My husband told you. *Leave our daughter alone.* Charles warned you what would happen otherwise. Now I am. *Stay away from her.*'

Jack sighed, once again recognising that Juliana was confused, her fragile mind slipping back through the decades to when Eloise and her father were both still alive — to when Sir Charles had banished fifteen-year-old Jack and his parents from the Roseland estate, after the scandal of his thirteen-year-old daughter falling pregnant.

'But Eloise is . . .' Jack hesitated, reluctant to remind the old lady of her grief. There were times when memory loss could be a comfort, he thought. He saw it in his patients; occasionally, he wished it upon himself.

'My only child! And I won't have her hurt any more.' Lurching to grab the door handle, Juliana almost tumbled out of the taxi. 'Go against my wishes at your peril, Jack Merchant,' she said crossly, frustrated again by her own frailty, and striving to mask it.

Jack frowned, finally closing the door and taking a step back. Immediately, Bob set off, eyes fixed dutifully on the road, while his mind whirled with this fresh gossip about Roseland. On mental autopilot, he drove down the lane past the busy little beach; he'd chauffeured Juliana many times and knew she loved to watch the children playing there.

Bob knew all about the tragic, premature death of Juliana's daughter; he'd also heard rumours about the adoption of her illegitimate first grandchild, four decades ago. Not that he would dare mention either event, nor relay local rumours about her two other, much younger granddaughters' brush with death ten years ago, when the twins were just five years old. Bob had a family to support; he valued his job too much to risk crossing a Trelawney, no matter how kindly Juliana appeared, and however charitable she always was to any locals in need.

As her driver discreetly digested Jack's news about the wedding, Juliana sat fuming about it. To calm herself, she let her eyes feast as usual on families enjoying a morning at the beach. Cornwall's coastline was blessed with many spectacular coves and bays, some rocky, others with miles of golden sand stretching as far as the eye could see. But always there were children, reminding Juliana of everything she had lost . . . and what she needed to protect.

'Jack Merchant getting married. At his age. Foolish man. But if he thinks he can hold his absurd wedding at my family home, where I raised my daughter, the woman he never saw fit to make a bride . . .' She thumped the seat beside her. 'Roseland shall welcome no other.'

It was only as the taxi finally turned into the grounds of the seventeenth-century manor house, bypassing sweeping lawns and lush botanical shrubberies to arrive at Juliana's beloved rose garden by the lake, at which point it veered off the main drive towards the farmhouse where she now lived, that Juliana realised she hadn't asked Jack who it was that he planned to marry.

He'd claimed the three of them had had tea together, but no such meeting had ever taken place. *Or had it?* Her mind had been playing tricks on her lately.

For weeks now, time had seemed to expand and contract without warning, flexing and tightening like a concertina. Whole days could pass in a flash, and then a single moment would feel like it lasted for weeks. *Years*. Sometimes, Juliana saw everything as clearly as the pretty scallop shells wedged into the sand beneath the crystal-clear water at Talland Bay. Other times, she'd walk into a room and forget how she came to be there, or why.

'If I'd met her, I would surely remember her. At the very least, I would know her name.' Juliana closed her eyes, concentrating hard. 'The invitation!'

Reaching for the pocket of her coat, she groaned, remembering that she wasn't wearing one. It was summer; she had on her best dress. The grey silk one, with the little covered buttons all the way up the back. Margaret had laid it out for her especially, this morning, as she always did before Juliana visited her daughter's grave.

'Darling Ellie. No bride could hold a candle to you.' Juliana closed her eyes again, picturing her beautiful face. 'Whoever this woman is, there's only one way she'll ever get married at Roseland. Over my dead body.'

2

Ten thousand miles away in Australia, Isabella sat on the veranda of her therapist's Byron Bay home overlooking Wategos Beach, gazing at a very different sea to the one that had entranced her estranged grandmother. No rock pools or playful children with fishing nets here. Surfers dotted the ocean, and the Pacific heaved and swelled, rather like Izzy's turbulent mood. She stared at it, then hooked her phone out of the pocket of her frayed denim shorts.

Usually, devices were banned from therapy sessions, but Sue flexed the boundaries for her most fragile and, secretly, her favourite client. She'd known Izzy for ten years, initially alongside her ex-husband when they came for couples counselling. Then, after the death of her biological mother, Eloise — and the bombshell revelations that followed — Izzy had come alone. The discovery that she'd been living a lie had left her with acute trust issues. Sue recognised her client's heightened need to feel in control at all times. She allowed the phone.

'Fuck.' Izzy uncrossed her slim, tanned legs and sat forward on the edge of her chair.

'Izzy? Are you OK? You've gone quite pale.'

'Yes. No. Actually, I don't know.' She continued to stare at her phone. 'It's . . .'

'Have you heard from Arthur?' Sue took a stab at what Izzy might be reading so intently; she'd spent many sessions agonising over her regrets and failings as a parent.

Izzy's mouth twisted ruefully. 'As if.'

'So what *is* it? I mean . . . Sorry,' she apologised, feeling flustered. She was letting her boundaries slip; blurring the line between counsellor and friend. 'Has something —'

'He's getting married,' Izzy cut in, her face flushing now. 'Next Friday, for God's sake.'

'Who? Arthur?' Mentally, Sue kicked herself. *She'd done it again*. But Izzy was such a complex, interesting client; she was fascinated by her eventful life story. 'You've mentioned before that your son has a girlfriend, but . . . Oh. Did you mean your ex?'

'No. I meant *Jack*. My . . . dad.' Izzy almost choked on the word. Having grown up being told that Jack was her big brother, not her father, calling him 'Dad' still felt wrong, even after ten years; even more so given that, at fifty-seven, he was only fifteen years her senior.

She scowled, fighting pain and anger that never seemed to ease: of missing a mum she hadn't even known existed, until she died. Her grandmother Juliana had seen to that; she'd cast Izzy out as a baby, leaving Jack's parents to raise her as their 'daughter' — conveniently, on the other side of the world, where Izzy couldn't discover her family's lies.

Sue kept her tone deliberately neutral. 'You sound angry. Is a wedding a bad thing?'

An impatient huff. 'I couldn't care less about it. Jack's had one wife already. I'm sure he's got his reasons for walking up the aisle again. I'm just cross he imagines I'd want to be there to watch. I mean, for God's sake, he expects me to fly halfway around the world at a week's notice. To chuck confetti over a woman I've never met. Never even *heard* of.'

'A week is certainly short notice.' Sue just about managed not to wince.

'Must be a shotgun affair. History repeating itself, right? Only, this time, Jack's decided to bite the bullet and actually marry the woman he's got pregnant.'

Sue allowed a few moments' silence, letting Izzy's hurt and anger fill it. 'Izzy,' she said gently at last, 'I remember you telling me your mum was thirteen when she had you. And Jack was fifteen. Look, I'm not defending your family's decision to conceal your adoption, but —'

'Good.' Izzy raised her eyebrows.

'*But,*' Sue continued carefully, 'I imagine they felt Eloise was too young to be a mother. Likewise, Jack a father. Or a husband. They were both underage, for one thing.'

'He didn't have to turn his back on her, though, did he? Bugger off to Australia and act like she didn't exist.'

'He was ordered to leave, as I also recall you telling me. And he took you with him.'

'His parents did, you mean.' Izzy scowled. They'd had this conversation many times, and she knew Sue was trying to help her cut through her anger to appreciate the facts of the situation. But finding out that she was adopted, and that the couple she'd always called Mum and Dad were actually her paternal grandparents, had been the biggest trauma in her life.

It had been a triple blow: Izzy had grieved for a mother she'd never known, but it had also felt like she'd lost her adoptive parents. They'd kept the truth from her, and now they were dead, too. Juliana Trelawney had plotted the betrayal, but Izzy's entire family had maintained it. She despised her grandmother Juliana, but she also couldn't forgive Jack.

'Jeez, is it any wonder I've been in therapy for a decade?' She dashed away a tear. 'My family is a joke, and this wedding will be a circus.'

'Will you go?' Sue asked softly.

'The hell I will! In fact, hell will freeze over before I ever set foot in Cornwall again.'

'Will Arthur?' Sue knew how badly it still hurt Izzy that her then sixteen-year-old son had decided to remain permanently in the UK, following his solo visit to Cornwall after his grandmother Eloise's death — prompted by the solicitor's letter about his inheritance . . . the letter that had first exposed Izzy's secret adoption.

'I guess so. Arthur lives in London now, but he's still very close to his grandpa. I suppose Jack's been more like a father to him.' Izzy paused, and Sue could see what it cost her to admit that. She glared at her phone again. 'In fact, according to this invitation, Artie's the best man. There's no mention of bridesmaids, but I expect the twins . . . Rose and Violet.'

Picturing their faces, Izzy chewed a strand of her long tawny hair, as ever feeling guilty at how she'd severed all contact with the girls, now teenagers. During her own brief visit to Cornwall ten years ago, Izzy had at first been thrilled to discover that she had younger sisters. But the situation was complicated, and she'd quickly withdrawn, returning to Australia and restricting contact mainly to Christmas and birthdays.

Jack himself had only just found out that the twins were his daughters, conceived during one final chance meeting with Eloise six years before. He'd been recently divorced at the time, but Eloise was married to someone else by then. She'd kept her pregnancy a secret from Jack — as she did her cancer diagnosis, six months after the twins were born.

But Izzy had no sympathy for Jack. During that visit, she'd seen his determination to be a good dad to Rose and Violet, then five years old, and she'd backed off from them all. Now, ten years later, she wondered if she'd been jealous of the twins being able to grow up knowing Jack was their real dad. She still loved her sisters, and she adored her son, but bitterness at the hand her family had dealt her remained a brick wall between them.

Sue watched the conflicting emotions flitting across Izzy's pretty, heart-shaped face. 'I know it's tough, being so far from home. Half your family on the other side of the world.'

Izzy shook her head. 'Home is *here*. In Australia. Not some crumbling old stately pile in deepest, darkest England. It has been my whole life. Apart from the first three months.' She frowned. 'And only half my family are there, anyway.'

'The Trelawney half.'

'Precisely.' She stared at her phone again. 'This wedding invitation . . . It feels more like a summons. To Cornwall. *Roseland.* I mean, for God's sake, that's where . . .'

'You were adopted as a baby,' Sue finished softly for her, as Izzy's voice dried.

'Juliana saw to that. I was the dirty little secret she wanted rid of, wasn't I? Now Jack expects me to go back there and play happy families. But I can't do it, Sue. I can't rock up at the family mansion and act like there aren't still more damned skeletons in the

Trelawney closet.'

'Skeletons?' A sudden breeze drifted off the water. It lifted Sue's short brown hair, and the back of her neck prickled with a growing sense that Izzy was hiding something big. 'And you're really not tempted to go back there? To dig up these . . . skeletons?'

'Oh, I'll go. Maybe not to the wedding, but certainly to Roseland.'

'Right. I see.' This time, Sue couldn't hide her surprise. She was used to her client's volatility, but this was a huge, sudden turnaround. 'May I ask what's changed your mind?'

'You may ask.' Izzy winced, knowing she sounded childish. She genuinely wasn't playing games; she'd had her belly-full of those with her ex-husband. Mostly, she confided freely in Sue, but there was one thing she wasn't ready to talk about: her secret mission. Her conviction that there were more scandals festering in the Trelawney family — and her determination to uncover them.

The email that had arrived late last night had been almost as big a shock as her dad's wedding invitation just now. After waiting weeks for a response from the ancestry-tracing website she'd registered with online, Izzy had practically forgotten about it. Now she couldn't get it out of her head. *A genetic match had been found!*

She had only registered with the website, and purchased their DNA test, as a late-night impulse after a particularly strained phone call with Arthur a few weeks ago. In the decade since the truth about Izzy's parentage had come to light, she'd felt lost, abandoned. But she also longed for connection. It had been a fleeting moment of curiosity, to know whether there were any other scandalous secrets in the Trelawney family tree.

And now, here was something. It had been a brief, sparse notification, with no further details beyond official confirmation that a 'significantly strong' DNA match with another applicant on their database had been determined.

As far as Izzy knew, her parents had both been only children, so this was a surprising and intriguing discovery. Being vague and anonymous — due to data protection — it didn't give her much to go on, but whatever it was, it was a lead of sorts. Now Izzy had two birds to kill — her father's wedding, and her own secret mission — and one stone: a return to Roseland.

* * *

'OK. Well, we're almost out of time today,' Sue said, after Izzy had sat quietly for a few minutes, deeply immersed in her thoughts. She didn't need to check her watch; the lifeguard on the beach in front of her home changed shifts at exactly the same time each day. 'I guess, if you're going to Cornwall, I won't see you for a couple of weeks at least.'

'Curiosity,' Izzy said abruptly, deciding that she owed Sue some explanation, even if not the entire truth. 'That's what's changed my mind. Curiosity to see my dad again. Meet his bride.' *And my mystery DNA match*, she thought, feeling her stomach churn with a mixture of anger, nerves, fear — and something she thought she'd long since given up on: hope.

Finally, Sue allowed herself a smile. 'Sounds like a good enough reason to me.'

'Oh, and karma. What goes around comes around,

yeah?' Izzy tucked her phone back into her pocket, and reached for her glass of water. She ended every therapy session the same way, as though to wash away the words that always left a bad taste in her mouth.

'You believe in fate, then? Or do we each forge our own destiny? Nature or nurture?'

'Both.' Izzy folded her arms, looking ready for battle now. 'My family screwed up my start in life. They set me on a path of *their* choosing. Now I'm taking back the wheel. I'm setting my own course, and I'm steering it right at them. It's payback time.'

Sue didn't usually offer her clients advice; it went against her ethical practice to interfere or try to influence decisions. But she'd come to care for this troubled woman; she couldn't let her leave without offering a note of caution.

'Izzy,' she said gently, staring into her fierce blue eyes. 'Do you know the truest thing I've heard said to anyone plotting revenge?'

Izzy huffed. She disliked being asked questions when she didn't know the answer. It made her feel at a disadvantage, and she hated that. 'Something about those in glass houses not throwing stones?'

Sue sighed. 'First dig two graves.'

3

Eve crawled into bed, still damp after her shower and with only a soft navy towel wrapped around her slim body, shoulder-length ash-blonde hair caught up in a loose ponytail. Yanking up the duvet, she groaned as she snuggled down, needing five more minutes before she had to get up and go find something quick and easy to throw together for dinner.

It had been a long, frenetic day at work, and she was starving — but too worn out to cook. She'd been feeling so tired lately. Bone-achingly so. Becoming an assistant producer on a breakfast TV show had been her dream job for as long as she could remember, but it was exhausting. Thank God it was almost the weekend. Just Friday to endure, then she could relax.

The heat didn't help; London was gritty and stifling in the summer. Eve longed to get out of the city; she also yearned for an iced latte with a double shot of caffeine for extra energy. The trouble was, she was too tired to get dressed and go back out to their local coffee shop.

'Hey, lazybones.' Her boyfriend appeared in the doorway. 'You look comfy.'

'I am. Come join me. Or better still, bring me a coffee. Extra espresso. Lots of ice.'

'Bossy boots,' Arthur teased. 'Good job I like strong women. Speaking of which, I have news. Two pieces, in fact.' He sauntered across the room, perching on the end of the bed.

Eve eyed him sleepily. 'Please tell me your witch of a boss has finally resigned. About time, too. She's stolen the credit for your last six features.'

'Oh, she's not that bad. I've actually learned a lot from her.'

'You're way too soft for your own good, Artie. Anyway, if not that, what?'

'It's Pops, actually. He called while you were in the shower.' Arthur rolled onto the bed now, stretching out next to Eve with a sigh. 'We had quite a chat. You were in there ages.'

Eve cuddled against him. 'I was waiting for you to come and soap my back.'

'Like I said, bossy boots.' Arthur chuckled, tickling her ribs.

Eve laughed too, then shoved his hand away. 'Don't make me laugh. I'm so tired, it hurts. Anyway, what were you going to say about your grandpa? Is Jack OK?'

'More than OK, as a matter of fact. He's getting married.'

'He's *what*?' Eve sat up, wide awake now. 'You're kidding.' She knew Arthur loved a good prank; he never took life, or himself, too seriously. He also never lied or played games, having spent his childhood watching his parents score points off each other and vowing never to do the same. Eve knew this, but he had to be joking about Jack.

'I kid you not. The invitation's in the post, Pops said. Only he wanted to call me first. Tell me in person, as it were. So it didn't come as such a shock, I guess.'

'Well, *that* worked. Not.' Eve rolled her eyes. 'But Jack's been single for ever. All he does these days is hang out with the twins. He's devoted to them.'

'And his work,' Arthur agreed affably, fiercely proud of his grandpa.

'Exactly. If anything, he's married to his job. In fact, come to think of it, I've never known Jack to have so much as a date. Now you're telling me he's getting *married*?'

'In a week's time.'

'No way! We only saw him a month or so ago. We stayed at his house, for God's sake. There's no way he could have snuck anyone in or out without us knowing. How can he possibly have met someone and proposed to them in the space of a few weeks?'

'I know. That's what I meant about strong women. Or woman, in this case. His fiancée can't wait, apparently. She has her heart set on being a June bride.' Arthur paused, looking thoughtful. 'And for the wedding to take place at Roseland.'

Eve shook her head. 'No way. Juliana will never allow that. You know she won't.'

'I do. Which brings me to my second piece of news. Pops has invited us down for the weekend. To meet his fiancée, I guess.' He paused again. 'And to, um, visit Gee-Gee.'

'You mean, he wants you to sweet-talk your poor old widowed great-grandmother into holding the wedding at Roseland against her wishes,' Eve said shrewdly. 'Very Machiavellian of him. He knows you have Juliana wrapped around your little finger.'

Arthur chuckled. 'She does have a soft spot for me, I can't deny it.'

The blush on his boyishly handsome face made Eve smile. 'Who can blame her? But even you will have your work cut out convincing Juliana to let Jack get married at Roseland. It's her home.'

'*Was* her home. The National Trust controls it now. Any member of the public can nose around it for the price of a cream tea. Legally, I'm not sure Juliana can *stop* Jack hiring it.'

'But she'll try. You know she will. She moved there as a new bride herself. That place has her heart. Jack must know that. He must realise he's in for a battle. Whoever he's marrying must seriously have him under her thumb for him to even risk upsetting Juliana.'

'Or he's madly in love and can deny her nothing. I know we're both cynical, hard-bitten media professionals.' Arthur winked. 'But true romance does exist, you know?'

'I'm not saying it doesn't,' Eve countered. 'It's just, Jack must really be head over heels to be getting married so fast. To someone you've never even met. I know he's your grandpa, but he's always been more like a dad to you. He talks *everything* over with you.'

'I know. To be fair, he did sound a bit sheepish about the whole thing.'

'I bet. He's, what, fifty-six? Fifty-seven? A bit old for acting on impulse. How did he even meet her? Please don't tell me on Tinder.'

Arthur shrugged. 'He didn't actually say. Could be she's a doctor, too, right? Maybe their eyes met across a crowded operating theatre.'

'Because surgical gowns are so attractive. Still, I guess he's good-looking. For his age.'

'He'll be flattered to hear it. And I won't dispute that he has good genes.' Arthur ran a hand through his thick blond hair, pretending to preen. 'Which I've obviously inherited.'

'You're gorgeous,' Eve agreed, blushing as he rolled closer to kiss her. After a few heated moments, she pulled away, leaning back on the pillow and letting out a long sigh. 'But can you believe your *grandpa* is getting married before you? Oh, the shame.'

'Oi! Is that a hint?' Arthur quirked one eyebrow. 'Only kidding. When I pop the question, I want it to be a surprise. Pops isn't the only one who knows how to sweep a woman off her feet, I'll have you know.'

'I hate surprises,' Eve said, but she kissed him again, and this time it was even longer before they broke apart. 'Right, we should get up. Cook. Eat. Tidy up. Pretend to be grown-ups. My mum's back tomorrow, remember? I haven't told her yet that you've moved in.'

Since graduating and starting her career in TV, Eve had lived in a converted studio at the end of her parents' garden. For the last two years, they'd been in Dubai, where her dad, an eminent psychiatrist, had been offered a golden career opportunity. Eve had been close to him as a little girl, but over the years they'd drifted apart. She spoke to her mum almost every day, though, and missed her badly. She couldn't wait to tell her that, despite her relationship with Arthur having been on and off, things were getting pretty serious with him now.

'What? You haven't *told* Cathy?' He leaped up and began hurriedly picking up his clothes, strewn all over the bedsit floor, and kicking trainers and newspapers under the bed.

'Don't panic, she won't be back till tomorrow lunchtime. Besides, she adores you. Your whole family. She'll be gobsmacked about Jack, too. Oh. I'm presuming he's invited her?'

'What?' Shoving dirty laundry into a cupboard, at the same time trying to prevent his colourful collection of surfboards tumbling out, Arthur glanced over his shoulder.

'To the wedding, Artie. Is my mum invited?'

'Ah. Pops didn't say. Or maybe he did. I was in shock. He asked me to be best man. It's a big responsibility.' He paused, staring at Eve, looking like a rabbit caught in headlights.

'What, arranging a stag night at the Talland Bay Hotel? It'll be just like every other weekend.' Eve laughed. 'Can you imagine what the locals will make of it? A wedding at Roseland. It'll be the biggest news in the village since . . .' She broke off, blushing.

'Since Ted tried to drown the twins ten years ago.'

Eve winced. 'Sorry, I didn't mean to put my foot in it.'

'You didn't.' Arthur shrugged. 'That's all ancient history. Dead and buried. Quite literally, in Ted's case.'

'It's not for Rose and Violet, though,' Eve said quietly.

'Oh?'

'Yeah. We text sometimes. Well, Vi messages, mostly. Just chat. Picking my brains about careers in TV. Anyway, apparently, Rosie is having bad dreams about it again.'

'I thought they were in Italy? Spending the summer at their friend's villa, lucky kids.'

'They are. But I don't think it's gone too well. Vi sounded anxious in her last text. She said Rosie's having panic attacks and night terrors again.'

Arthur squinted thoughtfully. 'They don't actually know what their stepdad tried to do, though, do they? Pops told me he's always been vague about it, to protect them.'

'I know. But they're fifteen now. They spend half their life online. Vi certainly does. God knows what she's seen on social media.'

'Well, they'll certainly never hear about all that from me. And everyone in the village adores them. No one would be tactless enough to mention what happened.'

'Not even when they're tipsy after a crate of champagne at the wedding reception?' Eve looked worried now. 'I presume Jack has at least told the twins he's getting married?'

Arthur wrinkled his nose. 'I forgot to check. I did ask about Mum, though.'

'Gosh, Izzy. Yes. Will she come, do you think?' Eve asked tentatively, knowing about the rift between them. Arthur rarely talked about it, but she knew it bothered him.

He shrugged. 'No idea. We haven't spoken properly in weeks. Months, even.'

'I bet she'll be curious, though. To meet Jack's mystery bride. I know I am.'

'Well, thankfully, you won't have long to wait. I said we'd get the train down straight after work tomorrow. That is OK with you, isn't it?' Arthur added anxiously, coming to sit next to her again. 'I wouldn't normally ask you to drop everything for me.'

'Is that right?' Teasingly, Eve waggled her towel, giving him a suggestive grin.

Blue eyes sparking, Arthur reached for her. 'On second thoughts, maybe we should just stay here all weekend. In bed.'

'What, and miss the inside scoop on the wedding of the year?' Eve poked him in the ribs. 'Not on your life.'

4

Cathy almost cheered with relief as she managed to hail a taxi straightaway at Heathrow Airport. It was frantically busy, and she was tired and jangled after the flight from Dubai. She smiled at the cab driver as he stowed her luggage, then climbed into the back seat, only relaxing as they set off and the familiar London landscape began to slide past the window.

It felt strange to be back, like she'd been on another planet rather than in a different country. Even more so because, this time, she wasn't returning to a busy family home. Her three children were all grown up now, with jobs and young families of their own. At least, Sam and Tom, her boys, were both married and settled in other parts of the country.

Eve was still living at home, although she seemed to spend most of her time at the office, working hard to establish her TV career. Her relationship with Arthur appeared to be going strong, maturing from the sweet intensity of a teen romance that began when Arthur first arrived in Cornwall, he and Eve both innocent but spirited sixteen-year-olds, to an adult partnership — with all the highs and lows that entailed. Cathy had lost count of the number of times her sunny but feisty and principled, highly independent daughter had called the whole thing off.

'*You* would never let a man's career come before your own, would you, darling?' she muttered, recalling her own dilemma about whether to accompany her husband to Dubai, when he'd taken the job there. She'd worried that she might be lonely; Chris was always busy appearing at conferences, or engrossed writing his books.

In the end, she'd decided to give it a shot, putting her own work as a freelance feature writer on hold for a couple of years. 'I tried my best,' she reassured herself, determined to stop feeling guilty about her decision to come home.

Closing her eyes, she pictured Chris's face after he'd dropped her off at Dubai International Airport. He'd embraced her warmly as they said their good-byes, but his manner had seemed preoccupied, and as Cathy watched him walk away, she saw him immediately take out his phone. She had never suspected him of infidelity; his only mistress was work. 'But I can't take second place to his job for the rest of my life,' she reminded herself.

Their marriage had always been a little choppy, but Cathy had still loved Chris enough to give Dubai a go, and it hadn't been so bad. Along with other expat wives, she'd busied herself setting up literary societies, organising talks and interviews with many bestselling authors. She was good at it, and, having long dreamed of writing a novel herself, she'd found it fun and interesting — only not enough to want to stay when Chris was offered another year's extension to his contract.

Telling him flatly that she was coming home, Cathy had been taken aback when Chris declared he was earning and learning too much to leave. Still, it hadn't seemed like the worst idea to have some time apart, and, confident that their marriage could survive a bit of distance, Cathy had stuck to her plan; as the cab pulled up outside her pretty pink-washed Edwardian terraced house in Chiswick twenty minutes later, she was very glad that she had.

'Home at last.' She sighed with pleasure as she closed the front door behind her. 'Damnit, what's all this?' Almost slipping on a pile of papers, she bent down to gather up what looked like a week's worth of post. 'Evie!' she called out. 'Are you here?'

It had been Cathy's idea for Eve to move into the studio at the end of their garden. Having survived its previous incarnations as a granny-annexe and teenage den for the boys, it had seemed wasted once they'd left home. When Eve returned from studying journalism at uni, struggling to afford London rents, the studio had offered the perfect solution on both sides: Eve retained her independence, but her parents could keep a watchful eye on her.

In fact, Cathy secretly hoped her daughter would never leave. She just wished she was a bit tidier and more organised. 'Some of these are *weeks* old,' she muttered, flicking through the stack of envelopes. Deciding the bills could wait, she wandered through to the kitchen and dumped them on the polished granite worktop, before checking the fridge. 'Please tell me you at least thought to get in some basics for me. Oh, Eve. When are you going to start acting like a grown-up?'

Rolling her eyes, Cathy surveyed the meagre supplies her scatty daughter had obviously picked up in a rush from the corner shop. Bread. Milk. A carton of chopped tomatoes; a slab of cheese. 'At least there's dried pasta in the cupboard. That's dinner sorted, I guess.' Then, spotting a bottle of Prosecco tucked at the back, a celebratory mood came over her. 'No, darn it. We'll crack open that bottle and get ourselves a takeaway.' Shutting the fridge, she was about to make her way upstairs to have a bath, when the landline phone rang.

'Mum! You're back!'

'Evie, darling. Yes, I'm home, thank goodness. Just this second walked in.'

'Sorry, I'll let you get sorted. I'm at work, anyway. About to go into yet another meeting. I've got to present this new feature idea I've been developing. Bad timing all round.'

'Actually, it's perfect timing. What do you fancy for dinner? I thought we might spoil ourselves with a takeaway. Catch up over a bottle of fizz.' A smile spread across Cathy's face at the thought. 'How's Arthur? What's the latest? Are you two on or off, right now?'

'Definitely on. In fact . . .' There was a pause, then: 'Look, I'd best go. I was just phoning to let you know I won't actually be home this evening. Artie and I are heading to Cornwall straight after work. Family crisis.'

Cathy squeezed the phone tighter. 'Crisis? What's happened? Is it Juliana?' Guiltily, she counted the months since she'd last been in touch with her late best friend's mum. Once, they'd been incredibly close; Cathy had practically grown up at Roseland. But after Eloise died, everyone's life had changed. 'Or the twins? Oh, Eve. Tell me, please.'

'Don't panic, they're all fine. It's actually Jack. He wants to talk to Artie. In person.'

'That sounds serious. Is Jack OK? Has something happened to him?'

'Sort of. I take it nothing's arrived for you in the

post, then?'

'Sorry?' Cathy crossed the kitchen to pick up the envelopes she'd stashed by the microwave. Wedging the phone under her chin, she flicked through them. 'Oh, this looks like Jack's writing.' Opening the envelope, her mouth fell open in shock. 'What the . . . ?'

'Exactly. Hmm, I guess he must have sent yours first. Ours hasn't arrived yet.'

'Jack's getting *married*? Who on earth to?' Scanning the small, square white card in her hands, Cathy was puzzled to see only Jack's name as the host scrawled beneath the date and details of the venue. 'Roseland. Oh my God. The wedding is going to be at *Roseland*?'

'Yep. A week today. In the great hall. With a family dress rehearsal the day before.'

'Wow.' Cathy paused, trying to digest this dramatic news. 'Sorry, darling, I know you're busy, but . . . Is it just me, or does this all seem rather rushed?' She peered closer at the scribbled card, then turned it over, wondering if Jack had written a personal note to her.

They'd been on the periphery of each other's lives since childhood — since Cathy's best friend Eloise secretly fell in love with the son of Roseland's estate manager, and one impulsive summer night resulted in accidental pregnancy . . . followed by Jack's banishment, and Eloise's heartache as she was forced to renounce him, and give up their baby.

Cathy had only got to know Jack properly ten years ago, when he'd returned to Cornwall after Eloise's death. Cathy had been grief-stricken at the loss of her best friend, and Jack's surprise and joy at discovering he was Rose and Violet's father was overshadowed first by grief for Eloise, then by terror when the twins almost drowned at Watchman's Cove.

Tragedy had forged a bond between Jack and Cathy, and even though she hadn't seen him in years, she cared deeply about his happiness, as much for the sake of her beloved lost friend, who had adored him. The twins, now fifteen, were also Cathy's god-daughters.

The thought brought on a rush of concern. 'Gosh. How do Rosie and Violet feel about this? They've had one disastrous step-parent. I hope their new stepmum will be less —'

'Murderous?' Eve cut in.

'Well, quite. So, who is she? Goodness, I knew things would have changed in London while I've been away, but not in Cornwall. Talland Bay has been the same for ever. I can't believe . . . This isn't some kind of joke, is it? A belated April Fool's prank?'

'That was my first reaction. But no. Jack's really getting married. Artie is his best man. The wedding will be at Roseland next Friday. Seriously, I wish they'd chosen somewhere less grand. I haven't a clue what to wear. Unless you happened to pick up any designer gear in Dubai that I can borrow? My wardrobe is empty.'

'Much like my fridge.'

A guilty chuckle. 'Sorry, Mum. Work has been insane. I've been too tired to shop.'

'It's fine. Like I said, I was thinking of getting a takeaway. Or . . .' Cathy looked around the kitchen, realising that with Eve away, there was nothing to keep her here. 'I could join you. Drive down to Cornwall tonight. We could even go clothes shopping together this weekend.'

'Really? Isn't the cottage all closed up? Artie and I

are staying at Jack's, by the way. He's meeting us off the train at Liskeard this evening.'

'That's no problem. I've got the keys. Somewhere.' Cathy opened a drawer and rifled through takeaway menus, wondering again when her daughter would learn to cook. 'The old Beetle is still in the garage. It's serviced and insured. I won't even need to unpack.'

'Are you sure? You've only just arrived home, Mum. You must be exhausted.'

'I'm fine, darling. And never too tired for Cornwall.' Cathy brushed away the thought of a long slog down the M4. 'I'll lock up here and drive straight down. Then I can see you tomorrow for breakfast. Or maybe brunch would be kinder to my jet lag.'

'Well, if you're really sure. That'd be fantastic. Then we can catch up at leisure.'

'Perfect. That's sorted, then. I can't wait to meet Jack's fiancée, too. What's she like?'

'No idea. I've never met her. Nor has Artie.'

Cathy practically dropped the phone in surprise. 'He . . . what?'

'I know. It's been a whirlwind courtship, apparently.'

'Which I imagine is causing quite a storm,' Cathy surmised.

'Put it this way, Juliana is spitting feathers. Hence Artie being summoned.'

'To smooth things over. Sure. Juliana has always doted on him. The twins, too. Family means everything to her. Gosh, I hope Jack knows what he's doing. I hope his fiancée is worth all this commotion. Well, I guess we'll find out soon enough. Tomorrow, hopefully.'

'Yes. In Cornwall. How long has it been since we

were all together there?'

'I don't know, but it feels like a lifetime.' Despite the heat of the day, goose bumps broke out on Cathy's skin as she stared down at the invitation again. A mixture of excitement, curiosity and nerves fizzed through her. 'I'll see you there, darling. I can't wait.'

5

Much later that evening, Cathy coaxed her old VW Beetle up the steep, quiet lane leading out of Talland Bay towards her family's long-time holiday home, and drove straight into an enormous pothole. 'Oh, for God's sake!'

Climbing out to take a closer look, she groaned. 'Where the hell has *that* come from?' Sighing, she remembered that she hadn't seen the place for a year now, and that had only been for a flying visit to escape the furnace-like Middle Eastern summer.

Winters in Cornwall could be lacerating, and even a summer storm could produce fierce gales that tore down trees, blew tiles off roofs and caused havoc in the most well-tended gardens, which Cathy's certainly wasn't.

When the decision had been made that they were going to Dubai, she'd wanted to appoint a property management firm, but Chris had said it was a ridiculous expense. He'd said the same about her suggestion that they hire a regular gardener, she recalled.

'Well, look at it now, Chris.' Not only would the pothole she'd just driven into require major repair, their pretty garden was badly overgrown. Cathy was dreading what state she'd find the house itself in.

Leaving the car, she picked her way anxiously towards it, battling rampant foliage. Her irritation vanished as she crested the familiar rise. 'Ah, there you are.' Nestled in a sheltered hollow was the quirky, once tumbledown cottage she'd spent weeks convincing her husband they should buy when the children were tiny — and then wholeheartedly resisted when he'd urged her to sell it ten years ago.

'Best decision I ever made, keeping this place,' Cathy declared, making her way down the steep, slippery steps towards the bright blue front door of the cottage she'd lovingly transformed over the years into a story-book hideaway. With its crooked roof and chimney, slate-roofed log store huddled at its side, and a profusion of clematis and fragrant wild roses winding around each window, it did indeed look like something out of a fairy tale. On the inside, though, Cathy had refurbished it into a comfortable home with all the mod cons.

Growing up, her children had spent most holidays here, and as Cathy opened the front door and walked inside, turning on lamps as she went, pictures of them rose up in her mind. She could almost see a sandy trail of child-sized footprints across the wood floor. 'Oh, enough of the nostalgia.' She brushed away a rogue tear. 'They're grown-ups with their own kiddies now. This is *your* time.'

A quick tour of the ground floor reassured her that everything was fine, if a little dusty, and she busied herself tidying and unpacking the groceries she'd brought from home. Cornwall was in the grip of a heatwave, and even at this hour of the day, it was stifling. *Please let there be wine*, Cathy thought.

After pouring herself a glass from the fridge, she opened the French doors at the back of the cottage and breathed deeply, inhaling the sweet scent of dusk and lavender from the terraced garden. Staring up at the rugged clifftop beyond, her eyes were drawn to the Celtic church silhouetted against the indigo sky.

She wondered if it was too late to take a stroll up there, just to look around, reacquaint herself with the glorious view. Visit Eloise's grave. It had been an age since she was there. 'Maybe tomorrow.' She yawned. 'I'm exhausted. I need to sleep.'

About to turn away, Cathy spotted a crow circling eerily slowly above the church tower. She shivered. Ten years ago, she'd been convinced Eloise was speaking to her from beyond the grave, urging her to protect her five-year-old twin daughters, while Chris had maintained that her unsettling visions were the result of a long, slow slide into depression.

'Stop it, Cathy. The past is over and done with. Leave it where it belongs.' Setting down her glass, she hurried to the kitchen. 'No more wine, either. It's making you fanciful.' Instead, she boiled the kettle for tea, then sat thoughtfully at the wide oak kitchen table, staring at the invitation she'd propped against the empty fruit bowl. Reading it for the tenth time, she felt sorry for Juliana, concerned about Jack — and burning with curiosity to meet his mystery bride.

* * *

That night, despite her exhaustion, Cathy barely slept, tormented by images of Eloise. Navy eyes flashing, long blonde hair rippling around her shoulders, she stood poised on the stairs above the great hall at Roseland. Waiting, as she'd done a thousand times; drawing everyone's attention, before gliding down to dance with a faceless partner. Exuberantly, she swished her gown, just as she used to at the costume balls she'd adored. Only, in Cathy's dream, her friend was dressed as a bride.

The dream felt so real that Cathy was certain she could smell Eloise's favourite lavender perfume, and hear the rustle of silk. It was only as she struggled awake the next morning that she discovered she'd left the window open all night. A gentle breeze was stirring the branches of the trees outside her bedroom, and scents from the garden drifted towards her on the balmy air.

The sounds and smells of Cornwall had invaded her dreams, she realised, pulling her back to the past, and Cathy felt unsettled and strangely on edge as she stumbled towards the bathroom and into a hot, reviving shower. 'Blasted jet lag. It's addled my brain.'

Glancing at her watch, she realised she had less than an hour to get ready, so it was a good job she only needed to stroll up the lane to the nearby Talland Bay Hotel. Eve had phoned late yesterday evening to check on her safe arrival and confirm that they were meeting there for brunch at eleven.

'How are things going at Jack's?' Cathy had asked cryptically.

'I haven't met her yet,' Eve replied drily, correctly guessing her mum's true interest.

Eager for the low-down on the bride-to-be, Cathy had been disappointed to learn that she'd been detained overnight for work, but would try her best to join them for brunch. 'Someone obviously likes to make an entrance,' she'd joked.

'Doesn't every bride?' Eve countered, and something in her voice had made Cathy wonder if Jack's wouldn't be the last wedding bells she heard this summer.

'You're right, love. It's one of the biggest days in

anyone's life.' She was dying to see Eve and suss out if she was planning her own.

Cathy told herself it was for that reason — the possibility of another surprise announcement — that she took care straightening her hair, before putting on a light touch of make-up and a pretty floral summer frock, but she was also conscious of a flutter of nerves as she thought of meeting Jack's fiancée. She wanted to look her best.

'I can't *believe* he's getting married,' she told her reflection, before eyeing it critically, at the same time trying to conjure up an image of the woman Jack had chosen as his new life partner. Although she hadn't seen him for years, it was impossible to forget her old friend's tanned, striking features, his thick blond hair and amused blue eyes.

She knew many hearts had been broken when Jack had remained loyal to Eloise, even after her death — even through his disastrous, short-lived marriage in Australia — and even more so when he'd decided to stay there, his years of sunshine and surf on the Gold Coast only enhancing his good looks. But time marched on, and who knew, Cathy thought: maybe Jack had lost his hair by now. Or run to fat.

Giving her neck and wrists a last spritz of perfume, she glanced at a framed photo of Chris on her dressing table. Her husband was tall, clever and looked like the formidably intelligent doctor he was, and Cathy had always loved the perceptive kindness that made him such a brilliant psychiatrist. Dark and intense, he was handsome, too, in a spare, ascetic way. But the warmth he reserved for his patients was now rarely extended to his wife — and Cathy had to admit that the spark of excitement she used to feel around him had dimmed over time.

'We've become like bookends, Chris,' she told his photo. 'Sitting at opposite sides of the same shelf, propping up our kids between us. But I'm only fifty-five. I'm not ready to be left gathering dust in a library.' She wondered where Jack had found his fiancée. Not in the ancient history section, she was prepared to bet.

Curiosity gave her butterflies once more, but as she left the cottage and strolled up the familiar lane, Cathy's dream floated back to her, and she was conscious of a pang of disloyalty to her late best friend. Glancing up towards the church, perched high on the clifftop, she felt a little shiver, despite it being another scorching hot day.

Eloise had blazed such a bright trail through life, and her loss had left a long, dark shadow. To have caught Jack's eye, his new fiancée must sparkle brighter than a thousand stars, Cathy thought. 'Who *is* she?' she wondered impatiently, walking faster now, eager to meet her — bracing herself to be dazzled.

6

As she arrived at the hotel a few minutes later, Cathy looked around eagerly, but there was no sign of Jack, or even Eve. She was the first there, but that was fine; it was good to have no one but herself to please, for once, and she felt comfortable and relaxed in the familiar surroundings.

The popular hotel had always been one of their family's favourite haunts, and Cathy was surprised but happy when the staff remembered her, immediately showing her to their former regular table under the shade of tall palm trees, then bringing her a chilled G&T with ice before she even asked for one. 'Now *this* is what I call pure bliss.' Tipping her face to the sun, Cathy made up her mind that, whatever Chris decided to do when his contract was up, she would never go back to Dubai.

'Mum!' A slim figure in white jeans and a yellow crop top darted towards her.

'Evie!' Cathy swivelled around to watch her daughter flitting along the gravelled path that wound through the pretty hotel garden, managing to stand up just in time before Eve flung herself into her arms. Sauntering along behind his girlfriend, Arthur grinned.

'Hi, Cathy,' he greeted her. 'You're looking as fabulous as ever. Positively glowing.'

She gave him a knowing look. 'OK, what have you two been up to? I know when I'm being buttered up.' She chuckled as Arthur blushed. A proposal must surely be imminent, Cathy decided, and nothing would make her happier. 'Lovely to see you again, Artie.' She turned back to Eve with a wide smile. 'How are you, darling? You look gorgeous.'

'Thanks, Mum, but you flatter me. I'm exhausted, and I have the eye bags to prove it.'

There was a cough from a few yards away. 'Your daughter is as modest as she is lovely. And so, may I say, are you. You don't look a day older than when I last saw you.'

Tiny hairs prickled on the back of her neck as Cathy turned to stare at the man behind the voice. Despite her earlier thought about time marching on, Jack was the one who didn't look a day older. In fact, he looked ten years younger.

Being engaged must agree with him, she thought, unable to stop herself glancing over his shoulder, eager to check if he was accompanied by the woman who had clearly put a spring in his step. Disappointingly, he wasn't.

'Jack.' The name felt curiously alien on her lips. 'Good to see you.'

'And you, Cath. It's been too long.' His light kiss on her cheek made Cathy blush.

So much for running to fat, she teased herself. Dressed casually yet smartly in a blue short-sleeved linen shirt, navy cargo shorts and deck shoes, Jack looked as handsome as ever. Lean and toned, his tanned legs fit and strong, he didn't look even close to his age, especially as his hair was still as thick and blond as Arthur's, although now with the odd silver streak at his temples that only served to give him a slightly distinguished air.

Cathy stepped back, feigning nonchalance, hoping

she hadn't been staring too obviously. 'How are you?' she asked pointlessly; he was gleaming with health and happiness.

Blue eyes twinkled. 'Never better. And you? Chris?'

'We're both good, thanks. Although, frankly, I'm all the better for being here.'

'This place is certainly a tonic. With or without the gin.' Jack chuckled, nodding at her drink. 'That's always been your favourite, Cath. Some things never change, hey?'

'And yet others do. Dramatically. I got your invitation. Is your —'

'Shall we get comfortable?' Jack cupped a hand under her elbow, steering her back to the table and grabbing a chair for himself, signalling at Arthur and Eve to join them.

'Oh. Sure.' Cathy felt awkward as she sat down. Jack's interruption had felt deliberate, as though he'd sensed she was about to ask about his fiancée, who clearly *wasn't* joining them.

Gazing around to cover her embarrassment, she scanned the clusters of families and friends enjoying the shady garden, a welcome oasis in the midst of one of the hottest summers on record. Recognising a few locals, Cathy wondered again who Jack was marrying — if she was from the village, or perhaps someone he'd met further afield through his work.

As a senior consultant, Jack had an extensive professional network. But picturing him with anyone other than Eloise was hard. Maybe he realised that. Maybe that explained the slight coyness Cathy was detecting. Perhaps it even accounted for his fiancée's non-appearance. She could be shy about meeting one of Jack's oldest friends, who had also been Eloise's *best* friend.

Cathy's mind whirled as she sat stiffly at the table, suddenly feeling as displaced as she had when she'd first set foot off the plane in London yesterday morning. Nothing looked any different, but everything was somehow slightly changed — as though she'd collected a favourite old coat from the tailors, and all the buttons had been re-sewn in the wrong places.

Taking a quick sip of her drink, she set it back on the table; tiredness, disappointment and something like hurt had suddenly made it taste sour. Jack was as warmly attentive as ever, and Cathy felt as much affection towards him as she always had. But there was no doubting the bride-shaped shadow lurking over their once easy friendship, and even without the soaring air temperature, Cathy's curiosity was beginning to reach boiling point.

'Man, would you look at that sea? I can't wait to get out on it. God, I've missed this place.' Arthur, as laid-back as ever, seemed oblivious to the awkward silence at the table. Drawing Eve towards the garden perimeter, he looped an arm around her shoulders, and the two of them stood gazing at the stunning view.

Cathy wished she could join them, rather than sit here with Jack, who crossed his legs, looking annoyingly relaxed. It would be rude to just walk away, but she was determined not to be the one to kickstart conversation. If Jack wanted to be secretive about his fiancée, so be it.

'It really is good to see you again, Cath.' His eyes, even bluer than the sea, crinkled at the corners. 'Artie's right. You're positively glowing. The desert must have agreed with you.'

'Not as much as this place,' she said honestly,

accepting the slim olive branch. 'I've missed it, too. I didn't realise how much until I drove through the bay. Saw Talland Church silhouetted up above.' She paused, remembering staring through the dusk at the medieval chapel, wondering if Jack ever visited Eloise's grave . . . if *that* was the reason he wanted to marry at Roseland, instead of at their local church. 'I hear we have a new vicar. Will they be the one to officiate at —'

'Cornwall gets in your blood, doesn't it? I don't think I could live anywhere else now.'

That was the second time he'd cut her off, Cathy registered, and she couldn't help her slight frostiness as she said: 'It obviously suits you. You look well.'

'I like peace and quiet,' Jack said affably. 'Although it's in short supply with those two around.' A comical eye-roll as he nodded at Arthur and Eve.

Cathy softened a little. 'I imagine so. But I gather the twins are in Italy?'

'Yes. Back tomorrow evening. I'm picking them up from Heathrow. They wanted to get the train down, but I can't wait. This is the longest we've been apart in ten years.'

'They must be so grown-up now,' Cathy said fondly.

'Fifteen going on twenty-five. But as different from each other as chalk and cheese.'

'Isn't it always the way with siblings? Same upbringing. Different personalities.'

'Nature versus nurture, Pops.' Arthur patted his grandpa's shoulder, as he and Eve finally joined them at the table. 'The age-old dilemma. I did a conversation piece on it recently at the radio station. *Do genetics pre-determine our fate, or can we forge our own destiny?*'

'It won an award,' Eve chipped in proudly, sitting

down next to him.

Arthur blushed. 'Evie's the real high-flier. She's about to be made lead AP.'

'Assistant producer,' Eve clarified, for her mum's benefit.

'I know.' Cathy rolled her eyes. 'I'm not that out of touch.' She reached for her daughter's hand. 'But you mustn't work too hard, love. You said you're feeling tired.'

'I want this promotion, Mum. Really badly. The trouble is, so do a dozen others.'

'Nothing wrong with ambition.' Jack smiled at Eve. 'Only not at the expense of your health. We all have our limits. Don't burn out, will you, Evie?'

Cathy flashed him a grateful look, her irritation dissipating. Over the years, their respective families had spent many happy hours chatting over drinks here, or enjoying lively dinner parties at Jack's house. The thought of a stranger infiltrating their little group was unsettling, but it didn't need to be the end of the world — or their friendship. She made up her mind to go easier on Jack and be welcoming to his fiancée, when she did finally show her face.

'Keep an eye on Evie for me, would you, Jack?' she pleaded. 'No burning the midnight oil doing work emails. I know what she's like.' She turned to her daughter. 'Do you have to rush back to London, darling? Or can you stay until after . . . ?' She glanced at Jack, seeing his jaw tense. 'I mean, just for a few more days.'

Eve pulled a face. 'I'll have to phone my boss and ask. It's not ideal timing. But with you being home now, I'd like to.' She leaned over to give her a hug. 'I've missed you, Mum.'

'Me too you.' Cathy hugged her back. 'And your dad sends his love.'

'Sure.' Eve shook her head. 'You don't always have to cover for him, you know?'

'I'm not,' Cathy lied. 'He specifically asked me to say so.'

'Every father finds it tough when their daughters grow up,' Jack said diplomatically. 'I can't wait for Vi and Rosie to be safely home. I need them back here, where they belong. And Izzy.' He turned to give Arthur a wry smile. 'Your mum may not believe it, but I miss her, too.'

'Fingers crossed we'll see her soon, hey?' Arthur said brightly. 'You know, at the *wedding*.'

7

Cathy glanced around the table, confused by everyone's smiles. She'd felt the word 'wedding' plummet like a stone. Was no one else conscious of yet another awkward silence? She almost held her breath as she waited for Jack to reply, then sighed in frustration as the hotel manager strolled over to greet them. Fond as she was of Harry, his arrival instantly let Jack off the hook.

'Welcome back, guys.' Harry beamed, oblivious to any tension. 'What can I get you?'

They all started talking at once, ordering fresh crab sandwiches and chilled beer — whisky for Jack — before sitting back to gaze silently at the view. The arrival of the food broke the ice a little, but still no one referred to the wedding, Cathy noticed. *So it wasn't just her.*

Determined to lift the mood, she was about to whisper to Arthur that he might propose a toast to the forthcoming happy occasion, when Eve stood up and excused herself, saying: 'Well, I don't know about you lot, but I'm stuffed. Fancy a stroll to walk it all off, Artie?'

'Sure.' He smiled. 'Race you down the hill. Last one at the beach buys the ice cream.'

Eve laughed. 'What are you, six? Besides, I'm way too full. And exhausted.'

Arthur frowned. 'You keep saying that, hon. You're starting to worry me.'

Cathy was worried, too, and as the two of them disappeared for their walk, she sat pondering, thinking it was a shame that Eve was staying at Jack's house. It was hard to chat with everyone around, and Cathy was itching to have a proper catch-up with her daughter.

'A penny for them,' Jack said, watching her.

'Sorry? Oh, I was just wondering about your fiancée.' It wasn't entirely untrue, and despite feeling hurt and baffled by his reticence about the wedding, Cathy didn't want to rain on his parade by dwelling on her niggling concerns about Eve. She smiled, adding a little self-consciously: 'The new love of your life.'

Jack reached for his whisky. 'You know who that was, Cath, and it will never change.'

'Then why are you getting married?' Immediately, Cathy clamped her mouth shut with one hand, horrified at herself. 'I'm sorry. That came out wrong. Ignore me, please.'

'No, it's fine. You were Eloise's best friend. I'd like to explain. I owe you that.'

'You don't owe me anything. And I'm your friend, too, remember? But OK, I admit I'm curious.'

'Of course you are. I get that. I've been single a long time. Sometimes it feels like for ever.'

'So it's loneliness?' Cathy knew what that felt like, and her husband was alive and kicking. 'Ellie's been dead for ten years. Naturally, you have to move on.'

'I do. And I won't deny that I've been lonely. Oh, I know I've still got the twins. But they're away at boarding school most of the time. Plus, you know, I'm not getting any younger.'

'Don't be daft. You're in your prime,' Cathy said, then felt herself blush again.

Jack laughed. 'Only a true friend would say so. You're too kind, Cath. But time marches on. Retirement and a solitary life were beginning to loom frighteningly close.'

'And so you've found someone to spend your autumn years with?'

'I think so.'

'You *think* so? Forgive me, but that's not exactly a ringing endorsement.'

'You're right. I'm being idiotic. I guess it's hanging out with Arthur and Eve, and now you. Please don't take this the wrong way, Cath. It just feels a bit like my past tapping me on the shoulder. Seeing you guys again . . . I suppose I look at you, and I can't help seeing Eloise.'

Cathy felt a slight shiver as, once again, she remembered her oddly vivid dream about her friend last night. 'Me too. I mean, whenever I come here, I think of her. Those times.'

'Where did the years go, eh?'

'They've been kind to you, though. You have a brilliant relationship with Artie. The twins adore you. I know things are complicated with Izzy, but . . .' Cathy hesitated, then thought, *In for a penny; in for a pound.* 'How does she feel about you getting married?'

'Izzy?' Jack shrugged. 'I haven't heard from her since I sent the invitation.'

'Air mail isn't the most reliable. Especially at short notice,' Cathy said pointedly.

'I emailed her.'

'Ah. Right.' Cathy frowned, thinking, remembering. Of Eloise's three daughters, Rose was the most like her mum physically, even more so than her twin: fey and willowy, while Violet was more robust and athletic. Izzy was a combination of the two, with the same blend of feistiness and fragility that Ellie had: bold and beautiful on the outside; broken on the inside. 'She'll come, Jack.' Cathy reached for his hand. 'I know she will.'

'I hope so. Life's too short to hold on to grudges. I'm reminded of it constantly. Patients wishing for just one more day. Even another hour. We have to look forward, don't we?'

'You're right. We do.' Cathy sighed. 'But why now? Why *her*?'

'It's hard to put into words, but . . . when you meet her, I think you'll understand.'

'Sure. Just tell me when, and where.'

For a moment, she thought Jack was going to brush her off again. Then he smiled, giving her hand one last squeeze, before letting it go and picking up his whisky. 'How about tonight?' he said casually, after taking a sip. 'Dinner at my place. Seven to seven-thirty-ish. It'll be just like old times, hey?'

Cathy smiled, too. 'Except I'm missing a husband, and you have a new wife.'

'Well, not quite. Not for another week. Not at all, if Juliana has anything to do with it.'

'Faint heart never won fair lady, Jack.'

'Very true. And I've picked the fairest of them all.' He raised his glass in a mock toast. 'Here's to new beginnings. Wait till you meet her, Cath. I know you're going to love her as much as I do. In fact, I'm counting on it.'

8

As the sun cooled that evening, Cathy drove the long way from the cottage to Jack's house on the opposite headland. There was a shortcut, but it was up one of the steepest paths in the village, and she didn't fancy puffing her way up there — not when she was wearing heels and a calf-length raspberry silk dress that she'd bought in one of Dubai's famous shopping malls.

Despite claiming that her wardrobe was empty, Eve had also dressed up — unusually for her. Cathy loved fashion and was always encouraging her daughter to wear more dresses, but Eve lived in jeans and trainers, claiming it was easier as she did so much running around between production offices at work. Tonight, though, she was elegant in a mauve jersey mini dress.

'You look stunning, love,' Cathy told her as they arrived at Jack's house. Pulling on the handbrake, she turned to reassure her daughter, who seemed oddly jittery. Come to think of it, she'd been in a strange mood since she'd turned up unexpectedly at the cottage a couple of hours ago, saying she preferred to stay there, after all, rather than at Jack's house. 'That's a gorgeous dress.'

'It's one of Violet's. I borrowed it. She has loads. Well, I think they're her mum's.'

'Probably. Ellie loved her designer clothes. She was always playing dress-up with the girls when they were little. Putting on pretend costume balls, and whatnot. Like Juliana and Sir Charles used to host at Roseland.' Cathy frowned, once again thinking of her dream last night. This wedding was clearly bothering her more than she realised. She hoped meeting Jack's fiancée would soothe her jitters.

'Yeah, Vi told me about that. She sounded a bit sad, actually. I texted to ask if it was OK for me to borrow a dress. I meant for tonight, but she said to help myself to whatever. She had no intention of getting tarted up for this — and I quote — *stupid wedding*.'

'Hmm. So that's how the land lies. You know, I'm not sure who I pity most. The twins or Jack. It'll be tough for the girls coming home to find a stranger in their home. But Jack's in for a rocky ride. Negotiating with teenagers is no picnic. I doubt they'll make it easy for him.'

'I don't blame them. Their dad's marrying a woman they've never even met.'

'They'll soon make up for lost time. And I'm sure Jack's fiancée will be sensitive to the girls' feelings. If she's around Jack's age, she may even have kids of her own.'

'Right, yeah. I hadn't thought of that.'

'She'll almost certainly be old enough and wise enough to realise no one can replace their mum. I actually feel sorry for her. I don't envy anyone trying to walk in Eloise's shoes.'

'She'd be stupid to try,' Eve said bluntly. 'The twins' bedrooms are a shrine to her. Eloise never lived in that house, but there are photos of her everywhere. Her books and paintings. Not to mention all those incredible dresses. I thought I might find something suitable for the wedding, as well as tonight. But this was actually the plainest dress I could find.'

'Well, it's lovely, sweetheart. Perfect for a summer

barbecue, if not a wedding at Roseland.' Cathy chewed her lip thoughtfully. 'If indeed it does take place there. I don't fancy Jack's chances persuading Juliana, do you? Even with Artie in his camp.'

'They're going to see her in the morning. A full-on charm offensive. Good job they've both got plenty of it. They'll need every drop, and then some.'

'I'll pop over to see Juliana myself tomorrow. Find out how it went.'

'But we can still go dress shopping, right?' Eve looked worried.

'Absolutely. Thank God for Sunday shopping hours. We can drive over to Plymouth. Shop. Have lunch. A good old gossip.'

Eve smiled, a little tearily. 'Thanks, Mum. I'm so glad you're home.' She leaned across to give her a hug, then sat back, wiping her eyes. 'God, I don't know what's wrong with me. My period must be due. Brilliant. Perfect timing for the wedding.'

'Don't worry, love. All eyes will be on the bride. Speaking of whom, shall we go in?'

9

As always, Jack's house took Cathy's breath away. It almost seemed to be carved out of the cliff, so high up that it was semi-veiled by near-permanent wispy clouds. Talland Church, dizzyingly far below on the opposite headland, looked like a tiny toy from this vantage point.

A rundown bungalow had once stood on the site, and Cathy knew that Jack had bought it purely because of its spectacular location, as he'd promptly demolished the old house to build a striking modern home made of glass and timber. A vast kitchen-diner and living room opened onto a wrap-around limestone terrace, specially designed to take in those incredible views.

When Cathy had first seen it, she'd teased Jack that he had built himself a James Bond hideaway, which he'd loved and immediately christened the place Goldeneye, after Ian Fleming's clifftop eyrie in Jamaica. Chris had been horrified, deeming both the name and house vulgar and pretentious. Jack had simply laughed and commissioned the name to be engraved in gold letters on a slab of black slate, which he then had mounted beside the gate.

There it stayed to this day. *Goldeneye.*

Cathy stared at it, as ever finding it deeply poignant, because she guessed why Jack had really built this house: brazenly unconventional and seemingly conjured out of raw, unfiltered nature, it reflected everything that had epitomised Eloise, and all she would have adored. 'Oh, Ellie. I wish you could have lived to see it,' she murmured.

'Sorry, Mum?'

'Nothing. Just thinking about Eloise. How she would have loved this place.'

Cathy was still thinking of her friend as they entered the gate and passed through the tall juniper and palm trees that stood sentry around the garden, protecting it from prying eyes and occasional battering storms. Ambling across the lawn, she felt wistful and on edge as she watched Jack laughing and chatting on the terrace.

Despite their conversation at the hotel earlier, she still couldn't believe he was getting married; she simply couldn't picture him with another woman. No sooner had she had the thought, than a throaty, feminine laugh drifted towards them. Squinting, Cathy could just make out long, slim tanned legs stretched out next to Arthur, who was leaning forward to tend a glowing fire pit.

'I guess that's her,' Eve said. 'She must have only just arrived. She wasn't here when I left Goldeneye this afternoon. Maybe you were right, Mum. About her wanting to make an entrance.'

'Well, I was only joking, really.' Cathy was determined to approach the evening with an open mind. She owed that to Jack. Forewarned was also forearmed. The more she knew about the twins' new stepmum, the better she could support them. She owed that to Eloise. 'What did Arthur say? He must have met her by now. Did you speak to him this afternoon?'

Eve hesitated. 'No. Actually, we had a bit of a fall-out. That's why I left and came home.'

'Ah.' Cathy had sensed something was off when Eve returned to the cottage, having initially gone back to Jack's house after brunch. She'd been hoping to have a proper chat with her daughter, but Eve had hidden in her old bedroom, claiming she had work to catch up on. She hadn't come out until they were about to leave, ten minutes ago. 'Nothing serious, I hope?'

Eve shrugged. 'He read some of my text chats with Violet, that's all. She's not happy about her dad's engagement. Neither is Rosie.'

'Well, like you said, that's not unexpected. In fact, it's completely understandable.'

'Exactly. That's what I told Artie. But he reckons I should be encouraging the girls to *think nice*. He had a right old strop when I said this engagement is suspiciously rushed.'

'Arthur likes to look on the bright side, that's all,' Cathy consoled.

'Tell me about it. He's such a peacemaker, and I love that about him. I do. But he can't fix everything with a goofy grin and positive thinking.'

'After all the ups and downs in his family, can you blame him for trying? Don't be too hard on him, love. He worships you. He's practically glued to your side.'

Eve blushed; she hadn't yet found the right moment to tell her mum that he'd moved in with her. 'Yeah. Sorry. Like I said, I'm worn out. Probably hormonal. I don't like it when Artie and I fight, that's all. Especially when I'm not sure why we're arguing in the first place.'

'Everything feels worse when we're tired. I should know. Jet lag has fried my brain. I'm sure I put my foot in it several times at brunch.' Cathy frowned, thinking back to her conversation with Jack. 'I just hope I didn't say anything too tactless about this engagement.'

'But it is weird, right?' Eve persisted. 'You were Eloise's best friend. This must all feel strange for you?'

'A little.' Cathy remembered her dream from the night before, Eloise radiant on the staircase at Roseland. 'But it's Jack's life, his choice. The wedding might even be fun. Clothes shopping for it certainly will be. Let's push the boat out for once, hey?'

Eve huffed. 'Sure. I'll buy the fanciest dress I can afford on my miserly salary.'

'Now, now. You'll get your promotion, darling. I have every faith in you. And you'll make it up with Artie. Everything is going to be fine. You'll see.'

'Thanks, Mum. You're the best.'

They continued across the lawn, and as they came closer to the house, Cathy gestured towards the clifftop. 'Perhaps we've both been guilty of getting things out of proportion. We might be in 'du Maurier country'' — she mimed speech marks — 'but Jack is no Max de Winter, and Juliana isn't Mrs Danvers. This is real life, not a murder mystery.'

'Although Roseland is every bit as spooky as Manderley. All those dark corridors, Sir Charles's ghost striding up and down them. I wouldn't get married there if you paid me.'

'Well, if you put it like that.' Cathy chuckled, taking her daughter's reference to getting married as a good sign. She and Arthur often had little tiffs; no doubt this one would blow over, too. Maybe Eve was jittery waiting for Arthur to propose; perhaps that was at the heart of their fall-out. 'Anyway, it remains to be seen if Juliana will allow it. She might be old, but she can be fierce. It would take a very determined bride indeed to stand up to her.'

10

'Bloody families.' Izzy stared dolefully into her third espresso from the complimentary bar. She shouldn't drink it; she had enough caffeine in her system to power the national grid as it was. But she needed something to cheer herself up, and she'd already had three doughnuts.

After guiltily downing the coffee, she set her cup and saucer down on the glass table next to her, and gazed around the brightly lit airport lounge. At least she could pass the time before her delayed flight in relative peace and comfort, away from the jangling noise and chaotic bustle of the main terminal.

As well as having good coffee on tap, together with a vast array of pastries, the lounge also provided spotlessly clean bathrooms, proper freshly cooked hot and cold food, and free high-speed WiFi, not to mention a massage facility on her chair. It was just a shame she wasn't in the mood to enjoy one. Attempting to relax anyway, she pressed her AirPods into her ears, before taking out her phone and scrolling through playlists in search of something soothing to muffle not only the hum of conversations around her, but also her own jangled thoughts.

Usually, Izzy hated being disconnected from her surroundings, especially in public places. As a reporter, she'd written about many tragic human-interest stories over the years; a part of her brain was always on high alert, ready to spring into action in case of emergency. Aside from that, she was also compulsively curious and loved tuning into other people's lives, their everyday conversations and domestic dramas. But not today.

Right now, Izzy was gripped by too big a crisis of her own to worry about anyone else's. 'Bloody families,' she muttered again, frustrated that not even the ambient chillout mix pulsing in her ears was softening the edges of her tension, or distracting her mind from picturing the faces that had been haunting her dreams for weeks: Juliana, Jack, Arthur, Rose and Violet.

Reaching into her hoodie pocket, she took out the notebook and pen she was never without, scribbling their names on the first page. Her therapist, Sue, always encouraged her to journal her feelings, as a way of purging and processing them, to help her feel more in control. 'I'm calling the shots this time,' Izzy reminded herself, doodling a picture of a house that began to look remarkably like Roseland. Angrily, she scribbled it out. 'Huh, maybe I should write a feature on dysfunctional families. At least that might make this ridiculous trip tax deductible.'

It had been an impulsive extravagance to pay for use of this lounge, on top of the price of her open-ended airfare. But when Izzy had landed after her fourteen-hour flight from Sydney to learn of an hour's delay on her connection to London, she hadn't been able to face the crowds of waiting passengers. The exclusive private suite had provided a welcome haven. Unfortunately, in its luxurious, genteel calm, her agitated thoughts clamoured more loudly.

Flicking to the back of her notebook, where she'd tucked her boarding pass, Izzy questioned herself again as to why she hadn't set a limit on her visit to the UK. She'd told herself it would be a waste of time — and her meagre savings — to travel all this way purely for a wedding she had no interest in; a wedding that would take place on Friday, after which she'd have time to do . . . what? Travel? Hang out with her son?

'Will Arthur even want to see me?' Izzy could count on one hand the number of times he'd been home in the last ten years, and their phone calls had become increasingly sporadic. 'He's probably hoping I won't come. The twins, too.' Automatically, Izzy glanced at her hand luggage: a compact holdall that was, in fact, all she'd brought with her. She flew fairly regularly for work — although only domestic flights within Australia — and had learned to save time by packing sparingly. That way, she avoided the queues at baggage claim.

The bulge in her bag's front pocket was the gifts she'd hastily picked up at Duty Free: aftershave for Arthur; perfume for the twins. She knew they weren't the most imaginative presents, but it had been so long since she'd seen all three of them that Izzy had been at a loss to know what they'd like. 'Artie better not have grown a beard,' she mumbled, still thinking of the aftershave as she scrolled through her phone again, studying photos of him on her camera roll.

Ironically, the first one that caught her eye was taken at another airport, ten years ago, when her sixteen-year-old son had left Sydney, fresh-faced and eager to get to know the Trelawney side of his family . . . to give life in Cornwall, and then London, a go. He'd never returned to live in Australia, and Izzy couldn't forgive Jack for that. Or Juliana. Especially her. She was Arthur's great-grandmother, and Izzy knew the old lady loved him, too. But she'd had Artie in her clutches long enough. Izzy wanted her son back.

Flicking to her emails, Izzy opened Jack's e-invite, anxiously scanning the details for the hundredth time. He hadn't even included his fiancée's name. 'Which tells you everything you need to know,' she lectured herself, feeling a jolt of anger when she re-read her dad's opening line: *To my darling Izzy.* Easy to be sentimental when you're on the other side of the world, she thought bitterly, wondering how Jack would react when he saw her in person.

A tannoy announcement made her jump, and despite the air conditioning, Izzy suddenly felt overheated as she realised her flight was finally ready for boarding. The butterflies in her stomach multiplied as she picked up on the buzz in the air around her. Passengers were hastily tucking away their books and papers, and TV screens flickered with updated departure times. Izzy scanned them rapidly, and there it was: the number of her gate.

God, what the hell was she doing? Glancing towards the exit, Izzy was on the verge of making a run for it. She could just go home. No one would ever know. She'd deliberately ignored the RSVP request on her dad's email, half wondering if that would provoke him into following it up with a phone call. It hadn't, and Izzy had taken that as yet another indication of his disinterest.

'If he was so bothered about me coming, he would have called,' she reasoned, taking one last look at her dad's rather rushed, jumbled message. Her heart thumped as she noticed the little flag indicating that she had new mail. Not one, but two new messages.

Quickly opening the first one, it took her a moment

to realise who it was from. Her dad's fiancée, writing effusively to say that she was *over the moon* about getting to meet Izzy, and how her *daffy dad* had sent out invitations in a such a rush that he'd forgotten to include her name, but that she *sincerely hoped* Izzy wouldn't hold that against her — that, in fact, she'd be *beside herself with joy* if Izzy would agree to be her maid of honour.

'Oh, sod it all to hell and back,' Izzy groaned, knowing she'd have to reply now and say that she was on her way to London. She was bitter and furious, but she wasn't rude. This woman, whoever she was, was planning her wedding. Izzy's own marriage might have turned sour years ago, but she wasn't so cruel as to deliberately cast a shadow over someone else's big day. It was Jack and Juliana she was mad at. She bore no grudge towards her dad's fiancée, who seemed friendly enough, if a little over-enthusiastic.

Dashing off a hasty reply, Izzy flicked back to her inbox, eager to check out the second new message before heading for the gate. Once on the plane, she wouldn't have a chance to log into email for hours, and she was desperate to know if she'd received a reply to the urgent message she'd sent to her mystery DNA match via the ancestry website.

Frustrated not to have been given any personal contact details for them — not even a name, how old they were, or whether they were male or female — Izzy had been forced to write to them care of the website representative, specifically asking for *her* phone number and email address to be passed on, together with a most particular request for them to *please be in touch*, as she was anxious to trace them . . . that she was, in fact, travelling to the UK especially to see them.

It had been a heartfelt plea, also calculated to engender curiosity in return, with Izzy using every journalistic trick she'd learned when trying to coax nervous interviewees into talking to her. But this was no witness to a banal, random local news story; this mystery person potentially held the key to open an entirely new, secret door into the seemingly perfect Trelawney family. Everything was riding on Izzy convincing them to meet. Or, at the very least, speak on the phone.

Mentally, she crossed her fingers, hoping the website representative had passed on her message promptly, and that their confirmation was waiting in her inbox, perhaps even — Izzy sent up a little prayer — including a few more personal details. A phone number, or . . . 'Oh. Damn.' Izzy's shoulders slumped in disappointment; the second email wasn't from them.

Like the message from her dad's fiancée, the email came from an address Izzy didn't recognise; unlike that gushing message, this short note was abrupt to the point of rudeness. ''Do not attempt to contact me again',' Izzy read aloud.

After a moment's satisfaction that her mystery relative had at least messaged her directly, bypassing the ancestry website, Izzy huffed crossly. 'Charming. So why register on the bloody website in the first place, if you don't want to be found?' It seemed ridiculous for anyone to put themselves out there to discover long-lost relatives, yet run for the hills when one was traced.

Buzzing with frustration now, Izzy tapped out a brief response: '*WHY NOT?*' Before she could change her mind, she pressed send. Almost instantly, a warning flashed up from the server that the message was undeliverable. 'Coward,' Izzy scorned, checking the IP address and immediately realising that whoever had sent the message must have set up a fake account.

Digging her nails into her palms, she forced herself to calm down. There was no point getting angry. She'd been raging at her family for years, and it had changed nothing. What she needed to do was come up with an alternative angle — another approach to solving the mystery. She had the bit between her teeth now, and, like the hardened reporter she was, Izzy refused to let go. 'Who are you, and what have you got to hide?' she tapped out in a fresh email, before deleting it.

Another tannoy announcement warned her that she was running out of time, if she still wanted to make the flight. Izzy hesitated. She didn't want to go to the wedding, and she didn't want to see her dad again. But she did miss her son, and her younger sisters. And if she'd been intrigued before about her surprise DNA match, she was burning with curiosity about them now.

'Maybe you've been hurt, too,' she speculated, wondering if this person was hiding behind anonymity because, like her, they'd been badly wounded by the Trelawneys . . . by Juliana. The woman who had done her best to ruin Izzy's life, and who needed to be taught a long-overdue lesson about the error of her ways.

Perhaps bitter experience had taught this person to be suspicious about *any* Trelawney — which, as fervently as Izzy rejected it, was irrevocably her own heritage. If so, she could hardly blame them for needing reassurance before they felt comfortable revealing whatever scandal had driven them into the shadows. 'I have to find you. But how?'

Looking again at the email address, she realised that while it was anonymous, it didn't appear to be a completely random combination of letters and digits, as she'd first thought. '*BS1beans4bytes*,' she mumbled, frowning as she attempted to decipher it.

Perhaps it wasn't a fake account, after all; maybe it had been sent from a public IP address that didn't accept incoming messages. 'Beans,' she pondered, glancing towards the buffet area in the corner of the airport lounge. 'Like, as in breakfast?' She chewed her lip, tasting espresso on her lips. 'Or coffee. Ground beans.' Tracing a finger over the next part of the address, she pondered the word *bytes*. Computers? Maybe a kind of internet café. But where?

With a groan, Izzy grabbed her holdall and almost raced across the lounge. Having vowed never to set foot in Cornwall again, she couldn't wait to get there now. All she had to do was get this stupid wedding out of the way, then she could concentrate on following the trail that *someone* seemed determined to conceal.

11

Jack spotted them and raised an arm in greeting. 'Cath! Evie! Perfect timing. Please, come and join us. The barbecue's all set. Artie here has excelled himself.'

Fixing a smile in place, Cathy stepped onto the terrace and was taken aback when Jack wrapped her in a bear hug. He was clearly in a buoyant mood, immediately hugging Eve, too, who responded half-heartedly, her attention focused on Arthur as she drifted towards him. 'Nice one, Artie,' she said shyly. 'I had no idea you were a budding Gordon Ramsay.'

'Rick Stein, you mean.' He waggled his eyebrows. 'We're in Cornwall now, babe.'

'Oh, but fish is strictly off the menu tonight,' said the glamorous woman at his side. She pulled a face as she uncoiled herself from her comfortable position on the rattan lounger, standing up elegantly, before swaying gracefully towards Jack. 'I can't abide the smell.'

Jack chuckled. 'My darling fiancée hates fish. Refuses even to have it in the house.' He smiled indulgently at her. 'Sweetheart, I'd like you to meet one of my oldest and dearest friends.' Turning back to Cathy, he said proudly: 'Cath, allow me to introduce my wife-to-be.'

Cathy had always lectured her children that it was rude to stare, but she couldn't help herself. What was it Jack said in the hotel garden earlier? *When you see her, I think you'll understand.* And she did. Now she knew exactly what Jack had meant, and why he'd been so evasive as they'd sat chatting this afternoon.

She understood, too, why Juliana was 'spitting feathers' about the wedding. Cathy couldn't blame her. For Jack's bride would not only replace Juliana's daughter at Roseland, she would surely also be a painful reminder of her . . . because with her honey-blonde hair falling in soft waves to her waist, and eyes as blue as the deepest part of the bay, Jack's *wife-to-be* was all but a carbon copy of Eloise.

Cathy stared at Jack, raising her eyebrows, waiting for him to acknowledge the resemblance. Make one of his self-deprecating jokes about it, even. Then the candles flickered on the terrace, the light changed, and suddenly the resemblance waned. Probably, it was just her projecting. After all, Eve had mentioned Eloise only moments ago, and, like her dream last night, their conversation had resurrected thoughts of her old friend. *Stop seeing ghosts*, she ordered herself.

Seemingly unaware of Cathy's inner turmoil, the source of her consternation stretched out slender, deeply tanned arms to envelop her in a welcoming hug. 'I'm so happy to meet you, Cath. Sorry I couldn't make it to brunch. I didn't mean to be rude. Work's just been crazy.'

Her body was lithe and toned, and as she stepped back, cherry-glossed lips parted to reveal perfect white teeth. Dark lashes swept over prominent cheekbones; violet eyes sparkled beneath smoky eye-shadow, black eyeliner *en flique*. With or without any slight resemblance to Eloise, Jack's mystery bride was stunning — and surely almost twenty years younger than him, in her late thirties, or early forties at most.

'Lovely to meet you, too,' Cathy said automatically, trying not to gawp. 'And please don't worry about brunch. We can have a good old chinwag now. Get to know each other.'

The cherry smile widened. 'Fabulous. Although, to be honest, I feel like I know you already. I've heard so much about you and your family. Jack never stops talking about you.'

'I wish I could say the same. He's been keeping you all to himself, for some reason.' Cathy suspected she now knew exactly what that reason was: not only was Jack marrying a woman with a passing resemblance to the love of his life, she was also around the same age as his eldest daughter.

What would Izzy make of her? Cathy fervently hoped she would come to the wedding, after all. Although her continued silence wasn't a good sign.

Jack, popping the cork on a bottle of champagne, grinned affably. 'Who could blame me? When you find something precious, you guard it with your life.' Setting the fizzing bottle back on the quirky driftwood bar strung with fairy lights tucked in one corner of the terrace, he pulled his fiancée snugly against his side. 'And you, my love, are priceless.'

A playful pinch of his chin. 'Very gallant of you, darling, I'm sure. Only, you know, I may be priceless, but I don't need wrapping up in cotton wool. I'm not one of Juliana's prized porcelain figurines. I won't break. I'm actually far tougher than I look.'

Cathy had to admire the woman's spirit, and at the mention of Juliana, she recalled Jack's meeting with her tomorrow: the great charm offensive. She wished she could be a fly on the wall for that; clearly, Jack was going to be caught between the wishes of two very determined women. 'Quite right,' she approved. 'Thankfully, the days are long gone when brides were handed over like helpless chattels.'

'Or lambs to the slaughter,' Jack's fiancée added, with a mischievous chuckle.

'Well, excuse me for believing in good old-fashioned chivalry.' Jack kissed her cheek, one hand curling around a taut waist exposed by a midnight-blue satin skirt that hung low on trim hips, while a matching camisole top left her midriff bare. 'And you *look* sensational.'

Cathy turned away, flustered by the obvious chemistry between them. No wonder Jack seemed high on life, more energised than Cathy had seen him in years. He was clearly mesmerised. *Bewitched.* She coughed to break the spell between them. 'You mentioned work being crazy. Do you work at the hospital, too? Are you a medic like Jack?'

'God, no. I'm far too squeamish. I work in TV. Although, come to think of it, there's probably as many scalpels. Definitely lots of back-stabbing. Marginally less gore.' A throaty chuckle. 'I'm a location manager for a production company. That's how Jack and I met.'

Gently arching eyebrows told Cathy that her subtle probing had been rumbled. 'Well, I didn't like to ask,' she said, flustered. 'But as I said, Jack here hasn't told us a thing.'

'Is that so?' A reproving pout at her fiancé. 'I hope you're not ashamed of me, darling?'

'I know better than to steal any woman's thunder,' he growled softly. 'You can speak for yourself. Although, actually, your beauty speaks for you.'

Cathy shuffled her feet, feeling like she was intruding on a private moment. 'Well, you've got me stumped. You work in TV. Jack practically lives at the hospital. So how did you two . . . Oh, wait. Were you scouting locations for a new medical drama?'

Indigo eyes widened. 'Wow.' A fleeting, stunned glance at Jack. 'You were right, darling. She *is* very intuitive. Seriously, Cath, you must have a sixth sense.'

'Hardly.' Cathy laughed, then felt awkward as she wondered if her leg was being pulled. Those dark, glittering eyes were hard to read. 'Well, if you guys didn't meet at the hospital . . .'

'We met at Roseland, appropriately enough,' Jack chipped in. 'I was visiting Juliana.'

'At the same time as I was checking out the grounds.' Another deep laugh. 'Before checking out the incredibly handsome stranger that quite literally knocked me for six.'

Jack took up the story, and it felt to Cathy that they were retelling it to each other, for their own satisfaction rather than hers. 'The twins had just flown out to Italy. I was looking forward to a rare evening home alone. I was rushing, not looking where I was going. In my defence, I did catch you before you fell.' His arms closed around his fiancée by way of demonstration. '*And* I gave up my quiet night in to cook dinner for you as an apology.'

A blissed-out sigh. 'And the rest, as they say, is history.'

Once again feeling like a third wheel, Cathy was thankful when Eve crossed the terrace to join in the conversation. 'Did I hear you say you work in television?'

A modest shrug. 'Nothing impressive. Strictly

behind the scenes.'

'Which is a sad loss to the viewing public,' Jack said, with a wink.

'I'd definitely have guessed you were an actress,' Eve continued, staring at his fiancée.

'Hmm, I'll take that as a compliment. I think.'

'Sorry, yes.' Eve blushed. 'I meant it as one. I work in TV as well, you see? I'm an assistant producer on a breakfast programme. But I know loads of people in the industry. Producers. Directors. Both current affairs and drama. Who did you say you work for?'

'Oh, they're just a tiny, independent company. Nothing impressive or mainstream like you. Commercial TV is so cut-throat, isn't it? I don't think I'm ruthless enough for it.'

'I'm not sure I am.' Eve sighed. 'Maybe that's why I haven't been promoted yet.'

'It's their loss,' Arthur said, sauntering to the bar to grab fresh glasses. 'Never change, hon. You're perfect as you are. More champagne, anyone?'

It was a general offer, but his eyes were fixed on Eve. Pleased to see that they'd made up, Cathy smiled and said, 'Being ruthless isn't always the way to get what you want.'

'I couldn't agree with you more,' Jack's fiancée approved. 'Brains not brawn, I say.'

'Although beauty helps,' Eve told her wryly. 'TV isn't only cut-throat. It can be incredibly superficial. Even when you're not in front of the camera.'

'Well, all I'll say is, it's a very good job I'm marrying into such a photogenic family.' A quick tap of a finger against her delicate nose. 'Just between us, a film crew is arriving at Roseland tomorrow. That drama series I was scouting for? It got the green light.'

'Wow.' Arthur's eyes widened. 'So our Roseland is to be the new *Downton Abbey*?'

'*Juliana's* Roseland,' Jack pointed out drily.

'But none of us will be on camera, surely?' Cathy felt a flutter of panic. Her husband was the one who loved giving TV interviews; she preferred to avoid the limelight, working for print media, not broadcast. The idea of a film crew at Roseland was ever so slightly terrifying.

'Only for the wedding movie.'

'Movie?' Jack's face was a picture of surprise as he stared at his fiancée. 'What's this?'

'Oh, darling, I *told* you. I have the best colleagues. Production doesn't start for a couple of weeks, so they have a tiny window. They need to get background footage at Roseland, but — and this is the generous bit — they're going to film our big day. As a wedding gift for us!'

'We're all going to be stars.' Arthur grinned, handing round champagne. 'Cheers to us!'

Cathy stood staring at Jack, convinced he was masking the same uncertainty that was rippling through her. He might be handsome, but he was deeply modest. Few people knew of his extensive charity work, or how he prioritised working for the NHS over private practice.

'Cheers,' his fiancée said huskily, clinking Arthur's glass. 'To Roseland.'

'To Roseland,' Cathy toasted automatically. 'And to you, Jack.' She smiled at him, and then turned to his fiancée. 'And . . . oh, I'm so sorry. I don't think I caught your name.'

Another teasing frown at Jack. 'You need to practise saying it, darling. We're exchanging our vows in less than a week. Honestly, let's start again, shall we? I'll introduce myself properly this time.' She thrust a hand towards Cathy; the candlelight caught each facet of the enormous ruby on her ring finger, making it sparkle. 'Hi, Cath. It's such a pleasure to meet you. I'm Rebecca.'

12

Juliana's shoes scraped rhythmically on the slate-flagged floor, as she paced up and down the kitchen at Roseland Home Farm. Her body was fizzing with a sense of expectation she couldn't put her finger on, and her mind was equally restless, yet annoyingly foggy. Nagging, half-formed thoughts pressed at the back of her mind; a feeling that she was forgetting something important . . . that something had either happened or was about to happen, but she couldn't recall what.

She'd been up since dawn. Pacing. Drinking tea. The heat made it hard to sleep, and her dreams had left her fractious. She was having them more often now, and last night's had been particularly vivid. It began as they usually did: with Eloise whispering in her ear; that melodic, lilting voice cajoling Juliana to follow her. Always, Juliana obliged; she would follow her daughter anywhere.

'God will reunite us soon,' she whispered, wringing her hands as she continued pacing. 'He knows I cannot bear the separation much longer.' Weariness stole through her, and she carried her tea to the kitchen table. As soon as she sat down, she glanced around the empty seats, wondering who was missing. 'Your husband and child are dead,' she reminded herself.

The grandfather clock she'd brought from Roseland awoke suddenly, singing out its Westminster chimes. Startled, Juliana knocked her teacup flying.

'Oh, you silly old woman.' Quickly, she reached out to rescue a book from the accidental spillage seeping across the table: a heavy, black leatherbound volume that had caught her eye at Roseland the other day.

As usual, Bob had driven her past the beach, where she liked to watch the children play. Afterwards, she'd asked him to run her over to the manor house, to make sure everything was as it should be. Almost immediately, she'd forgotten why she was there, wandering in a daze through room after room, mingling anonymously with summer tourists, until she found herself inexplicably in her husband's old library, situated in part of the house closed to the public.

Even when she'd lived at Roseland, it wasn't a room Juliana had been in often. Sir Charles had been a traditionalist, always disappearing there after dinner, leaving his wife and daughter to their own devices. 'It's all your fault, Charles. If you had been a more loving father, Ellie would never have fallen for that boy. *Jack*. She would never have had Isabella. Or given her up. Her body and soul wouldn't have been ravaged by sadness. She'd be alive today!'

Rocking to and fro in her chair, Juliana cradled the book thoughtfully. 'My little Rosie will appreciate this,' she murmured. 'She at least respects the history of Roseland. Oh, I need to see my girls.' Forgetting they were in Italy, and that they'd spent the afternoon with her before they'd left, Juliana grumbled: 'Damn Jack, keeping them from me.'

'Juliana?' Margaret bustled into the kitchen, hobbling slightly; she was almost as old as her employer and had known her for most of their lives, first as a friend and now as companion housekeeper. 'Your visitors have arrived. Will you see them in here, or shall I —'

'Visitors?' Juliana stared at her, waiting for the fog in her mind to clear. 'Oh! You mean Cathy, come to play with Eloise. Bless her, she comes every Sunday. Tell John Merchant to let the ponies into the meadow, would you? Or perhaps the girls will swim in the lake today.'

Briskly, Margaret mopped up the spilled tea. 'No, no. It's not —'

'Don't fuss, Maggie,' Juliana cut in impatiently. 'Cathy is like one of the family. Roseland is her second home. She takes us as she finds us. She won't mind a bit of mess.'

Relieved that Juliana at least remembered what day it was, if not the year, Margaret didn't point out that they were no longer at Roseland, nor that Cathy was now a grown woman with a family of her own. 'It's *Arthur* come to see you. Your great-grandson.' Tactfully, she didn't mention that his grandpa was with him. Juliana had been ranting about Jack for days.

'Gee-Gee!' On cue, Arthur bowled into the kitchen, striding energetically across the room. His blond hair shone in the morning sunshine, and he brought with him the sweet earthy smell of outside. Stooping to kiss his great-grandmother on both cheeks, he said brightly: 'You're looking particularly beautiful today.'

'Nonsense, you silver-tongued flatterer,' Juliana reproved fondly. 'But you're a good boy. I was saying to your grandmother Eloise only yesterday, how charming you've grown up to be.'

'Yesterday?' Arthur glanced over his shoulder, discreetly shaking his head at his grandpa, who was hovering in the kitchen doorway, waiting for a sign that Juliana was calm enough for him to enter and begin the delicate process of negotiating wedding arrangements. After her fury at the church the other day, Jack didn't want to risk distressing Juliana again.

'At my daughter's *graveside*, Arthur.' Green eyes twinkled mischievously now. 'I haven't completely lost my marbles, you know? Despite what you all think.'

'Oh, Gee-Gee. Don't be daft.' Arthur sat down next to her at the table and took hold of her hand, squeezing it gently. 'We all adore you. Me, the twins. Pops.'

'Ah, yes. Your grandpa. You can come in now, Jack Merchant. I won't bite.'

'Juliana. Good morning.' As Jack crossed the kitchen, he smiled and gestured to Margaret that it was safe for her to leave. Her round face was pinched in concern, and he understood why. His last visit here, with Rebecca, had been an unmitigated disaster.

It had started off well enough. Rebecca was beautiful and vivacious, and, at first, Juliana had seemed mesmerised by her. Trancelike, with a faraway expression on her face, her eyes had remained fixed on her lively visitor.

In fact, for a full ten minutes, she'd barely said a word, and while Jack had grown increasingly concerned that something was badly wrong, Rebecca filled the silence by chatting brightly about her plans for the wedding at Roseland. Immediately, it became obvious that Juliana was indeed following every word, and bitterly resenting each one.

Jack blamed himself. Naturally, Rebecca didn't yet understand the subtleties of their family history. He'd explained some of it, but not all, and he was in no rush to do so. They were still getting to know each other, and Jack was fine with that. There was plenty he didn't know about Rebecca, too, but what meant the most to him was that she made him feel good. *Alive*. She breathed colour and energy into his life, and he couldn't get enough of that.

Now, as Margaret left the kitchen, they exchanged a knowing look, and Jack intuited that she was also recalling how she'd had to dash to Juliana's side in this very kitchen a few days ago, to calm her down while he and Rebecca beat a hasty retreat. Yes, it was safe to say Juliana hadn't taken to his fiancée. But Artie was different. Juliana doted on her great-grandson, and he knew exactly how to handle her. Between the two of them, they would manage to smooth things over. Jack was confident that all would be well.

'Loitering in corners is bad manners,' Juliana told him haughtily.

'Excuse me. I didn't want to barge in and intrude.'

Juliana gave a curt nod, which Jack took to be a sign of her tacit approval. He breathed out in relief, pleased to have sidestepped an early confrontation. He knew Juliana still saw him as the son of a humble employee on the estate, although she would never allude to it. Not to his face. Then again, she didn't need to. The past coloured every atom of air, both here and at Roseland.

An elegant, slightly condescending tilt of her head. 'Tell me, Jack, when is Isabella arriving?'

Jack hesitated. He still hadn't heard from his eldest daughter.

Juliana gave him a tight, knowing smile. 'I see. Well, I imagine she's not best pleased about your marriage. She'll have felt neglected enough by your decision to remain in Cornwall these past ten years. Now your absence is to be compounded by a new claim on your time and affection.'

'Izzy no longer needs me in the same way the twins do.' Sitting down opposite his grandson, Jack raised his eyebrows, signalling to Arthur that he would handle this. But he had to draw on all the reserves of patience he'd cultivated through his years as a surgeon not to retaliate to Juliana's gentle goading. 'Besides, Izzy's happy in Australia. She's forging her own path now. But as I told you at the church the other day, we're very hopeful she'll make it over for the wedding.'

'And as I told *you*, Jack, you're deluding yourself. Isabella hates us all. Surely you know that? But you disappoint me. I thought you were here to tell me you've come to your senses.' A dismissive wave of her hand. 'Oh, I have no objection per se to you getting married.'

'Thank you,' Jack interjected drily.

'After all, there's no fool like an old fool.' Juliana gave him a tart look. 'You're welcome to throw your life away, if you so choose. But you can parade your bride in front of me as many times as you like, my answer will remain the same. My home is not for hire.'

'So you *do* remember meeting her?' Jack raised his eyebrows, gently challenging.

Sensing a fight brewing, Arthur quickly intervened. 'Gee-Gee, you remember the National Trust takes care of the estate for you now? They manage the house. The gardens. So many people want to visit there. It's still the most beautiful stately home in the whole of Cornwall. In England. The entire world,' he exaggerated comically, as Juliana remained rigid.

'There's nothing wrong with my memory, Arthur dear,' she said, but her voice was softer as she addressed him. 'The Trust has done a fine job. Their stewardship is impeccable.'

'And legally binding,' Jack pointed out.

'Piffle. It's all just paperwork. Roseland has been in the Trelawney family for generations. In every way that counts, it belongs to me. I was the last bride to marry there. My daughter would have been the next. If she hadn't been duped into another unsuitable match. If the natural course of her life hadn't been so tragically derailed.' A sharp glance at Jack tangibly laid responsibility for both events at his feet.

'We all miss Eloise,' he said quietly. 'But would she have wanted us to grieve for ever? She was one of the most joyful people I've ever met.'

Juliana's back was ramrod straight. 'I don't need you to tell me about my daughter,' she said, looking teary-eyed now. 'She shone brighter than the sun. She eclipsed *everyone*. Your fiancée isn't fit even to walk in her shadow. Marry her if you must. In the church. At the beach. On the moon, for all I care. But mark my words. This wedding shall *never* take place at Roseland.' Thin shoulders quivered in a little shudder. 'I can feel it in my bones.'

13

Despite the thick stone walls of the farmhouse, built to keep it warm in winter and cool in summer, the temperature in the kitchen seemed to rise, as though the old brick bread oven in the corner was at full blast. The mid-morning sun was already high in the sky; light blazed through the leaded windows, streaming towards the rows of antique French crystal lining a huge pine dresser along one wall, fragmenting into dancing rainbows on the twinkling glass.

Closing her eyes to hide her tears, Juliana welcomed the sunshine on her face, feeling in its warmth the gentle touch of Eloise's hand. She felt it often; she always had. Her presence was all around her, ingrained into every familiar object that Juliana had brought from Roseland to keep her daughter's memory alive.

Opening her eyes, she took a soothing inventory of them. The grandfather clock that had once stood in the great hall, where Eloise had so frequently danced until dawn. The vases bequeathed to Juliana by her mother, which Eloise had filled with lavender from the garden.

As her gaze came to rest on the rocking chair by the Aga, Juliana let out a sigh, picturing her daughter swinging on it as a child, pretending that it was a boat on the high seas. In her imaginary play, Eloise had always been a pirate, an artist or adventurer. Never a princess, despite her beauty; despite the pretty dresses

Juliana had loved to have made for her.

So much promise, all for nothing. Jack should have known better, she thought fretfully. They'd both been far too young to fall in love, but hard work had already opened Jack's eyes to the ways of the world. He must have realised Eloise was destined for a more suitable marriage. He'd known full well that her father was a hard master. He should have anticipated Charles's rage at discovering their daughter's secret, improper romance with the teenage son of his estate manager.

When Charles turned his back on their daughter, banishing her baby, it had broken Juliana. She would never forgive him for that, even as she understood his objections to her unfortunate attachment to Jack. But while she blamed her husband, Juliana also blamed herself for not having been strong enough to stop him.

Mostly, though, she blamed Jack. For letting Ellie love him in the first place. For breaking her heart when he was forced to leave. Worse, for being the cause of her subsequent, inconsolable misery that allowed her to fall prey to that awful man. *Ted*. The local artist who'd coveted Eloise's fortune, trying by fair means and foul to steal it from her.

He'd failed, but it had all but destroyed Juliana when Ted had turned his attention to her twin granddaughters instead. Not even Jack's valiant rescue of them from the rising waters at Watchman's Cove could redeem him in Juliana's mind. Her poor, darling girls. They'd lost so much; she at least had to preserve Roseland for them. Their mother's childhood home; their heritage. *Their* destiny, not Jack Merchant's imposter bride's.

As if reading her thoughts, Arthur said softly: 'Just imagine, Gee-Gee, the wedding will be a true Trelawney celebration. Four generations all back together at the old ancestral home. What could be nicer?'

'My dear boy.' Juliana rested a hand on his arm. 'I'm afraid you're quite mistaken. This won't be a Trelawney wedding. Jack isn't one of us. Nor is his second-rate bride.'

Jack heard his own gasp of shock, and felt his blood boil. 'Now, hang on a minute, Juliana.'

Arthur shook his head, signalling that *he* would handle his great-grandmother this time. 'You're right, Gee-Gee. Neither Jack nor Rebecca are Trelawneys. But think of the twins. Rosie and Violet. And my mum, Isabella. Jack is their father. He's my *grandfather*. We're all descended from you and Sir Charles, aren't we? We all have Trelawney blood flowing through our veins.'

'*You* do. And if you or one of my granddaughters wanted to marry at Roseland, nothing would please me more. You'd be carrying on our esteemed name. Our family bloodline. Lord alone knows who this woman is, or where she's come from.'

'Her name is Rebecca,' Jack said quietly. 'And I don't care where she's from. I only care about her future. *My* future. I deserve to find happiness again.' He was telling himself as much as Juliana, and his words, so carefully thought out up to now, began to run away with him as his desperation for everything to be settled grew. 'So does my family. Rebecca will be an important part of that. She'll be good for Rose and Violet. They need a loving maternal presence in their lives. They've been without one far too long.'

As soon as he'd said it, Jack realised his mistake.

He had only meant to reassure Juliana that he was acting in the best interests of her granddaughters, but as he saw her shoulders slump and read the shock and distress on her face, he kicked himself for his tactlessness.

Despite their strained history, Jack had always respected Juliana. Once, he'd pitied her desperately. Sir Charles had been the one to banish him and his family from Roseland, and despite the pride and family loyalty which had kept Juliana silent at the time, Jack had seen how deeply it affected her. She may not have approved of her daughter loving him, but Juliana wasn't cruel. If she'd had her way, Jack was certain he would have been treated with far greater tolerance and kindness.

Pride was indeed one of Juliana's flaws, but Jack had also seen its benefits. He knew of the quiet acts of charity Juliana carried out in the village — her unseen, often unrecognised generosity within the community. As someone who was equally uncomfortable accepting gratitude, Jack perceived a sort of kindred spirit in the way Juliana silently went about noticing and helping others. More than that, he would for ever be connected to her through their intense love, and devastating loss, of Eloise.

Jack owed it to Ellie to keep an eye on and care for her grieving mother; he also shouldered his part in causing that grief, by failing to protect Eloise when she was alive. He refused to shirk his own guilt, and while Juliana's manner towards him often rankled, he shared and understood the unspeakable pain that lay beneath it. Watching the colour drain from her already pale face, Jack was furious with himself for upsetting her. Again.

'The twins have only one mother.' Juliana's voice was barely a whisper. 'You cannot replace my daughter in their affections. Even if this *Rebecca* has replaced her in yours.'

'I know. I'm sorry, Juliana. I honestly didn't mean to suggest . . .'

'She does realise she'll never be mistress at Roseland? I trust you haven't held out a false promise of riches, Jack. As you well know, my estate is held in trust for my grandchildren. You may give your bride your own name, for what it's worth. But she will never be a Trelawney. Nor inherit my fortune.'

'She doesn't want or need it, and neither do I.' Hearing the faintest snort from Arthur, Jack glanced across the table at him, reading the same thought in his blue eyes. Jack was rich. Not from old money handed down through generations of Cornish landowners, but from new money, earned through his own hard work, first through farming the land he'd bought in Australia, and now from being a highly esteemed oncologist.

'Rebecca isn't a gold-digger, Gee-Gee,' Arthur chipped in. 'She's a successful career woman. She works in television. Like my Evie. You remember Eve, don't you?'

'Of course I do. Cathy's girl.' A plaintive sigh. 'Where is Cathy? I want to see her.'

'She'll be at the wedding too,' Arthur encouraged, spotting a new angle for persuasion. 'She's here right now, as it happens. In Talland. You'll see her later, I'm sure.'

'Perhaps with Rebecca?' Jack suggested tentatively. 'It might help if you two have another chat. Get to know each other a little.'

'That's a great idea, Pops.' Arthur beamed in relief; he was running out of ideas. 'Eve and Cathy are going shopping this afternoon. I'll drop Evie a text. Suggest they drive over here first.' He looked questioningly at his grandpa. 'Or maybe we can pick them up when we leave here? After we've stopped off at Roseland, I mean. We could collect Rebecca at the same time.'

Juliana glared at Jack. 'Your fiancée is at *Roseland*?'

'She's working there, Gee-Gee.' Arthur groaned inwardly. He was trying to help, and it had seemed they might finally be getting somewhere. Now he'd made things worse again. 'Organising the filming,' he explained, almost immediately realising that he was digging himself into an even deeper hole. Juliana looked as though she might erupt with fury.

By contrast, her tone was pure ice as she demanded: 'Filming? What filming?'

For a moment, Jack wished that Rebecca had never set eyes on Roseland — never fallen in love with it and convinced him it would be the perfect place for them to get married. *Serendipity*; that's what she'd called it. They had met there by chance; they would marry there by design. Nothing could be more romantic, she'd insisted, and Jack had agreed.

Now he felt caught between two strong women: one he deeply respected, and one he loved to distraction. 'Rebecca isn't there planning our wedding,' he reassured Juliana. 'She's talking to the estate manager. This heatwave is turning the lawns to tinder.' Deliberately, Jack seized on what he hoped might distract Juliana: her beloved garden.

In fairness, it was half true: Rebecca *was* finding out what could be done to revive Roseland's drought-stricken grounds. Now wasn't the time to explain that she wanted them to look perfect not only for their wedding, but for the cameras that would be arriving any day.

'That's why Pops and I are heading over there next. After we've had a good long visit with you, of course,' Arthur continued, scrabbling to regain lost ground. 'To make sure the estate manager puts up warning signs around the estate.'

'Visitors need to be reminded that while picnics are permitted, barbecues are not,' Jack clarified truthfully. 'One stray match, and Roseland could go up in flames.'

He knew it was a low blow; deliberate emotional blackmail. But he was growing increasingly desperate to get Juliana on side. Only, as she sat up straighter, green eyes glinting now, Jack sensed that his attempt had backfired, and any concerns he had about the old lady's mental sharpness vanished as, gleefully, she threw down her trump card.

'Then *no* one could get married there,' she declared triumphantly. 'What would your precious Rebecca do *then*?'

14

'So, that went well,' Arthur joked as they reached Jack's car. After bidding a strained farewell to Juliana, they'd walked over to Roseland Hall in tense silence. Picking up on his grandpa's mood, Arthur had stayed quiet when Jack turned to stalk towards the car park, rather than going into the manor house to find Rebecca as agreed. 'Sorry, Pops. I did my best.'

'Oh, it's not your fault.' Jack unlocked his BMW and climbed in. 'I knew it was a long shot.' As soon as Arthur had fastened his seatbelt, he gunned the engine, reversing swiftly. Gravel spun up from his tyres as he accelerated up the drive to the tall iron gates at the exit.

Arthur swivelled in his seat for one last, lingering look at Roseland, then turned back to stare curiously at his grandpa. 'Where will you get married now?'

Jack gripped the steering wheel. 'At Roseland. The wedding will go ahead as planned.'

'Really? But how can it, if Juliana refuses to give her permission?'

'I don't need it. As you reminded her, she signed the manor over to the National Trust after Sir Charles died. In point of fact, it's *their* call. And they've already made it. The house will be closed to the public on Thursday and Friday. Roseland is ours for forty-eight hours.'

'Seriously?' Arthur looked hurt. 'Then why get me

all the way down from London to try and charm Juliana into agreeing? You know, that does make me feel a bit . . . used.'

'Sorry, Artie.' Jack sighed. 'That really wasn't my intention. But I can see it looks like that from where you're sitting, and you're right to be cross. I put you in an awkward position.'

'Juliana, too. I think she actually believes she still lives at Roseland. The look on her face when I said Rebecca was already there.' Arthur winced. 'I felt awful.'

'Me too, believe it or not.' Jack changed gear, wrenching too hard, and the engine roared. 'Damnit. It's just a bloody wedding. Everyone needs to chill the heck out.'

'You know it's not that simple, Pops. Getting married is a big deal. Holding the wedding at Roseland is huge. Juliana was as white as a sheet by the time we left. She looked like she'd seen a ghost.'

'It probably feels like that,' Jack acknowledged. 'It stirs up a lot of memories for me, too. To be honest, that's why I wanted you along for the ride. Your great-grandmother adores you. I thought she might find your approval of the wedding comforting.'

'Right. Sure. I get that.' Arthur could never stay mad at his grandpa for long.

'I don't need her permission, but I suppose part of me wanted her approval.' Jack shook his head. 'At my age! Still trying to court favour from a family that considers me a black sheep.'

'Well, I guess you were a sheep farmer, back in Oz,' Arthur quipped weakly, then frowned. 'Which reminds me. Have you heard from my mum yet? Maybe if she does come, that'll make Gee-Gee feel better. Juliana might adore me, as you say, but she never stops talking about her *long-lost granddaughter Isabella*. She thinks Mum hates her, though. Maybe she does. Who knows?'

'Your mum is pretty complex,' Jack said evasively. 'But no, I haven't heard from Izzy. Rebecca was going to follow up my email to her. Apparently, I forgot to put my lovely fiancée's name on all the invites. I know, I'm an idiot,' Jack said, when Arthur chuckled. 'I was rushing, OK? I just put my name down as the host. Although I did add that you're my best man.' He grinned. 'I thought that might win favour with your mum.'

Arthur shook his head. 'You're becoming seriously Machiavellian in your old age, Pops. Evie said it, and I'm beginning to think she was right.'

'I just want everyone to be happy. There's too much tragedy in life. We have to seize the good bits. Cherish and enjoy them while we have the chance. Like you do with Eve, yes?'

Driving in Cornwall, Jack never took his eyes off the road for a second; the narrow lanes meandering through miles of hedge-bordered fields could twist or drop away into a dyke without warning. Even knowing them like the back of his hand, Jack never took safety for granted. He was not only a doctor by profession; he was a protector by nature.

Having lost so much, Jack held on extra tightly to everything he had left. Juliana wasn't the only one clinging on to her loved ones. Rebecca had been right to tease him about trying to wrap her up in cotton wool. He wanted to do the same with his girls. With Arthur. Scanning the road to make absolutely sure it was clear, he turned to look at him, studying his reaction, needing to feel he had someone on his side, but also keen to know that his grandson was happy.

'Eve?' Arthur beamed. 'Yeah. She's the one, Pops. No doubt.'

'Good man. That makes me happy.' Reassured, Jack returned his eyes to the road, enjoying the purr of the BMW's engine, the freedom of empty country lanes. His peripheral vision took in acres of farmland that, sun-scorched and freshly harvested in a pre-emptive bid to avoid heatwave damage, reminded him of Australia . . . of Izzy. He hoped his eldest daughter really would come for the wedding. Not only for Juliana's sake, but his own. And Arthur's. His grandson might hide it well, but he'd had a tough ride, too. He needed his mum. 'Eve's wonderful, Artie. Perfect for you.'

'I know, Pops. Now keep your eyes on the bloody road, would you?'

Jack chuckled affectionately, slowing the car and deftly turning into the steep lane leading to Talland Church. As they passed it, he remembered Rebecca's gasp of horror when he'd suggested they hold the ceremony there. She'd looked so shocked that he had immediately dropped the idea, and, in truth, he couldn't blame her for vetoing it.

Everyone had adored Eloise. Even strangers had been captivated by her. Her down-to-earth friendliness, despite her privileged upbringing. Her startling beauty and quirky exuberance. Her death had shocked the whole community; every guest in the church congregation would have been thinking about her, buried in the graveyard outside.

Rebecca deserved to be the star at her own wedding, and the twins deserved to be bridesmaids without people whispering about them behind their hands. A private ceremony and reception for close friends and family at Roseland was not only Rebecca's dream, it was Jack's priority. But he genuinely didn't want to upset Juliana. He'd deliberately gone to find her at the church to acknowledge and pay respect to her enduring grief. Even as her stubbornness frustrated him, he was moved by her vulnerability and was now feeling torn.

'You tried your best with Juliana, too,' Arthur said, staring at the pretty chapel as they drove past it and continued up the hill. 'I know you care about her. You spend more time with her than any of us. Not that she remembers it. Her dementia is getting much worse, isn't it?'

Jack didn't reply until they reached Goldeneye, and he'd parked. 'Perhaps.' He wasn't entirely convinced; he had a niggling sense that Juliana had just outplayed him. 'Old people tend to live more in the past than the present. Sometimes they confuse the two. Roseland symbolises the life Juliana had. Everything she once held dear, as well as what she's lost. It does for me, too.' He gripped the steering wheel tighter, even though the engine was off.

'You sound like you don't actually *want* to get married there, Pops.'

'It's . . . tricky. Roseland is where I fell in love with Eloise. It's where I lost her, too.'

'And where she gave up my mum when she was a baby.'

'Exactly. At some level, I guess I hoped the wedding might be an occasion for healing. For all of us. You said it yourself, Artie. Four generations together again.'

'If Mum comes, that is.'

Jack winced. 'I know she's still mad at me.'

'Mum's mad at everyone.'

'Izzy's been through a lot. But if I've learned anything from meeting Rebecca, it's that love can heal.' Jack shrugged. 'Without wishing to sound trite or soppy.'

Arthur grinned. 'What you sound like is a man in love. I'm happy for you, Pops.'

'I wish everyone felt the same. I realise our family is complex. But, well, between you and me, Rebecca doesn't have one of her own. I think that's another reason she loves Roseland. Family tradition. She wants to be part of that. She can't wait to be a stepmum to the twins.'

'I'm not sure they quite share her enthusiasm,' Arthur said honestly.

'I handled that badly, too. I know I did. I should have waited to talk to the girls in person this evening, not on the phone. Stupidly, I thought they might be excited. A wedding at Roseland. They love that bloody place.'

'They love you more. I guess the idea of sharing you is tough for them.'

'The twins will always come first for me. They're actually a big part of the reason I'm getting married, to be honest. I want to give them more stability. Maybe a female influence in their lives, as well. Like I said to Juliana.'

Arthur pulled a face. 'Yeah. Don't remind me.'

'Juliana is a wonderful grandmother,' Jack said diplomatically. 'She loves seeing Rose and Violet. But she can't help them practically anymore. The twins are growing up, but I'm not ready to cut them loose just yet. Only, I'm at the hospital so much. Rebecca's work is far more flexible. She travels a lot, working here and there. She can work entirely remotely, if she needs to.'

'It's the modern world, Pops,' Arthur teased.

'Sure.' Jack gave his grandson a rueful grin. 'Fine, I'm an old fuddy-duddy. The twins are always telling me so.'

'I bet they are. I can't wait to see them. Hey, I can come with you to Heathrow, if you like? Keep you company. I'm not in any rush now. Eve's spending the day with her mum, and neither of us have to be in the office tomorrow. We both phoned our bosses. It's a done deal. We'll be working from Talland all week. Through the miracles of modern technology,' he joked.

'Ha. Thanks. I'd love that. Both the company and you guys being here till the wedding.'

'After the hash you made of the invitations, Pops, I could hardly leave you to organise your own stag do.'

'Hmm. That's the least of my worries.'

'Oh, I wouldn't worry too much. By this time next week, you and Rebecca will be married and jetting off on honeymoon.'

Jack shrugged. 'Before today, I would've agreed with you. Now, I'm not so sure.'

'Trust me. Actually, trust your *fiancée*. Juliana may not have spent much time with Rebecca yet. She hasn't had a proper chance to get to know her. But I have. She's a tough cookie. I reckon she'll get the wedding she wants, or die trying.'

15

'I'm an idiot.' Cathy groaned as she parked her car in a lucky space on Plymouth's pretty yet bustling waterfront, where they planned to have lunch after shopping. 'There I was, rabbiting on about us not being in a du Maurier novel, all the time having no clue that she's called *Rebecca*.' She turned to look at Eve, groaning again as her daughter laughed. 'It's not funny!'

'Well, it is a bit, you have to admit.'

'I blame Jack. She must be laughing at us up her sleeves. Not that she had any. Or much of a skirt, either.' Cathy laughed too, now. 'Do I sound like an old fuddy-duddy?'

'No more than usual.' Eve grinned. 'Anyway, she didn't hear us talking about her. She has no idea we thought she might be as psychotic as her fictional namesake. But I'll be sure to avoid getting in any boats with her. I'll even hide all the matches at Roseland on Friday.'

'Thursday,' Cathy corrected. 'The rehearsal is the day before the wedding, remember?'

'Right. I guess we'd better get a move on, then.' Reluctantly, Eve released her seatbelt.

Cathy watched her in concern. 'Are you quite sure you're up for this?'

'Totally. I'm actually looking forward to it. The pomp and ceremony. Even the cameras. The last wedding I went to was over in minutes. My boss got married at Richmond Register Office. No fuss, no frills. Straight back to work. Rebecca was right about one thing: TV is cut-throat. You have to be constantly on your game. My boss never even went on honeymoon.'

'Your boss sounds exhausting. But I meant are you too tired for shopping?'

'Never. I want Artie to see me in a posh frock. It might even prompt a proposal. Ha, I could do with a honeymoon. I haven't had a holiday since I came out to see you in Dubai.'

'I wonder where Jack and Rebecca will go,' Cathy mused.

'Somewhere expensive. Did you see the size of that ruby on her ring?'

'That was Eloise's,' Cathy said quietly. 'Juliana gave it to her on her fortieth birthday. You must have seen paintings of her wearing it? They're all over Roseland.'

'Really? Bit tactless of Jack to give it to Rebecca, then. How did he get it, anyway?'

'Eloise gave it to him before she died. Along with the matching necklace. She actually told him to give them to the new love of his life. Although I doubt Juliana knows that.'

Cathy frowned, thinking back to her flying visit to the farmhouse before they'd set off for Plymouth. Fully expecting Jack and Arthur to have charmed approval from Juliana, she'd been concerned to find her in a state of distress and mental confusion. Margaret was trying to calm her, but it had quickly become clear to Cathy that Juliana wasn't in her right mind.

She'd looked half wild, fretting about the ponies escaping from the meadow, then insisting Cathy take a dip in the lake with Eloise to cool down. Realising she'd come at a bad time, Cathy had hugged Juliana and promised Margaret she would return later in the afternoon, once Juliana had rested. Physically, she was frail, but she'd always been as sharp as a tack. Perhaps she'd be better after a nap. Cathy hoped so, feeling a niggling worry about dementia.

'So this wedding has Eloise's blessing, at least,' Eve said. 'That makes me feel a tiny bit better. The fact that Eloise knew Jack would move on, and she was OK with that.'

'Ellie only ever wanted Jack to be happy. And you know what? I think, finally, he is.'

'Really? He struck me as a bit *too* hyper last night. Don't you think? Like he was trying extra hard to be funny. Make us all like his fiancée. But you know him better than I do.'

'Jack and I go way back. He's happy,' Cathy said simply, picturing the sparkle in Jack's blue eyes at last night's barbecue — remembering the look of almost bewildered joy on his face, as though he couldn't quite believe his luck.

Cathy had to admit that she'd warmed to Rebecca more as the evening had worn on. After an awkward start, with Rebecca performing her own introduction, she'd been the perfect hostess, charmingly attentive to her guests, witty and teasing with her fiancé. But it wasn't the electric spark of sensuality between the two of them that had finally convinced Cathy her old friend was in a good place. It was the hug he'd given her before she'd left.

To Cathy, it had almost felt like a goodbye. Jack had told her over brunch that when he looked at her, he saw Eloise. After strolling across the moonlit garden with her, while Eve and Arthur helped Rebecca clear up after the barbecue, he'd held her close as he said goodnight. Cathy had sensed him letting go of something. Not their friendship, she hoped, but perhaps her connection to Eloise. She had almost felt him mentally closing that door, to open a new one.

'Well, I'm glad he's happy,' Eve said. 'He deserves it. Not all men of Jack's age are as laidback and lovely as him. Jack's definitely one of the good guys.'

Cathy gave her a knowing look. 'You're thinking of your dad, aren't you? Don't judge him too harshly, sweetheart. He cares about all of us, in his way.'

'From a distance, you mean. Where he doesn't have to get his hands dirty, as it were.'

'Not for much longer. I called him this morning, while you were still in bed. Don't worry, that wasn't a dig,' she added quickly, as Eve opened her mouth to protest. 'I told you, you need to rest. Anyway, your father's coming over for the wedding.'

'You're kidding.'

'Nope. Jack suggested it last night. He and Chris are old friends, too, remember?'

'And you're happy about that? Dad coming to Talland?' Eve rolled her eyes. 'Doesn't he hate the cottage? Didn't he try to make you sell it once?'

'A long time ago. He was worried that Cornwall makes me go loopy. In fairness, it does stir up a lot of emotion for me. This place is part of me, darling. It shaped who I am.'

'Exactly! And Dad wanted you to give that up.' Eve huffed.

Cathy thought for a moment. 'Maybe. But I never will.' She laughed, then squeezed her daughter's arm. 'Come on. That posh frock won't buy itself. Let's hit the shops. Find something that will knock your boyfriend for six.'

'Like Rebecca did Jack, you mean? Or was it vice versa?'

'Both, I suspect. They looked equally besotted. Mind you, Artie couldn't take his eyes off you. Maybe Rebecca won't be the only bride at Roseland this summer,' Cathy teased.

'Oh, God, no. I told you, Mum. You couldn't pay me to get married there. That place is definitely haunted. Sir Charles is guarding it from beyond the grave.'

'There's only one ghost at Roseland,' Cathy said quietly, thinking once again of her dream about Eloise. 'For Rebecca's sake, I hope she doesn't make an appearance.'

16

Later that afternoon, Cathy headed back to the farmhouse to see Juliana, as promised. She had hoped that Eve would come with her, but after returning from their shopping trip, her daughter had suddenly seemed tense and distracted. Hearing her phone ping repeatedly, Cathy realised that work — and the promotion she was chasing — must be playing on her mind. Sure enough, Eve said she had a million emails to answer. Cathy had sighed in resignation and left her to it.

It was such glorious weather, she drove the long way round to Roseland, sticking to country lanes rather than main roads. With the sunroof pulled back, she filled her lungs with soft air sweetened by the scents of honeysuckle, mint, elderflower and jasmine, while her eyes feasted on cheering bursts of bright red fuchsia, yellow zinnias and purple foxgloves that jostled for space in the hedgerows, like the colourful dresses of fine ladies at a summer ball.

The breeze wove its fingers through her hair, tousling her usual neat blonde bob, and Cathy felt happier than she had done in ages. She was pleased to see Juliana calmer, too, as she arrived an hour later to find her sitting in the shade of the ancient oak tree nearest the manor house, where Margaret had set up afternoon tea for them and was bustling around, making sure Juliana was comfortable.

'This is lovely, thank you so much.' Cathy gazed

with pleasure at the pretty wrought-iron table where Juliana was already settled, a cream silk shawl draped over her lap, despite the dry, scorching heat even this late in the day.

'Cathy, so good of you to come.' Juliana held out both arms, inviting a hug.

'You're looking much better. You were a little tired earlier,' Cathy said tactfully.

'I was furious, not tired.' Green eyes twinkled. 'You don't need to humour me, dear.'

'Of course not. Shall I pour? This cake looks deliciously tempting, too.' Cathy sorted refreshments for each of them from an impressive home-baked selection, then settled down in her seat with a sigh. 'It's lovely to see you both again. And you really are looking well, Juliana.'

'Thanks to Maggie here. She's a godsend. Without her, I'd be like Miss Havisham, surrounded by tattered curtains and dusty old furniture coming apart at the seams. Like me.'

'Nonsense.' Margaret clucked in gentle disapproval.

'Maggie's right,' Cathy said, feeling herself blush as she remembered likening Juliana to Mrs Danvers last night. Even so, she was happy to see her usual sharp humour back in evidence, along with her neat chignon and elegant clothes: a floral dress not dissimilar to her own, except in soft cream, as opposed to Cathy's favourite pinks. 'You look as fresh as a daisy, Juliana.'

'Sweet of you to say so, Cathy dear. But sand is for children to wiggle their toes in and build castles. No point burying our heads in it. I hate getting old, but it is what it is.'

'Well, you seem in fine form to me.'

'One tries.' Juliana let out a sigh. 'I walk over to Roseland most mornings. Tend to my roses. Keep my mind and body active, just as Jack is always nagging me to.' She raised her eyebrows. 'Still, I suppose he'll have his bride to boss about now. Or is it the other way round?'

Cathy smiled. 'Oh, Rebecca isn't so bad. She comes on a little strong at first, I grant you. But this must all be pretty daunting for her.' She gestured expansively with one arm.

Even having grown up spending weekends and summers at Roseland, exploring the sprawling grounds and playing hide-and-seek in the many rooms, Cathy found it slightly intimidating. Not spooky, as Eve had said earlier, but definitely awe-inspiring.

Rebecca had talked incessantly about Roseland at the barbecue last night; it had clearly made a big impression on her. Perhaps that accounted for the glamorous front she seemed determined to put on, Cathy speculated: as Jack's fiancée, maybe she felt obliged to live up to what might be expected of a bride at one of Cornwall's most prestigious stately homes.

Juliana didn't bother turning to look. She'd cherished Roseland for six decades; she could recall every inch of it as effortlessly as her daughter's face. 'Rebecca is a painted harlot. All that make-up. It's a mask, I tell you. She's as fake as her nails.'

'That's a bit harsh,' Cathy chided softly. She had to admit that she hadn't been able to take her eyes off Rebecca's striking face last night, but she'd watched enough of the TV programmes Eve had worked on, and read the magazines she devoured for research into new feature ideas, to know that such an overtly sultry look was the latest trend. 'It's the fashion nowadays.'

Juliana frowned. '*Eve* doesn't look like that. She doesn't dress like a whore.'

That shocked Cathy, but she didn't want to get into an argument about Jack's fiancée. She barely knew the woman, and while Eve had also seemed convinced there was something false about her, Cathy was still determined to give Rebecca the benefit of the doubt. 'Evie prefers jeans to dresses, that's all,' she hedged. 'Although, as it happens, she's just bought a gorgeous green silk one to wear to the wedding.' *Damnit*. She'd resolved on the drive over not to bring it up so soon.

'She'll find another occasion to wear it,' Juliana dismissed loftily. 'I've made my wishes on that subject perfectly plain.' She fell silent for a few moments, then said brightly: 'Perhaps Arthur will take her dancing. He's extremely good at it. Rhythm is in his blood. Oh, how Ellie loved to dance.' She waved her hands, as though conducting music only she could hear.

'She had natural grace,' Cathy agreed, relieved to change the subject. 'And she loved a good party. Even pretend ones.' She remembered Eloise sneaking her into Roseland after dark when they were children, so they could waltz around the great hall, giggling as they curtsied to pretend suitors.

'Now *that's* a wedding I would have no objection to.' Juliana thumped the table. 'My Arthur and your Eve. It's what I've always hoped for. Isn't it, Maggie? Ever since my darling Ellie left us. Her grandson settling down with her best friend's daughter. Those two were made for each other.'

Cathy nodded. 'We all said so, didn't we? From the moment they met.' She sighed, remembering that day on the beach, her then sixteen-year-old daughter coming home giddy with excitement after meeting

Arthur — tanned and charming, fresh off the plane from Australia — for the first time. They'd both had other relationships over the years, and a fair few ups and downs, but they had always come back together.

'Their love was written in the stars,' Maggie said fondly.

'That's a lovely thought.' Cathy smiled. 'Although, they did just have another of their little tiffs,' she added thoughtfully. 'I was actually thinking of suggesting a day at the beach tomorrow. Invite Artie along. Just to make sure the two of them are OK. Force Eve to take a break from working so hard, too.' She hesitated. 'I don't suppose you still have the twins' kayak, do you, Juliana?' She knew there was no need to reference why the girls didn't keep it at their own house, nor why Rose and Violet refused ever to set foot on a boat again.

'Funny you should ask that,' Margaret chipped in, propping her hands on her ample hips. 'It must be something about the hot weather. Makes everyone fancy themselves a sailor, doesn't it? I was only saying to Maureen at the bakery this morning. Talland is growing more like Newquay by the day. Hundreds of colourful skiffs are bobbing all over the bay, and —'

Juliana huffed impatiently. 'Oh, do get to the point, Maggie.'

'I was coming to it, Miss Impatience,' her long-suffering companion scolded.

Cathy laughed, enjoying the good-natured bickering of their lifelong friendship. 'Don't tell me someone else has borrowed the boat?' she said, with a groan of disappointment.

'Clever you. That's exactly it,' Margaret looked surprised. 'Just this morning, in fact.'

'Really? That's a shame. Never mind. We can hire one at the little café on the beach.'

'Oh, you won't need to do that,' Margaret continued quickly. 'I'm not one to spoil a surprise, but since you've already mentioned a picnic . . .' She blushed at the pleasure of having news to share. 'Apparently, that's the plan. A day at the beach to celebrate the twins coming home.'

'What a brilliant idea,' Cathy said happily. 'Good on Jack. I know he can't wait to see the girls, and they love the beach. If not the sea itself. For obvious reasons,' she finished quietly.

'Actually, it wasn't Jack's idea.' Juliana's eyes glinted. 'It was Rebecca's.'

Cathy was surprised, but pleased. 'Was it? Well, that was very kind of her.'

'Indeed.' Juliana's head tilted. 'I'm sure she believes it made her *seem* so. She was quite plaintive in her request when she came here earlier. She's a talented actress, I'll say that for the woman. In fact, if you ask me, she should be in front of those wretched cameras, not behind them.'

On cue, the sound of an engine rumbled across the peace of the afternoon, and the three women turned to watch a convoy of trucks weave its way steadily towards Roseland.

'I wonder what they're filming,' Margaret said wistfully.

Juliana frowned. 'I couldn't care less. Damned ridiculous inconvenience.'

'Now, now. They won't bother us, if we don't bother them.'

Cathy didn't turn to look, keeping her eyes fixed on Juliana's face, still bothered by her animosity towards

Rebecca. After Friday, she would be the twins' stepmum. They adored their grandma and would need to know she was at peace with the idea of their dad getting married. 'You've said a couple of times now that you think Rebecca's hiding something,' she said cautiously. 'Putting on some kind of mask. I know she's very beautiful, but do you have any particular reason to suppose her kindness is an act?'

Juliana lifted a thin arm in a sweeping gesture. 'Look around my garden, dear. Some of the most beautiful flowers also carry the deadliest toxins. *Nerium oleander*. Morning glory. Hemlock. Deadly nightshade. Their beauty belies their poison. It's Mother Nature's way, isn't it? Dazzle her victims. Lure them into a honeytrap.'

Cathy frowned. '*Dazzle*. Wait a minute, are you suggesting . . . Juliana, I really don't think Rebecca is trying to *trap* Jack. Why on earth would she do that? Unless you mean because he's rich. That she's after his money. That's certainly not the impression I get, but —'

'But you're far too trusting, Cathy. That is your only failing, while Jack Merchant's is pride. His arrogance and vanity have blinded him. He's invited the very devil into his home, and he's too busy congratulating himself on his conquest to see the danger.'

'Danger? Devil? Now, steady on.' Cathy knew Juliana visited Talland Church every week, but she was also aware that she rarely went inside. Her visits were to remember Eloise, not honour God. Religion, for Juliana, had always been more about family tradition.

Vividly, she recalled her and Sir Charles taking their place on the front row every Sunday, but their presence had owed more to social patronage:

the Trelawneys had always been philanthropists; local benefactors. This biblical fervour was new, and slightly disturbing.

Juliana nodded wisely. 'The Lord is watching. And so is my daughter.'

Cathy glanced back at the manor house. Despite her awe of it, she didn't believe it was haunted. Her comment to Eve that there was only one ghost at Roseland had been a throwaway, somewhat flippant one. 'Juliana . . .'

'My Ellie will never stop looking after her girls. She isn't fooled by this woman. Don't let her deceive *you*. Rebecca may have the face of an angel, but she's the devil incarnate. And like the malevolent serpent, she will bide her time. Then, when everyone least expects it, she will bite.'

17

Rose was so cold, her body felt numb. She sat rigidly, paralysed by fear and the freezing water swilling around her legs, rising ever closer to where she was perched precariously on a rough stone shelf, carved out of the rocks over hundreds of years by the ferocious sea. Faster and faster, it rose, almost up to her waist now.

It was so dark, she couldn't see anything above, below or around her. All she knew was that her twin sister was right beside her, grasping her hand, whispering to her that everything would be OK. 'Help. We need help, Letty,' Rose whimpered.

'I'm here. It's OK,' came the muffled response.

Everything sounded muffled, and Rose shook her head from side to side, trying to clear it. She thought she heard shouting in the distance. Male voices. No, *one* voice. It came louder now, ordering them to stay where they were; that he was coming to get them. Rose opened her mouth to reply, but a sudden hard push in her back sent her tumbling into the ice-cold sea. She tried to scream, but water filled her lungs, choking her.

Coughing violently, she kicked her legs and arms, clawing desperately with her hands as she saw a flickering light ahead of her . . . The sun? No, it wasn't that. It was . . .

'Shush, Rosie. It was just a bad dream.' Violet's voice was clearer now, low and urgent, but her hand was gentle as she stroked back her sister's tangled, long blonde hair.

The bright light was her bedside lamp, Rose realised, blinking rapidly and looking around. Only, this wasn't her bedroom. 'Where are we?' Her heart began pounding faster again, as panic returned. 'Where's Dad? I want Dad!' It had been his voice calling to her; she was certain of it.

'Dad's at home. We're in Italy, remember? We're going home today.'

'Oh. Right. Yeah.' Rose sat up, rubbing her eyes. 'Of course.'

Violet continued to watch her sister in concern. It was ages since Rosie had experienced nightmares so bad that she'd called out in her sleep. It was all their dad's fault, she thought crossly. His phone call had ruined everything: their holiday; their entire life. 'Anna's dad is taking us to the airport in an hour, so you'd better hurry up. I'm all packed and ready to go.'

Rose didn't move. 'I *want* to go home. I've really missed Dad. But . . .'

'I know. I get it. I feel the same.' Violet pulled a face. 'It's not just Dad anymore, is it?'

'How could he get engaged without even telling us? Who is she, anyway?'

Violet shrugged. 'Dad said on the phone that he wants to tell us everything in person. Explain it all properly. He was just calling ahead because he didn't want it to come as a shock.'

'Well, it is.' Rose wrapped her arms around her thin body, hugging herself. 'Anyway, I don't care who she is. She's not our mum. We don't need a pretend one.'

'No. We don't,' Violet agreed fiercely. Then, seeing her twin's blue eyes fill with tears, she added more gently: 'Don't worry, I can fix this. I'll make everything OK again, I promise. I always do, don't I?'

Rose relaxed a little. 'Grandma says you're the brains of the family.'

'And you are its beating heart,' Violet quoted softly, remembering what Juliana always told them. 'Just like Mum was. Dad knows that. He won't want to upset us. He'll come around. He always does. I bet you my secret stash of Italian liqueurs we can get him to call off this stupid wedding.'

Rose smiled weakly, climbing out of bed now, wincing as her feet touched the cool terracotta floor tiles. Their friend's villa was beautiful, but old and traditionally built. Rose had loved staying here, but after so many weeks away, she was homesick now: for her own bed, and for the comforts of their modern house. She hated the idea that they would return to find a strange woman living in it. 'Do you really think so?' She frowned doubtfully. 'But how?'

'Knowledge is power,' Violet quipped, checking her phone. 'I texted Eve after Dad's phone call. Asked her to do some digging around. See what she can find out about his fiancée.'

'What, you mean like on Facebook? Embarrassing old photos? Ex-boyfriends?'

'Maybe. But I was thinking about more important stuff. She works in TV, apparently.'

'Like Eve.'

'Exactly. Evie said she'll ask around. Phone some of her contacts. Find out any interesting gossip. Anything incriminating.' Violet scrolled through her phone, reading her text chats, frowning at how little Eve had managed to find out so far. Basically, nothing.

Rose frowned, too, still looking dubious. 'Dad won't care if she's messed up at work. He says people make mistakes all the time. How would that split them up?'

'I guess it depends on what I find out,' Violet said, more confidently than she felt. 'But don't you worry, Rosie. I've got this.'

* * *

In truth, Violet had no plan beyond trying to suss out the enemy. That was the only thing she knew for sure: this *Rebecca* was a threat to their happy life with the dad who'd been everything to them since they lost their mum. They didn't need or want another woman bossing them around, or telling their dad what to do. Everything was perfect just as it was.

And Rosie was right: although they were identical twins, Violet had always felt older than her sister. She felt responsible for her, and considered herself the smart one — the one who saw through people, and who got things done. Rosie was too soft, too trusting. She was a daydreamer; a bookworm who believed life should be like it was in the novels she loved reading.

Their dad was like that, too. Always seeing the best in people. Believing in happy endings, even though he wasn't a big reader. Except for the stories he'd read when they were little. Violet knew he'd secretly edited out the sad bits, making characters seem much nicer than they were. But losing their mum had destroyed all her faith in fairy tales. They had to write their own happy ending now, and it definitely didn't include a wicked stepmother.

Yes, she needed to protect her sister, and her dad — even from himself. He'd sounded so soppy and loved-up on the phone, but Violet knew he hadn't really met his Cinderella. She'd bet her new iPhone that his *incredible fiancée* was only interested in him because he was rich. And if there was a way to make their dad see that this woman was a toad not a princess, Violet was determined to find it.

18

Twelve hours later, Jack hummed happily as he wandered into his study, leaving his daughters to unpack. They'd been chatty enough with Arthur on the long drive from Heathrow, but Jack had picked up that they were giving him the cold shoulder, answering all his questions about their holiday in monosyllables. As soon as they arrived home, they'd sloped off to their rooms.

Jack didn't mind too much. 'They'll come around. They always do,' he consoled himself. He was over the moon to have them home again; it felt like they'd been away ages, and he hated being apart from his girls. They went to boarding school, but it was only across the border in Somerset, and this was the first time they'd been on holiday without him.

At first, he'd resisted the idea. As a single parent, he was fiercely protective; he would run through fire to keep his children safe, and he worried about them constantly. But they'd begged him to change his mind, and eventually Jack had given in, reassured that they'd be well looked after by their best friend Anna's parents, who owned a villa on the Amalfi coast.

'I should have been a banker, not a surgeon,' he huffed ironically, sitting down at his desk and opening his laptop, to catch up on work correspondence. Both Anna's parents managed hedge funds, hence her being at boarding school: they worked longer hours even than Jack. 'But I'd rather save lives than make millions,' he reminded himself.

Even so, he flicked away from his emails to run a quick search for Italian villas. Maybe Rebecca would fancy that for a honeymoon. They hadn't actually discussed it yet; planning the wedding at Roseland had taken all their energy, especially with Juliana throwing a spanner in the works. As far as Jack was concerned, he would happily forgo one. He didn't want to be away from the girls again, and, besides, there was nowhere he loved more than Cornwall.

'Please come, Izzy,' he implored, returning to his emails, disappointed to find that there was still no reply from his eldest daughter. His first instinct had been to call her, but he'd resisted it, not wanting to put her on the spot. But perhaps he should. Picking up his phone, he was about to dial her number when Violet marched into the study, her face a picture of discontent.

'Oh, not you as well.' She rolled her eyes.

'Sorry?' Jack swivelled round on his chair, tucking his phone away.

'You're always working. So is Eve. We were *supposed* to meet up. I've got a present for her, and everything. But she's bailed on me. Apparently, she's got, like, a zillion emails.'

Jack gave her a sympathetic smile. 'Wishing you were back in Italy already, hey?'

'Of course not.' An indignant glare. 'I couldn't wait to get home.'

'Right. Well, that's good.' He pondered for a moment, grappling with the mysteries of teenage logic, drawing a blank. 'So why the long face, then?'

An exasperated huff. 'Don't you *know*?'

Noticing Violet's fleeting glance at the framed

photo of Rebecca on his desk, Jack sighed. 'I might have an inkling. But I'd prefer it if you could tell me in your own words.'

'Fine. I'm mad at you for getting engaged behind our backs. I'm worried about Rosie. I don't want to be a dumb bridesmaid, and I —'

Jack held up his hands in surrender. 'Woah! OK, I get the picture.'

'You asked.'

'I did. And I'm glad you've told me. Thank you for being honest.'

An exaggerated eye-roll. 'Did you even miss us? Or were you too busy with *her*?' Another, even more disdainful glance at the photo.

'Of course I missed you. Loads. Both of you. I phoned you every day, didn't I? For a whole month.'

Violet scowled, throwing herself onto the sofa. 'Exactly. A month. And you never mentioned Rebecca before that. So you're saying you met her after we left?'

'Yep. The day you flew to Italy, as it happens. I went to see your grandma, after dropping you at the airport. Then I was planning a quiet night in, when I bumped into —'

'Yeah, yeah. Rebecca told us that bit just now. We got the works about how it was fate, the two of you meeting at Roseland. Blah, blah, blah. She's trying really, really hard.'

'That's a good thing, yes?' Jack frowned, flummoxed again by teenage contradiction.

'Maybe.' Violet shrugged. 'But it's still weird. The whole thing has freaked Rosie out completely. She's had nightmares again ever since you phoned and told us.'

'Oh?' Jack frowned in concern. 'I'm sorry to hear that. I'll talk to her.'

'She's asleep.'

'OK, well, I'll chat with her tomorrow.' He risked a smile now. 'I've taken the day off especially to spend with you guys. We've got plenty of time. I'm all yours.'

'Yeah, right. Until Friday. I mean, what's the rush? She's not pregnant, is she?'

Jack stared at Violet, too shocked to reply. The thought of having a baby with Rebecca hadn't occurred to him; he'd well and truly moved on from that life stage. But perhaps she hadn't. She was still in her early forties; maybe she had expectations they hadn't yet discussed.

Jack wasn't sure how he felt about that, but, for the first time, the age difference between them gave him pause for thought. He hesitated, and Violet, sensing weakness, went for the jugular.

'She's trapped you into marrying her, hasn't she? Because you're rich, and she works for a totally lame TV company. I asked Evie to look her up, you know? She works on *proper* programmes. Anyway, she hasn't found out a single thing about Rebecca. It's like she doesn't actually exist. Or doesn't want anyone to know about her. What's she hiding?'

'Hang on a minute. You asked Eve to *investigate* Rebecca?'

A careless shrug. 'I meant google her, Dad. Not call the FBI.'

'Well, you could always just ask Rebecca yourself. Whatever you want to know. She'd love to tell you. She's dying to get to know you and your sister.'

'God, that's so cringe, Dad. You sound just like her. I mean, we've only just got home, and she's already done the gushy stepmum thing. Rosie didn't buy it, and nor do I.'

'Where's Rebecca now?' Guilt surged through Jack, not only for the upset he'd caused his daughters by not breaking the news of his engagement in person, but also for the stress his fiancée must be feeling. Taking on two teenagers was no picnic. He was worried about her.

'She went out.' Violet smirked, happy to take credit for scaring her off.

'Right. Well, I'll talk to her later. And I'll chat with Rosie tomorrow. She's obviously tired from travelling. You must be, too. Why don't you head off to bed as well? You'll need all your energy tomorrow.' He paused for effect. 'We're going to the beach.'

'We are?' Finally, a glimmer of approval.

Jack was dying to laugh; he could read Violet's excitement, even if she refused to show it. 'Actually, it was Rebecca's idea,' he added, craftily hoping to score brownie points for her.

'Huh. Well, it hardly takes a genius. We live in Cornwall. There's nothing else to do.'

Jack rolled his eyes; his daughter was clearly determined not to approve of anything connected to his fiancée. He made one last attempt to win favour for her. 'She also suggested a picnic. Ice creams afterwards.' Jack grinned; the twins loved ice cream. 'Oh, come here and give your old dad a hug.' He opened his arms as Violet held fast to her stubborn impassiveness.

'You're such an idiot, Dad.' Finally, she stood up from the sofa, taking her time as she sauntered towards him, obviously trying her hardest not to smile back.

Jack continued to swallow his laughter, hiding his

amusement at her determination to act cool. The twins were growing up so fast, but both of them still hovered on the verge of being daddy's girls. For ten years, they'd been inseparable. He knew it would be hard welcoming a new woman into their lives, but if anyone could win them over, Rebecca could.

'You're probably right.' He pretended to sigh. 'I'm an idiot. But a lucky one to have such gorgeous, clever daughters. I'm proud of you, Vi. Everything will be all right, I promise.'

As she nestled against him, Jack caught sight of them both in the mirror above the sofa, and smiled. All three of his daughters had the same golden hair and cobalt eyes as their mum, yet even though Rose and Violet were identical twins, they were vastly different from each other. While Rose usually had her nose stuck in a book, in truth it didn't surprise Jack that Violet had been googling his fiancée. Rosie was fey and dreamy, but Vi was sharp and savvy.

'Sorry, Dad. It's not really your fault. You can't help being an old softie.'

'Well, I'm your father. The buck stops with me. I'm sorry I sprung Rebecca on you, but, you know, I honestly think she'll be good for all of us. Give her a chance, sweetie pie.'

Violet pulled back, looking up at him. 'Rosie thinks you've forgotten Mum.'

'Never. I know you both miss her terribly. I do, too, and I wish, every day, that she hadn't died. But you remember how joyful she was. She loved life. She loved her girls. And me. Even though I'm an idiot.' He smiled. 'She wouldn't want us to be sad for ever.'

'Would she like Rebecca, do you think?'

Jack pondered for a moment, not wanting to give a

glib, knee-jerk response. 'The most important thing for your mum was that you two are loved. I'm sure, if she's looking down on us now, and sees how much Rebecca cares about you, she'll be happy.'

'Well, she isn't,' said a tremulous voice from the doorway.

Jack started. He hadn't noticed Rose appear in the doorway, and he wondered how long she'd been there. Visibly shivering in her nightdress, his daughter had an unfamiliar, strangely blank expression on her face — vacant and somehow detached. He couldn't tell whether she was awake or sleepwalking; he had no idea if she was dreaming when she continued hoarsely: 'In fact, Mum's furious.'

19

'Sleep OK, love?' Jack breezed into the kitchen the following morning, hoping Rosie would be feeling calmer after a night back in her own bed, determined that not even her stubborn refusal to look up from her book could put a dent in his mood. The sun was shining, he had the day off, and they were headed to the beach. Even better, his oldest friends were joining them.

He'd phoned Cathy late last night, inviting her and Eve to meet them at their old favourite picnic spot, while Arthur was already assembling a feast. Best of all, he'd had a long heart-to-heart with Rebecca after the girls were finally in bed, and they'd agreed that there was nowhere in the world more beautiful than Cornwall. Their honeymoon would be a staycation.

'Artie!' Rose finally looked up from her book as Arthur sauntered into the kitchen.

'Hey, how's my favourite bookworm?' he greeted, before turning to grin at Violet, who strolled into the kitchen a second later. 'And here comes your partner in crime. Although in those Snoopy pyjamas, she looks more like a grumpy toddler.'

Violet gave him a playful punch. 'You know, *technically*, I'm your aunty. So behave yourself, or I'll ground you. Anyway, there's no rush to get dressed. We're going to the beach.'

'We're all going on a Cornish holiday,' Arthur sang.

'Calm down, Artie,' Jack said, then laughed as his

grandson waltzed Violet energetically around the kitchen.

'I hope you've practised your first dance, Pops,' he said breathlessly. 'You can't let the side down. I bet Rebecca dances like a prima ballerina.'

'Prima donna, more like,' Violet muttered, abruptly pulling away from Arthur.

'Give her a chance, Vi,' Jack pleaded, determined that today would be a turning point in his daughters' relationship with his fiancée. 'Rebecca's trying, isn't she?'

Violet shrugged. 'Whatever.'

'Did I hear rightly that she's planned a fun dress-up session with you two?' Jack also knew that Rebecca had told the girls — generously, but slightly foolishly, in his opinion — that they could choose her dress for the wedding rehearsal. She was doing everything in her power to get close to them. His daughters needed to meet her halfway.

Violet looked down. 'We used to do that all the time with Mum,' she mumbled, taking out her phone and scrolling rapidly.

'Of course.' Jack sighed. Kicking himself, and realising that he was getting nowhere, he turned his attention to her sister. 'Rosie, do me a favour, would you? Pop out to the garden and check if Rebecca's ready to go. She was making a quick work call.'

'Whipping that production crew into place, is she?' Arthur grabbed a leftover piece of toast from Rosie's plate. 'I heard a few grumbles earlier,' he said with his mouth full. 'Some of the guys were chatting over their full English. Wishing for their old boss back. Rebecca is definitely cracking that whip, if rumours are to be believed.'

'Which they generally aren't.' Jack poured himself a coffee. 'Where did you hear this?'

'The café on the high street, where I picked up our picnic food. It was crawling with TV bods. Pretty soon there'll be more production staff than locals in the village. Good for business, I guess. Keeps the gossips happy, too. This filming has really set tongues wagging.'

'Rebecca has, you mean.' Jack rolled his eyes. 'Work isn't a popularity contest.'

'Good job. By the sound of it, I'm not sure she'd win it.'

'My point exactly,' Violet muttered, without taking her eyes off her phone.

'But she's tough,' Arthur added, spotting his grandpa's frown. 'She can handle a few nosy parkers.' He grinned. 'Your ears must have been burning, though.'

Abruptly, Jack put down his coffee. 'Sorry?'

'Oh, come on, Pops. You must know you're a minor celeb in Talland. Everyone knows you. Or wants to. They're all bursting to know why you're getting married.'

Jack huffed. 'Juliana's already given me a thorough interrogation on that subject. I shall take no further questions at this time.'

'Case closed, eh?' Arthur laughed. 'Seriously, though, maybe you should get some security at Roseland. From what I gather, half the county's planning to turn up and watch. Hey, you know what? You should sell your wedding video in the gift shop. You'd make a killing.'

'Or I'd kill someone. I'm getting a tad fed up of being grilled about my life choices. Who I marry, and where, is no one's business but mine.'

'Are there really cameras all over Roseland?' Finally, Violet looked up. 'Can I see?'

'Why don't you ask Rebecca?' Jack said deliberately. 'Here she comes now.'

'I have to get dressed.' Abruptly, Rosie stood up and strode towards the kitchen door.

'So, are we good to go?' Rebecca wandered in from the terrace, looking stylishly beach-ready in a scarlet kimono that ended mid-thigh, jewelled flipflops and nails painted to match. She smiled at Rosie, who ignored her, stalking out of the kitchen. 'Right. I guess that's a no.'

'She's probably forgotten her suncream.' Instinctively, Jack covered for Rosie. He was determined to use all his diplomacy skills to negotiate a peaceful rapprochement today.

'Good job she's remembered before we left. Her skin is so fair, bless her. Yours too, Vi.' Rebecca turned to her with a concerned expression, before stooping gracefully to grab her own straw beach bag from under the kitchen table. 'No matter. I've got plenty to spare.'

'Violet has a favour to ask you.' Jack nodded encouragingly at his daughter. 'She was wondering if you might wangle her a backstage tour with the film crew at Roseland.'

Rebecca wrinkled her nose. 'Might be tricky. It's a closed set. But sure, I'll see what I can do. Maybe tomorrow. Although we're having our little dress-up session then, aren't we?'

Violet shrugged. 'Whatever.'

'Sweetheart, Rebecca said she'll try, OK?' Jack gave his fiancée an apologetic look.

'And I will,' she promised, holding out her arms to

Violet for a hug.

'I've got to get changed, too,' Violet muttered, side-stepping her.

'Right, then.' Jack clapped his hands together. 'Let's mobilise. Take those out to the car, would you, Artie?' He pointed at the bulging baskets. 'Best stow them in the SUV.'

Arthur looked offended. 'Hey, I didn't buy that much.'

Jack laughed. 'You did. You always do. But I meant the BMW won't make it down to the beach. That slip road is like a ski slope. Only with sand instead of snow.'

'First-world problems, Pops,' Arthur teased, then groaned as he tried to pick up both baskets at the same time. 'Maybe you're right. I hope Eve and Cathy haven't packed too much.'

'Sorry to contradict, but I hope they have,' Rebecca said. 'I don't know Eve, of course, but don't you think she was looking a little thin and pale at the barbecue on Saturday?'

Arthur's blond eyebrows puckered. 'She does keep saying she's tired.'

'Cath reckons she's working too hard,' Jack chipped in. 'I know you're both logging on remotely this week, Artie. Take some time off as well, though, hey? Slow down a bit.'

'Cornish time. That's what we're on now.' Rebecca groaned. 'I've been trying to book a carpenter for days. We need to set up camera gantries in the great hall. Not one single person has returned my calls. I'm beginning to think I'm blacklisted, or something.'

Jack chuckled. 'The locals are a suspicious bunch. You'll get used to them, darling.'

'It's the same in Australia,' Arthur said. 'You remember, Pops?'

'On the farm, sure. Sydney's an entirely different kettle of fish.' He flashed a grin at Rebecca, holding up his hands. 'Sorry to mention the unmentionable.'

'As long as we steer clear of the harbour today.' She shuddered. 'That smell.'

'We're headed for the quietest spot in the bay. Not a fishing boat in sight.'

'Just the little kayak.' Rebecca beamed at Rose and Violet as they returned to the kitchen, both now dressed in denim shorts and bright T-shirts. Turning back to Arthur, she added: 'Don't forget to stow *that* on the SUV, will you? I can't wait to get out on the water.'

The twins looked horrified. 'We're not going on a boat!' they said in unison.

Arthur stared at Jack, who in turn stared at Rebecca. He gave a subtle shake of the head as he saw her open her mouth to say more — no doubt to apologise for putting her foot in it. Because Jack could tell from her blush that Rebecca had recalled, too late, everything he'd told her about the twins nearly drowning ten years ago, along with his plea not to mention it.

He didn't blame her; she was only trying to plan a fun day out. It had been an unintentional slip, and no harm had been done. He needed it to stay that way; he needed today to go well. 'No one has to do anything they don't want,' he said brightly. 'There are only two rules today. Have fun.' He grinned at the twins. 'And eat your body weight in ice cream.'

20

Cathy watched Eve haphazardly shove a selection of fruit, drinks and snacks into a large cool bag, resisting the urge to take over and organise it properly. She despaired of her daughter ever becoming domesticated, but she didn't want to upset her by being bossy. Eve still seemed edgy and distracted, repeatedly checking her phone.

'How's the project coming along?' she asked. 'I heard you working late last night.'

'Just checking in with my boss. Catching up on a few calls. Everything's fine.'

Cathy wasn't convinced. 'Did you speak to Artie?' Perhaps they'd had another fight.

Eve shrugged, zipping up the cool bag. 'Briefly. He was busy yesterday. Then he went up to Heathrow with Jack in the evening, to collect the twins.'

'Ah, right. I can't wait to see them again.'

'Me too,' Eve said quietly. 'I bet they're supertanned after Italy.'

'I expect so. A month in the Mediterranean. Even their fair skin will be golden.'

'I know. I'll look like a ghost in comparison.' Eve glanced at her reflection in the mirror over the kitchen table, frowning at herself.

'A bit of sun will be good for us all,' Cathy said tactfully, determined to keep the conversation going. She was afraid that if they stopped talking to each other, a gulf might open up between them that would soon be too wide to bridge. Out of nowhere, she thought of Chris, and how their lives seemed to be progressing on parallel lines.

'I'd have thought you had enough sun in Dubai,' Eve said, as though reading her mind.

Cathy smiled. 'I did. But nothing beats summer in Cornwall.'

'You're right.' At last, that brought a smile in return. 'Hopefully, we'll have a good day. Like old times, hey? All hanging out at the beach. Vi wants me to pop over to Roseland with her and Rosie tomorrow, too. She texted just now.' Another glance at her phone.

'Ah, that will please Juliana. She'll love to see the girls. She misses them so much. She was asking after you yesterday as well, darling. I drove over to the farmhouse in the afternoon, after we got back from our shopping trip. You were busy working on your project,' she added, seeing Eve frown. 'Otherwise, I'd have invited you along.'

'Sure. No problem. I'll pop round there later. I want to ask Juliana about . . .' She hesitated. 'About the filming. How she's finding it, now the production crew have arrived.'

Cathy sensed that Eve had been about to say something else, but she decided to roll with it. Anything to keep her talking. 'Yes, it was all go there yesterday. Roseland looks more like a movie set than a stately home right now. Crew everywhere. Lights. Cameras. Action.'

'Did you see any actors?' Eve's face lit up now. She loved working in TV, and she couldn't hide her genuine interest in the filming.

'No. But I kept hoping.' Cathy chuckled. 'Mr Darcy galloping across the fields on a stallion, perhaps. Or emerging from the lake with his shirt plastered to his chest.'

'Ha! Rosie would love that. I reckon she's Jane Austen's number one fan.'

'Clever girl. She's a proper bookworm, isn't she? Violet, not so much.'

'She wants to be a reporter. Like Izzy. Or a producer.'

'Like you,' Cathy said proudly.

'Assistant producer.' Eve looked glum again. 'Anyway, Vi wants me to go with them tomorrow. Rebecca's showing them the film set. The twins asked if I'd tag along. Although, to be honest, I reckon I'm just being used as a decoy.' She pulled a face. 'Apparently, Rebecca's planned a dress-up session for them. Vi's desperate to get out of it.'

'Oh, that's a shame. It sounds like fun. It might also be a chance for them to bond.'

'Which is exactly what Vi's afraid of. Cringey mother–daughter pep talks.'

'Stepmum,' Cathy corrected softly, then frowned, wondering if that's what Eve felt about their own chats. She was summoning up the courage to ask, when Eve's phone beeped.

'Speak of the devil.' She rolled her eyes. 'Rebecca wants to know if we have any spare picnic blankets. They're en route to the beach and forgot theirs.'

'You two text, then, do you?' Cathy was surprised. She hadn't got the impression that Eve was keen on Rebecca. Quite the opposite, in fact.

'Absolutely not. Artie must have given her my number. See what I mean? He's always so compliant. He should have checked with me first.'

'I've never really got into the habit of texting,' Cathy

said, trying to divert a potential outburst. Things were definitely still not right between Eve and Arthur, she decided. Either that, or her work project wasn't going as well as her daughter claimed. 'I prefer to hear the sound of someone's voice. I'm so glad you taught me to video call in Dubai, love.'

She waited for Eve to say something like *me too* and was disappointed when she remained quiet, eyes still fixed on her phone. 'Right. Well, I'll go fetch those blankets.'

'Sure. I'll take this lot out to the car. See you there.'

Grabbing the cool bag, Eve brushed past Cathy and stalked through the hall to the front door. Moments later, it banged shut, and the noise echoed through the cottage; it reverberated even more jarringly in Cathy's heart, as it seemed to her that Eve wasn't only slamming the door on their home, but also any *cringey mother–daughter pep talks*.

Walking slowly upstairs, she wondered if Rebecca knew what she was taking on by becoming a stepmum. 'But she has Jack,' Cathy reminded herself, wandering into her bedroom and sitting down on the bed, feeling inexplicably low . . . and lonely.

Reaching for the pillow on her side, it occurred to her that Chris no longer had a 'side'; he hadn't visited Cornwall for years. Her last few visits had been alone, or with the children, while her husband stayed in London, too busy to take time off.

Cathy sighed, glancing at the phone on the bedside table, recalling their conversation yesterday afternoon before she went to see Juliana, while Eve worked in her bedroom. That, too, had been dominated by talk of *his* latest work project.

As if her thoughts had telepathically reached

across the miles, the phone rang — the number on the screen instantly identifiable as their apartment in Dubai. Cathy stared at it, heart thumping. She didn't pick up.

21

Half an hour later, Cathy dug her feet into soft, silky sand, and released a sigh that felt like it had been trapped inside her for days. 'Good call picking this beach, Jack.' She turned to smile at him. 'Do you remember how the kids used to moan when they were little? That extra ten-minute walk to get here. But it's so worth it. This place is next door to heaven.'

Talland Bay was blessed with two pretty coves, the first a little rocky and ideal for shell-seeking, while the second was more popular with families, being sandy and dotted with rock pools, with a wide fresh-water stream running down to the sea. It also had the added advantage of public toilets and a gorgeous little café and shop.

Both beaches were accessed via a steep, narrow slipway, where Jack had parked his SUV, while Cathy left her old Beetle on the lane higher up, not wanting to brave the drive — or the tricky three-point turn needed on the way home. But to get to where they were sitting, there was still an extra walk. A hundred metres more rewarded them with a stretch of sand perfect for picnicking, with stunning views across the bay.

'I beg to differ.' Jack leaned back on one of the blankets Cathy had brought. 'This isn't next door to heaven. We've arrived, Cath. This is paradise on earth.'

She laughed at his comical exaggeration of getting

comfortable, stretching out his tall body and wriggling his shoulders. For a moment, Cathy found her eyes drawn to his strong, tanned chest, lightly covered with soft blond hair, and legs that were taut and muscular from all the swimming, running and cycling he enjoyed to keep fit.

She'd seen Jack in his swim shorts many times, but not for years, and suddenly Cathy felt unaccountably shy being alone with him, both of them semi-naked. Forcing herself to focus on the gorgeous view ahead, rather than at her side, she said: 'You know what? I think you're right. If there is an afterlife, I sincerely hope this is what it looks like.'

Eve and Arthur were in her sightline, strolling along the shore, and Cathy squinted, trying to make out if they were talking. They were more than an arm's length apart, which was unusual for them, she thought, while the twins were falling over each other like playful puppies as they splashed excitedly in the shallows, for once forgetting to act cool.

Their giggles carried across the beach, and Cathy smiled, relieved to see them happy. With Rebecca checking out the gift shop, insisting on having a browse before it got too busy, she decided to seize the moment and ask Jack how the twins felt about his engagement — perhaps even suss out if he'd picked up on any tension between Eve and Arthur.

'The kids have no idea how lucky they are,' Jack said, before she could speak. 'Being able to hang out here. All this freedom. It's everything I ever wanted for them.'

'If only we could wrap up moments like this, hey? Keep them in our pocket for ever.'

'I wish.' Abruptly, Jack sat up. 'I wish I could protect them from pain, always.'

Cathy rested a hand on his arm. 'You're a good dad, Jack. No one could have coped better with the hand life has dealt you. Ellie would be proud of you. I know I am.'

'Thanks. The credit isn't all mine, though. For all her foibles and eccentricities, Juliana's a good grandma.' He sighed. 'Sometimes I think I can't do right for doing wrong.'

'Your engagement has rocked the boat a little, hasn't it?' Cathy smiled, indicating that she meant it kindly. 'I wanted to talk to you about that, actually. How the twins are taking it.'

'Hey, don't you two look the glamourous couple?' said a lilting voice behind them. 'Sunning yourselves on the Cornish Riviera. I'll be expecting an invite onto your yacht later.'

Rebecca had arrived from behind, and it wasn't until she dropped to her knees behind Jack, leaning into him and sensuously massaging his shoulders, that Cathy spotted her. *How much of their conversation had she overheard?* Feeling flustered, she laughed to cover her awkwardness, saying: 'Glamorous? Well, I haven't been called that in a long time.'

Jack's fiancée was the glamorous one, she thought, watching her shrug out of her kimono to reveal a tiny scarlet bikini. Glancing down at her own cerise one-piece, Cathy wished she'd been braver in her choice of swimwear. Only, she'd been thinking of comfort rather than vanity. Her skin already had a golden sheen; she wasn't interested in tanning every inch of her body. Unlike Rebecca, it seemed, whose perfect body was an even toffee colour all over.

'Nor me.' Jack dipped his head to allow Rebecca to

work on the knots on his shoulders. 'I spend most of my days masked up and dressed in scrubs. The very opposite of glamour.'

'You're too modest, Jack.' Rebecca bent to kiss the back of his smooth neck. 'I've seen the looks other women give you.'

Cathy wondered if she'd imagined the sideways glance at her. 'You're right, Rebecca,' she said lightly. 'You're marrying a minor celebrity. At least, that's what Artie calls him.'

Jack snorted. 'My grandson spends way too much time on social media. He thinks anyone who posts pictures of their breakfast is famous.'

'I think he's extremely savvy, actually,' Cathy countered. 'Eve, too. Far more than I was at their age.' She glanced towards the two of them again, frowning as she noticed her daughter gesticulating, as though arguing heatedly. 'It's the modern world, isn't it? Twenty-four-hour media bombardment. Growing up in London probably has a lot to do with it, too, in Eve's case.'

'If you can make it there, you can make it anywhere,' Rebecca quipped. 'Either that, or it'll eat you up. London is brutal. Still, as they say, what doesn't kill you makes you stronger.'

'Are you from London, then?' Cathy asked curiously, realising she didn't know.

'Perish the thought.' Rebecca shuddered. 'Pass me that oil, would you? Oh, and thanks for bringing the extra blankets. Jack built a house that has everything. Except blankets.'

Cathy smiled, handing over the bottle. 'No problem.' She wanted to ask Rebecca where she'd lived before moving in with Jack, but the deliberate change of subject wasn't lost on her. 'I used to love the city,' she commented instead.

Jack huffed. 'Until you came to your senses and got the hell out.'

'Temporarily, alas.' Cathy sighed. 'This is a holiday for me, not real life.'

'Does it have to be?'

'What?' She stared at him, taken aback by his question. 'Well, I took time off in Dubai. But I can't be a lady of leisure for ever. My freelance contacts are mostly in London.'

'Exactly. *Freelance*. The clue's in the name. You have the freedom to work anywhere, Cath. Besides, it doesn't have to be for ever. But maybe for now? Until Chris comes back?'

If he comes back, Cathy thought. 'I guess we'll see,' she prevaricated.

Jack picked up on her hesitation. 'He's coming for the wedding, though, right?'

'Flying overnight on Wednesday. He'll pick up a hire car at Heathrow. All being well, he'll be here Thursday morning. In time for the rehearsal, hopefully.'

'I can't wait to meet him,' Rebecca said eagerly, handing the bottle of oil to Jack. 'Now do me,' she instructed, scooting around to sit cross-legged in front of him.

'Chris is looking forward to it, too. He was thrilled to hear about your wedding,' Cathy lied. He'd actually told her on the phone that it was the most ridiculous thing he'd ever heard: Jack getting married when he was *almost across the finish line* — his kids practically grown-up.

A wide, cherry-glossed smile. 'He sounds great.

Actually, a friend of mine teaches at the uni in Dubai. She often mentions a *dishy famous psychiatrist*. I wonder if it's your Chris.'

'Dishy?' Cathy laughed. 'He'd be flattered to hear himself called that. But famous, a little. He does quite a bit of media work. Mostly radio. Some TV. You know, opinion pieces on psychiatric tragedies in the news. Controversial legal defences around alleged accidental killings. Diminished responsibility, that sort of thing.'

Rebecca looked intrigued. 'Killings. I'll have to put him in touch with our scriptwriters.' Scooping her long hair into a ponytail, to give Jack better access to her shoulders, she glanced back at him. 'Don't stop. You have magic hands, Mr Merchant. That feels so good.'

'Oh, is it a thriller, then?' Cathy stared at Rebecca, then looked quickly away. The woman was enjoying Jack's shoulder massage a little too obviously — and vocally.

'You could call it that,' Rebecca said cryptically. 'It's a period piece, of course. But modern in theme and tone. Although, in my experience, all the best dramas have the same ingredients, no matter when or where they're set. Roseland will be perfect for all of them. You know. Love. Greed. Jealousy.' She paused, arching her back in pleasure as Jack's hands pressed into her shoulder blades. 'Revenge.'

22

Cathy reached for a bottle of water to disguise her reaction. The back of her neck was prickling as she remembered Juliana's somewhat paranoid suspicions yesterday, but she didn't want to spoil the day by asking Rebecca if she'd made comments like that to her — which would explain why the old lady had been so rattled by Jack's fiancée, imagining dark and dangerous things about her.

Clearly, Rebecca was being frivolous. Cathy got that. But maybe Juliana hadn't. Although she was quick-witted, she was old-fashioned. Cathy could recall taking her teenage children to Roseland, frequently watching them roll their eyes after being told off for 'roasting' each other, as they called it. To Juliana, their teasing had come across as bad manners.

'The girls are desperate to see the film set,' she blurted out, realising that Rebecca was staring at her. 'They want to know what happens behind the scenes. Vi's been texting Evie non-stop questions.' Too late, she remembered Eve saying the twins had actually been trying to avoid spending time with Rebecca. She kicked herself, hoping she hadn't put her foot in it.

Jack frowned. 'Questions about the filming, right?' He knew his daughter had been googling his fiancée; he wondered if she was still investigating her.

'Yes. The filming,' Cathy confirmed quickly, feeling caught in a tricky spot. It was one thing chatting to Jack about his daughters' collywobbles over his engagement; she didn't want to come straight out and tell Rebecca that Rosie and Violet were dead set against it.

Rebecca smiled. 'I can't wait to give them a tour. I know the twins practically grew up at Roseland, but it looks very different now. Transformed for our wedding. Especially for you, darling,' she added huskily, catching Jack's hand and pressing it to her lips.

'Get a room, you two,' Arthur joked, approaching. 'Public displays of affection are strictly forbidden. Didn't you read the signs? They're right next to the shark warnings.'

'No sharks in Cornwall, mate,' Jack told him, noticing Cathy's anxious look.

He needn't have worried. Cathy got the joke. It was actually her daughter's whereabouts that was troubling her. 'Where's Evie?' she asked, looking up at Arthur.

He nodded towards the slip road. 'Headed home just now.'

'But we've only just got here.' Cathy clenched her jaw, biting back more questions. She was concerned to know if they'd had yet another fight, but she didn't want to pry.

'Yeah. It's a shame.' Arthur smiled, but it seemed a little forced. 'I did my best to persuade her to stay. But it's so hot. She said the sun was making her migraine worse, so . . .'

'I told you she was looking a tad peaky,' Rebecca chipped in, looking worried.

'But why didn't she say anything to me?' Cathy frowned. 'I should go check on her.'

'You stay and relax,' Arthur said quickly. 'It's ages

since you've got to hang out here. I come all the time. I told Eve I'd follow her. Just as soon as I've dunked the twins.' He waggled his eyebrows. 'They challenged me to a water fight, and I need to remind them who's boss.'

Cathy hesitated. 'Well, if you're quite sure she's OK.'

'Absolutely. I promise you I'll take good care of her,' Arthur said earnestly, and it seemed to Cathy that he was referring to more than her daughter's headache.

Immediately, she felt herself relax a little. 'I have no doubt you will,' she said sincerely. 'Just don't leave her alone too long, OK? She hasn't seemed herself for a couple of days now.'

'One good dunking, and I'll be off.' He gave a comical salute. 'Scout's honour.'

As he turned to leave, Rebecca held out her hand. 'Actually, before you go, Artie, would you mind doing me a favour?'

Cathy stared at Rebecca, curious to know what it was — suspecting she was rarely refused anything. Sure enough, Arthur dipped his head gallantly. 'Of course,' he said eagerly, reminding Cathy of Eve's lament that her boyfriend was too compliant.

'Great.' Rebecca clapped her hands in excitement. 'I just need help fetching the kayak. I'm desperate to get out on that water. Sharks or no sharks.'

'I'll help, son,' Jack offered immediately.

Rebecca reached over to pat his thigh. 'No need, darling. You stay with Cathy.' She winked. 'I saw how you both struggled down that slip road. Wouldn't want you to pull a muscle now.' She lowered her voice suggestively. 'I need my bridegroom on top form.'

'Ha, you've been roasted, Pops.' Arthur laughed at

the look of indignation on Jack's face. 'We won't be long, anyway.' He glanced anxiously towards the slip road. 'I need to head back ASAP to check on Evie.'

'We'll be five minutes, tops,' Rebecca assured him. 'Behave yourselves, you two, OK?' She gave a throaty chuckle, navy eyes glittering as she stood up, hooking an arm over Arthur's.

Cathy blushed, somehow feeling the comment was aimed at her. *As if she would flirt with Jack!* He was her oldest friend, and practically a married man.

Feeling a bubble of naughty rebellion, she waved at the departing pair, calling out teasingly: 'Have fun and play nicely, kids!'

23

Heads turned as Rebecca swayed across the beach, her red bikini looking even more minuscule now that she was moving — no, *undulating*, Cathy thought. Turning to Jack, about to suggest they go find the twins and buy ice cream, her merriment faded as she saw his expression.

His eyes were fixed on his fiancée, too. *Bewitched*, Cathy thought, once again remembering Juliana's warning. There was no doubt that Rebecca's beauty was intoxicating, but if for whatever reason she was trying to trap Jack, he was an entirely willing victim.

Despite her teasing comeback after Rebecca's jokey warning, Cathy suddenly felt thoughtful about his engagement — for his sake, as well as the twins'. Did the age difference with his fiancée really not matter to him? Wondering how to raise the subject, she busied herself setting out picnic things, ready for when Rose and Violet did return.

They were clearly off having fun, and although conscious of a twinge of concern, Cathy told herself not to fuss. The girls were smart and independent, used to being at boarding school. Besides, she knew they'd never venture into deep water; they always stuck to the shallows.

As she unfolded yet another blanket and spread it across the sand, Cathy noticed a family settling down close by for their own picnic. A young couple with a daughter who looked about five years old; the same age as the twins had been when their mum died.

'Hey, are you OK?' Jack placed a gentle hand on her shoulder.

'Totally.' Cathy gave up on the cool bag and sat back, surreptitiously wiping her eyes.

'Right. So those are happy tears.'

'Sorry. I guess I'm still worrying about Eve.' It wasn't a complete lie. 'There's definitely something up with her. I wish I knew what it was.'

'Artie will take care of her. She's his whole world,' Jack said simply. 'It's good to see.'

'It really is,' Cathy agreed wholeheartedly. She turned to Jack. 'We did OK, didn't we? Managed to raise our little humans to be reasonably kind, intelligent people.'

'You did more than OK, Cath. Eve is a credit to you. And she's perfect for Artie.'

'As he is for her. Thanks to you. Oh, I know he's your grandson, but you've been an incredible mentor for him. He's a lot like you were when you were younger, you know?'

'Poor guy.' Jack chuckled. 'There's no hope for him, then. It's all downhill from here.'

'You're too modest.' Cathy laughed, too, before realising that with Arthur heading home to Eve, and Rebecca taking the boat out, this might be her best chance yet to talk to Jack in private. 'And Artie's a star. To be honest, it's Rosie and Vi I'm really worried about.'

'Oh?' Jack raised a hand, shielding his eyes as he stared intently towards the sea.

'I don't mean right now.' *Oh, do get to the point*, Cathy mocked herself, recalling Juliana's instruction to Margaret at Roseland yesterday. 'I mean, I'm worried they're missing their mum.'

Jack frowned. 'Of course they are. They've never stopped missing her.'

'Yes, but now that Rebecca . . .' Seeing Jack's face close off, Cathy almost lost her nerve. She wanted to talk to him about the twins; she didn't want him to think she was questioning his judgement about getting married.

Yes, Rebecca was a lot younger than him, and Cathy was all too aware of both Eve's and Juliana's reservations about her. So far, though, neither of them had come up with any more substantial concerns beyond that the woman was too beautiful, and therefore not to be trusted — which was, of course, ridiculous, albeit understandable given their staunch allegiance to Eloise.

Cathy realised their suspicions arose mainly from loyalty: Juliana to her daughter's memory, and Eve to Jack and his family, especially the twins, whom she adored. But although Rebecca hadn't shared much about herself, she seemed nice enough. She had a few sharp edges, perhaps, but those only seemed to excite Jack more; Cathy hadn't seen him so upbeat in years. Perhaps, in time, Rebecca's vivacity would win over Eve and Juliana — and the twins, too.

'She'll be their stepmum, yes,' Jack said mildly. 'The twins are still adjusting to that.'

'Exactly. Any change takes getting used to. I realise that,' Cathy pacified quickly. 'Juliana is struggling with the idea of the wedding, too. As you well know.'

'Indeed. She thinks Rebecca is replacing her daughter.' Jack huffed. 'As if anyone could. As if Rebecca is seriously interested in Juliana's bloody fortune, either.'

'Or yours.' Cathy pulled a wry smile.

'Huh. She fired off the same nonsense at you, too, did she?'

'With both barrels.'

Jack sighed. 'I respect Juliana's protectiveness. Of the twins. Eloise's memory. Even bloody Roseland. I've tried to be reassuring. I actually thought I'd dodged a bullet by speaking to the National Trust about the wedding first. Stupidly, I thought it would help Juliana to know that Roseland will be handled with kid gloves.'

'I guess it's all she has left. Along with her memories. And her grandchildren. Arthur, too. I completely understand that.' Again, Cathy hesitated. 'I just wonder if the twins do. Or if they feel the same as Juliana, that Rebecca is taking the place of their mum. And they're not ready for that.'

'They will be,' Jack said confidently. 'I know Rebecca comes on a bit strong. She grabs life with both hands. Frankly, it's what I love most about her. I wish I could be so brave. It's taken me years to stop dwelling in the past, and . . . Anyway, I realise our engagement was fast.'

'Hmm. You could say that. I think you broke the land speed record.'

'Ha, well, seize the day, and all that. Like I said to you before, Cath, time waits for no man.' He shrugged. 'Juliana was actually the one who reminded me of that. I thought she'd be happy to see her granddaughters loved and looked after.'

'I'm sure she is. Or will be. Once she's got used to Rebecca. Rosie and Vi, too.'

'I know they're putting up walls right now. But there's no rush. Rebecca's here to stay.'

Cathy took that as a gentle warning. 'I'm sorry if I'm speaking out of turn.'

'Of course not. The twins are your goddaughters. You love them, and they adore you.'

'I promised Eloise I'd always look out for them. Sorry, I know that's your job.'

'You don't have to keep apologising, Cath. It's always good to talk things through with you.' Jack reached for her hand, giving it a squeeze. 'Thank you for looking out for my girls.' His blue eyes twinkled. 'And me. Your grumpy, *old* friend,' he said, with ironic emphasis, referencing Rebecca's comment just now. 'We go way back, don't we?'

'We do. And I guess being back in Talland stirs it all up. Both our families have a lot of history here, don't they?' Cathy looked curiously at Jack. 'Does Rebecca know it all?'

He shook his head. 'Parts. Not all. I don't want to scare her off completely. Some baggage is best left in the hold, isn't it?'

'Maybe.' Cathy turned to look out across the sea, shivering as a flash of memory from a nightmare last night came back to her. She'd forgotten all about it this morning, distracted by picnic preparations; now, distressing images rolled over her in waves, and she knew exactly where the dream had come from. 'Although, no matter how deeply we bury the past,' she continued quietly, 'it has a funny way of coming back to bite us.'

24

She must have nodded off, worn out by worry and lulled by the warmth of the sun, along with the soothing, repetitive rush of the waves. The lingering after-effects of jet lag rippled through her, and Cathy had a strange, dizzy feeling, as though she was tossing and turning on the deck of a boat, like one of the little skiffs in Talland Bay that Margaret had talked about yesterday at Roseland.

Slipping back into last night's dream, Cathy imagined herself standing on the deck of one of them, cowering as waves crashed over her, sweeping her away and pulling her under. Opening her mouth to groan, her lungs felt tight, as though they'd filled up with sea water.

Well and truly in the grip of nightmare now, Cathy scrabbled around for something to hold on to, feeling a rush of relief as she saw a pair of hands reach out towards her. They were painfully thin and bony, but Cathy grabbed them anyway, staring into wide, terrified blue eyes in front of her. She heard a voice cry out for help, and realised it was her own. The sound of it woke her up.

'Rosie?' she whispered, immediately realising whose eyes she'd imagined silently pleading with her. 'Oh, God. What a horrible nightmare.'

Sitting up, Cathy rubbed her eyes, feeling calmer as logical thought returned, and she recognised that her dream just now — a continuation of last night's —

had been merely a throwback to the past, stirred up by her visit to Juliana yesterday . . . and the old lady's paranoid fear for her granddaughters.

'Aunty Cath! Aunty Cath!'

'Rosie?' Cathy said again, turning in confusion now. Her fingers clenched, and she half imagined the feel of those cold hands within hers. But it had been a dream. Hadn't it?

'Aunty Cath!' The voice came closer. *It was real.* 'She took her! She took Rosie!'

It wasn't Rose calling out, but her twin sister.

'What?' Violet's distraught face finally crystallised in front of Cathy's blurred eyes. 'Who did? Took her where?' Still, she battled the remnants of her nightmare, fighting tiredness to focus on what the white-faced teenager in front of her was saying.

'*Rebecca.* She said the best way to conquer our fears is to face them. She made Rosie get on the boat. They went out on the bay. Ages ago. And they haven't come back. Oh, Aunty Cath, I'm scared. Where's my dad? Where did he go?'

Frantically, Cathy looked around, but her eyes were drawn in terror to the darkening clouds rolling in ominously over the sea. 'After the heatwave comes the storm,' she whispered, feeling fear tighten her chest — a very real fear, this time, not part of some fantastical nightmare.

She stared at the waves crashing to the shore, breaking with such force against the sandy beach that they surged upwards. Shocked by their power, in contrast to the tranquillity before she'd nodded off, Cathy scanned the boats bobbing erratically, perilously, further out to sea, just as they had in her dream. No. It was a premonition, she thought irrationally.

Cathy wasn't sure she believed in such things. Not anymore. *You had one before, and it came true*, she reminded herself, trembling as she remembered the events of ten years ago. 'Phone him. Can you phone your dad, Violet?'

'I didn't bring my phone!' the teenager wailed. 'Dad told me to leave it behind, for once. To be in the real world for the day.'

Cathy groaned. 'I don't have mine, either. I'm always forgetting it. Eve is forever reminding me. She's glued to hers, of course. If only she was here,' Cathy burbled on, trying to reassure Violet by chatting as normally as possible, in the circumstances.

But as she scoured the beach for Jack once again, she noticed that it was all but deserted. There was no one to ask for help. Most of the tourists would have scuttled back to their hotels and guesthouses at the first clap of thunder, she realised, while the locals, more attuned to the rapidly changing Cornish weather, had no doubt already headed home before the looming storm hit.

The keening of the wind at the clifftop was growing louder now, the eerie, almost human cry screeching through rocky crevasses. Violet clung to Cathy, who in turn hugged her closer, trying to think what to do for the best, cursing herself for not having gone to look for the girls sooner, for nodding off and not noticing the sudden change in weather.

'We need to find your dad. I don't understand where he's gone. Where *is* he?' Cathy looked around, unable to conceal her panic as lightning crackled furiously over the horizon, the rumbles of thunder growing closer and more frequent now.

Once again, Cathy's nightmare rose up, and she

couldn't stop herself picturing Rosie out there on the water. Petrified. In fear for her life.

'I've called the coastguard!' The voice came from twenty feet away, barely audible.

'Jack?' Cathy screened her eyes with one hand; the wind was picking up, whipping sand into her eyes. Her heart thudded painfully in hope. 'Is that you?'

'I couldn't get any mobile reception,' Jack panted, sprinting towards them. 'I had to run to the café. Violet, stay here with your Aunty Cath. I'm going to find your sister.'

Another jagged bolt of lightning ripped the sky open, exposing yet more threatening darkness. '*Now*, Jack,' Cathy urged. 'Please. Don't hesitate this time.'

Only Jack would have known what she meant. Ten years ago, no one had believed Cathy when she'd pleaded that the twins were in danger. Everyone had discounted her seeming premonition as the by-product of depression. Jack had believed her, but he'd hesitated, reluctant to accept that any living soul would want to harm his tiny, beautiful young daughters.

Rebecca wasn't a monster, Jack thought, as he raced across the sand. She wasn't *Ted*. But she had unwittingly taken Rose into danger. *And it was all his fault*. He should have made it clearer to his fiancée that the twins were not to go out on the water. Not under any circumstances.

He'd told Rebecca about what had happened to them, but perhaps he hadn't explained strongly enough the lasting impact on his girls. Jack trusted his fiancée; he knew she would only have been trying to help, by encouraging Rosie not to be frightened of the water anymore. But it was a mistake. A bad one. He prayed they both lived to put it right.

25

Hurrying after Jack, with Violet still locked against her side, refusing to let go, Cathy saw the full force of the changing tide, stirred into a frenzy by a vicious gale. Instantly, she realised the insanity of anyone going into the water.

She knew Jack's first instinct was to search for Rosie himself; it was Cathy's, too, but it was suicidal to dive into the sea during this storm. Cathy had never seen anything like it, in all her years coming to Cornwall. They needed to wait for the coastguard.

'Jack!' she screamed. 'Come back!'

But Jack was beyond hearing, deafened not only by the wind, but by dreadful memories of his own. With every step, they rose up to torment him: plunging into the freezing, churning water, heart pounding, lungs almost bursting as he dived deeper and deeper, all the way down to the secret caves at Watchman's Cove, desperately hunting for five-year-old Rose and Violet, with time fast running out before the rising tide swallowed the pocket of air where they were hidden, kidnapped by their stepdad Ted and held for ransom.

'No! Stop!'

Jack's cries were stolen by the wind, but in any case, his barked orders were only to himself: to stop picturing his daughters' dead bodies floating face down on the water. He'd *found* them; they had *survived*. Now he would find Rose and Rebecca.

'I can't lose you, too,' he gasped, clawing his way

through the swirling shallows — the sea, so inviting only half an hour before, now as hostile as though it really was shark-infested. Jack was a strong swimmer. He'd grown up surfing; in Cornwall, and in Australia. He was confident enough to tackle the toughest conditions. These were tougher.

'Dad!'

His head jerked up, eyes frantically scanning the rolling waves. 'Rosie?'

'Jack! Over here!'

Two voices, one reedy and high-pitched, the other lower, throatier. Both instantly recognisable.

'I see you!' Water gushed into Jack's mouth as he called out, and he felt the undercurrent drag at his legs as he tried to swim towards them.

The orange kayak bobbed twenty feet from the shore; it might as well have been a mile away. The power of the water caused it to pitch and roll, and Jack could see Rose in the front seat, soaking-wet long hair shrouded around her terrified face like seaweed.

He knew that Rebecca, as the adult and more experienced paddler, would have seated herself in the rear, but while Jack could hear her voice, calm and low, repeatedly reassuring Rose, he couldn't see her.

His body shuddered as yet more adrenalin pumped through him. 'I'm coming!' he yelled, half swimming, half clawing his way towards the boat. Several times he was dragged under, swallowing more great salty mouthfuls that rushed into his stomach, already churning with fear. He fought the impulse to retch; there was no time for nausea.

'Hold on! I've got you!' With an almighty effort, he threw himself at the boat, managing to grab hold with first one hand, then the other. 'I'll tow you in!'

Only, the fibreglass vessel, so light on land, usually so mobile on the water, became slippery and uncontrollable as it swelled and dipped, tossed around by waves that continued to drag Jack in all directions. His bones ached as he dug his fingertips into the side of the kayak with every ounce of his strength.

If it flipped, he would be pulled with it; if he went under, he might never come back up. Already, he could feel the riptide ensnaring his body, until he was barely in control of his own movements. Extricating Rose and Rebecca from their seats would be that much harder beneath the weight of the water, too. If they were tipped overboard, either they would be trapped beneath the kayak, drowning in seconds, or swept away by the fierce current.

Desperately, Jack tried again to get a grip on the boat, but he could feel his energy flagging from repeated, ineffectual attempts to steer it. Lifting his eyes to the furious sky, he screamed his rage at the heavens.

'No! You can't have them! They belong to me!' Then, as his fingertips lost their grip once again, he rested his cheek against the slippery fibreglass, and whispered in despair: 'Please, don't take them. Take me instead.'

He was about to attempt one final push, drawing on sheer willpower rather than any remaining reserves of energy, when the loudest thunderclap yet exploded directly overhead. Suddenly, the tide seemed to turn, throwing the kayak towards the beach in one great, heaving surge. Jack was dragged along with it, pulled beneath the boat, for a moment completely submerged beneath its base . . . trapped, just as he'd feared.

Water was sucked painfully up his nose, and

rubbery dizziness stole through him. For a moment, he was tempted to give in to it. Then, as though a giant, invisible hand was lifting him from below, he felt his body move upwards.

Kicking with what little strength he had left, he pushed himself back to the surface, emerging spluttering and disoriented, but thankful to feel his feet touch solid ground. 'Rose? Rebecca?' he gasped, as water streamed off every inch of his body.

'Oh, Jack, she's *gone*.'

His ears were blocked, his vision still clouded by salt water and fear. The voice sounded muffled, seeming to come from a distance, but as he shook his head and scrubbed at his eyes, he could see the boat was close by. Rebecca was out of her seat, straddled across the middle of the bobbing kayak. She was drenched, white-faced. And alone.

'*No!*' Frantically, Jack dived again. His eyes were stinging like crazy now, and his chest felt like it was about to explode. Again and again, he dived and resurfaced, each time dragging a hasty mouthful of air into his lungs. 'Stay there!' he yelled at Rebecca, as his head breached the surface once more, and he saw that she'd managed to climb onto the beach.

Before he could scream at her to go find Cathy and Violet, a wave caught him, tossing him around like a piece of driftwood on the foaming surf. The next thing he saw was algae-covered stones; swirling tangles of dark-green seaweed. His daughter's floating, lifeless body.

26

'I'm so sorry. I can say it a million times, and it still won't tell you how sorry I am. I know you can't forgive me, Jack. *I* wouldn't forgive me. I don't forgive myself.'

Rebecca sobbed quietly, head in her hands, elbows propped on the table, a thick blanket wrapped around her shoulders. Despite the blanket, and the heating turned on full blast by the café owners, her slim body was trembling uncontrollably. It was shock, Jack said, repeatedly insisting she try to sip the hot drink kindly provided for her by the anxious young couple.

They were the ones who had called the coastguard, handing the phone to Jack so that he could bark his whereabouts and predicament down the line, before watching him sprint back to the sea. Neither had said a word as they'd stood at the window; having both grown up in Cornwall, they were all too familiar with the sea's deadly power, as well as its beauty.

Their hearts had been in their mouths as they'd waited for the flashing lights of the coastguard vessel, praying it would arrive in time. But Jack had got there first, and the next time the couple saw him, his eyes were as dark and tortured as though he'd been to hell and back. He looked exhausted; half-dead himself. Almost as lifeless as the body in his arms.

Rosie. The café owners had known the teenager all her life; the sight of her skinny arms and legs hanging limply, eyes tightly closed, skin tinged with blue, broke their hearts. Grabbing the phone once again, the husband had insisted on calling an ambulance, but Jack stopped him.

It would take longer for the paramedics to get there than it would for him to treat Rosie himself, he'd said. He was a doctor; he was her *dad*. Only his hands would coax his little girl's heartbeat to return; only his breath would fill her lungs and bring her back to life.

He worked on her for ten minutes — the longest of his life — until he heard her first cry, and the sound of it was as joyous and terrifying as watching a newborn baby take their first breath. Jack hadn't seen Rosie being born; he hadn't even known she was his daughter until she was five. Then, he'd almost lost her — and Violet. What happened today was too close to history repeating itself. Cathy had been right, he thought: *sometimes the past returns to bite us.*

'Jack,' Cathy said gently, breaking into his agonised thoughts. 'You need to drink, too. You're as white as a sheet. Rosie's going to be OK. She's safe. You did well.'

He shook his head. 'I nearly lost her. It's my fault.'

Cathy couldn't help glancing at Rebecca, sitting at Jack's side on the opposite side of the table. She still had her head in her hands, while Violet sat huddled against Cathy. The girl hadn't stopped trembling, nor had she taken her eyes off her sister, stretched out on a camp bed the café owners had fetched.

The blankets Cathy had swaddled her in were the extra ones she'd brought for the picnic, and she wanted to laugh hysterically, and then cry, at the horrific change in circumstances. Today had been intended as a fun day out; it had almost ended in tragedy. *Would it also signal the end of Jack's engagement?* Cathy watched him stand up to check on Rosie again, his shorts and the T-shirt he'd hastily pulled on clinging damply to his body.

After checking her vital signs, he returned to sit next to Rebecca. Whatever questions he had for his fiancée, Cathy had plenty herself — and as Rosie's godmother, she considered it her place to ask them. 'What happened?' she demanded.

'There was a hole in the boat,' Rebecca said quickly, as though she'd been waiting to be asked. 'I didn't know. I only saw it when Jack pulled it out of the water. But I couldn't control the kayak. Even if there hadn't been a storm, it was going under. I tried everything. But the hole . . .' She trailed off, burying her face in the blanket, sobbing quietly again.

'I should have checked it.' Jack clenched his fists. 'That boat has been stashed in Juliana's hayloft for ages. There would have been substantial wear and tear. It wasn't Juliana's responsibility to maintain it. I should have made sure it was safe.'

Cathy shook her head. 'It's not your fault, Jack.'

'Isn't it?' His blue eyes were desolate. 'It's my responsibility to look after my family.'

'You didn't expect Rosie to go out on the water. For obvious reasons.'

'She didn't want to go. You *made* her!' Violet yelled, glaring across the table at Rebecca. 'I told her, no. Don't go, Rosie. But you said it would help. Just to sit in it.'

'*Exactly*,' Rebecca almost squeaked. 'I just thought she might sit in it for a while.'

'That's actually dumb.' Violet's furious eyes narrowed. 'The kayak isn't a stupid inflatable. The sea isn't a swimming pool. It's *dangerous*.'

Jack leaned across the table to take hold of her hands. 'It's OK, Vi. Your sister's going to be fine.' He glanced at Rosie. 'I don't want to move her just yet. We'll let her sleep a little, then I'll take you both home, OK?'

'She didn't want to go on the boat,' Violet repeated flatly.

Rebecca groaned. 'I'm so, so sorry, Letty.'

'Don't call me that. Only *Rosie* calls me that.'

'Sorry,' Rebecca said again. Then, after a long pause: 'Honestly, I was trying to help. I didn't realise. I genuinely thought it might be good for Rosie to try. I only meant for us to paddle in the shallows. Just for her to know that the sea isn't something to fear.'

'But it *is*,' Violet insisted. 'Especially when Rosie's already feeling fragile. You *knew* she's been having nightmares.'

Rebecca looked stricken. 'No, I didn't. Honestly, I had no idea that she —'

'I'm sorry, sweetheart. This is all my fault.' Jack ran a hand through his hair. He didn't entirely blame Rebecca; he meant what he'd said, that he should have checked the boat's condition himself. But while it had been a well-intentioned mistake, it was a bad one. 'We need to talk, and we will. Later. When Rosie's recovered. *All* of us.' He glanced at his fiancée, and although it wasn't an unfriendly look, it was serious.

As furious as she was, Cathy felt sorry for Rebecca in that moment. The woman seemed genuinely distraught, and despite Jack making all the right noises, it was obvious that he was angry, too — in his usual restrained way. Turning to Violet, she said: 'I think all

Rebecca's trying to say, love, is that it was a genuine accident.'

Cathy believed that, even though she was certain Juliana wouldn't; that when she found out what had happened, the old lady would insist Rebecca had deliberately tried to harm Rosie.

Silently groaning in frustration, Cathy mentally replayed Juliana's scathing insistence that Rebecca had set a 'honeytrap' for Jack. She could almost hear her railing about Rebecca's greed and ambition — her determination to get her hands not only on Jack's money, but the twins' inheritance.

Cathy frowned, surreptitiously studying Rebecca's pale, beautiful face. She was cross with her for taking Rosie in the boat, but she refused to believe there had been any sinister intention behind it. For one thing, that wouldn't make any sense. After marrying Jack, control of the twins' trust funds would inevitably fall partially to Rebecca as his wife. But they weren't married yet, and if the worst had happened, and Rosie had died, they surely never would be.

'It truly was an accident,' Rebecca whispered, giving Cathy a grateful look. 'A horrible, thoughtless mistake. I'm so, so sorry,' she said for the hundredth time. 'Jack?' She turned to stare at him, her blue eyes pleading. 'You believe me, don't you? You forgive me?'

Cathy looked away now, feeling uncomfortable and even more sorry for Rebecca. This was a moment that should take place in private between her and Jack. Deliberately averting her eyes, she gazed around the cosy, retro-styled café, with its driftwood counter, colourful tables and chairs, a breakfast bar set against the window, giving a panoramic view of the beach.

She hadn't been here for ages, but it was poignantly familiar. When her children were younger, she'd brought them every day during holidays, most often with Eloise, who had spent hours at the beach with Rosie and Violet, and occasionally Juliana, paddling and building sandcastles — Eloise and the twins had explored the bay on that same kayak, both of the girls tucked into the front seat, while Ellie sat in the rear, watching over them with eagle eyes.

Cathy shivered, then glanced up at the door, wondering if someone had just entered the café. The coastguard, perhaps, come to speak to Jack. There was no one there, but an odd chill lingered, and Cathy hugged Violet a little tighter, before turning to check on Rosie.

Sleeping peacefully now, she looked achingly vulnerable, and Cathy's eyes filled with tears as she remembered her mum begging her to look after her girls. If Juliana was right, and Eloise truly was still watching over the twins, she must be spinning furiously in her grave right now.

Ellie, are you here? Cathy wondered. An ear-splitting clap of thunder was the only answer.

27

'Sweetheart, your grandma is here to see you.'

Immediately, Rose turned her face away from the pale-faced woman hovering at her bedroom door. She hated the fake look of apology on Rebecca's beautiful face; she didn't want to talk to her, ever again. Or anyone. In fact, she hadn't said a word since her dad had brought her home last night. Especially not to him. He was a liar, and his fiancée was an evil witch.

Violet hadn't left her side, mutely interpreting and anticipating her every need. They'd always been able to guess each other's thoughts, although Violet dismissed Rose's theories about twin telepathy. She insisted it was the closeness of their bond — their shared experience of childhood tragedy — that kept them on the same wavelength.

Rose knew deep down it was more than that. Her grandma claimed to possess a sixth sense and always insisted that she, too, was *intuitive* — just as her mum had been. Rosie believed that now more than ever. She believed she could sense the presence of loved ones, even when they weren't there; she was convinced she could hear their voices, even feel their touch.

It was as though Violet had been with her on the boat yesterday, holding her hand, exactly as she had done in that underwater cave ten years ago, experiencing the same terror — and now the same shock and rage at the things Rebecca had said to her. *No. She couldn't be.* Rosie hadn't told Violet about any of that yet. It was all still too raw; too devastating.

She couldn't bring herself to tell her dad, either — to call him out on his lies. But she was more determined than ever to find a way of stopping his wedding; to force this woman out of all their lives, for good. She had brought nothing but trouble.

Turning back to glare at Rebecca, Rose was startled to find that she'd disappeared. In her place was her grandma, quietly watching her. Rose frowned. 'Is she gone?'

Juliana didn't need to ask who she meant. 'Not yet. But don't worry, darling. I'm sure she soon will be.' Walking into the room, she looked around curiously. She had only been inside Jack's house once, briefly, and this was the first time she'd seen the photo wall dedicated to Eloise in her granddaughter's bedroom. She stepped closer to it, letting out little mews of pleasure as she spotted familiar memories. Then a grunt, one finger stabbing at a gap between the pictures. 'There seems to be one missing.'

'I know. It was my favourite, too. One of Mummy at Roseland. At a party, when she was younger. It was gone when I got back from Italy. The frame probably fell off and broke. Dad must have taken it and not told me. Like everything else he's kept secret.' Rose frowned. 'I just want everything to go back to how it was, Grandma,' she added tearfully.

'That's why I'm here, darling,' Juliana soothed. 'To help.' She reached into the linen bag looped over her shoulder, pulling out a black, austere-looking leather-bound book.

'What is that?' Rose eyed it curiously. 'It looks like a book of spells.'

Her grandma huffed. 'I'm no witch, my love.

Although I suspect I've been called worse. No, it's just something to keep you entertained. You need to rest after your terrible ordeal.' She handed her the book. 'I thought you might like company.'

'Thanks,' Rose mumbled, disappointed that it wasn't a book of magic, after all. Although it seemed to be very old. She flicked through the thin, almost tissue-like pages without much interest. 'Anyway, Letty's here. She won't leave me alone with *her* again.'

'But your sister's spending the afternoon at Roseland, isn't she? Visiting the film set.'

'What?' Rose sat up in a panic. 'Oh. Yeah. That's right. So I'll be stuck here with —'

'Rebecca will be at Roseland, too,' Juliana said firmly. 'As she was at pains to tell me, the second I arrived.' Thin white brows arched ironically. 'I think she was hinting that my visit was ill-timed. As if I need an appointment to see my granddaughters!'

Rose stared down at the book. It was kind of her grandma to think of something to entertain her, and to make a special effort to visit; she didn't get out much these days. Their dad usually drove them over to the farmhouse, so she and Violet could visit their grandma, chat and eat cake. 'What's it about?' she asked, without much interest.

Juliana sat down slowly on the bedside chair, making herself comfortable, taking her time to answer. 'It's actually a love story,' she said at last.

Rosie winced. 'I don't really read romance novels. I prefer thrillers.'

'Well, every good love story has a dash of tragedy, and vice versa. I think you might enjoy this one. There's even a mystery. Quite a shocking one.' Juliana paused, watching Rose slowly turn the pages again.

'You see, it's your grandfather's journal.'

'Grandpa Charles?' Rose's interest was piqued now. 'He kept a diary?'

'Apparently so. It was a surprise to me, too, darling. I only found it the other day.'

'But you said it's a love story.' Rose flicked through the pages more eagerly now, eyes narrowing as she tried to decipher snippets of the small, neat, closely printed handwriting. 'Is it about you and Grandpa, then? Wow. That *is* romantic.'

'Gosh, isn't it?' said a familiar voice from the doorway. Rebecca nodded at the journal. 'Sir Charles must have had quite a tale to tell. I've never seen such a big fat diary.' She crossed the room, closing the curtains slightly against the bright stream of morning sunshine. Then she sauntered to Rose's bedside. 'It looks like a blockbuster. May I see?' She held out a hand.

'Journals are private.' Rose hugged the book to her chest.

'Oh. Of course. Sorry.' Immediately, Rebecca let her hand drop. 'I didn't mean to pry.'

Rose knew Rebecca's interest wasn't genuine — that she was just trying to smooth things over after what she did yesterday — but being horrible to her would only make things worse. As Violet had said, they needed to bide their time and be clever. 'You'll have to ask Grandma if you can read it,' she said politely, glancing towards Juliana, who smiled tightly but said nothing.

'Oh, don't worry.' Rebecca smiled, too, then nodded at Rose. 'Your dad has told me bits and pieces about the Trelawneys, that's all. They certainly do sound . . . colourful.'

'Right. Here we are,' Jack said in a rather strangled

voice, entering the room at that moment, a breakfast tray wedged against his chest. After setting it down on the dressing table, he strode towards Rose, bending down to give her a hug, frowning as she turned away. 'Did you sleep OK, darling?' he asked, tactfully ignoring the snub. 'How are you this morning?'

'Alive, at least,' she mumbled, scowling.

'And thank God for that.' Jack let her sarcasm pass, too. She'd been through a lot, and he forgave her grumpiness. 'I think we all learned a lesson yesterday. I know I did. I've just booked both cars in for a full service. I should have done the same for the kayak, only —'

'I have that kayak serviced regularly,' Juliana cut in indignantly, sitting up straighter.

'I'm sure you do,' Jack said, determined to avoid an argument. Rose needed to rest.

'But *are* you sure?' Rebecca challenged softly, giving Juliana a sympathetic smile. 'Perhaps you muddled up the dates.' She raised her eyebrows at Jack, reminding him how they'd batted this point back and forth last night: Juliana's dementia; her forgetfulness. The way she hadn't even recalled her first meeting with Rebecca, or their chats about the wedding.

'I most certainly did not.' Juliana bristled. 'I keep a diary of my own.' She glanced at the book Rosie was still hugging. 'Not as extensive as my husband's, of course. Nevertheless, I make a note of all pertinent dates. Well, Margaret does. And as I believe I told you when you came to ask about the boat, it was serviced a month ago. Regular as clockwork.'

'That's not quite how I remember our conversation,' Rebecca said silkily. 'But never mind. What's done is done. Rosie is safe. We all need to move on.

The wedding rehearsal is in two days. Violet and I are going over to Roseland later to make sure everything's in order. There's a lot going on, isn't there?' She tilted her head sympathetically. 'We all have little memory lapses from time to time. Especially when we're busy.'

Juliana gripped the arms of her chair, until her knuckles turned white. 'Are you suggesting I don't remember my own words?'

'It's not your fault, Grandma,' Rose said heatedly. 'It's *hers*.'

Rebecca's face paled again. 'Wait, I didn't mean . . .' She sighed. 'I'm sorry if I spoke out of turn. This isn't the time for squabbles. It's just, I'm so worried about you, Rosie. Please don't upset yourself. You already sound as croaky as a little frog. We don't want you to lose your voice entirely, do we?'

Rose glared at her. 'Really? I bet you'd actually like that. But you know what? Even if I *did* lose my voice, that doesn't mean I can't tell.'

Self-consciously, Rebecca flicked back her hair, giving a nervous laugh. 'Tell what? What on earth are you talking about, sweetheart?'

'You *know* what. What you said on the boat. Before I fell into the water. You weren't supposed to tell me, were you?' She turned furious eyes on Jack now. 'I was never supposed to find out what really happened ten years ago. That it wasn't an accident at all. That our stepdad tried to drown me and Letty.' Despite her angry bravado, tears rolled down Rose's face now as she turned to Jack. 'And that you've been lying about it ever since.'

28

'I know your sister's still mad at me, Violet. And at your dad. I get that, I do. But no hurt was intended. Truly. What I told Rosie . . . I blurted it out without thinking. I was completely overwrought. Terrified. The kayak was sinking. All I could think about was what your dad told me happened when you were little. Like he said, I was praying history wouldn't repeat itself. That Rose wouldn't be pulled under the water. That she wouldn't —'

'Drown?' Violet rolled her eyes as she cut across Rebecca's impassioned tirade. She didn't believe a word of it. Surreptitiously, she flicked a sceptical glance at Eve, sitting next to her in the back seat of Rebecca's Mini as she drove them both over to Roseland.

After Rose's tearful outburst earlier, Jack had encouraged his fiancée to bring forward their visit to the film set — to give him a chance to make up with his daughter alone, having gently and patiently explained everything in detail to her and Violet.

It wasn't that he hadn't wanted to talk to Violet, too; he'd been devastated that the truth had come out so horribly, after ten years of shielding his daughters from their late stepfather's crimes. But Violet had repeatedly reassured him that she was fine, and to focus on Rosie.

Surprisingly, Violet realised that it was true: she wasn't upset. At first, it had been a shock to discover that Rosie's nightmares weren't the legacy of an innocent childhood accident, after all, but rather a kidnap-and-ransom attempt by Ted, the man who had stood in place of a father to them for the first five years of their lives. But while she was shocked, she wasn't as devastated as her twin. In fact, she felt the quiet satisfaction of a mystery solved.

Violet's long-held ambition was to be a reporter, like her big sister Izzy. Learning of Ted's crime had given her a taste of what it felt like when the missing pieces of a puzzle fell into place. She wanted to repeat that with Rebecca; she was hell-bent on finding out what she was hiding. She simply didn't believe that what happened yesterday was an accident. Every instinct told her that no one was as perfect as this woman was pretending to be.

'I'm sorry again,' Rebecca said, smiling ruefully at Violet in the rear-view mirror.

'So am I,' Eve said quietly, reaching over to take hold of Violet's hand. 'All of us only ever wanted to protect you. Keeping secrets isn't a good thing, but sometimes it's for the right reasons. Some things are hard to tell.' She frowned, looking thoughtfully out of the window.

'Thanks, Eve,' Rebecca said gratefully. 'And thank you for coming with us today. It's good to have your company. I know you've been super busy. How are things coming along with your big project? Any closer to that elusive promotion, do you think?'

Deliberately changing the subject, Eve thought, replying vaguely: 'Work's good. How about yours?' She flicked a sideways glance at Violet, who just managed to repress a snigger.

For the last few days, they'd both been trawling the internet to see what they could find out about

Rebecca. So far, neither had come up with anything. Eve had exhausted her list of TV contacts now, but all her calls had drawn a blank. No one had even heard of Rebecca, and she was beginning to think the woman must have faked her CV to get such a plum job.

Being honest, she'd added a little extra gloss to her own, when she'd applied for promotion. But the basics were there: she did a good job, day in, day out. Seeing Rebecca at work would hopefully flush out any lies. Eve had worked with lots of production crews, and she knew they could be brutally honest. She was certain she'd be able to read any scepticism on their faces. Artie had already mentioned that he'd heard a few grumbles.

While Eve was intending to watch and listen, Violet was secretly plotting a more direct approach. *She had a new plan.* If Rosie almost drowning yesterday hadn't opened their dad's eyes to Rebecca's true nature, she needed something even more shocking — and she was convinced she'd hit on the perfect thing.

'Things have stalled slightly,' Rebecca admitted, pulling a face. 'In fact, you won't see any of the crew here today.'

Violet couldn't suppress a moan of disappointment. 'Why not?'

'Has the production been cancelled?' Eve frowned. 'What about filming the wedding?'

'Not cancelled, but slightly postponed,' Rebecca told her. 'As for the wedding, the guys will be back for that on Friday. Then it will be all systems go.'

'Don't they need to rehearse camera angles?' Eve pressed. In her experience of TV productions, the final run-through was always done with the cameras rolling.

'Don't worry, it's all in hand.' Rebecca smiled. 'I just thought you guys might be more comfortable having our dress rehearsal in private. Not everyone is used to cameras, are they? Apart from you, of course, Eve. I'm sure this is all familiar territory for you.'

'Sure.' Eve wasn't entirely convinced.

Rebecca sighed. 'OK, you got me. I guess I should come clean. Things are actually a little fluid at the moment.' She pulled a face. 'There's been a change of director. I need to check in with the producers, actually. But later. Once we've had fun playing dress-up. OK?'

'OK,' Violet agreed immediately, eager to put her own plan into action now.

'Great. Oh, look. Here we are.' Rebecca nodded as they turned sharply into the approach road leading to Roseland. 'We made good time, didn't we?'

Eve didn't reply, sitting quietly as the car pulled up in front of the tall, ornate iron gates, feeling unexpectedly overawed by the impressive sight ahead. She'd visited Roseland so many times, over the years, and nowadays she barely noticed its grandeur. But something about it this morning struck her as ominous. No, *melancholy*.

The solid, grey granite walls were cloaked in shadows as the morning sun shifted westwards, and the windows were strangely dark, like once glittering, now sightless eyes. Or perhaps Eve was projecting her own sombre mood onto the manor house. She needed to talk to Arthur, and her mum, she realised. But she couldn't face it. Turning over her troubled thoughts, she jumped as Rebecca slammed the steering wheel, then leaned on the car horn.

'Darn it.' Rebecca tutted irritably. 'There's supposed to be someone guarding the entrance.'

Eve exchanged a glance with Violet. Usually, Rebecca was so calm and controlled. She wondered what was putting her on edge. 'It's OK. We can open the gate ourselves, can't we?'

'It's locked. We've had to bring in security. Too many of those suspicious locals hanging around.' Rebecca wrenched off her seatbelt. 'Damn. Wait here, OK? I'll be right back.'

29

Eve and Violet sat quietly until Rebecca had climbed out of the car, but as they watched her stride towards the gates and begin talking energetically to a man in uniform, Violet whistled and said: 'Jeez, man. Temper, temper.'

'Dodged all my questions again, too, didn't she?' Eve huffed.

'I don't get it. What's the big deal?'

'No idea. I haven't found any mention of this production in the trade press, either,' Eve said thoughtfully. 'Usually, there are write-ups. Cast listings. Brags about PR and marketing junkets. Although it sounds like things are a bit chaotic, if there's been a change of director.'

'I couldn't find anything on Google, either.' Violet sighed. 'Nothing recent about Roseland. Nothing at *all* about Rebecca. Maybe she's using a fake name.'

'Yeah, good point. Although I did find her on Facebook. Look.' Eve held out her phone, loading Rebecca's profile.

'Wow. She likes sunsets, doesn't she?' Violet rolled her eyes. 'And frothy coffees.'

'It's the same on Instagram.' Eve switched websites. 'More sunsets. Artfully posed cappuccinos. A few beach shots. At least they tell us where she's been, if not where she lives. That's definitely Newquay.' She pointed to a photo of a pretty high street. 'There are a couple of recent ones of Talland, too. See? There's the church. And the graveyard.'

Violet frowned. 'God, that's freaky. Who the hell takes photos of people's graves?' She peered closer as Eve continued scrolling. 'There are none of her, though. Or any friends.'

'Maybe she hasn't got any. But more to the point, there isn't a single picture of your dad. Which is *very* odd, I'd say. Most people can't resist posting engagement photos. I can't find Rebecca's professional history, either. Which is probably weirdest of all. Every single person I know who works in the media keeps an up-to-date profile online. Most of us constantly have an eye on the next potential job opportunity. But not Rebecca.'

Violet groaned. 'It's like she's a ghost.'

'Or a fraud.' Eve looked at her phone again. 'Although I do remember her saying she works for a tiny independent company. Perhaps that means she's freelance.'

'So?' Violet looked doubtful. 'How does that help?'

'Well . . . you could check the Companies House website. Maybe Rebecca's registered a business there. Even an address. Maybe not her home one, but it could be something?'

'Brilliant. Thanks, Evie. I knew I could count on you. I can't put this on Rosie. She's too poorly after what happened yesterday. It's up to me to fix this. I promised her I would.'

Eve gave her a high-five. 'We're a team, Vi. If there's anything dodgy about Rebecca, we'll find it.' She looked back at her phone. 'Not having any friends is sad, but hardly a crime.'

'Dad said she doesn't have a family, either. But that doesn't give her the right to muscle her way into ours.'

Violet stared through the front windscreen, watching Rebecca, who was all smiles now as she rested a hand on the guard's arm, charming him into opening the gates.

'She can turn it on and off like a tap, can't she?' Eve mused, watching too.

'She thinks she can twist *everyone* round her little finger. She's fooled Dad. And Artie. Even your mum. And Aunty Cath knows Dad better than anyone.'

'She knew your mum, too,' Eve said softly.

Violet frowned, remembering why they were at Roseland: not only to see the film set, but to check out the wedding arrangements. It was only a couple of days away; it was now or never for her big plan. 'Well, she doesn't fool me. She's bad news. And I'm going to prove it.'

30

Ten minutes later, Violet wasn't feeling quite so confident.

Pausing at the entrance to Roseland's great hall, she gasped in awe. She'd expected to see cameras and elaborate lighting rigs; she hadn't been prepared for the entire house to look as though it was staged for a seventeenth-century aristocratic wedding, rather than a modern ceremony. If this was all Rebecca's handiwork, she must be very clever indeed.

Perhaps she'd underestimated her, Violet worried. 'I bet this is what it looked like when Grandpa and Grandma got married,' she said, strolling around, trying to take it all in.

'They must be filming something historical,' Eve surmised, gazing around too.

It felt like stepping back in time. Alabaster plinths topped with rose-filled urns stood alongside a red-carpeted aisle, with dozens of rows of wainscot chairs arranged either side, each one draped in white organza, with a crimson velvet bow at the centre. Garlands of white roses were looped around the tall, stone-mullioned windows, while candle-lit sconces lined the walls, casting a romantic, slightly eerie glow. The place looked like a cathedral.

For a moment, Eve felt tearful as she tried and failed to picture walking up such an aisle herself, with Artie at her side. She badly needed to talk to him; she had to talk to her mum, too. She was fully aware that she'd been pushing them both away, claiming to be working hard on her presentation — the promotion she'd been chasing for months.

In truth, Eve had barely thought about her job for days, other than systematically reaching out to her colleagues in an effort to help Violet investigate Rebecca. She'd actually been preoccupied by a far more personal problem, only, as she'd said to Violet in the car just now, some things were hard to tell.

'Eve? Are you OK?' Rebecca rested a hand on her arm.

'Sorry? Oh. Yes. Just bowled over by . . . well, all this.' She gestured around the room.

'Which bits are for the filming, and which for the wedding?' Violet asked, making a beeline for a camera in the corner, lifting the dust sheet covering it, peering underneath.

'Careful, sweetheart,' Rebecca cautioned. 'The new director will have my head on a block if I disturb anything. She said we could have a look around, but not to touch anything.'

'But you're getting married here on Friday,' Violet pointed out. 'And the rehearsal's on Thursday. What if one of the guests accidentally knocks something over?'

'The crew are acting as ushers,' Rebecca told her. 'They'll shepherd everyone around.'

'Wow. Your colleagues are really pushing the boat out for you,' Eve said drily.

Rebecca smiled. 'I'm very lucky, I know. And thankful for everyone's support.'

'Production crews do tend to become like family,' Eve acknowledged. 'Mine's a close-knit bunch. It's a competitive industry, but people look out for each other. Don't you find?'

Rebecca screwed up her nose. 'There have been a few wobbles on this project.'

'Artie said he heard some of the crew moaning in the café,' Violet said bluntly.

'Really?' Rebecca frowned. 'That's a shame. Well, I suppose I did come on board at the last minute. I wasn't even supposed to be at Roseland. Or scout it as a location in the first place. You see, my boss got ill right before she was scheduled to come here.'

Eve stared at her; this was the first piece of solid information Rebecca had volunteered; cynically, she wondered if she had an ulterior motive for doing so. 'Is your boss very ill?'

'Enough for a spell in hospital. Listeria. Dodgy sandwich.' Rebecca winced. 'I had to stand in for her at the last minute. Very unfortunate for her. Although lucky for me, I guess.'

'Very lucky,' Eve agreed. 'You get the plum job. Bump into Jack.' She gestured around the great hall. 'Then all this happens.'

'Yes. Like I said, I'm extremely thankful.' Rebecca smiled. 'Just extraordinarily busy.'

'Sure.' Eve took the hint and checked her watch. 'Look, why don't you show Violet around? I've seen enough production sets in my time. I'll wait here. Put my feet up for a bit.'

Rebecca looked at her in concern. 'Artie said you've been feeling worn out. We were all so worried about you, the other day. When you left the beach in such a hurry. Is there anything I can help with? You do still look rather pale, you poor thing.'

Eve gritted her teeth, feeling patronised. 'I'll live.'

'Actually, Rebecca, I wanted to show *you* something,' Violet said, strolling back towards them. 'You know you wanted us to try on dresses, pick outfits for the wedding rehearsal? I know where there's a whole stash. The Trust has been collecting stuff for a living history exhibition. It's upstairs. Want to see it?'

'Wow, that sounds amazing.' Rebecca looked pleased at Violet's unexpected helpfulness. 'You think we might borrow something?' She glanced around the hall, eyes sparkling now. 'That would be perfect. Clever you,' she said, before giving Violet an impulsive hug. 'Oh, I'm so happy that you and Rosie are my bridesmaids.'

'Sure.' Violet flinched at the hug, feeling a jolt of guilt. She sensed Eve's gaze on her, too, and knew she'd be wondering what she was up to. She hadn't had a chance yet to share her big plan.

It had only come to her this morning, after chatting with her grandma, while their dad had his heart-to-heart with Rosie. As soon as Margaret had arrived to take Juliana home, Rebecca had driven Violet over to Cathy's cottage, where they collected Eve — then heading directly to Roseland. There had been no time to talk in private.

'Everything's going to be perfect,' Rebecca continued happily. She smiled as she straightened one of the organza covers, fussing with the bow. 'Especially with Izzy as my maid of honour. The three Trelawney girls all together, hey?'

'If she comes.' Violet felt her spirits drop. She'd so been looking forward to seeing Izzy, but their dad said he still hadn't received any reply to his invitation. Izzy hadn't responded to Violet's texts, either, and her continued silence was desperately disappointing.

'Well, between you and me.' Rebecca leaned towards her, whispering conspiratorially, 'Your sister is already on her way. In fact, she'll be here tomorrow.'

'What? But how do you . . . ?' Violet stared at Rebecca, then Eve. 'Did *you* know this?'

'No, I didn't. Honestly,' Eve insisted, when Violet gave her a sceptical frown. Discovering the truth about Ted had probably damaged her trust in everyone, and Eve couldn't help flicking a rather pointed glance at Rebecca. 'I'm dying to see Izzy, too. So is Artie.'

'Does *he* know?' Violet demanded, swivelling around to glare once more at Rebecca.

Her smile turned sheepish. 'As a matter of fact, yes. He does. But I begged him to keep it a secret. You both won't mind keeping it under your hats a little longer, too, will you? I really want to surprise your dad.' Her voice softened. 'Call it an early wedding gift to him.'

'Sure. He'll be over the moon,' Violet admitted, her mind going into overdrive now.

Izzy was smart. She was also a hot-shot reporter. Surely, she would see through their dad's fiancée, too? As Rebecca herself had said: the three Trelawney girls would soon be all together — plus Eve, who was like an honorary sister.

Between the four of them, they had to be able to find *something* to convince their dad that he was making the biggest mistake of his life. Something like hope curled in Violet's stomach. She had her secret plan; her big sister was finally coming. Things couldn't get any better.

31

'Could things get any worse?' Izzy stared up at the departures board. 'Four and a half hours. On a train.' The plane from Dubai had only taken three or so more, and Izzy groaned in disbelief that it took so long to cross the UK. She looked around for a bench; there wasn't one. But she didn't want to risk sitting on her holdall, not with the aftershave and perfume bottles inside.

After the relative calm and comfort of her air-conditioned flight, emerging from Heathrow to hail a taxi to Paddington Station had been a shock to the system. London was noisy and sweaty in the summer; every pore of her skin already felt clogged. At this rate, it would be quicker to hire a bloody car and drive to Cornwall herself. Although, in truth, she was too exhausted and jet-lagged to drive, even if she had a clue about the route.

Taking out her phone, she scanned her contacts list, trying to think of an alternative plan but drawing a blank. She refused to call Jack. Even if he wasn't about to get married, which undoubtedly meant he'd be busy and preoccupied, Izzy was in no hurry to see him.

Her finger hovered over Arthur's number. Had he already gone down to Cornwall, getting a head start on his best-man duties? If he was still in London, perhaps they could travel down on the train together. Or maybe he owned a car and could give her a lift . . .

Izzy sighed, recognising how little she knew about her son's life now. Deciding not to make the call, she tucked her phone away. It wasn't that she was worried he might be unfriendly; she was the one who felt weirdly nervous about contacting him. They hadn't spoken properly for weeks, perhaps months, and she hadn't seen him in person for a couple of years. It seemed bad manners to pop up out of the blue, begging a favour after all this time.

'So near and yet so far,' she murmured, struck by the irony that, geographically, she was closer to her son than she'd been in ages, and yet she felt more distant from him than ever. *This* was home to Arthur now. Not Byron Bay; not even Australia.

Yes, they were poles apart, and it made Izzy sad that she was feeling as anxious about seeing her son again as the rest of the Trelawneys. More so, perhaps, because she had zero expectations of them, which was the reason she'd had no qualms about emailing Rebecca from Dubai, rather than getting in touch with Arthur. There was no emotional baggage in that quarter. Izzy didn't know this woman, and she didn't plan on getting to know her.

As soon as the ink was dry on her dad's marriage certificate, Izzy planned to get on with her real purpose in coming here: tracing whoever it was that had suddenly and suspiciously got cold feet about being found, and sussing out what they were hiding.

'Knowledge is power,' she muttered to herself. 'Juliana Trelawney has had the upper hand long enough. It's time I knocked her off her pedestal.'

Despite her bravado, Izzy felt an annoying prickle of tears as she watched a young woman crouch down to cuddle a little girl, reassuring her that their train would arrive soon. From the quantity of their bags, it looked like they were running away, rather than going on holiday. *At least she's taking her child with her*, Izzy thought. She's not packing her off to the other side of the world with strangers. Lying to her about who she is and where she belongs.

'Mum?'

Izzy's heart was pounding as she swivelled around. 'Artie? Oh my God. Is that you?' She stared in shock at the tall, handsome young man standing in front of her. He looked almost the same as the dozens of framed photos lining the walls of her apartment in Byron Bay, but not quite. Still blond, still gorgeous, but with an air of confidence she wasn't used to seeing. *He looked like Jack*, she realised. When he was younger; when she'd still believed he was her charming, playful big brother, not her lying father. 'What the heck are you *doing* here?'

'Yep. It's me. And I've come to see you, of course.' Arthur raked a hand through hair that was shorter than Izzy remembered.

He was less surfer dude now, more laidback reporter, she thought, in his faded jeans, white T-shirt, leather messenger bag slung across his lean body and aviator sunglasses pushed back on his head. Thinking of the aftershave in her bag, Izzy was relieved to notice he was still cleanshaven. She couldn't stop staring at him, thrilled yet baffled.

'But how did you know I'd be here?'

'Rebecca forwarded your flight details to me.' He shrugged. 'I get the train down to Liskeard from Paddington regularly. I knew you'd be here at some point. Once I found out what time you were landing at Heathrow, it wasn't hard to figure out roughly when.'

There was a slight, uncharacteristic coolness in her son's usually ebullient tone. Izzy picked up on it immediately and recognised his hurt that he'd had to learn about her journey second-hand.

'I only decided to come at the last minute,' she said defensively.

'Sure.'

'I was going to call you,' she lied. 'It was just crazy, wrapping up work. Booking flights, a hotel. Everywhere was sold out. Cornwall's popular, hey?' As Arthur remained silent, she said softly: 'I nearly didn't come. Then I thought it might be nice to surprise you.'

'Huh. Well, you've done that, all right.' Finally, Arthur yielded a crooked grin.

Izzy smiled back, happy for any ray of sunshine. 'How's Eve?'

'Fine. I guess.'

Sensing trouble, Izzy asked casually, 'You two are still an item?'

'We're living together. I guess that classifies as being itemised.'

'Well and truly.' Izzy laughed. Then before she knew it, she was crying lunging towards her little boy, who was suddenly a grown man of twenty-six with a live-in girlfriend and a career, and the wherewithal to live halfway around the world without his mum. Half falling, half grabbing, she lurched in his direction, and, somehow, they met in the middle.

'I've missed you, Mum.' Arthur was lean, but his arms were strong.

Izzy didn't want the hug to end, but she needed to breathe, and he was squeezing her so tightly. 'When did you get so buff?' she teased, pulling back. 'Have you been working out?'

'Swimming, mainly. Surfing. The occasional run. You know.'

'No, I don't,' Izzy said sadly. 'But I'd like to. I want to know *everything*.'

'Lucky for you I've hired a car, then. We've got a good five hours ahead of us. Time to listen to my entire Spotify playlist. And put the world to rights while we're at it.'

Izzy gave him a watery smile. 'I only care about your little corner of it. Oh, I've missed you, Artie. I'm so glad you're here. I was dreading the train. Clever you. Thanks for coming.'

'Someone has to carry your bags.' He grinned, reaching for her holdall. 'You obviously *haven't* been working out. Look at you, Mum. You're tiny. You need to eat more.'

'I've been too busy to cook. Besides, you know I hate it.'

'So does Evie. Terrific, so I'm to be chef as well as chauffeur, for the foreseeable,' Arthur teased. 'Good job I do love cooking.'

Izzy laughed. 'You're a foodie now, hey? You know, I'm not actually sure five hours will be long enough. We've got months and months to catch up on.'

'Yeah. I guess we'd better hit the road, then.'

'Can we grab a coffee first? After twenty-four hours on the go, I'm half zombie. I'd hate to nod off in the middle of anything interesting.'

Arthur pointed at a nearby kiosk. 'I know it doesn't look like it, but that place does the best espresso. Or do you need somewhere to freshen up, too?'

Izzy's jeans and T-shirt were sticking to her, but now that she'd seen Arthur again, she didn't want to be apart from him for a single moment. 'Later.' She beamed at him again.

'It's cool if you want to sleep in the car, Mum. I know what it feels like stepping off that plane. Like your body is here, but your mind is stuck somewhere over the Indian Ocean.'

'Thanks, but you know the best way to combat jet lag. Embrace the new time zone. Trick your brain into thinking it doesn't actually need to sleep. It's true. I did a feature on it.'

'A sugar fix also helps,' Arthur chuckled, taking out his wallet as they approached the kiosk. 'I did a feature on that, too. For the radio station I work at now.'

'Great minds think alike, Artie. And you know me.' It felt good to claim that familiarity, after being apart from him for so long. 'I never say no to a doughnut.'

'Yes, I know you, and I'll be sure to buy extra for the journey.' Arthur winked. 'Seriously, though, it's no problem if you do want to grab a bit of kip in the car. I've kept tomorrow completely free. We can hang out.' A slight pause. 'Catch up with everyone.'

Izzy was convinced she detected the same nervousness on his face that was suddenly churning in her stomach. Immediately, she changed her mind about that doughnut. 'Sure.' She forced a smile; it came out more like a grimace. 'I just hope they're ready for me.'

32

'How did you sleep?' Arthur asked eagerly, the following morning. 'You picked the best hotel. I'm amazed they had a room.' As good as his word after he'd dropped Izzy off late last night, he'd arrived in the elegant foyer of the Talland Bay Hotel bang on eleven. Aware that his mum was nervous about seeing everyone, he'd suggested they have brunch together first.

'Luck must be on my side. For once.' She gave him a hug. 'Last-minute cancellation. Shall we eat in the garden? The guy on reception said we could. It's too gorgeous to be inside.'

'Sure,' Arthur mumbled, dreading they might be shown to his family's usual table. Sure enough, they were soon seated in the same shady spot where he'd had brunch only a few days ago. With Eve. At the reminder, he sighed, wishing she was with them.

'Gorgeous place, isn't it? I can swap with you and Eve, if you like?' Izzy teased, seeing his glum expression. 'Although you're hardly slumming it at Jack's. I seem to remember he lives in some kind of *Grand Designs* clifftop glass mansion. Must be an upgrade for you guys. Don't you share a broom cupboard somewhere in west London?'

'Studio,' Arthur corrected. 'But Eve's staying at her mum's cottage here.'

'Ah.' Tactfully, Izzy didn't ask why. She'd gathered on the long drive yesterday that something was going on between the two of them. She wanted to know all about it, but only when Arthur was ready to tell. 'I guess you could check into Roseland a couple of days early.'

'Oh, it's not being opened up for wedding accommodation. It's closed to the public for forty-eight hours, too. Although there's film crew everywhere.'

'Film crew? What, like, TV reporters? Don't tell me Jack's marrying a member of the royal family.'

Arthur shook his head. 'Rebecca's a location manager for a production company. That's how she and Pops met. At Roseland. They're filming a new drama there. And the wedding. But that's just a side hustle. A wedding gift from the crew. Nice, hey?'

'Incredible.' Izzy stared at her son. 'She sounds like some kind of superwoman.'

Arthur didn't reply until they'd given their breakfast order to a hovering waiter, then he lowered his voice as he said: 'To be fair, we're all still getting to know her.'

Izzy glanced suspiciously around them, before leaning forward to whisper theatrically: '*Why are we whispering?*' Then, more loudly: 'Don't tell me the wedding has set tongues wagging? Is it all very scandalous? Are the locals up in arms, gossiping about them?'

Arthur winced. 'Keep your voice down, Mum, OK? I know you're joking, but yeah. As it happens, there's loads of gossip flying about. You know how well-known Jack is in the village. And what with everything that happened to Eloise . . .'

'Everyone is burning with curiosity about Rebecca.' Izzy rolled her eyes. 'Poor woman. I almost feel sorry for her. Anyway, you said you don't know her very well. How come? I thought you were down here most weekends?'

'Yep. But not recently. Work's been full-on. Eve's chasing a promotion. Anyway, to be honest, Pops kind of sprung his engagement on us. He's only known Rebecca a month or so.'

'You're kidding.' Izzy lowered her voice again. 'She's not pregnant, is she?'

Arthur looked shocked. 'You know, I hadn't thought of that. But no. I don't *think* so.'

'So she's pushy?'

'Well . . .'

'Oh, come on, Artie. There must be a reason it's all happened so fast.' Izzy folded her arms, giving him a knowing look. 'I'm jet-lagged, not stupid. There's something you're not telling me. My reporter radar is twitching. Come on, spill.'

Arthur shrugged. 'There's nothing much to tell. Honestly. Rebecca seems lovely. I've never seen Pops so happy. But you can check out the happy couple for yourself this afternoon.'

Izzy gave him a stern look. 'Oh, don't you worry, Artie. I intend to.'

* * *

Twenty minutes later, Izzy pushed away her empty plate, sighing in satisfaction. 'That was the best mushroom omelette I've ever eaten.' She leaned back, staring up at the cloudless, azure sky over the bay. 'And I suppose the view's not bad, either,' she added grudgingly.

Arthur grinned. 'Almost beats Bryon Bay, hey?'

'I wouldn't go that far.' She wasn't here as a tourist;

she'd come reluctantly, her purpose being to investigate her family, not admire their homeland. 'But you look tired, Artie. Sorry, it's my fault. That was a hell of a drive yesterday. Were you too wired to sleep after you dropped me?'

'Uh, no. It wasn't that.' He didn't meet her eyes.

'Right. I see. So you got a grilling for bringing home the prodigal daughter.'

'Is that really how you see yourself?'

'Darling, please don't answer questions with a question.' Izzy arched her eyebrows. 'You're not a politician. Or my therapist.'

'You're still seeing Sue, then?' Arthur frowned.

'Artie, you did it again!' Izzy huffed. 'Look, just give it to me straight. Is Jack surprised I'm here? I'm pretty sure he only invited me out of politeness. I bet he never actually expected me to come. Juliana must be beside herself, too. The illegitimate brat returns.'

'Mum, you don't have to act tough with me. I know it must be weird coming back, but everyone's dying to see you. Pops. Eve. Her mum Cathy. You remember her?'

'Ah, Cathy. Yes, I do.' Izzy smiled. 'She was very kind to me once, a long time ago.'

'She's still lovely.'

'Good to know.' Izzy mimed drawing a tick in the air. 'Seeing as she's your future mother-in-law.' She winked, then said more seriously: 'But tell me about the twins. How are they doing? What do *they* think of their dad getting married?'

'They're coming round to the idea,' Arthur said diplomatically.

'Enough said.' Izzy rolled her eyes. 'So how do they feel about seeing *me* again?' She heard her own voice break and was surprised at how anxious she felt about Rose and Violet's reaction — if they would ignore her, just as she hadn't replied to their texts and emails for weeks.

Although she hadn't seen her sisters in person since they were five, she'd chatted occasionally with them on FaceTime, mainly at Christmas and on their birthdays, but enough to stay in touch. She hadn't meant to break off contact completely — at least, not with them. But even though they were teenagers now, the twins had been through too much for Izzy to feel comfortable grilling them about family secrets. Only, with so many questions burning in her mind, she'd found it hard to talk normally with them; it had felt easier to keep her distance.

Arthur sighed. 'As far as I am aware, the twins don't actually know you're here. I'm not sure anyone does. Rebecca wanted it to be a surprise. I don't think she's even told Pops yet.'

'Seriously? Jeez. I can't wait to meet this woman. She sounds as big a control freak as I am. I hope she bosses Jack about. He deserves a taste of his own medicine.'

Arthur heard the hurt in his mum's voice, and he wasn't fooled by her tough act. 'He's missed you too, you know? Pops talks about you all the time.'

'Yeah, right. So that's why my ears have been burning. Sorry, love. I know you think the world of your grandpa. Jack's practically brought you up, whereas your own dad —'

'Is not on the agenda right now,' Arthur cut in.

'Sure.' Izzy got the message, and she didn't push the subject. It meant a lot to her that Arthur had come to meet her; she didn't want to scare him off. 'You're

OK, though, Artie? You really do look knackered.' She smiled. 'I'm your mum. I'm allowed to say it.'

'I'm fine. Just stuff on my mind.' He jumped as his phone buzzed, frowning as he checked his messages. 'OK, I'm worried about Eve. She gave me the brush-off *again* when I called her last night. Said she was still up to her ears in work and wanted to crack on.'

'Sounds reasonable? You said yourself she's chasing promotion.'

'Yeah. But we always bounce work ideas off each other. It doesn't make any sense. I don't know, I just feel like she's pushing me away.' He put his phone down again, disappointed that there was still no message from his girlfriend. 'Making up excuses not to see me.'

'I'm sure that's not the case.'

'What if she's thinking about breaking up with me?'

'From everything you told me on the drive down, I doubt it. Go talk to her, Artie. Forget about hanging out with your old mum today.' Izzy forced a laugh to cover her disappointment; she'd been so looking forward to spending time with her son.

Despite what she'd told him, Izzy had barely slept last night, spending most of it online, still attempting to trace the mystery email address. She'd had a brainwave around dawn, wondering if the 'BS1' might be a postcode. Bristol, perhaps.

For a moment, she'd felt pleased with herself — until she ran a search for internet cafés in that area and discovered there were dozens. It was impossible to know which one the email had been sent from, or even if it had come from Bristol at all. 'BS' might be someone's initials. Or a company logo. But her repeated searches had found no matches. She was no further forward, which, this morning, felt crushingly like she'd taken ten steps backwards.

'I told you, Mum.' Arthur cut across her thoughts. 'Eve doesn't *want* to see me. Besides, I took the day off to be with you. Soon as we're done here, we're heading over to Roseland.'

'Roseland?' Izzy's heart jumped. She wasn't ready to see Juliana yet; not until she'd uncovered the scandal that she felt certain was enmeshed in the conundrum of her DNA match. Before she saw the old woman, she needed more ammunition in her back pocket. If Juliana had more secrets in her past, Izzy wanted to know them. 'I thought we were going to Jack's house?'

'Later. I promised Pops I'd check on Juliana first. She doesn't do well in this heat.'

'Right. I guess she's quite elderly now.'

'Eighty-five. But not a day over sixty, if you ask her.'

'I wouldn't dare.'

Arthur smiled. 'She's still fierce, but she has a heart of gold.'

'She keeps it well hidden. But then, you were always her favourite. You must be fond of her, too,' Izzy forced herself to say, even though the idea of her son's affection for Juliana Trelawney hurt. 'You lived with her while you did your A levels, didn't you? Before uni.'

'Yeah. She took me in when I first came to Cornwall.' He shrugged. 'We rubbed along OK together. But it's Rosie and Violet she dotes on now. She talks a lot about you, though, Mum. She's been convinced you wouldn't come for the wedding.'

'She was very nearly right.'

'Sure. Well, I for one am glad you're here. And Gee-Gee will be, too. But if you want a tip, don't mention the wedding. Or Rebecca. Juliana is incandescent with rage about both.'

33

'That's some convoy,' Izzy said, two hours later, watching a steady stream of trucks and vans heading up the long, winding drive towards Roseland. The logos on the side of each vehicle told their own story: caterers, florists and equipment transportation.

'I did warn you.' Arthur locked the hire car, then leaned against the roof, staring too.

'Not quite Roseland as I remember it.' Even so, as they left the car park and made their way up the drive, before cutting across the grounds towards the farmhouse, Izzy felt a wave of nostalgia — and regret for not telling her son the whole truth about why she'd come here.

She wasn't being deliberately underhand. If she'd learned one thing as a reporter, it was to check her facts and only run the story when it was bulletproof. The thought made her reach into the back pocket of her denim shorts for her phone.

There were no messages; no further emails. The softer and slightly more conciliatory one she'd sent after waking up in the middle of the night, her body clock telling her it was morning, had once again bounced back. Izzy refreshed her inbox, frowning as nothing new popped up.

'Oh, it's not so changed,' Arthur said. 'Gee-Gee still prunes her rose garden. The lake is the same. It's pretty much identical inside the house, too. We won't get to go in there today, though. They're setting everything up. For the filming and the wedding. But you'll see at the rehearsal on Thursday. I hope you've brought your glad rags. And remembered how to smile,' he added drily.

'I'll put my game face on when it's needed, Artie. Don't you worry about that.'

Arthur sighed. 'I'd rather it was the real thing, Mum. I hate seeing you unhappy.'

'Is that how I seem to you?'

'It's hard to know,' Arthur told her honestly. 'You're just like Pops. Impossible to read.'

'Yeah, well. The big difference is, he's a good liar. I'm not. I've never learned to bite my tongue. I speak as I find. It's what makes me a good reporter. And a lousy daughter.'

'Oh, Mum. Pops adores you. I know you've found it tough to forgive him. It wasn't exactly easy for him, either, you know? Being forced to live a lie all those years.'

'Funny, he made it look effortless.'

'He chose to look on the bright side, you mean. He kept you in his life. That's what mattered most to him. Happiness is a choice, isn't it? That's what Gee-Gee always says.'

Izzy laughed out loud at that. 'Easy for her to say, too. All the choices were hers to make. Things look very different when you're the one having decisions made for you.' She stopped walking and leaned against the tall trunk of a beech tree, sheltering from the hazy afternoon heat.

Arthur joined her, reaching up to grab a slim branch, fanning himself. 'It's too bloody hot. I can't think straight. All I know is that family matters more than what we call each other. Names are just names.

It's love that really counts.'

Izzy smiled. 'When did you get to be so wise, Baby Yoda?'

'We've all lost too much already, haven't we? Not just people, but time.' Arthur gave his mum a wry smile. 'I'm so thankful you and I have the chance to make up for that. But the clock's ticking for Juliana. Go easy on her, OK?'

* * *

Roseland's finest bone china graced the rustic oak table in the farmhouse kitchen, and as Izzy eyed the incongruously elegant tea laid out for them, she knew instantly that they'd been expected, even though Arthur had implied over brunch that it was to be an impromptu visit, purely to check on how the old lady was coping in the heatwave.

Despite promising that she'd go gently, Izzy was disappointed. She'd *wanted* Juliana to be surprised — to feel even an ounce of the shock that had devastated her when she'd learned about her adoption ten years ago. Yet, once again, her grandmother was the one calling the shots. Izzy ground her teeth as she sat down at the table, deliberately not waiting to be invited. 'Hello, Juliana.'

'Hello, Isabella.' Green eyes softened as she turned to her great-grandson. 'Arthur, dear. Would you mind fetching me my cane from the living room?'

'Of course.' Arthur walked slowly across the kitchen, reluctant to leave the two women alone — both fiery and strong-willed; both with fragile hearts and egos. Before closing the door behind him, he mimed an exaggerated grin, pointing first at his face and then at Izzy.

Obediently, she smiled, but the moment Arthur left the room, she propped her elbows on the table and said: 'I see you've still got my son wrapped around your little finger.'

'Arthur's a good boy. He takes care of his great-grandmother.' Juliana reached for the teapot, but her hand trembled and she was forced to set it down again.

Izzy held fast for a moment, watching her struggle, then groaned inwardly. 'Fine. Here, let me help you.' She poured tea for them both, and then, as though to counteract her reluctant act of kindness, said: 'Arthur forgives far more easily than I do.'

'*Forgive us our trespasses, as we forgive those who trespass against us*,' Juliana quoted softly. 'God will judge me for my sins soon enough.'

'Oh, spare me the violin strings.' Izzy's temper snapped now, even though she felt an unexpected jolt at the idea of her grandmother dying. Arthur was right; there had been too much loss in their family. 'You outlived your husband. Even your daughter. You'll outlive us all.'

Juliana gave her a straight look. 'You came here ten years ago to find your family. We obviously weren't good enough for you, as you scuttled off again, back to Australia. So tell me, Isabella, what is it that brings you here now?'

Izzy bristled, even as guilt made her blush. 'Jack's wedding, of course,' she said defiantly, recalling Arthur's warning not to mention it. But she refused to sit here and take all the flak; her dad deserved to be the one in the firing line, not her.

'That wedding. It won't happen. Jack needs to accept that.'

'Why does he? You can't stop it,' Izzy pointed out. 'You may have been able to rule your daughter's life, but Jack's a free agent. He can do what he likes, and marry whom he chooses.' It felt odd to be defending her dad, but Juliana's controlling manner riled Izzy.

'Not while my granddaughters are in his care. Not while Jack is the de facto guardian of the Trelawney fortune.'

Izzy rolled her eyes. 'Not *his* fortune, though. It hardly affects his choice of wife.'

'It most certainly does.' Green eyes, still sharp despite the eighty-five years of turbulent life they'd witnessed, fixed on Izzy. 'I take it you've not met her yet, then?'

'Jack's fiancée? Not yet. But I'm sure she's lovely. I bet she comes from a nice, normal family and has absolutely no idea what she's getting herself into. I actually feel sorry for her.'

'Save your pity. She's a shallow, heartless gold-digger.'

'Steady on, Gee-Gee,' Arthur said, returning to the kitchen at that moment. 'Sorry, I couldn't find your cane anywhere.'

'Couldn't you, dear?' Instantly, Juliana was all gentleness. 'Oh, silly me. That's right, I don't have one.' She smiled. 'I forget so many things these days.'

'Here, let me help you with your tea,' Arthur offered, while Izzy rolled her eyes again.

Juliana waved him away. 'Thank you, but I don't want it. All I want is that wretched woman gone. Roseland is my *home*. I won't let her steal it!'

'I've told you before, Gee-Gee. Rebecca isn't trying to steal anything,' Arthur pacified.

'Have a drink, Juliana.' Despite the resentment

she'd carried for so long, Izzy was shocked and saddened by her grandmother's agitation. Only recently, she'd visited a care home to interview people living with dementia. She was certain she recognised the signs in Juliana. Taking hold of her thin hand, she was surprised to feel a wave of pity.

'Let go of me! You're all the same. Vultures hovering around a wounded animal, waiting for it to die.' Pulling her hand away, Juliana slammed it onto the table. 'Maybe you'll get your way. I'd rather watch Roseland burn to the ground than see that woman living in it.'

Arthur looked worried now. 'You don't mean that, Gee-Gee.'

'That's never going to happen,' Izzy said flatly. 'Jack would never move into Roseland. Not even if he was legally permitted. You know why.'

'On the contrary. I bet he can't wait to take his place at the head of the Trelawney table,' Juliana said fiercely. 'The son of a lowly estate manager, finally getting his hands on Roseland? He's bided his time very patiently. I'll say that for him.'

Arthur opened his mouth to speak, no doubt to defend his grandpa, but Izzy shook her head. 'We'll leave you to rest now,' she said quietly.

'It will all be yours, one day,' Juliana told her plaintively.

Izzy frowned. 'Roseland means nothing to me. I haven't come here for that.'

'Then I'll ask you again. Why *have* you come here, Isabella?' Shrewd green eyes glinted as they studied her face, but a glimmer of tears hinted at unexpected vulnerability.

'To see my son,' Izzy said deliberately. 'Save your

money for him, OK? Or the twins. Roseland, too. I don't want it. Any of it.'

'I'm sorry you feel that way.' Juliana sighed. 'I wish I could make you understand. The things I regret . . .' She trailed off, eyes closing. 'Your mother . . .'

'You need to rest, Gee-Gee.' Arthur kissed her cheek. 'We'll see you again on Thursday, OK? At the rehearsal.'

'No, you won't.' Juliana's head rocked from side to side, her lips moving as though she was having a silent conversation with someone.

Izzy watched the old lady with narrowed eyes, suspecting her frailty was exaggerated: a deliberate distraction from unwanted, probing questions. Or perhaps simply an act put on to gain sympathy. Izzy felt her own evaporate as quickly as it had appeared.

What other secrets are you hiding, Juliana? she thought, glancing back as she followed her son out of the room. *And who else knows them?*

34

'So, that went well.' Arthur rolled his eyes, acutely conscious of a sense of déjà vu. It was only a couple of days since he'd said the same thing to his grandpa; now it was his mum who had provoked Juliana almost to the point of hurling her favourite antique teapot at her.

Izzy carried on striding down the path, away from the farmhouse, at breakneck speed. '*Scuttled off*. Like I'm some sort of measly coward for going back to Australia, away from the family who disowned me in the first place. What the hell right does she have to think of *me* as a coward? She's the one who quailed in the face of public judgement. Who gave away her first grandchild to avoid a scandal.'

'Mum . . .'

'Perish the thought that tongues might wag. Oh, no, we couldn't risk the precious Trelawneys being the subject of gossip. Yet Juliana has the gall to accuse *me* of running away.'

'She was overwhelmed to see you, that's all,' Arthur jumped in, as Izzy was forced to pause for breath. 'It made her crotchety.'

'Crotchety!' Izzy threw up her arms. 'I'd hate to see her truly mad.'

'At least she got out her best china. That shows how much she loves you,' Arthur quipped, trying to placate her. 'I usually get my tea in a chipped mug. Without so much as a buttered scone in sight.'

'Funny way to show you love someone. What happened to a good old-fashioned apology? You know, *I love you. I'm sorry I fucked up.*'

'She did kind of apologise. At least, she seemed to be heading that way.'

'She played the sympathy card, you mean. All that *woe is me, I regret everything* rubbish. And the crazy head rolling. What the heck was that about? I can see she has dementia. Maybe early onset, but it's there. She's not physically ill, though, is she?'

'Not as far as I'm aware. But you're right. Her behaviour is a little . . . erratic.'

'And the rest.'

'You know what, though, Mum? You two are more alike than you realise.'

'What the hell?' Izzy stopped walking and turned to stare at her son.

'I mean it. You and Gee-Gee are both volatile. Impulsive and a bit unpredictable. Not to mention stubborn and hot-headed. Oh, come on,' Arthur said, when Izzy glared at him. 'Remember the grief you gave me when I came to the UK? But it was the right thing to do. If I hadn't come here, I'd never have found out the truth about our family. Nor would you.'

'Do I even know the *whole* truth, though? Juliana's hiding something. I can sense it.'

'Now you sound even more like her.'

'I'm serious, Artie. She didn't attack me because she felt overwhelmed. She feels *guilty*. It's the classic behaviour of every cornered animal. Strike first to protect yourself. I'm no vulture, but Juliana is definitely nursing a secret wound.'

'I think it would help if we talk to her again,' Arthur said cautiously. 'Now the first meeting is over, it'll be easier. But let's maybe wait until *after* the wedding, OK?'

'You heard what she said. There won't *be* any wedding. Not if she can help it.'

'Pure bravado. She can't stand the thought of anyone but her daughter getting married at Roseland. Especially not Rebecca.'

Izzy raised her eyebrows. 'What exactly is so wrong with this woman? You said the twins aren't keen on her, either.'

Arthur shrugged. 'Nothing. I guess she's just not everyone's cup of tea.'

That made Izzy smile. 'Oh, Artie. You couldn't sound more English if you tried.'

'You say that, but I'll always be an Aussie as far as most people are concerned. That's probably all it is with Rebecca, too. She's not from here. It's a tight-knit community.'

Izzy looked at him curiously. 'Wait, you mean it's not just the great Trelawney family that's taken against her?'

'Let's just say she'd caused a few ripples. I've heard the odd spiteful word. Although, to be fair, it's mostly because of the film crew. They've pretty much taken over the village.'

'Sure. I saw some of them last night at the hotel. Reading scripts. Drinking whisky.'

'Yeah. They're nice enough, and mostly keep to themselves. Which is probably what's driving everyone mad.'

Izzy frowned. 'I don't follow.'

'Juliana might be possessive of Roseland, but so are the villagers. A few aren't best pleased about all the commotion. Especially as no one knows what's being filmed.'

'You mean, aside from the wedding of the century.'

Arthur let his mum's sarcasm pass. 'Everyone's desperate to know. Will it be another *Downton*? Or *Brideshead*?'

'Or *The Woman in Black*,' Izzy said drily. 'They've definitely missed a trick in their casting. Juliana has that part nailed. So who are the lead actors? Anyone I've heard of?'

'That's just it. No one knows. Rebecca's given strict orders for the utmost secrecy.'

'Like I said, control freak.' Thoughtfully, Izzy reached into her lightweight crossbody bag, taking out a packet of cigarettes and her lighter. She rarely smoked these days, but after the unsettling encounter with her grandmother, she needed something to steady her nerves. 'Sounds like this Rebecca's ruffling a few feathers. Good for her. In fact, the more I hear about her, the more I like the sound of her.' Lighting up, she took a long, slow drag on the cigarette.

'Mum! You can't smoke here,' Arthur said urgently. 'Look at the grass.'

'Ah. Right. Shit.' Izzy glanced around, taking in the drought-stricken lawns.

'One flick of that ash, and you'll start a fire.'

'What, you mean like *this*?' Mischievously, she lobbed her cigarette towards a tree, where scrubby grass sprouted at its roots like a bad haircut. Immediately, a tiny plume of smoke curled upwards, followed by an orange flame. 'What was that Juliana said? That she'd rather see Roseland burn than let Rebecca live here? Maybe this could be my good deed of the day.'

'Jesus, Mum.' Arthur hurried towards the flame, stamping it out with the soles of his deck shoes. 'What the hell were you thinking?'

Izzy didn't know. She hadn't really intended to start a fire. She'd lived her whole life in Australia and had seen the devastation caused by bushfires. All she knew was that she wanted, somehow, to leave her mark on this place where her mum had played as a child, conceived her as a teenager, only to give her away.

Night after night, Izzy dreamed about it, imagining her mum Eloise running through Roseland's corridors. She'd even tried to picture Jack as a child, growing up on this beautiful, exclusive estate, tolerated for the sake of his hard-working father, yet not considered good enough to love a Trelawney, let alone become one of them.

Izzy had lied when she'd told Juliana that Roseland meant nothing to her. In fact, it meant everything. She realised now that it had got under her skin ten years ago, when she'd first returned as an adult, after being banished as a baby. It was in her blood, and this infuriating mystery about the family who ruled from its rolling acres had become an obsession; an itch she had to scratch.

The whole situation was driving Izzy mad. She couldn't understand how it was possible to feel at once such longing and such loathing for a place. 'Last night I dreamed I went to Roseland,' she muttered, watching Arthur continue to stamp out the flame she'd started.

'Seriously, Mum.' Hands on hips now, he shook his head. 'Don't do that again.'

'Sorry, love.' Izzy frowned. 'But you have to admit, it would solve a heck of a lot of problems for everyone, if Roseland really did go up in flames.'

35

'Roseland has become an obsession for Juliana. She thinks anyone who comes near it wants to steal it. Even though she's already given it away.' Rebecca sighed. 'Although considering her state of mind, I'd seriously question the validity of that contract. Anyway, she's made up her mind about me. She won't change it now. I know that.' She reached for her coffee. Her third.

'She's a stubborn old bird,' Izzy told her, pulling a face. 'Like me, according to my darling son.' She rolled her eyes. 'It must run in the Trelawney blood. Whoever they don't like simply becomes persona non grata. As far as my family's concerned, you're either in or you're out. There are no half measures.' She lifted her own cup of espresso, holding it out towards Rebecca's. 'Cheers to you, anyway. From one Trelawney reject to another.'

'And right back at you. From a fellow coffee addict,' Rebecca said, laughing.

'Is this a private party for two, or can I join in?' Jack picked up his tumbler of whisky, raising it in a toast. 'Here's to the two most beautiful women in the whole of . . . this hotel.' He chuckled, in a playful, indulgent mood. 'My darling daughter, and my very clever, extremely cunning wife-to-be. How you managed to keep quiet about Izzy's arrival, I'll never know.'

Rebecca's brows furrowed. 'Good surprise, though?' she asked tentatively.

'The best early wedding present ever,' Jack confirmed, leaning across the table to kiss his fiancée's cheek softly. 'I couldn't be happier.'

'The twins will be mad, though,' Rebecca worried. 'They wanted to come tonight, too.'

'I know.' Jack sat back in his chair with a sigh. 'But Rosie still needs to rest. It's too soon for her to be out and about, after her ordeal. And I could hardly invite Violet without her.'

'They'll blame me, though.' Rebecca's eyes filled with tears. 'I just can't seem to win them over. I know I've made mistakes, but . . . Sorry. This is supposed to be a happy reunion. I don't want to spoil the mood for you guys with my silly woes.'

'Vi seemed chipper enough last night,' Jack said. 'It sounds like you had a good day with her at Roseland.' He took hold of his fiancée's hand, giving it a reassuring squeeze.

'The best.' She gazed shyly at him from beneath her lashes. 'You know, I think she's actually getting excited about being a bridesmaid. She adored our dress-up session. You wait, darling. You won't believe your eyes when you see us in all our finery. Rosie, too.'

'But will she be well enough for the rehearsal?' Izzy asked in concern. She'd been shocked when Arthur had told her about Rosie almost drowning. 'It sounds terrifying, what happened.' She addressed the comment to Rebecca, still avoiding looking directly at her dad.

Their first meeting had actually gone much better than she'd expected, but she still felt uptight and on edge around him. There were things Izzy needed to have out with Jack, but she didn't want to launch straight into conflict — especially not in front of his fiancée, who did indeed seem as lovely as Arthur had said, not to mention surprisingly beautiful and glamorous.

The moment Izzy had spotted her across the hotel lobby, wearing an eye-catching silver mini dress, she'd felt scruffy and under-dressed in her T-shirt and denim shorts. She *had* planned to be wearing something smarter the first time they met, but there hadn't been time to change. Arthur had sprung this dinner on her, just as he had the visit to Juliana this afternoon.

At first, Izzy had been irritated, sensing that she was being 'managed'. Finally, she'd conceded that Artie had a point: if he'd told her in advance that he had invited Jack and Rebecca to have dinner with her this evening, she would have pleaded jet lag — anything to put off the confrontation she'd been dreading throughout her long journey.

'Terrifying is the word,' Rebecca said, pulling Izzy's attention back to their conversation about the boat accident. 'The storm came out of nowhere. I was petrified.'

'I bet you were.' Izzy gave her a sympathetic look. 'The sea is lovely to look at, but it can be lethal. It has to be treated with respect. It's the same back home. You have to think of the ocean as a capricious, fair-weather friend. Beautiful when the sun shines, but it can turn on you at any moment. We need to get to know its moods. Figure out its patterns of behaviour. Artie always used to check and double-check tidal times before he went surfing at Bondi. You guys have something similar here, don't you? That little yellow book. Oh, what's it called?'

'*Tide Times*,' Rebecca supplied. 'At least, I think so,'

she added quickly. 'I don't actually own a copy. I must have seen one lying around at Jack's, I suppose. Not that I've read it. Personally, I tend to just look out the window and check the weather.' She laughed.

Izzy laughed, too. 'The good old-fashioned way. *Red sky in the morning, shepherd's warning*. Do they say that here, too?'

'Absolutely.' Rebecca beamed at her. 'I love watching the sunrise. And sunset. At Goldeneye, you can see for miles across the bay, and the light is just so —'

'I haven't known a storm like that on this coastline for years,' Jack cut in, frowning now. 'I didn't see any sign of it on the weather warnings. I *did* check. And double-checked.'

'Of course you did,' Rebecca soothed immediately. 'No one doubts that.'

Jack gritted his teeth, not liking the feeling that he was being humoured. 'That was up there among the worst days of my life, and there have been a few.' He glanced at Izzy, knowing he didn't need to spell out to her what was also on that list.

Despite their years apart, and although he recognised that his daughter was stubbornly holding herself aloof from him, he'd been relieved to sense that their connection wasn't entirely broken. He'd felt it in their first, awkward hug when they met in the hotel lobby.

Jack was beyond thrilled that Izzy had come for the wedding; it filled him with hope that they could repair their relationship. And despite his flicker of irritation with Rebecca, he was happy to see his fiancée and eldest daughter getting on like a house on fire. Things were tricky with the twins; Rebecca needed someone in his family on her side.

'Anyway, it wasn't your fault. It was mine.' Rebecca

held up her hands. 'It was my idea to go out on the boat. Although I'm still convinced Juliana was mistaken about having it serviced. I really do think her state of mind is deteriorating. I don't know her that well, of course,' she added, wrinkling her nose, 'but . . . Tell me, Izzy. How did you find her this afternoon?'

'Quite mad.' Izzy grinned. 'In fact, are you absolutely sure you want to join *the clan*? Apples don't fall far from the tree, do they?' She waited, fully expecting Rebecca to joke along. They'd enjoyed plenty of banter over dinner, discovering they had more in common than a love of coffee. Both were self-confessed workaholics, and they counted many of the same books and films on their top-ten lists. She was taken aback by Rebecca's sudden seriousness.

'I've waited a very long time to feel part of a family,' Rebecca continued, and there was a catch in her throat. 'I don't have one of my own, you see? My parents died when I was a little girl. I was brought up by my grandma till I was old enough to fend for myself.'

'Wow. I'm so sorry to hear that. Tough on you. And your grandma, I imagine.' Izzy pulled a face. 'I hope she wasn't as bonkers as mine.'

Rebecca raised her eyebrows. 'They threw away the mould when they made Juliana.'

'Now, now, girls. Be nice.' As soon as the words had left his mouth, Jack wanted to bite them back, feeling like a grumpy old man out with his teenage daughters.

Glancing around the restaurant, he wondered if that's what other people were thinking — if they were all talking about the age gap between him and his fiancée. It hadn't bothered him before; nor had what

Artie told him about gossip in the village. But tonight, for some reason, he was concerned about both. Catching the waiter's eye, he signalled for the bill.

'Spoil sport.' Rebecca pouted.

'We'd best get back to the girls,' Jack said quietly. 'But we'll see you tomorrow, Izzy? Any time from midday onwards.' He frowned when she didn't reply. 'For the party.'

'*Engagement* party.' Rebecca's blue eyes sparkled now.

'Oh, right.' An engagement party, followed by a family dress rehearsal, and then finally the wedding itself. *How long were they going to drag out this ridiculous charade?* Izzy thought churlishly, recalling her prediction to her therapist that the wedding would be a circus. But who was the ringmaster?

As if she could read her mind, Rebecca said: 'Sorry to drag you out of your hotel again, Izzy. You were probably hoping to rest before the wedding. But we didn't get around to having stag and hen dos, you see? I think this little party tomorrow is your dad's way of making it up to me. Actually, not so little, I hope.' She turned to Jack with a sultry smile. 'In fact, I'm expecting very big things.'

36

'I take it that's not your dress for the wedding rehearsal,' Jack chuckled as Violet strode towards him, the following afternoon. He was still working hard to get back into her good books, firstly after the revelations about Ted, and secondly for not inviting her to dinner with Izzy last night.

'Duh, course not. I got this in Italy. Like it says.' Violet rolled her eyes, pointing to the slogan embroidered in red and white across her neon green jersey mini dress. But she could tell it was the length, not the design, that had caught his attention. He was such an old fuddy-duddy.

'Ah, of course. So . . .' Jack racked his brains for less controversial small talk. 'Rebecca tells me you had a nice time at Roseland, yesterday. I hear you've got everything planned. Right down to the last secret detail.'

'Exactly. *Secret*,' Rebecca teased, overhearing their conversation as she swayed across the terrace to join them. 'Mum's the word, OK?' She smiled at Violet, before handing Jack a glass of champagne. 'I told you. We want everything to be a surprise. Don't we, sweetheart?'

'Absolutely.'

'Now I'm really worried.' Jack mimed an expression of mock horror.

Rebecca clinked glasses with him. 'It's all going to be perfect. You have your suit ready, don't you? How about you, Artie?' she added, as he emerged from the kitchen.

'Sorry?' Artie blinked in the bright sunshine, looking miles away.

'Your suit? For the wedding?' Rebecca repeated patiently.

'Oh, right. Yeah. I'm good to go. Shoes polished. Speech written. Complete with lots of bad jokes at your expense,' he teased his grandpa, but his eyes were fixed on the garden.

'Eve will be here soon,' Jack told him, guessing what lay beneath Artie's uncharacteristic tension. 'Cath's driving them. She said they'd pick Izzy up from the hotel en route. You know what your mum's like. She's probably keeping them chatting.'

'Sure.' Arthur helped himself to champagne, trying to get into the party mood. But he was still worried. He hadn't seen Eve since Monday, and they'd barely spoken since.

'She's a fool if she doesn't appreciate you, Artie,' Rebecca said softly. 'You're such a darling. Eve is lucky to have you.'

'I'm the lucky one,' Arthur mumbled. 'Anyway, I'd best go check on the party food.'

Strolling back into the kitchen, he checked his phone, at the same time casting a critical eye over the platters of fresh salad, crusty bread from the local bakery, along with bowls of spicy pasta and fragrant rice, plus a selection of cold meats, cheeses, olives and miscellaneous other snacks laid out on the worktops. Remembering Rebecca's preference, there was no seafood, which he knew would disappoint his mum.

As well as having a sweet tooth, Izzy loved chargrilled fish. So did Eve, and usually Arthur would have done a barbecue. Tonight, though, he didn't want to be tied to cooking; he wanted to be glued to Eve's side. His mum had wanted to know all about his world; well, that was the little corner where he was happiest. He only hoped Eve still felt the same.

* * *

An hour later, Arthur was beginning to think that his mum, Eve and Cathy must have forgotten all about the party. Miserably, he gazed around the terrace. Rosie was curled up on a sun lounger, engrossed in the enormous book she'd scarcely put down since Juliana had given it to her, while Violet was glued to her phone, as usual. Rebecca and Jack stood gazing across the bay, drinking champagne. His grandpa's favourite jazz music played softly in the background.

The romantic scene seemed to taunt his aloneness, and Artie wished he didn't have to be here. But he was his grandpa's best man, and Pops had always been there for him. Arthur owed it to him to make today special — and tomorrow, and the day after. The trouble was, he was dreading it all. Not the rehearsal or wedding per se, but Eve dumping him just when he needed to be on top form. Engrossed in his thoughts, he jumped when someone tapped him on the shoulder.

'Mum! At last.' Arthur gave her a hug. 'Where's Eve?' he asked immediately.

'Don't panic, she's on her way. Cathy's just parking the car. Sorry, love. We got chatting at the hotel. I guess we lost track of time.' Izzy frowned, glancing around the terrace with narrowed eyes, looking as sceptical about the romantic scene as Arthur had been feeling a moment ago. 'Here they come now. And there are the twins.' She raised a hand, waving at them. 'I must go say hi.' And with that, she disappeared.

Cathy laughed as she stepped onto the terrace. 'Your mum hasn't changed, Artie. Never sits still. Never stops talking.'

'Tell me about it.' Arthur laughed, too, then turned to Eve with a shy smile. 'I hope she didn't wear you out.'

Eve frowned. 'Why would she? I'm absolutely fine. I told you, I've been busy with work, that's all. I'm not ill, or anything.'

'Good. Sorry. Yes.' A long pause. 'You look lovely, anyway.'

'Thanks.' Eve stared pointedly at her ripped black jeans and faded Blondie T-shirt. 'As you can see, I dressed up for the occasion.'

'Well, you look wonderful to me, whatever you're wearing. You always do.'

'You too.' She smirked at his even scruffier jeans and Rolling Stones T-shirt.

Arthur laughed. 'Heck, if Pops wanted black tie and tiaras, he should've booked the Savoy.' He nodded towards the kitchen. 'Although I reckon my food's better. Are you hungry?'

Eve grinned at that. 'You read my mind.'

Cathy smiled too, watching fondly as the two of them sauntered into the house. Over the last couple of days, she'd become increasingly worried that something had gone very badly wrong between them. Eve had barely left her bedroom at the cottage, claiming work pressures, and Arthur had sounded more bereft each time he'd phoned. It was a relief to see them chatting normally again.

'Hi.' A gentle hand on her shoulder.

'Oh! Jack.' Cathy felt her heartbeat race as she spun around. 'You made me jump.'

'Sorry. I just wanted to say hello. And thanks for coming. I was getting worried you'd had a better offer.'

'Of course not. This is your engagement party. I wouldn't miss it for the world. Thank you for asking me. I mean, *us*.' Cathy looked away, finding it weirdly hard to meet Jack's eyes.

He looked almost unbearably handsome in his caramel chinos and white shirt. Classic, unshowy, confident in his own skin. By contrast, Rebecca seemed determined to claim the spotlight, wearing a sparkly red gypsy-style dress that left her shoulders bare, with perilously high heels and her hair flowing in soft waves to her waist. She looked like a flamenco dancer.

'Hi, Cath,' she greeted, sashaying across the terrace. 'You look lovely. Pretty in pink. As usual.' She double air-kissed Cathy, before hooking a hand over Jack's arm. 'We're so glad you could make our little party at such short notice. Strictly speaking, it wasn't on the To Do list, but spontaneity is good, right?' She smiled up at her fiancé.

'Right,' he agreed. 'Always more exciting to swim against the tide.'

Rebecca laughed. 'Well, I don't think I'll be swimming anywhere for a while. Rosie and I have a little pact. No more boat trips. We're sticking to shell-seeking.'

'That sounds lovely,' Cathy said politely. *Although a little tactless*, she couldn't help thinking. 'Eve and I always used to pick a handful as souvenirs before we went home. I've got some pretty ones in my suitcase already. Along with a load of dirty laundry.' She pulled a wry smile. 'No prizes for guessing what I'll be doing when I get home this weekend.'

Jack frowned. 'You're leaving this weekend?'

'Well, Evie has to get back to London for work. I said I'd drive her.' Cathy feigned a nonchalance she didn't feel.

She was worried that it wasn't actually work pulling Eve away, but that something else was pushing her to go: a quarrel between her and Artie that may have been temporarily put on hold, but not fully resolved. Plus, Cathy couldn't bear the thought of leaving Cornwall.

Rebecca smiled. 'That's nice. And your husband's arriving in the morning?'

'All being well,' Cathy said tightly, prickling at the heavy-handed reminder.

'So you'll be all together again. Happy families. How wonderful.' Rebecca gazed at the twins, who were chattering excitedly with Izzy now, their three blonde heads leaning close together. 'Look at them. Aren't they gorgeous?'

'Beautiful,' Cathy agreed, and her voice cracked. She didn't want to leave them, either.

'They so are. They take after their dad. In fact, I don't know what I've done to deserve such luck.' Rebecca's blue eyes turned misty. 'I not only have the world's handsomest groom. I have the three prettiest bridesmaids. I'll be a thorn between roses.'

Jack lifted her hand, kissing it gently. 'Darling, without wishing to diss my wonderful daughters, you'll be the belle of the ball. Roseland itself is hardly worthy of such a bride.'

'Oh, Jack,' Rebecca sighed. 'This is lovely, and

everything.' She gestured around the terrace, taking in the champagne and roses on each table, fairy lights woven around the garden, with candles ready for the party to stretch into the evening. 'But I can't wait for the morning. I know it's only the dress rehearsal, but I've got butterflies just thinking about it.'

'Me too,' Jack said honestly. He'd barely slept, his stomach having been in knots since they got home from dinner last night. He couldn't put a finger on why he was feeling this way; he certainly couldn't blame the food at the hotel, which had been excellent, as always.

Sure, he'd had a wobble worrying about what people were thinking of the age gap between him and his bride, but it wasn't like him to pay attention to other people's opinions. Jack racked his brains, still having no clue what was causing him to feel so on edge.

Rebecca laughed. 'You mean, you're not quite the tough guy you pretend to be.'

'Do I?' Jack looked quizzically at her. 'The twins always tell me I'm an old softie. Anyway, you know I'm not one for bells and whistles. But you've worked so hard planning this wedding. I hope it's everything you've dreamed of, and more.'

'Oh, it will be. I know it,' Rebecca said huskily. Once again, she gazed across the terrace to where Izzy, Rose and Violet were falling about with laughter now. Her eyes glittered in the afternoon sunshine, and her glossy mouth curved in a soft smile. 'The whole Trelawney family gathered together at Roseland. Yes, I truly think it will be a day to remember.'

37

'Hi, Aunty Cath. So you've found Letty's secret smoking hideout.'

'Rosie.' Cathy turned around at the sound of her voice. 'Smoking?' She arched her eyebrows. 'I know your dad let you and Vi have a little champagne today. But cigarettes?'

'Oh, no. Not cigarettes. I wouldn't let her do that.' Rose pulled a face. 'Violet play with matches? Seriously bad idea. Anna just gave her some nicotine-free vapes in Italy. But please don't tell Dad. Letty only wanted to try them. Promise you won't tell?'

'I promise. As long as she doesn't make a habit of it.' Cathy chuckled. 'Or get caught. Although, she's certainly chosen her hideout well.' Looking back towards the house, she realised that they were indeed completely hidden from sight here.

At the far edge of the garden, surrounded by trees and lush flowerbeds, she could see only a glimpse of the party continuing on the terrace. A few local friends had joined them now. Cathy thought she recognised a couple of faces from Jack's previous dinner parties; hospital colleagues, she recalled. And it looked like the new vicar chatting to Rebecca.

It had been a lovely afternoon, and Cathy was happy to hear the sound of laughter and clink of glasses. But from their secret corner, it all felt very far away, as though she and Rosie were in a separate room. To one side of them lay the pristine lawn, rolling towards the terrace; to the other, the sheer drop of the cliff, and the glistening blue of the bay beyond.

Drinking it all in, Cathy envied Rebecca for getting to enjoy this stunning view, every day, for the rest of her life. 'Lucky Rebecca,' she murmured, just as she'd said when Eve relayed how a bout of food poisoning had landed Jack's fiancée the job at Roseland — followed by a whirlwind engagement with Jack. *We make our own luck*, Eve had replied darkly.

Cathy knew her daughter could be cynical, and she hadn't been surprised when Eve had suggested that Rebecca most likely had a hand in her boss's misfortune. But Cathy found it hard to believe anyone could be so devious. She'd had her own scruples about Rebecca, not to mention serious concern about the whole boat incident. But, somewhat surprisingly, Izzy seemed to have taken to her dad's fiancée immediately, which went a long way to reassuring Cathy. If Izzy, who had spent the last couple of hours complaining about the Trelawney family, and everyone within their orbit, actually liked the woman, Rebecca couldn't be all bad.

'It's lovely to see Izzy again, isn't it?' Cathy said, turning to Rose. But her expression was blank, her eyes half-closed. 'Rosie? Are you OK?'

'What? Oh. I'm a bit tired, that's all.' She dug her hands into the pockets of her pink denim pinafore dress. 'Actually, I might go to bed and finish reading my book.'

'Ah. That sounds like a good idea. It's a big day tomorrow, isn't it? The dress rehearsal.'

'Yeah.' Rose's eyes flicked to the church now, high above on the clifftop.

Cathy gave her a swift hug. 'I know you still miss

her, darling. We all do.'

'Dad doesn't. He never talks about her anymore. It's like he's forgotten her. And Rebecca keeps trying to have *little chats* about her with us. But I don't want to.'

'It's tough getting used to a new woman in your dad's life. I guess it's probably the same for Rebecca. Give her a chance, hey?'

'That's what Dad says. But why should we? Why should *she* get to dance around drinking champagne, while Mum . . .' Rose frowned. 'I can't bear thinking of her in that place.'

'I know, love. Although, in a way, I find it brings me comfort,' Cathy said gently. 'It's such a beautiful church. Your mum used to love going there. The view is so tranquil.'

'Not underground, it isn't. That's where Mum is. Buried. *Suffocating*. Just like me and Letty nearly did in that cave when we were kids.'

'Sorry?' Cathy stared at her in horror. 'Oh my God, Rosie. How did you . . . ?'

'Rebecca told us. Well, she told *me*. When we were on the boat. Apparently, she was so scared, she just blurted it out. Pretty lame excuse, don't you think?' Rose huffed. 'But it wouldn't have been a problem if Dad had told us in the first place.'

'Please don't blame him, darling. He was only trying to protect you. We *all* were. But it must have been dreadful, finding out like that.' Cathy gave Rose another hug, feeling awful. 'I'm so sorry. Have you talked to your dad about it? How are you feeling about it all now?'

'Yeah, he said sorry. And that he'd been planning to tell us everything when we were older. I'm OK, I guess. I don't think Ted really meant for us to die. He only wanted our money. He knew Dad would pay anything to get us back.'

'Your dad would give his life for you and your sister,' Cathy said croakily.

'He almost did, didn't he? Ten years ago. Then again on Monday. I just wish . . .'

'You wish?' Cathy prompted softly, suspecting what was coming next.

'I wish he could have saved Mum's life, too.' Rose stared up at the church again. 'I still can't believe she's gone. I can picture her so clearly. Especially at bedtime. Her hair was so soft. She always smelled so good. I remember her lavender perfume.'

'Me too,' Cathy said, recalling her dream on her first night in Cornwall — when the sounds and scents drifting in from the garden had made her think Eloise was in her bedroom.

'I used to think she was looking after us,' Rose continued wistfully. 'But how can she be? If she was, she wouldn't let Dad marry *her*.'

Cathy followed Rose's gaze in the other direction now, towards the bar in the corner of the terrace, where Rebecca was raising a champagne toast to Izzy. She had her head tipped back, laughing. Izzy was laughing, too, while Jack looked indulgently between the two of them.

Be happy for him, Cathy told herself. He had been reunited with his eldest daughter, and he'd found love again, after years alone. She thought of Chris, arriving in the morning, and felt a sinking anxiety. But he was her husband; Jack could never be more than a friend.

Cathy gasped, gripping the balustrade tighter.

What on earth was she thinking? Jack was getting married in two days. She needed to stop mooning over him and concentrate on her own husband — who had always told her that she *went loopy* whenever she came to Cornwall.

He was probably right, Cathy admitted, and as she'd told Jack: as soon as the wedding was over, she would go home. Back to London. That was where she belonged, not here, watching Rebecca drape herself all over Jack. She glanced back at the terrace, watching her do just that. 'Your dad loves Rebecca,' she said deliberately. 'And she's OK. No one's perfect.'

'She pretends to be,' Rose scoffed. 'But Letty said she's hiding something. She's going to find out what it is. *Expose* her.'

'Gosh. That sounds a little harsh,' Cathy said, feeling a bit sorry for Rebecca now. 'You know, you don't get to be a grown-up without making a few mistakes.' *Like telling a fragile teen about her murderous stepfather*, she thought grimly.

'But people have to own up to them, don't they? And apologise. Like Dad did. Unless they're dead, obviously.' Rose shrugged. 'Grandpa Charles did some pretty nasty stuff. I bet that's why Grandma gave me his diary to read. So I know the truth. Even if Grandpa can't say sorry now.'

'Sorry for what?' Cathy asked curiously.

'Well, I've only read half, but so far . . . Drinking too much. Shouting at people. Firing them for giving bad looks. He brags about it all. *Daring to disrespect a Trelawney*, he wrote in one bit. I know he was our grandpa, but he doesn't sound very nice. I feel sorry for Grandma.'

Cathy suspected that was most likely Juliana's

intention in giving Rose the diary. 'Well, your grandma has lived a very long life. I'm sure she's made a few mistakes, as well.'

Rose stared back at the terrace. 'Izzy reckons she's got secrets, too. She's so mad at Grandma. About the adoption. She hasn't forgiven Dad for it, either.'

Cathy sighed. 'I know, sweetheart. And it's very complicated. But at least you're all together again. Talking to each other. That's what counts.'

Rose shook her head. 'Izzy said actions speak louder than words.'

'She did?' Cathy turned to watch her, chatting happily with Arthur now, as though she didn't have a care in the world. Then again, she'd watched Eve do exactly the same over the last few days: pretend she was completely fine, when she clearly wasn't. 'Rosie, have you seen Eve?'

'Nope. Not since earlier. With Letty. Having their little detective debrief.' She laughed. 'Oh, wait. I did see her after that. She helped me look for Mum's photo. A special one that Dad had framed for me. It's gone missing from my bedroom.'

'Oh, dear.'

'Yeah. Evie looked everywhere for it. She even got Izzy to help. Then she said she had a headache and was going to lie down for a bit.'

'Eve seems to be having a lot of headaches,' Cathy worried. 'I think I'll go and find her. Check she's all right. I've got some paracetamol in my bag, too.' She gave Rose a hug. 'Try not to worry, OK? Maybe you and Violet will feel better after the rehearsal tomorrow.' *Maybe we all will*, she thought ruefully.

'Thanks, Aunty Cath.' Rose smiled, but Cathy noticed the tiniest hint of a smirk on her pretty face as she added: 'I have a weird feeling you're probably right.'

Watching her stroll across the lawn, hands in pockets, whistling softly, Cathy pondered whether she'd just been subtly manipulated by a teenager. To what end, she had no idea, but she knew from experience with Eve how clever girls could be at that age.

She certainly knew that Jack was finding it hard to navigate the rocky path of parenthood right now. She needed to get her head out of the clouds and help him, she decided. Eloise had asked her to look after her girls, and that's exactly what she would do. Because despite Rose's heartfelt wish, she wasn't here — and she was never coming back.

About to head towards the house, Cathy caught movement out of the corner of the eye, and heard an odd rustling in the trees. Looking up, she was certain she heard her name being whispered. Immediately, her gaze was pulled back to the church on the clifftop, and she felt the back of her neck prickle. Above the tower, a solitary black crow rose in the air, silently circling.

38

The holiday cottage was comfortable and spacious, and, like their Chiswick home, it had been stylishly modernised for family life by her mum. But it was still an old, characterful building, and several of the floorboards creaked. Eve recognised every single one.

From her position at the kitchen table, where she'd been sitting ever since they'd left the party early — Eve having feigned a migraine — she had known exactly when her mum moved from her bedroom to the bathroom, having a quick shower after taking off her party dress. She'd heard each footstep as she made her way downstairs to join her . . . and make her the mint tea she'd said might help soothe her headache. But Eve didn't have one.

'OK, love?' Cathy yawned as she strolled into the kitchen. 'I can't believe how tiring it is, chatting to people. I'm with Rose. I need an early night before our busy day tomorrow.'

Eve frowned. She didn't want to think about the rehearsal. 'I know,' she said tightly.

'I'm sorry you have another migraine.' Cathy screwed up her nose. 'Although, I wasn't actually sorry to leave the party early,' she confided. 'I think —'

'Mum,' Eve cut in. 'There's something I need to tell you. Only it's not easy to say.'

'Oh? Well, take your time, darling. I can make you that mint tea first, if you like? It'll only take me a minute.'

'No. Thanks, Mum. But, please, just sit down.'

'Is it your promotion? Sorry, love. Didn't you get it? There will be other opportunities, I'm sure.' She knew she was burbling, but Eve's sudden intensity was beginning to scare her.

'No. It's not about that. But, please, don't talk. Just listen. I need to say this now, before I lose my nerve again.' Eve took a deep breath. 'You know I've been feeling really tired?'

'You've been working too hard,' Cathy said, coming to sit next to her at the kitchen table. 'Haven't I told you? All these late nights chained to your laptop. You need to *rest*.'

'Sure. But the thing is, no amount of rest will fix this. You see, it's not work making me so tired. It's not my promotion. Or even my period. It's . . .' She took a deep breath. 'I found a lump.'

'A . . . what?'

'In my left breast. On Sunday. Well, I felt something a few weeks ago, actually.'

'A few . . . Why didn't you tell me?'

Because I was in Dubai, Cathy thought guiltily. *I was halfway around the world, when I should have been here, with my family.*

'Well, it wasn't very big. Or noticeable. I know, I know. That doesn't mean anything. I've done enough features about it on the bloody programme. I guess I was busy. Stressed. Over-tired. I thought I'd imagined it. It actually seemed to go away. Then when I was trying on those dresses in Plymouth. For the wedding . . .'

'Go on, love,' Cathy encouraged, even though every word pierced her heart.

'Well, the assistant was fiddling with the bodice.

You know, figuring out if it needed to be taken in. She was young. Chatty. I just came out with it. I told her I thought I might have felt something. I honestly thought she'd laugh. Tell me not to be daft. But she didn't. She went really pale and said her mum died of breast cancer, and did I mind if she felt it.'

Cathy dug her nails into her palms, sensing what was coming. 'And did she?'

Eve nodded. 'She said I should get it properly checked out. Immediately. But Mum, I can't. I'm too scared. And I've been too frightened to tell you. Or Artie. Because you both know what comes next, don't you? You watched it happen to Eloise. She found the tiniest lump. And then she died.'

39

'Sweetheart, let's try not to get ahead of ourselves, OK?' Even as she spoke the words, Cathy was conscious that she was saying them as much to herself. Her body felt like it had gone into shock; she felt boiling hot, then freezing cold.

She stared at her daughter, but it was Eloise's beautiful, pale, gaunt face that she saw. Years ago, after her friend's illness had begun to take its toll, Eve had been poorly, too. Immediately, Cathy had feared the worst for her little girl: that she'd been struck by cancer, too. It turned out to be a grumbling appendix, but Cathy had never forgotten how Chris berated her for being hysterical and always assuming the worst.

The whole episode had been distressing for Eve, too, and Cathy was determined not to make that mistake again. She had to stay calm, even though her mind was spinning. All she could think about was the crow, circling above the church last night. She forced a smile. 'I know it's scary, love. Finding a lump. But it might not be serious.'

'Not serious?' Eve's voice simmered with indignation, but her eyes were shadowed, full of fear that tugged at Cathy's heart. 'How the hell can it not be?'

'Well, it could be a cyst. Something benign. It's not necessarily cancer.' Cathy sent up a silent prayer. 'Like the shop assistant said, we need to get it checked out first. And we will. As soon as possible. Then we'll figure out what to do. Let's take this one step at a time, OK?'

As Eve held her head in her hands, sobbing quietly, Cathy stroked her daughter's hair and thought back to their shopping trip on Sunday. With the benefit of hindsight, she realised now that something had changed in Eve from that day — even from the moment she'd bought the green silk dress for the wedding.

At first, Cathy had assumed that was the reason for her daughter's change in mood. *Perhaps she was wondering if Artie would ever propose*, she'd speculated. Then, as Eve had buried herself in work, barely speaking, hardly leaving her room, refusing to take any phone calls, she'd guessed it was her promotion that was bothering her. Or a row with Artie.

Only now, as Cathy recalled that shopping trip, the boutique assistant's oddly tense manner came flooding vividly back to her — along with Eve's unusually subdued responses — and all the pieces clicked into place. 'You're not alone, darling,' she said, squeezing her hand. 'We all love you to bits. I'm right here, and so is Artie.'

'I'm not telling him,' Eve said immediately. 'After the wedding, maybe. But not now.'

'But why ever not? He'll want to support you. You know he will.'

'He's got enough on his plate. He's Jack's best man. Izzy is here. The twins need him, too.' Eve frowned. 'He has too much on his mind to cope with more of my rubbish.'

'It's hardly rubbish, love. It's important. *Very*. And think of the strain it's put you under already, trying to pretend everything's fine.' Cathy wrapped an arm around her shoulders, hugging her. 'I've been so worried about you. So has Artie. Honestly, you should tell him.'

Eve shook her head. 'You *know* why I can't, Mum.'

Yes, Eve's boyfriend knew all about breast cancer, too, Cathy acknowledged: it had stolen his grandmother's life, and changed his own for ever. It was after Eloise's death that Arthur had come to Cornwall as a teenager, searching for the missing pieces in his family, and, in the process, found Eve. 'But you're his life, Evie,' she said quietly, remembering Jack saying the same thing at the beach, before the day had gone so badly wrong. 'Let him be there for you.'

Selfishly, Cathy wanted every possible drop of love and support around her daughter; she couldn't bear to see her struggling alone like this. In her mind, Eve had obviously gone from A to Z in a heartbeat — just as Cathy had always tended to do. *Like mother, like daughter*, she reflected. Eve hadn't even seen a doctor yet, but already she was ripping up her mental scrapbook of future plans: the promotion she'd been chasing; marrying Arthur and having children with him . . .

'It will tear him apart,' Eve said sadly. 'He hates drama. He's had so much with his own family, he can't handle any more. He'll run scared. I know he will.'

'Don't give up, darling,' Cathy urged. 'Not on yourself, and not on Arthur. He's a good, kind man. And he's strong, too. If you haven't seen that before, you will now. It's in our darkest moments that we discover who we can truly lean on.'

'Only if they're stable in the first place,' Eve said morosely. 'Artie and I have been on and off more times than a light switch. What if things between us just . . . crumble?'

Cathy pondered, not wanting to give a glib, knee-jerk answer. 'No one knows what goes on in other people's relationships. But from where I'm standing, I don't think it will. It seems to me Arthur has always been your rock. You may have been a bit on and off. That's actually no bad thing. You have to kiss a few toads to know a prince when you find one.'

That finally made Eve smile. 'You mean frogs. Oh, Mum.'

'Besides, he's moved in with you, hasn't he? That says something. And it's going well?'

'Better than ever,' Eve admitted. 'I've never been happier. In fact, I had a call from my boss this afternoon. They loved the presentation I've been working on. I've got the promotion.'

'Oh, darling, that's *wonderful*.'

'It really is, Mum. And Artie's helped me so much. He's my lucky charm.'

'There you are, then.'

Eve frowned. 'Or is he? Look at his family. Let's be honest, they're a bit of a mess. Izzy loathes Juliana. The twins are mad at Jack. No one likes Rebecca. And she's *definitely* not as sweet and innocent as she pretends to be.'

Cathy sighed. She'd only just had this conversation with Rose, and she was starting to feel like Rebecca's personal PR, constantly having to defend her. It was time to let the woman fight her own battles; she had Eve to worry about now. 'Well, it's Jack's decision who he marries.'

'He doesn't have the best track record, though, does he? None of them do. Look at that old diary Rosie's glued to. It's the size of a doorstep. The Trelawney history reads like a Greek tragedy. Artie's always saying he thinks his family might be cursed.'

'Cursed?' Cathy looked at Eve in concern. 'I know you're upset, darling, but —'

'But what if he's right, Mum? And what if his bad luck rubs off on *me*? Maybe it's best I don't tell him. If I don't even see him again. Everyone good and kind in his family seems to die. Yes, the more I think about it, the more certain I am. Marrying a Trelawney would be like signing my own death warrant.'

40

The knock on the front door was so soft, Cathy almost ignored it, until it came again. 'Jack.' She only just managed to stop herself falling into his arms in relief, as she opened the door to see her old friend's familiar, handsome face. 'What are you doing here?'

'You left without saying goodbye,' he said simply, and his blue eyes were clouded in concern. 'I was worried about you.'

'But I told Rebecca. Eve had a headache. We needed to come home. She . . .'

'Cath, what is it?' Immediately, Jack reached out to her, then let his hands drop as she turned away. Following her into the living room, he said anxiously: 'Has something happened?'

Glancing towards the kitchen, where Eve was finally drinking the soothing mint tea Cathy had made for her, she sighed. 'Yes. No. To be honest, I don't know.'

'Has Eve's headache got worse? Is she unwell?'

'I'm not sure. Oh, Jack, it's happening again, and I don't think I can bear it. Eve's found a lump. She thinks it might be cancer.'

* * *

'You won't be long, will you?' Eve's eyes filled with tears as Jack stood up.

Cathy, sitting next to her daughter on one of the hard, uncomfortable plastic seats lined up outside the treatment room, squeezed her hand. 'I'll wait with you. Don't worry, love. I'm not going anywhere.' She checked her watch.

There were still a few minutes until the emergency biopsy Jack had arranged over the phone within moments of her telling him about Eve, just two hours ago, and she appreciated that he was needed elsewhere. It touched her deeply that he had not only set up the appointment so fast, but that he'd abandoned his own engagement party and driven them to the hospital himself.

Cathy was also moved to see Eve's obvious trust in him. Still not wanting to tell Arthur what was going on, she was leaning heavily on his grandpa's kindness.

'I'll be back in two shakes of a lamb's tail,' Jack told her now, as though Eve was a little girl feeling scared before the dentist.

Cathy knew he was deliberately downplaying the gravity of the situation, to normalise it. As they'd arrived, she had glanced into the small, white-painted room, feeling sick with nerves at the sight of the enormous mammography unit. Still, it was a heck of a lot more welcome than the operating theatres they'd passed further along the corridor, she decided.

After the oncologist — a colleague of Jack's — had examined Eve, he'd explained that a biopsy under general anaesthetic would be their usual practice. Then Jack had discreetly taken him aside for a private discussion, and Cathy knew it was thanks to his intervention that they were performing a vacuum-assisted keyhole excision under local anaesthetic instead.

'Thanks, Jack.' Cathy smiled warmly at him. 'For everything.'

'If they call you in, tell them to wait for me. I won't

come in the room, but I want to be nearby. In case you need me. Either of you.' He placed a gentle hand on Cathy's shoulder.

'I appreciate that. We both do.' Cathy turned to smile at her daughter, speaking for her, sensing that fear had dried Eve's voice. Her skin was so pale, it seemed almost translucent, and her eyes were wide and terrified as they fixed on Jack, silently begging him not to leave.

'It'll be over before you know it, Evie,' Jack said softly. 'I work with these guys every day. They're the best. They'll take excellent care of you. I can't say it isn't an uncomfortable procedure, but in clinical terms it's pretty fast. And painless. Trust me.'

'Always,' Cathy whispered under her breath, as she watched him stride down the corridor, noticing heads turn his way — not because he was handsome, still smartly dressed in the chinos and shirt he'd worn for his engagement party, but because he was respected.

The looks directed at him here were very different to those she noticed in the village, Cathy thought. As Arthur had said, his grandpa was a minor celebrity in Talland Bay; as Jack himself had admitted, he had a lot of baggage. All the locals knew his history: at Roseland, and with Eloise. Naturally, they were intrigued about his wedding; by all accounts, gossip in the village was rife. But the hospital was Jack's domain and had nothing to do with any of that.

Here, he was admired for his professional expertise, and it showed. Had he been any less revered, Cathy knew they wouldn't have got an appointment so fast, the very same evening — possibly not for days. *It's in our darkest moments that we discover who we can truly lean on*, she recalled saying to Eve, and it dawned on her that she hadn't given so much as a passing thought to phoning Chris.

How had it come to be, she wondered, that when the chips were down, it wasn't her husband she was leaning on, but Jack? *Because he's a first-rate oncologist,* she told herself. Then: because Jack had lost Eloise to breast cancer, and he knew exactly how that felt — how Cathy was feeling right now.

Yes, Jack understood her fear, and Eve's panic, and he wasn't judging either of them. He was reassuring Cathy, and treating her daughter with as much kindness as he did his own girls. More than that, he'd moved mountains to help her.

Chris would have, too, Cathy acknowledged. If she'd called him . . . Guiltily, she remembered that she'd deliberately missed several calls from him now. Before she could question herself about that, Eve's name was called — and, as though thinking about him had conjured him up, Jack returned. 'Sorry about that. I just had to make a quick call.'

To his fiancée, Cathy guessed. She hadn't been able to avoid overhearing Jack's conversation when he'd phoned from the cottage to tell Rebecca that an emergency had come up, and that he'd been called urgently into the hospital.

Despite the heated complaints Cathy could hear on the other end of the line, Jack hadn't revealed anything about Eve, and Cathy was grateful for his discretion; she knew he'd endured major flak from his disappointed fiancée. Fleetingly, she wondered if Rebecca would call off the rehearsal tomorrow . . . even the wedding. Butterflies whirled in her stomach at the thought.

'I'm the one who's sorry, Jack,' she said. 'For

dragging you out like this.'

'You didn't. I insisted,' he pointed out calmly, before turning to Eve, smiling reassuringly. 'All good? Ready to go?'

'As I'll ever be.'

'Good luck, darling.' Cathy gave her hand one last squeeze. 'I'll be here when you get out. Everything will be fine.' She blinked away her tears, trying not to think about what would happen if it wasn't.

As the door closed behind her daughter, Cathy squeezed her eyes shut, mentally searching for her happy place. But all she could see was a slideshow of Eve growing up; rapid snapshots of chaotic family life in quick succession. Her children paddling at the beach, Eve's hair tangled in the wind and her skin dusted with sand, eyes shining as she devoured her favourite ice cream.

Suddenly, her thoughts turned to Roseland, and somehow her daughter's image merged once again with Eloise's — this time, when she was a child, long before the shadow of cancer blighted her life. Memories rose up of Eloise riding her pony, and tumbling through the gardens; playing hide-and-seek in the bushes. Then the two of them throwing stones into the lake, before sneaking into the great hall, pretending to be grand ladies at a ball.

In the next moment, Cathy pictured herself at Goldeneye, gazing out over the glorious view that had so captivated her this afternoon, reminding her of everything she would soon be leaving behind — for weeks; months. Perhaps for ever. Whatever happened with Eve, they would be going home to London this weekend; saying goodbye to Cornwall . . . and to Jack.

Cathy gasped, and her mind's eye looked up. The

church seemed to glow more brightly, as though lit from within. She gritted her teeth as, yet again, she saw the crow, as black as death, silently looping around the church tower in ever-decreasing circles.

41

The roses smelled divine, but Juliana felt sick as she bent closer to examine them, the following morning. Instantly, she recognised them from her own garden, gathered without her permission and arranged in crystal urns similar to the one she'd placed at her daughter's grave. 'Very appropriate,' she muttered, with bleak satisfaction. 'This wedding will be Jack's funeral.'

The urns were staged on top of gleaming alabaster plinths lining the aisle that stretched almost the full length of Roseland's great hall. A plush crimson carpet filled the space in between, and even though today was the rehearsal rather than the wedding itself, the carpet was already scattered with fresh petals, waiting for the bride and groom to crush them as they walked, releasing their scent as they made their way to the altar at the end.

'That was my mother's,' Juliana grumbled, eyeing the heavy mahogany sideboard that had stood unnoticed in Roseland's grand vestibule for centuries. But Jack's fiancée had spotted it; she'd spotted all the finest Trelawney heirlooms, pilfering them from throughout the manor house to stage the high-ceilinged great hall for the wedding event of the year. *Her* wedding.

'Greedy, scheming, *evil* woman.' Juliana crushed the soft head of a rose, before turning to glare at the clusters of candles flickering on gilt console tables throughout the vast room.

She suspected it was no accident that they were arranged to illuminate valuable oil paintings on the panelled walls above: showing off the Trelawney ancestry to her guests. 'How dare she? She's a fake. A social-climbing charlatan.'

At the other end of the hall, as yet oblivious to Juliana's fury, Jack entered through the heavy oak double doors, his attention focused on his cufflinks. 'Blasted, fiddly things.' He'd been determined to wear them, though, and not only because the tailored white dress shirt Rebecca had bought to go with his black dinner suit required them.

The gold cufflinks had belonged to Jack's late father; today of all days, they felt like a lucky charm, and Jack needed all the luck he could get. He also needed help to fasten them; usually steady-handed and dextrous, with a surgeon's skilful precision, he was so nervous that each of his fingers felt like thumbs.

It was his own fault for telling Arthur to meet him here, Jack reminded himself, rather than having breakfast together at Goldeneye. Only, after his late night at the hospital, he'd wanted some quiet time alone with his thoughts before the rehearsal; he also needed privacy to take the call from his colleague. 'Come on, damnit,' he muttered, taking out his phone.

He was about to give up waiting and press redial on the number he'd called a dozen times already this morning, when a noise made him look up. 'Juliana? Is that you?'

Dressed in grey silk, with her silver hair flowing loose down her back, the slight figure standing at the altar appeared almost ghostlike, her ankle-length gown shimmering ethereally in the candlelight. Then she turned to glare at Jack, and the flash of her green eyes was unmistakeable. 'Jack Merchant. Well, well. I see you've come dressed as the lord of the manor.'

Jack bit back his automatic response to her sarcasm; he couldn't handle conflict today. 'You're early,' he said instead, striding towards her. The rehearsal didn't start for another two hours, and he was surprised to see Juliana here so soon — at all, in fact. He wondered what had changed her mind about coming.

'This is my home,' she said haughtily, holding herself even more upright as Jack approached. 'No one enters it without my being present.'

Jack didn't point out that hundreds of people did exactly that every day; it was the reason they'd only been granted exclusive access to Roseland for the Thursday and Friday; weekends were for tourists, and the fundraising necessary to maintain the ancient manor house.

'Ah, so you're playing gatekeeper. Quite right. Did you see the twins? Rebecca drove them over earlier. She thought they'd like to get changed here, while she did her final checks. Made sure everything's perfect. She's done an amazing job, don't you think?'

'Self-indulgent frippery.' A dismissive wave encompassed the elaborately dressed hall. As her eyes came to rest on the altar, Juliana stared thoughtfully at the tapered white candles flickering in the silver candelabra at its centre.

'Beautiful, isn't it?' Undaunted, Jack ploughed on with his charm offensive. 'Of course, Roseland has been brought into the twenty-first century by the wonder of electricity.' He frowned at the tall, rather ugly TV spotlights positioned around the hall. While Rebecca was thrilled about the wedding being filmed tomorrow, he was less keen. 'Not quite so romantic, but necessary. No electricity; no filming. No movie; no money to pay Roseland's bills. But Rebecca thought the candles would be a nice touch. A nod to the history of the place.'

'Ridiculous fire hazard. Utterly uncalled for. Nothing about this wedding is remotely authentic. Certainly not historically.' An ironic eye-roll. 'One presumes the woman isn't getting married in fancy dress. Some kind of elaborate Jacobean costume.'

'And if she does? Surely, it's a bride's prerogative to pick her own outfit? Actually, I think Rebecca very kindly allowed the twins to choose for her. For the rehearsal, at least.'

Juliana tutted. 'The trial run, you mean. Another new-fangled idiocy.' Stepping closer to the altar, she stroked its French lace runner with trembling fingers. 'This belonged to my mother. She had it specially made for my wedding. My father gave me away. He walked me up the aisle. Handed me over to Charles. It was a very simple affair.' She gave Jack a sad look. 'Where there's true love, there is no need for spectacle.'

Jack frowned. 'Rebecca works in TV. She's artistic. OK, fine, she enjoys a sense of drama. Nothing wrong with that, is there? Look, Juliana. These next couple of days are supposed to be special. I want them to *feel* special. Not for me, but for the girls. Izzy, too. She hasn't flown halfway round the world to watch me sign my name in a register office.'

'But then, Isabella coming to Roseland has nothing to do with your wedding. Haven't you realised that yet, Jack? Your daughter has her own agenda. Principally, punishing me.'

'Nonsense. Izzy's had a lot to come to terms with,

I grant you. But she's working on it. She's letting go of the past. We all need to. Roseland doesn't exactly bring back the happiest memories for me either, you know?'

He stared around the great hall, desperately trying not to think of the last time he'd seen it so lavishly decorated — trying to blot out memories of dancing with Eloise at her fortieth birthday ball. The ruby necklace and matching ring she'd worn, gifted by Juliana for her birthday, and later given to Jack; the swish of her scarlet silk ballgown as she'd waltzed and whirled, hair flying wildly around her beautiful face, glittering violet eyes locked on his.

She was pregnant with the twins at the time, only she hadn't known it. Nor had Jack. He hadn't even realised he was their father. He'd certainly never dreamed that, a year later, Eloise would be diagnosed with breast cancer. 'Stop it,' he ordered himself, furious that he was allowing the shadow of the past to cloud what was supposed to be a relaxed, happy family day. It was time he let go of it all, for good. He needed today; he needed *Rebecca*.

'She's not her equal, Jack. She isn't half the woman Eloise was,' Juliana said, as though she could see into his mind. 'Deep in your heart, you know that. Oh, you can keep trying to fool yourself. But Rebecca doesn't fool me.'

'Juliana . . .'

'This wedding is an insult to Eloise's memory. I'm not here to rehearse or celebrate it. I'm here to *stop* it. With my daughter's help.' Clinging on to the altar for support, Juliana closed her eyes, her lips moving slightly as she whispered something inaudible.

'Whatever. I have to get on.' Jack's patience was

wearing thin now. 'If you choose not to be a part of today, that's up to you. But my family will be here any moment. My friends, too. They care about me. They want to see me happy. If you don't, I'm sorry, but I can't waste any more time or energy trying to persuade you.'

'You may be happy, Jack. But are the twins? My granddaughters? You must know you've made their mother angry, too.' Juliana opened her eyes to glare at Jack. 'Can't you feel it? Can't you feel her presence here? She danced her heart out in this room. Look at her!'

Juliana gestured towards the centre of the hall, where a pale circle of light pooled beneath an enormous French crystal chandelier, suspended from the high, vaulted ceiling criss-crossed with oak beams. Her eyes shone, and her too-thin body swayed in time to a symphony in her mind. 'She's with us, always. She loved you so much, Jack. How can you betray her, disrespect her memory, and for what? A cheap imitation bride.'

'OK, that's *enough.*' About to walk away, Jack was taken aback when Juliana turned away from the vision that only she could see, and stalked towards the staircase at the end of the hall. He hadn't seen her move so fast in years, and her sprightliness surprised and, in truth, annoyed him. He felt as though, yet again, he'd been played by her. 'Great start to the day,' he muttered. 'At least it can't get any worse.' Then his phone buzzed.

Jack braced himself. His colleague must have worked through the night. The biopsy results were in.

42

'Grandma!'

The twins' excited voices made Jack look up. 'Hey, there you are.' He watched them skip down the staircase and hug Juliana, who instantly reverted to her usual stooped frailty.

'Darlings,' she said feebly. 'You both look so beautiful.'

'Your grandma's right.' Jack gave Juliana a wry glance, letting her know that he'd registered her Oscar-winning performance. 'I can't believe how grown-up you look. Where are my little girls? I turn my back for a second, and suddenly you're young women.'

'Exactly what I told them,' said a melodic voice behind them.

'Izzy!' The twins spoke in unison, hurrying to their big sister's side.

'Sorry, guys. The taxi took for ever. I meant to get here sooner. Well, don't you both look utterly edible?' Izzy stared wide-eyed at their flouncy, long white dresses. 'Two perfect meringues. Although, isn't that kind of stealing the bride's thunder? I deliberately wore black.' She patted her fitted sleeveless dress. 'OK, I'll admit I didn't bring anything more festive with me.'

'You look like you're going to a funeral, Mum. Not a wedding,' Arthur teased, crossing the hall in long strides to join them now. Eve followed slowly behind, looking tense.

'Wedding *rehearsal.* But less of the cheek, hey, or it'll be *your* funeral.' Izzy gave him a playful punch on the arm. 'But you look gorgeous, Artie, so I'll forgive you. Not as gorgeous as your girlfriend, of course. I love your dress, Evie. That green silk looks amazing on you.'

'Thanks.' Eve smiled faintly, before drifting away from the group.

Jack was about to go after her, when he noticed Juliana wringing her hands, looking confused. His grandson had been right, he thought; her dementia was getting worse. Feeling bad that they'd quarrelled, he was torn between comforting her and speaking to Eve.

He understood Juliana's grief, but there was a time and a place for it, and that wasn't here. It wasn't the best moment to speak to Eve, either — here, in front of everyone. But Jack didn't want to draw attention to her by calling her away. He had to say something, though. Only, suddenly, his mind had gone blank. All he could think of was the text message replaying on a loop, over and over. He felt shell-shocked and tongue-tied.

At least the twins had no such problem, and, not for the first time, Jack was thankful for their chattiness — Izzy's, too. All his daughters had a lot to say for themselves, he thought, sighing as he watched them cluster around their grandma. Three generations of Juliana's family. Four, if he counted his grandson, which was exactly what Arthur had tried to point out to his beloved Gee-Gee: this wedding would be a true Trelawney celebration.

Surely, that would soften Juliana? No one had forgotten her daughter; quite the opposite. Rather than having angered Eloise, he was pretty sure she would be proud and happy, if she could see her daughters today. Families needed to stick together, no matter what life threw at them, be that good, bad or utterly terrifying. Grinding his teeth at the reminder of the test results, Jack turned to look at Eve again — and found she was already staring at him.

'Eve!'

For a moment, Jack thought he was the one to have spoken her name, then he saw Izzy stepping quickly towards her son's girlfriend, having noticed that she'd silently pulled even further away from the group.

'Are you OK?' Izzy asked her. 'Where's your mum?'

Once again, his daughter had taken the words out of Jack's mouth. *Where was Cath?* He guessed that, like him, she would have had a sleepless night, after their long, difficult evening at the hospital yesterday. But he'd promised her he would impress on his colleague that speed was of the essence, and that he'd let Eve and Cathy know as soon as he had the results. Automatically, he glanced at his phone.

'Mum's still at the cottage,' he heard Eve tell Izzy. 'She's waiting for Dad to arrive. Artie drove me in his hire car.'

'Ah, that's right.' Izzy nodded. 'Your dad flew in this morning, didn't he? How is he?'

'Actually, he's not here yet. His flight was delayed. So he says.' Eve rolled her eyes. 'Mum's not happy. For one thing, his text woke her up in the middle of the night. For another, she thought the message was something urgent.' Another sideways glance at Jack.

'Poor Cathy,' Izzy sympathised. 'She'll be wiped out. So am I, after the party yesterday. I was sad you had to leave early, though. I hope your headache's better? Rosie told me you had another migraine.'

'I'm fine. But thanks,' Eve said quickly, feeling uncomfortable lying to Izzy. 'Did Rosie find that missing photo of your mum? I know she was upset about it.'

Izzy shook her head. 'Well, we found the frame under her bed. But not the picture.'

'Weird.' Eve frowned. 'Perhaps Jack took it.' Another tense glance towards him.

'Hmm, I reckon that would be weirder. Given that he's marrying Rebecca tomorrow.'

Eve smiled at that. 'Yeah. I dread to think what she'd do if she saw her fiancé gazing longingly at a photo of his ex.' She winced, recalling Rebecca's flash of temper yesterday, after finding Roseland's gates locked.

'Murder on the dance floor?' Izzy suggested darkly. 'Oh, look. Here's your mum.'

'Darling, am I late? Have I missed anything?' Cathy was breathless, after hurrying across the hall. 'I couldn't wait any longer for your father to arrive. He'll have to find his own way here now. If he bothers to show up.' She tutted.

'Didn't he call you?' Eve said indignantly.

'I called him. He didn't pick up.' *No doubt playing tit for tat*, Cathy thought crossly.

'Well, it's his loss if he misses the rehearsal,' Eve said irritably. 'But you haven't, so don't worry. Everyone's just mingling right now. Waiting for Rebecca, I guess.'

'Ah. Right.' Cathy looked across the hall, spotting Jack sitting next to Juliana. 'Has he spoken to you?' she whispered. 'Is there any news? Right. I'm going over there to ask him,' she said, as Eve shook her head, chewing her lip anxiously.

'Mum, not now.' Eve grabbed her arm. 'At least let him get married first.'

'But like you said, darling. This is only a dress rehearsal. It's not the real thing.' She gave her daughter a quick hug. 'Wait here. I'll be right back.'

43

As Cathy headed across the hall, her heels clacked on the parquet floor, resonating in her chest with the dull, anxious thud of her heartbeat. She almost lost her nerve; only the thought of Eve spurred her on. She knew her daughter had barely slept, worrying about the results. Neither had she. Although, in all honesty, it wasn't only the biopsy that had kept her awake.

Keeping her eyes fixed on Jack, trying to read his expression, Cathy felt again that same fizz of excitement she'd had last night when he had wrapped her in his arms outside the cottage, giving her a reassuring hug after driving her and Eve home from the hospital. Something fundamental had changed between them, she realised — at least, on her part.

Slowly, gradually, without her even noticing, Cathy's feelings for Jack had crossed a line between friendship and something far, far deeper. It was more than affection for his family, and it went beyond gratitude for his help with Eve. It was crazy, impossible love.

He's getting married tomorrow, she reminded herself. Nothing but a bomb falling on Roseland could stop the wedding now. Even if Jack wanted to, which he obviously didn't. He was an honourable man and deeply loyal. And he loved Rebecca; he'd told her so himself.

If Cathy had imagined his arms lingering around

her as he'd said goodbye last night, she was mistaking kindness, perhaps pity, for something more. Jack had been comforting her, that was all. Undoubtedly, they shared a bond that stretched back years, resurrected now through worry about Eve's biopsy, which brought back memories for them both about . . . '*Eloise*. Oh my God.'

Cathy stopped walking and stood staring towards the grand staircase at the end of the room — more specifically, at the half-landing, where the portrait of Eloise that Juliana had commissioned for her daughter's fortieth birthday still hung in pride of place. It was a beautiful piece of art, gilt-framed, and a striking likeness of Eloise. But it wasn't the painting of her late, lost friend that made Cathy's heart thunder in her chest; it was the shimmering figure standing in front of it.

Gleaming honey-blonde hair rippled in soft waves over slim shoulders exposed above a ruched bodice threaded with gold; fine crimson silk clung to gentle curves, the Bohemian-style ballgown falling to a delicate handkerchief hemline. Slim fingers toyed with a ruby pendant necklace, artfully showing off the matching gold filigree ruby solitaire ring — the playful, slightly coquettish pose exactly matching that in the painting above. Cobalt eyes stared boldly across the great hall, softly alluring and yet at the same time curiously defiant.

There's only one ghost at Roseland, Cathy remembered saying, convinced that she'd conjured up her presence through worry and fear about Eve's cancer scare. Eve, too, had mentioned Eloise several times over the last few days, Cathy recalled. Now, finally, she understood why her old friend's life and death had been playing on her daughter's mind.

Looking around the room, searching for Eve, needing to reassure herself that she was OK, Cathy was puzzled to see everyone else standing equally transfixed. Turning back to Jack, she was bewildered to see him, too, staring towards the staircase. His handsome, tanned face looked oddly pale, and his tall frame seemed rigid with shock. *But how could that be?* Surely, this unearthly figure existed only in Cathy's imagination?

Slowly, she turned to look at her again — this metaphysical echo of her deep-rooted fear and yearning — fully expecting the shimmering image to have vanished, ethereal atoms evaporating, imploding into the depths of her own tortured mind. Only, she was still there, and as Cathy caught the familiar scent of Eloise's lavender perfume, she thought she might faint.

Jack felt Cathy's eyes on him, but he couldn't move. He stood gaping at the apparition before him. For, surely, that had to be what it was: the portrait of Eloise made three-dimensional through an optical illusion created by candlelight, shadows and deep, never-ending grief. Yes, this was some kind of weird alchemy; a kink in the physical laws of the universe.

As the bright blaze of morning sunshine collided with the gloom of the seventeenth-century stairwell, it had distorted the particles of light hitting the back of his retina, triggering false electrical signals that appeared to breathe false life into this figment of memory. He didn't believe in ghosts; this was simply a mirage. A conjuring.

And then it spoke.

44

'Jack?' A throaty, nervous giggle. 'What's going on? You all look like you've seen a ghost.'

'Rebecca.' Recognition flooded through Jack like ice water. He took a step forward, then another, until he was striding towards his fiancée. At last, one foot on the bottom stair, he was close enough to see that her hair was lighter, her face oval, not heart-shaped. Blue eyes glinted boldly, rather than with the carefree spark that, despite everything, Eloise never lost.

As Rebecca walked slowly down the stairs to meet him, those glittering eyes remained fixed on his; her body swayed, only not with Eloise's fey gracefulness, but rather with a sultry energy that almost crackled like electricity in a thunderstorm. Jack could see it now — he could see everything, as clearly as if the great hall had been lit up by a thousand TV spotlights.

There was a myriad of tiny differences between his fiancée and the lost love of his life, but, dressed in the ballgown that had been Eloise's favourite, the similarity between them was unnerving. The impersonation was unforgivable. 'Where the hell did you get that dress?'

'I . . . I borrowed it.' Eyes widened; high cheekbones flushed. 'Don't you like it?'

'Borrowed it from where?'

A barely perceptible flick of her eyes towards Violet. 'Upstairs. In one of the bedrooms. There was a whole closet of old dresses. Rails and rails of ballgowns.

I . . . I didn't think anyone would mind. It was supposed to be a bit of fun.'

'Fun?' The word almost stuck in Jack's throat.

'OK, a surprise tribute to Roseland's past. Like the roses and candles.' Another glance at Violet, this time more anxious. 'This ballgown . . . it's from Roseland's collection, isn't it? Clothes being curated for a special display. A day in the life of the Trelawney aristocracy.'

Jack stood stiffly, staring at the beautiful face he'd fallen in love with only four weeks ago, and the reason he'd felt such an instant connection with Rebecca hit him like a thunderbolt. From the moment they'd met — here, at Roseland — he'd felt as though he had known her for years. Because his unconscious mind *had* known her, he realised; it had recognised the subtle resemblance between her and Eloise, and his desire to feel happy and fulfilled again had fired every synapse in his brain, setting off a network of electrical connections that had made him feel, finally, as though he'd found peace; that he'd come home. That Eloise had returned.

It wasn't Rebecca he'd fallen in love with, he understood now, but a transference of all the joy and passion stolen from him when Eloise died. Meeting at Roseland had powerfully, subliminally, reinforced that feeling; Rebecca had brought to life everything Jack had lost and still, unconsciously, yearned for. It was a chemical reaction; a mere placebo effect.

Only moments before, Rebecca's pale face and trembling mouth would have aroused his deepest concern; now Jack felt strangely detached. His scientific, clinical instincts had taken over, and he found himself dispassionately dissecting their relationship. Specifically, he questioned when her resemblance to

Eloise had dawned on Rebecca. Because, dressed as she was, it was surely indisputable that it had.

Four weeks ago, she couldn't have known. They'd met as strangers, literally bumping into each other at random, as Rebecca was so fond of reminiscing. He also remembered her surprise at the speed of their engagement. After two days and nights spent at Goldeneye, she'd never returned to her own flat; a week later, he had given her the ruby ring she now wore, asking her to be his wife. Rebecca had never questioned his urgency, and nor had Jack.

No, not at any point over the last month had his fiancée's similarity to Eloise consciously registered with him. So when had it struck *her*? When she'd officially moved into his home, while the twins were in Italy — their bedrooms plastered with photos of their mum?

With a groan, Jack recalled Rose quizzing him yesterday, before the party, about a framed photo missing from her wall. The twins were always redesigning their rooms, and he'd assumed Rosie had forgotten that she'd switched things around. He'd thought no more of it.

Now he couldn't help wondering: had Rebecca taken it, deliberately copying a picture of Eloise, playing on their superficial resemblance for the rehearsal today, exaggerating it even further by dressing like Eloise's portrait? And, if so, to what purpose? To remind him of what he'd lost, so that he would appreciate his new love all the more? Or to prove herself better than what he once had?

She claimed it was intended as a fun surprise, but that seemed too glib, too easy. Rebecca had planned every second of this wedding; every last detail had been calculated for maximum impact. What possible effect had she been aiming for with this stunt?

For that is how it struck Jack, and he had to know the truth. Not that it would change anything, he recognised in despair. He could never unsee the resemblance now; the walls of his self-delusion had come tumbling down. *There's no fool like an old fool,* Juliana had taunted him. Jack had to know whether he had, indeed, deluded himself — or if he'd been played.

'Look over your shoulder,' he said sharply.

'What? Why?' Slowly, Rebecca turned, staring up at the painting for a few moments, before turning to Jack again. Beneath her make-up, her face had turned white. 'Is that . . . ?'

'Eloise,' Jack gritted out. 'On her fortieth birthday. Wearing the very ballgown you have on now. That ruby necklace. That ring. Standing in that exact spot on the stairs.'

'Oh.' Rebecca's eyes widened. 'No wonder you all look so . . . you must have thought that Eloise . . .' Her eyes filled with tears as she glanced around the room, seeing the shocked faces staring back at her. 'Sorry, guys. I'm not a ghost.' She lifted her shoulders in a helpless shrug. 'But I am an idiot.' Her tears spilled over now. 'I genuinely didn't realise . . .'

'Are you absolutely sure about that?' Jack said in a low, strained voice.

For a moment, he thought again of Juliana — the frailty and forgetfulness she seemed able to turn on and off at will. Well, her acting skills had been far surpassed by the woman she despised. It was a bitter irony; it would also vindicate every insult Juliana had thrown at Jack.

Turning to look at her, he expected to see the old lady's eyes flashing once more with scorn and derision. Perhaps even a sense of victory. *She had been right*. He'd been a fool, just as she'd called him. Instead, though, he saw a broken woman who, for a whisker of time, had fallen prey to the same delusion — the same deliberately staged illusion — just as Jack had.

Juliana was already convinced that her daughter's presence was all around. The shock, confusion and desperate longing written on her gaunt, pale face told Jack that, for a flickering moment, she too had believed that Eloise had somehow risen from the dead. 'Fuck,' he muttered under his breath, hating himself for having been so stubborn. So blind.

'Jack. Perhaps Rebecca should go back upstairs and get changed.' It was Cathy; calm and gentle as ever . . . equally shocked, but obviously trying not to turn a drama into a crisis.

'Cathy's right. Please go.' Jack stared at his fiancée, too angry to feel sympathy for her distress. Whether deliberate or accidental, what she had done was devastating. To him, and to his family and friends. He wasn't sure where they went from here; he needed time to think.

'No. I'm not going anywhere.' The confidence of Rebecca's low voice was at odds with her crumpled expression. 'I don't run away from my mistakes.' Her chin tilted. 'I stay and face them. I *belong* here. I'm not leaving.'

Jack ground his teeth together, fighting the impulse to yell. He could see Rosie, still seemingly transfixed, staring open-mouthed at Rebecca, while Violet stood at her sister's side, eyes narrowed and arms folded, looking stony-faced and yet . . . *triumphant*?

She would be happy to see his fiancée disgraced, Jack admitted sadly. Then, in the next moment, he recalled how Violet had spent hours with her at Roseland, the other day — and how she'd returned in an unusually perky mood, all sweetness and smiles, even towards Rebecca.

Had this been his daughter's idea? Jack gave her a quizzical look, sighing as Violet immediately looked down, refusing to meet his eyes. He groaned, not in anger but in self-recrimination, aware that he'd continually brushed both the twins' concerns aside, and in doing so had possibly driven Violet — always the more go-getting one — to take desperate measures.

But now wasn't the time for post-mortems, even though he recognised that his love affair with Rebecca had just been dealt a death blow. The rehearsal was ruined, but tomorrow was another day. He didn't believe in defining people by their mistakes. As Rebecca had just told him: she didn't run away from hers. And nor did he.

45

'It worked, Rosie. My plan.' Violet's cheeks were still flushed from the look her dad had given her, but she didn't care. 'I *knew* if Dad saw her in that dress he'd realise she's a fake.'

'That was rather cruel, sweetheart,' Cathy said sternly, watching Rebecca flee tearfully back up the stairs, while Artie ushered his grandpa out of the hall. There was no sign of Izzy — or Eve. Looking around, Cathy realised the hall was empty, apart from herself and the twins. 'Rosie? Are you OK?' The teenager still seemed frozen to the spot, reminding Cathy of her semi-trance yesterday, as Rosie had stared up at the church where her mum was buried.

'It's her. I know it is.' Her eyes were wide and fixed.

'That wasn't Mum,' Violet said, but less belligerently now, picking up on her twin's shock. 'She just dressed up to *look* like her.'

'I'm not talking about *Mum*.' Rose shook her head until fine strands of golden hair, so beautifully styled by Rebecca earlier, came loose from its high ponytail. 'I meant, it's *her*.' She spun around on her heel. 'Where's Grandma? I have to tell her.'

'I think she left.' Cathy glanced around, too, feeling a jolt of concern for the old lady. 'I saw Margaret earlier. Hopefully, she's taken your grandma home.'

'*This* is her home,' Rose said faintly. 'And *she* has come to steal it. Grandma was right all along. I know who she is now. It all makes sense. I can't believe Dad was fooled by her.'

'What the heck are you on about?' Violet said impatiently. 'You're talking in riddles again, Rosie. This isn't one of your novels. You need to get your head out of that stupid book Grandma gave you, and into the real world. We've won, haven't we? I *told* you I'd fix it.'

Rose frowned. 'Not yet, we haven't. Like I told *you*, I read about her. It's *her*. I've got a bad feeling about this, Letty. I know you think this was your idea. I'm scared it was actually hers.'

'Rubbish. I tricked her. I laid out all the dresses. I told her the red one suited her best. She totally bought it. She had no idea why I gave her that ballgown. It was a *honeytrap*,' Violet declared gleefully. 'And she fell headfirst into it.'

Cathy shook her head. 'Vi, I know you don't like Rebecca, and I appreciate this situation is difficult. But it's really not kind to take pleasure in someone else's misfortune.'

'Huh!' Violet threw her hands up. 'Her *fortune*, you mean. Look at this.' She took out her phone, scrolling to an official-looking website.

'What's this?' Cathy looked over her shoulder. 'Oh. It looks like a list of planning applications.' She'd spent hours on one herself, when they converted the little studio annexe at the bottom of their garden for Eve to live in.

'It is,' Violet confirmed eagerly. 'I actually found it by accident. Eve suggested I check out the Companies House website. To see if Rebecca has registered a business. You know, to find out who she really is. Where she comes from.'

Cathy sighed, fully aware that Violet had enlisted

Eve's help in investigating Jack's fiancée. She didn't entirely blame them; she'd been frustrated, too, by Rebecca's evasiveness — her seeming reluctance to divulge anything personal. 'OK. So tell me what you've found. Has she been planning a mega extension to Goldeneye? That's hardly a crime.'

'No, it isn't. But plotting to sell Roseland is. *Look.*' Violet held the phone closer for her to see. 'That's Rebecca's name. And that's the name of a property developer. I googled them. Rebecca's hired them to develop Roseland into luxury apartments. Then I bet she's going to sell them, and make millions.' Eyes narrowed, Violet said: 'I *knew* she was up to no good.'

'She must be marrying Dad to get control of us,' Rosie said, staring at her twin. 'Grandma was right. Rebecca is only interested in our inheritance. She wants to steal it from us. She's planning to take Grandma's *home*.'

Cathy clearly recognised Juliana's influence now, and Violet's use of the phrase 'honeytrap' a moment ago suddenly rang a bell, reminding Cathy of that unsettling conversation with Juliana at Roseland on Sunday afternoon. She'd hinted ominously then about Rebecca trying to trap Jack — for his wealth, Cathy had assumed.

There had been no particular reference to Roseland, but of course Juliana prized it beyond everything. She'd do anything to stop a stranger stealing her family legacy . . . even putting her granddaughters up to this devious scheme with Eloise's ballgown? 'I know it's your grandma's biggest fear,' Cathy said carefully. 'But there are no grounds to her suspicions.' She glanced at the website again. 'Although that's definitely Rebecca's name. And Goldeneye is listed as her address.'

'You have to help us convince Dad,' Violet said urgently. 'He won't listen to me.'

'He will, darling,' Cathy contradicted gently. 'But try not to worry too much. This application is listed as pending, see? It's highly unlikely to get approved. For one thing, to sell something, you have to actually own it.'

'And we will. Don't you see?' Violet was getting impatient now. 'Grandma said she's leaving everything to me, Rosie and Izzy. Her fortune will all come to us.'

'Exactly. Her fortune,' Cath said calmly. 'But not Roseland. Your grandma signed it over to the National Trust after your grandpa died. At least, I'm pretty sure she did.'

'She definitely did,' said a voice behind them. 'Except, I reckon that contract isn't worth the paper it's written on.' It was Izzy, striding towards them across the hall. 'I'm sorry to say I think my clever little sister here is right. Ownership of Roseland is a grey area. As things stand, the twins still have a claim over it. And whoever has guardianship of them has a say in it, too.'

'*Thank* you, Izzy.' Violet rolled her eyes. 'At least someone believes me.'

'Sorry?' Cathy stared at Izzy in shock. 'Grey area? What do you mean?'

'Any evidence of mental compromise when a contract is signed immediately invalidates it.' Izzy sighed. 'Juliana is . . .'

'Losing her marbles,' Violet said bluntly.

Cathy raised her eyebrows, but let it pass. 'Her dementia is recent, though.' She frowned, pondering how infrequently she'd seen Juliana over the last ten years. 'Isn't it?'

Izzy shrugged. 'I have no idea. Except she signed that contract right after her husband died. She was a distressed, grieving widow. Or maybe she was absolutely fine. Whatever. If there is the tiniest loophole, I suspect Rebecca will find it. God, it all makes sense now. I wondered why she kept banging on about Juliana's state of mind over dinner the other night.'

'She blamed Grandma for the boat being damaged, too,' Rose pointed out.

Cathy cast her mind rapidly back over the last week, wishing she could turn back time so easily. For every niggle of doubt that she'd had about Rebecca, there had been an excuse — *she* had made excuses for her, repeatedly telling Eve, and the twins, that the woman wasn't so bad. Now Cathy feared she was far worse even than any of them had imagined.

She had to tell Jack. Only, she knew him — better than anyone, as Eve had said to her, after that first awkward brunch, when Jack had seemed so reluctant to talk about his fiancée. Maybe he'd suspected, deep down, that something was off with her, Cathy speculated. He wasn't a stupid man; on the contrary, he was fiercely intelligent. He was a man of the world.

He was also a man of his *word*, Cathy reflected. He'd promised to marry Rebecca, and he would. Only, did Rebecca know that? If she was prepared to marry purely to get her hands on Roseland, what might she do if she feared that prize was about to be snatched away?

'We have to stop her.' It was Rose who spoke the words everyone was thinking.

'We do,' Izzy agreed.

'Well, my plan obviously wasn't as clever as I thought,' Violet admitted. 'It's your turn now, Rosie. So come on. What's your brilliant idea?'

Rose didn't hesitate. She reached for her twin's hand, dragging her towards the staircase where Rebecca had stood only moments ago. 'Come with me, and I'll show you.'

'What's upstairs?' Izzy said curiously.

'That *stupid book* Grandma gave me.' Rose rolled her eyes. 'I need it. For evidence.'

'Evidence?' Cathy exchanged a glance with Izzy, who looked as baffled as she felt. 'What sort of —'

Rosie shook her head. 'Actions speak louder than words.' She turned to her big sister. '*You* told me that, Izzy. And you were right. Mum warned me in my dream, too. She told me she wasn't happy. Now I know why. We've done enough talking. It's time for us to actually *do* something.'

46

Cathy had never needed a cup of tea so badly. Watching the twins dash upstairs, she was about to ask Izzy if she fancied a restorative coffee, when she saw her striding back across the hall in the direction she'd just come from. 'Izzy?' she called out, wondering where she was going.

'I won't be long, Cath. I'm just going to check on Juliana.'

'Oh. Right. That's good.' Cathy was relieved; she'd been planning to do the same.

Looking around, she realised that after all the commotion, she was entirely alone. She wondered where Eve had gone — and Artie. She hoped they were together; she hoped Eve was finally telling Arthur about the lump in her breast. Cathy was desperately worried about her daughter, and the biopsy results, and she was eager to speak to Jack and find out if there was any news. She was worried about him, too. Was he with Rebecca right now, arguing?

Wandering through the hall, Cathy sighed as she took in the extravagant wedding decorations that now seemed so horribly fake. 'Please don't let Jack forgive her,' she muttered, recognising that he had such a good heart, she wouldn't put anything past him.

Thinking about his kindness reminded Cathy of how gentle he'd been towards her and Eve last night — which, in turn, further increased her already crushing fear about the biopsy results. *Forget about tea*, she thought; she needed a bloody whisky.

Once again, Cathy pictured Jack's handsome face and twinkling blue eyes as he enjoyed his favourite drink. 'There has to be a bottle in here somewhere,' she mused, strolling into the kitchen at the back of the hall.

As soon as she entered the small but well-equipped room — an annexe to the commercial kitchen that catered for the visiting public — Cathy saw more evidence of Rebecca's grandiose plans. Every surface was loaded with gourmet delicacies obviously intended for after the rehearsal, while stacks of white china bearing Roseland's crest, along with trays of crystal glasses, were arranged on a serving trolley for the wedding itself. A tall, glass-fronted fridge was stocked with champagne.

Cathy rolled her eyes. 'Living in the style to which she intends to become accustomed.'

'Why eat bread, when you can have cake?' acknowledged a dry voice behind her.

'Jack!' Cathy whirled around. 'You're still here.'

'Of course. What is it they say? Only the guilty flee the scene of a crime.'

Cathy didn't laugh. She knew he was putting on a brave face, but he didn't have to; not with her. 'None of this is your fault, Jack. What Rebecca did . . .'

'Sure. The whole situation is . . .' He frowned. 'Anyway, I'll find the right way to deal with that in due course. It's not actually Rebecca I've come to talk about, Cath. It's —'

'Eve,' she cut in breathlessly, feeling her heart pound as Jack took out his phone.

'Yes. Cath, I'll come straight to the point. I have news.' Deliberately, Jack concealed his nervousness by adopting what the twins called his *doctor's voice*. 'As promised, my colleague fast-tracked his diagnostic examination. I've got the biopsy results. There are no abnormal cells, Cath. None whatsoever. Eve doesn't have breast cancer.'

'Oh my God.' Cathy reached for the worktop as her legs turned to jelly. 'Are you *sure*?'

'One hundred per cent.'

'Oh, Jack. I'm so relieved.' Cathy drew in a deep breath. 'But the *lump*?'

'Was purely hormonal.' Jack hesitated, worrying how to tell Cathy the next bit, uncertain how she would take it. Once again, he hid behind his clinical mask, albeit that he was dressed in a dinner suit and bow tie, rather than a white coat. 'Aside from being a touch anaemic, Eve's in perfect health. As a matter of fact, she's . . . pregnant.'

'What? Oh my *God*.' Cathy stumbled now, but Jack grabbed her arm, steadying her just in time. Her legs felt like they were about to give way. 'It was just a hormonal lump,' she echoed faintly, her eyes filling with tears. 'That's what Eloise thought hers was, at first,' she added huskily. 'A milk lump. She was still breastfeeding the twins when she was diagnosed.'

Cathy covered her face with her hands, and she wasn't certain whether she was weeping in sadness for her lost friend or joy and relief for her daughter.

'I didn't know that,' Jack said gruffly. 'But it makes sense. It's actually a common mistake. I'm glad Eve told you about it when she did. Eloise didn't get checked soon enough.'

'She was in denial. The twins were only six months old.' Cathy groaned, and then laughed — and then wiped away more tears. 'Eve pregnant. I can't believe it.'

Reaching for a stool, Jack encouraged her to sit down. Then he dragged a second one across the kitchen, perching opposite her. 'I'm really sorry to break it to you so bluntly. I got the text half an hour ago. But, well, events took over.' He gave a wry smile.

'Yes, of course. I mean, obviously, what with the rehearsal. And Rebecca.' Cathy was aware that she was babbling, but her head was spinning. Should she tell him now about what the twins had discovered — and what Izzy had said? 'Jack, about Rebecca . . .'

'I also wanted to tell Eve first. I hope she won't mind that I've told you. Although, as it goes, I think it's probably best this way. Far better that the news comes from you, her mum.'

'Yes. Thank you. I think you're probably right, but . . . How? I mean, obviously, I know how it happened.' Cathy felt herself blush.

'I should hope so, at our age.'

'But how could Evie have had no idea?'

'Oh, that's simple. And again, not uncommon. Before the biopsy, Eve told the nurse she couldn't remember when she'd had her last period. It seems her cycle has been somewhat irregular. She works too hard. Always rushing around. Not eating regularly.'

'She's lost weight,' Cathy agreed. 'I put it down to her working all hours. Plus being hopeless at cooking.' She laughed, suddenly feeling giddy and euphoric.

'Exactly. And what with that and finding a lump. Feeling exhausted. Headachy. It's little wonder Eve put two and two together and made ten.'

'I can't believe it. My little girl is going to be a mum.' Cathy stared at Jack, beaming. 'But what on earth made you do a pregnancy test? Just to rule it out? No one mentioned that at the hospital.'

'They didn't do one then. Not specifically. But my colleagues were very thorough, as I asked them to be. Along with X-rays and tissue extraction, they did multiple investigative blood tests. Those often reveal the hCG hormone earlier than urine samples.'

'Ah. Right. Gosh. The miracle of medicine.'

'The miracle of *life*.' Jack's eyes shone with what looked suspiciously like tears.

'Yes. Oh, but poor Artie. Eve's been pushing him away. She's got this irrational idea in her head. That being with him might bring her bad luck.'

'Really? But those two are so good together. Artie told me Eve's the one.'

'Did he?' Cathy felt the bubble of happiness inside her grow almost to bursting point. 'That's so lovely. And I'm sure, deep down, Eve feels the same. Only . . . after everything that's happened in your family . . .' She hesitated, suddenly feeling awkward. 'You see, lately, Eve's become gripped by the idea that there's some kind of curse on the Trelawneys.'

Jack looked puzzled. 'A curse?'

'I know it sounds a bit . . .' Cathy pulled a face, bracing herself for Jack to react in the same way her husband always did to *hysterical hunches*, as he called them.

'Actually, it sounds to me like the hyper-sensitivity of an intelligent woman in the early stage of pregnancy. Completely natural and understandable.'

'Yes. You're right,' Cathy agreed, happily surprised.

'But Artie won't take offence, any more than I do.' Jack smiled. 'He's a good man. He'll understand everything Eve's been going through.'

'I hope so. Yes, I'm sure he will. They'll figure it all out. Oh, Jack. I still can't believe it.' Desperate to hug him, Cathy folded her arms to stop herself, determined not to be that sad, pathetic person, madly in love with someone who obviously didn't love her back.

Jack looked thoughtful now. 'I have to admit, as thrilled as I was to give Eve the all-clear, I was worried about telling her. She and Artie are twenty-six. Both on the cusp of careers they're passionate about. Having a baby is a huge life change.'

'They won't be on their own. They'll have plenty of family support around them.'

'Absolutely. More to the point, they'll have us.' Jack winked. 'We're old hands at this parenting malarkey, aren't we, Cath? I mean, look at my three girls. I've barely put a foot wrong.' He rolled his eyes, chuckling ironically.

Cathy laughed too. 'Oh, I have to go and find Eve and tell her.'

'Of course.' Jack stood up. 'I have one or two things I need to take care of myself.' He looked around, his expression turning serious. 'You should get the hell out of here, Cath. Go find Eve.'

Cathy reached up to him now, saying shyly, '*Thank* you, Jack.'

'No thanks needed,' he said gruffly, squeezing her hand, before striding towards the kitchen door. At the last moment, he turned back. 'Congratulations, Cath. You'll be a grandma again by Christmas.' His blue eyes twinkled. 'Best present ever, hey?'

'Yes, it is,' Cathy said softly, sighing as she watched him leave, closing the door behind him. 'I only wish we could be together when it's delivered.'

47

Cathy felt like cracking open a bottle of champagne; she wanted to dance around the kitchen, singing at the top of her voice. In the next moment, she felt like sweeping everything off the worktops, destroying Rebecca's stupid feast — lighting the stove and setting fire to the whole damned place, so that the wedding could never happen at all. 'Get a grip of yourself, Cathy.'

Deciding to take a shortcut through the kitchen's fire exit, she blinked as she emerged into bright sunshine, for a moment feeling disoriented. Gradually getting her bearings, she realised she was at the back of the house, in a courtyard opposite the old stable block. Memories rose up. The smell of the hay; the clatter of the ponies' hooves in their stalls.

The past stirred again in her unconscious, and Cathy felt almost tearful as she pictured her old friend proudly mounting her pony, before riding around Roseland's estate, scorning the need for a helmet, letting her long hair stream behind her like a golden victory flag.

'Oh, Juliana,' Cathy sighed, remembering the old lady's confusion on Sunday, when she'd thought Cathy was a child again, come to play with Eloise. 'You may not be losing your marbles, but grief is a cruel imp. It's played tricks on your mind, made you suspicious of *everyone*.' She hoped Izzy had found her — and that they at least had finally managed to put their differences aside.

'What the . . . ? Yuck.' Feeling something squelch beneath her high heels, Cathy looked down, groaning as she realised that she'd stood in something that looked like mud, but probably wasn't, given that the summer heatwave had baked the earth to a dry crust.

Scouting around for an outside tap or hose, she noticed the row of old sawdust buckets, deliberately hung close to the stables, in case of fire. There was no longer any need for them; Roseland was well-equipped with smoke alarms, modern extinguishers and a sprinkler system. But Cathy recognised them fondly as being part of the public tour — along with the wardrobes of clothes in the upstairs bedrooms, where Violet must have found Eloise's ballgown.

Perhaps that was where the twins had gone now, she speculated. 'Poor Vi.' It couldn't have been easy looking through her mum's old belongings. Cathy was actually surprised that any of Eloise's dresses were still here at Roseland, rather than at Goldeneye or the farmhouse. Juliana had always been most particular about her daughter's clothes and jewellery.

Had Juliana had a hand in Violet's little plan? Cathy wondered again. Was she shrewder than they all thought, pulling her granddaughters' strings, after all? Cathy remembered her surprise that Juliana had given her husband's old diary to Rose, and the girl's insistence that she had discovered something important. What had she found?

Turning possibilities over in her mind, but coming up with nothing sensible, Cathy carried on walking through the courtyard, beyond the stables, desperate to find Eve now and share the good news. Her feet seemed to lead her of their own accord, guided by muscle memory through the labyrinth of paths winding between Roseland's extensive outhouses.

Lost in thought and sporadic memories, it was only as she spotted the lake in the distance that she realised how far she'd walked. 'Eve, is that you?' she murmured, squinting against the bright sunlight at an indistinct figure she spotted striding to and fro beside the lake.

Eager to talk to her daughter, Cathy headed quickly in that direction. She was about halfway there, when she felt a vibration against her side — an insistent buzzing coming from the peach silk handbag that matched her dress, and which she'd almost forgotten was looped over her shoulder. She hated carrying a phone, but Eve always insisted it was important for safety.

At the reminder of her daughter, Cathy glanced once more in her direction, frustrated by the interruption. Digging impatiently into her bag, she took out the phone. 'Who on earth could be calling me now? Talk about the worst possible timing.'

Shielding the screen from the glare of the midday sun, Cathy waited for her eyes to adjust to the light. Immediately, she recognised the number. It was Chris.

This time, she picked up.

48

Eve felt bad that she hadn't spoken to her mum before running out of the great hall. She knew she'd be worried about her, but she hadn't been able to stand it any longer. Seeing Rebecca posed on the staircase, dressed as Eloise — who had died so tragically of cancer — all her fears about the biopsy had come crowding in on her.

Had Jack had the results yet? Eve was desperate to know, and she was burning in frustration that, yet again, his stupid fiancée had dominated the limelight, taking all the attention for herself. 'There are other things going on in the world apart from this ridiculous wedding,' she muttered, hurrying out into the black and white tiled foyer.

Scowling up at yet more gloomy, gilt-framed portraits of Trelawney ancestors lining the panelled walls, she thought again of the curse she was convinced hung over Arthur's family — even more so now, after the farce of the wedding rehearsal. 'They should burn this bloody place to the ground,' she muttered, feeling a buzz of adrenalin as she stared at a flickering candelabra on an antique chest of drawers. 'One little flame. That's all it would take.'

Startled by footsteps behind her, she hurried out through the grand front door, skipping down the steps and across the drive. Striding off in a random direction, she pulled up short as she reached what looked like the back of the kitchen block. The door was open, and what she assumed to be a member of catering staff stood leaning against it, puffing on a cigarette.

'Hi,' Eve said, frowning as she registered that he was dressed not in kitchen uniform, but scruffy jeans. An incongruously flashy camera was looped around his neck. He looked Eve up and down, saying nothing. 'Fine. Whatever. Have it your way,' she snapped.

Was he a reporter? She remembered the locked gates at the entrance to the estate, and wondered if he'd snuck into the grounds to take photos. Feeling self-conscious in her long silk dress, she hurried off, desperate to get away. Glancing back once, she groaned in irritation as she noticed the man still watching her. He grinned, then made a big show of dropping his cigarette to the ground, stamping it out. 'Idiot,' Eve growled, hurrying onwards, not caring where she ran now.

'Eve, wait!' It was Arthur, sprinting behind her.

'Oh, Artie.' She whirled around. 'I thought you were with Jack.'

'I was, but I saw you leave, and . . . Sweetheart, what is it?' He reached for her hand, his eyes narrowing in concern as Eve burst into tears.

'*Eloise*.' Eve screwed her fists into her eye sockets, trying to blot out images of the woman who had haunted her imagination more over the last few days than she had throughout the last decade since her death. 'I mean . . .'

Arthur shook his head. 'No, sweetheart. It was *Rebecca*.' He huffed. 'God alone knows why she was dressed like that. But that's for Pops to deal with, yeah?'

'No. I mean, yes. I know,' Eve stuttered. 'What I mean is . . .'

'It's me, isn't it?' Arthur's head dropped.

'What?'

'It's OK. You don't have to spare my feelings. I'm not an idiot. I can see it for myself.'

Instinctively, Eve folded her arms across her chest. 'See what?'

'*You.*' Arthur raked a hand through his hair. 'You haven't been yourself since we got here. Everything was fine in London. Then it changed. Something has changed between *us*.'

'I'm sorry.' Eve felt dreadful that he was blaming himself.

'You don't have to apologise. I only want you to be happy. If I don't make you feel that way anymore . . . If I've done something, *anything*, to upset you. Please, just tell me.'

'Honestly, it's not you.' Eve bit her lip, hating the anguish on his face, but still feeling unsure how to tell him the truth. 'Well, it sort of is. But it's more your family.'

'My family?' Arthur looked baffled now. He glanced over his shoulder, looking cross. 'Has someone said something to upset you? Because if they have, I'll go and —'

'No.' Eve shook her head, dislodging the loose chignon her mum had styled for her so carefully this morning. 'No one has said anything. I'm not talking about your family right now. I meant, in the *past*.'

'OK, you've totally lost me now.'

Eve gestured back towards Roseland's grand frontage. 'Look at this place, Artie. This is your heritage. The grand Trelawney family seat. History stretching back centuries. It's in your blood. Ancestral aristocrats. Trust funds. The . . . family curse.' *There, she'd said it.*

'Curse?' Arthur gave her a quizzical look. 'What curse?'

'You were the one who mentioned it,' Eve muttered, feeling silly now.

'I was joking, sweetheart.' He frowned. 'Is that what's been worrying you?'

'Partly.' Eve looked away again, unable to meet his eyes. 'You're right. Coming here has changed one thing for me. Maybe everything, I'm not sure. But, yes, it was being at Jack's house that first made me think of it. Think of *Eloise*.'

Automatically, Arthur glanced back at the manor house again, remembering the shock of seeing Rebecca dressed up like his grandmother's painting. 'I know it was upsetting, what happened just now. But . . .' His brows furrowed. 'What does Eloise have to do with *us*?'

Eve sighed. It had taken her days to pluck up the courage to tell her mum. She owed Arthur the same honesty. Only, she couldn't come right out and say it; she needed to explain herself — the superstitious fear that had gripped her over the last few days.

'Eloise's death was tragic,' she said quietly. 'But it didn't stop there. There's Juliana. She'd already lost her husband. Then she was forced to send her first grandchild away.'

'*Chose* to send her away,' Arthur corrected. 'According to Mum.' He shrugged. 'Anyway, that's all in the past. And I'm pretty sure Gee-Gee regrets having her adopted. But Mum's had a pretty good life. OK, my dad's a loser. But she had *me*, didn't she?' he joked.

Eve didn't smile. 'I know, Artie. But look at the bad will her adoption caused. Izzy is still furious with Juliana. She despises Roseland, too. Honestly, she loathes this place.' *Even more than I do*, Eve thought. 'She hasn't stopped ranting about it since she got here.'

'Tell me about it.' All too easily, Arthur recalled his mum almost setting fire to it.

'Roseland doesn't even belong to Juliana anymore. She's lost *everything*.'

Arthur thought for a moment. 'I can see where you're coming from. But there's a logical explanation for all of it. There is no curse. *I'm* not cursed, if that's what you've been worrying about.' He gave Eve a lopsided grin. 'You know, Sir Charles was proper old school. He practically drank himself to death. As for Roseland, you can blame the government for that. Inheritance taxes. Subsidy cuts. Stately homes all over the country are struggling. In fact —'

'It's not about all that,' Eve cut in, sensing Arthur was launching into one of his favourite rants about the state of the nation. She took a deep breath. 'Artie, I found a lump.'

'What?' Above his charcoal dinner suit and crisp white shirt, his tanned face paled.

'In my left breast. Jack helped me get an emergency biopsy. Last night. He's still waiting for the results. I thought . . . somehow, I got it into my head . . . being with you might bring me bad luck. I'm sorry. Saying it out loud, it sounds so idiotic.'

'Oh, Evie.' Arthur pulled her against him. 'It doesn't sound idiotic at all. You must have been so worried. Why on earth didn't you *tell* me?'

'Because I didn't want it to be real,' she sobbed against his chest.

Arthur held her, absorbing her tears. 'I'm right here, babe, and I'm going nowhere. Whatever the future brings. Good or bad. Let's hope it's good, hey?' He pulled back, giving her a gentle smile, but she could see tears in his eyes, too. 'Let's face it, with Pops on the case, there's every reason to be confident. He's always been my rock. He'll be yours, too.'

His words reminded Eve of what her mum had said: that in the darkest moments, she would discover who she could lean on. Jack had already been amazing; his grandson was equally so. She gave him a watery smile. 'Thanks, Artie. I don't deserve you.'

'You deserve everything. In fact . . .'

'Artie, wait . . . what?'

Arthur dropped down on one knee. 'Evie, I love you with all my heart. I have done since I was sixteen. From the moment I met you, in fact. I flew halfway around the world looking for something. I had no idea what. Then I found you, and I knew in that moment you were going to change my life. And you have. For the better. We've had our ups and downs, I know. But we ride them together, don't we? We're meant to *be* together. For ever. Please, marry me?'

Eve was so shocked, she couldn't speak. She stood staring at Arthur, lost for words.

He gave her a cheeky grin. 'See, I told you I'd surprise you with a proposal one day, didn't I? Now for God's sake say yes, because this bloody gravel is killing my knee.'

'Yes. *Yes*,' Eve said, and then burst into tears. 'A thousand times, yes. I'll marry you.'

Immediately, Arthur straightened up, pulling her back into his arms. 'For better, for worse. Trust fund or no trust fund. Lump or no lump. Family curse optional.' He tilted her chin, looking seriously into her eyes. 'I love you, Evie. If you let me, I want to take care of you, always. No matter what.'

'Oh, I do want. You. Us. All of it,' Eve stuttered joyfully, before Arthur's lips pressed against hers. 'Only, please,' she said after a few moments, 'don't even think of suggesting we get married at Roseland, OK? Actually . . .' She turned to stare broodingly towards the grand old manor house. 'Tell me I'll never have to set foot inside that wretched place ever again.'

49

In a daze after ending the brief phone call with her husband, Cathy carried on wandering towards to the lake, still reeling from everything Chris had just told her.

Rebecca had been spot on, she thought bitterly, recalling the woman's arch hint at the beach, about her friend at the university in Dubai who talked constantly about a *dishy psychiatrist.* Cynically, Cathy wondered if Rebecca had known all along about her husband's affair but had been too polite to tell her the truth. Or if she'd simply kept that particular trump card up her sleeve to play when she needed it . . .

Nothing would surprise Cathy now. About Rebecca, or her husband. She thought back to their muted farewell at the airport — Chris's preoccupied manner then, and her own reluctance to take his calls ever since. 'I *knew* he wasn't coming to the wedding.' Deep down, she'd probably also known that their marriage was heading towards a dead end, Cathy admitted to herself now. She just hadn't wanted to admit it to her family.

The thought made her heart race in panic. 'They'll be devastated. Maybe they'll blame me for leaving him in Dubai,' she worried. 'Oh, what a mess.'

Taken aback as she was by her husband's revelation — and unhappy about the cowardly way he'd delivered it over the phone — Cathy realised she bore no ill will towards Chris for having found passion elsewhere. After all, she had, too, albeit unrequited. No, she refused to be bitter; it was a waste of energy. This was simply their time to move on from each other.

They'd raised a gorgeous family together, and the children would always connect them. Chris had been thrilled to hear about Eve's pregnancy, which in the spirit of parental fairness Cathy had felt obliged to share with her husband — also, at some level, testing if the happy news would finally nudge him to come and see his daughter. His *family*. It hadn't, and, moreover, he'd insisted Cathy should be the one to tell Eve, and her brothers, about their intended divorce.

All things considered, Cathy had agreed it was for the best. The only thing she was uncertain about was whether to keep or sell the cottage. Chris had left it up to her, stating flatly that he intended to stay in Dubai, whatever. But could Cathy really stay in Cornwall now? Much as she loved this place, she loved Jack more. It would be ridiculous to torment herself by staying here, watching him and Rebecca live happily ever after.

'She doesn't deserve you,' Cathy bemoaned, recalling the twinkle in Jack's eye as he'd congratulated her on becoming a grandma again. He'd been excited, too; she could tell. But he hadn't hung around to celebrate, or crack open a bottle of champagne.

His thoughts had returned almost immediately to Rebecca; he had *one or two things to take care of*, she recalled him saying. Were they together right now, making up — even making plans for Jack's new great-grandchild, who they would welcome into the world as husband and wife?

'I can't bear it.' Cathy made up her mind at last.

Once she'd spoken to Eve, they would immediately drive back to the cottage and pack — and leave a day earlier than planned.

She had no intention of staying in Cornwall for the wedding. Nor was she prepared to put herself through the torture of saying goodbye to Jack. Maybe she would even find a local tenant for the cottage. If so, she would never need to come here again . . .

Feeling distressed at the thought, Cathy speeded up now, frowning as she drew closer to the figure still pacing up and down the lakeside. 'Oh. That's not Eve.'

'Hi.' The throaty voice drifted towards her. 'Brave of you to come and find me, Cath. I'm guessing my name is mud.'

A light breeze drifting off the lake caught Rebecca's hair, spinning it around her beautiful face. Once again, Cathy was reminded of Eloise, and she felt sad and angry all at the same time. She wasn't sure what her best friend would have had to say about Cathy falling in love with Jack, but she had no doubt she'd be furious that this woman was obviously marrying him out of greed, all the time planning to steal Roseland from the twins and sell it for profit.

'Hardly surprising, wouldn't you say?' she said pointedly. 'When you've lied and schemed to get what you want. Do you even *love* Jack?' She saw Rebecca's surprise at her uncharacteristic directness, but there was little point in beating about the bush now.

'Love.' Rebecca's mouth twisted scornfully. 'People say it all the time, don't they? *I love you*. But what does it really mean? I fancy you? I'm scared of being alone? I need someone to pay my bills, or help me with the kids? There's a power dynamic in every marriage. All relationships are a form of bargain.'

Cathy decided not to challenge her on that; she was more interested in flushing out Rebecca's agenda. 'Well, I can see what you'd gain from Jack. But what's in it for *him*?'

Rebecca flicked back her hair. 'Isn't it obvious? Jack's pushing sixty. I'm the best offer he's had in years. He won't find many other younger women prepared to share his bed. Or put up with his kids.'

'Put up with . . .' Cathy glared at her. 'The twins were right about you.'

'I'm sure they were,' Rebecca said, looking surprisingly sad, rather than offended. 'They're smart girls. They've had the best education money can buy, haven't they? The most amazing home. Exotic holidays. Family all around them. Food on the table. They've never known a day's hunger in their life.' She turned away now, staring back across the lake.

Cathy frowned, puzzled by Rebecca's sudden change in mood. Her scathing comments about Jack had been as brittle and heartless as they were ill-founded. Now she looked strangely crestfallen; defeated, even. As though she was tired of being angry. She looked . . . different. Or was this yet another tactic to win sympathy, and get her own way?

'Yes, Jack has worked hard to give the twins a good life,' Cathy said cautiously. 'But you have an amazing job, Rebecca. You must have been well educated.' Once again, she realised how little she knew about Jack's fiancée — her life before she met him.

'I had *nothing*, OK?' Her jaw clenched, and her eyes were bright with tears.

If her distress was an act, it was a very convincing one, Cathy thought. 'I'm sorry. You've always sounded so . . . positive,' she said diplomatically.

'Don't patronise me. And don't you dare judge me. You don't know me. You haven't walked in my shoes. None of you have.'

'Sure. You're absolutely right.' Cathy took a step back as it occurred to her that, with the wedding on hold, and her plans to control Roseland potentially in tatters, Rebecca had nothing much left to lose. She looked almost wild — totally unlike her usual polished, controlled self. 'You're right. I know hardly *anything* about you. Perhaps it's time you told me.'

50

'Rosie? Violet? Is that you?' Cutting across the great hall, Jack followed the voices towards the almost hidden door next to the staircase at the end of the room, sparing one last glance up the stairs at Eloise's portrait. Immediately, it reminded him of Rebecca. He had no idea where she'd gone — he hadn't been able to find her — but, right now, he honestly couldn't care less.

All he cared about was making sure his daughters were all right. After his initial flash of temper towards Violet for having tricked Rebecca into wearing Eloise's ballgown, he had cooled down enough to realise that she'd only been trying to help. He had no idea if Rosie had been in on the plan, but he was fully aware that neither of the twins liked his fiancée. He should have listened to their concerns, he realised now; he shouldn't have rushed into this wedding.

He didn't blame Rebecca, but he didn't love her. That much had become blindingly clear to him. Only, that was no excuse for cruelty. 'I should have been kinder,' he berated himself, replaying his harsh words to her. 'I humiliated her. I *provoked* her,' he thought, feeling a frisson of anxiety about how she might retaliate. He had no idea.

How little he knew her, he realised now. What he'd felt, these last weeks — it had been excitement. Novelty. The opposite of what he'd felt with Cathy just now in the kitchenette: ease, comfort, the sense of solid ground beneath his feet. He wondered if she'd found Eve yet and told her the good news.

Chris would be thrilled, too, Jack knew, guessing that his old friend must have arrived by now. Picturing that happy reunion, he was conscious of an unexpected pang that felt uncomfortably like jealousy. His own family seemed to be falling apart.

'We're in the old library, Dad!'

Jack shook himself out of his maudlin thoughts, and carried on down the dark corridor, realising that it was taking him deeper into the inner sections of Roseland — the former family rooms generally closed to the public. He felt goose bumps break out on the back of his neck, but it took him a moment to realise why.

'Not just any old library. Sir Charles Trelawney's private, personal domain,' he realised, as he spotted the brass plaque on the heavy, oak-panelled door. 'Well, well. I never thought I'd set foot in here again.'

As he reached out to turn the handle, a sick feeling churned in the pit of Jack's stomach. This was where he'd been summoned as a fifteen-year-old to see the baronet, and where he had stood, proud but terrified, at his father's side, while Sir Charles ordered them both never to set foot in Roseland again — while Eloise was banished, and their baby daughter adopted.

'Wicked old goat,' he muttered. 'Thank God he's dead and gone. If I knew where his grave was, I'd dance on it.' Giving himself a stern reminder that he'd come here to cheer his daughters up, not bring them down, he forced a smile as he stepped into the room.

'I'm sorry, Dad,' Violet said immediately, leaping up from the red leather chesterfield sofa where she'd been sitting. 'I only wanted to show you that Rebecca was a trashy fake.'

Jack almost laughed at her bluntness. 'Well, if you put it like that. OK. I forgive you.'

'Letty's found out the truth about her,' Rosie said, rushing to her sister's defence.

'Ah, that's right. Your investigations.' Jack nodded wisely at Violet. 'So you called in the FBI, after all, DI Merchant?' He winked, letting her know he wasn't cross, then pointed at the book Rosie was hugging. 'That must be quite a story. You've hardly put it down for days.'

'You should read it, too, Dad.' Rosie stood up from the sofa, holding out the heavy black volume. 'Before I have to put it back. Grandma asked me to leave it in here when I've finished it. In Grandpa Charles's desk.'

Jack followed the direction of her gaze to the traditional, leather-topped mahogany desk in the corner, and more memories rose up like phantoms.

Lit only by a Tiffany standard lamp next to the sofa, the large but somehow claustrophobic room was gloomy and windowless, deliberately so to protect Sir Charles' valuable first editions from the ravages of sunlight. Jack stared at them — row upon row of books that had so intimidated him as a child — and the more he looked, the angrier he felt.

His life had been changed for ever, after that bitter, furious meeting, more than four decades ago. He had long since forgiven Juliana, who could have stopped it if she'd chosen to — if pride and loyalty hadn't silenced her. But he knew Izzy never would.

That moment had changed her life, too, and nothing Jack said could ever make up for what his eldest daughter had been through. He didn't care about Sir

Charles, or his diary. He wanted nothing more to do with the Trelawneys. He couldn't wait to see the back of Roseland.

'Another time, darling, OK? I was thinking we should have a chat. About what happened back there. And where we go from here.' He raised his eyebrows, looking around the room. 'Why don't we do it somewhere a little less gloomy, hey?'

'Good idea,' said a voice from the doorway. 'I was about to suggest the same thing.'

'Izzy!' Violet called out. 'We were wondering where you were.'

'Sorry, guys. Things to do. People to see.' Izzy strode into the room, glancing around. 'Jeez, I've seen funeral parlours less spooky. You should come outside. It's a gorgeous day. Let's not waste it. I know this morning was shitty, but we still have the afternoon.'

'Sure,' Violet agreed. 'But we have to go see Grandma first.'

'She was worried about the book,' Rosie added. 'I have to tell her —'

'What's it about?' Izzy cut in, staring curiously at it. 'Is that the same one I saw you reading at the party? So it's Juliana's, yeah?'

'Actually, it belonged to Grandpa Charles. It's his journal. You should read it yourself.' Rosie offered it to her sister now, flicking a grumpy glance at Jack. 'Seeing as Dad won't.'

'Maybe later,' Izzy said, before relenting as her sister frowned. 'OK, then. Hand it over.' Reluctantly, she took the book, flapping open the cover. '*The private journal of Sir Charles Trelawney*,' she read aloud. 'Is it good, then? Find out any juicy scandals?'

She asked the question flippantly, but her heart was pounding now. *Could this be the elusive, missing clue she'd been searching for all these weeks?*

So far, all her own lines of enquiry had drawn a blank, and she'd heard nothing more from the person whose DNA had been matched with hers; not since that one email warning her to back off. The next step of Izzy's plan was still to travel to Bristol, after the wedding. She wasn't fully convinced that the 'BS1' in the email address was actually a postcode, but she hadn't been able to come up with any better ideas.

Now, suddenly, she had her grandfather's private diary in her hands. Surely, if Juliana was hiding something scandalous, her husband would have known about it? Eagerly, she scanned the opening page. She was dying to find out her grandma's secret; she couldn't wait to throw it in her face — claim a moral victory over her.

It had to be something awful, for no one else to know about it. Over the last couple of days, each time Izzy had subtly probed her sisters, and Artie, about any other scandals in the family, they'd looked at her like she'd gone mad. Maybe Juliana had got pregnant before she married Sir Charles, Izzy speculated — and, out of shame, she'd hidden it from her husband — from everyone.

She knew Juliana had given birth to Eloise during her first year of marriage, which meant that any previous illegitimate baby would now be close to the age her mum would have been, had she lived. Around Cathy's age, Izzy estimated, wishing that data protection hadn't prevented the ancestry website from revealing the birth date of her anonymous DNA match.

Perhaps that explained this person's reluctance to be found. The social stigma of illegitimacy that dogged the older generation. It might also account for Juliana's disgust when her own daughter had an illegitimate baby years later . . .

And if Juliana had punished Eloise out of her own repressed guilt — made her give up her baby, give up *Izzy*, as she'd felt compelled to give up her own first child — the time had come to call her out on that hypocrisy. Force her to confront and admit her own sins. Teach her a lesson for inflicting the consequences of them on others. On her.

Vindication. *Revenge*. It was so close, Izzy could almost taste it.

51

'What exactly do you want to know?' Rebecca began wandering along the lakeside again. Spotlights around the perimeter caught the scarlet silk of the ballgown she was still wearing, making it glow; the flowing skirt snagged on a tall bulrush. Impatiently, Rebecca pinched its fat, cigar-shaped flowerhead, snapping it off and tossing it away.

'The truth,' Cathy said simply, following her. 'From the beginning.'

'Fine.' Rebecca stopped walking and turned to face her, arms folded. 'I was born poor. I grew up poorer. Then I worked my socks off to better myself. I took every opportunity that came my way, and when there were none, I made my own. Is that what you want to know?'

'We make our own luck,' Cathy said softly, recalling what Eve told her about the food poisoning that had put Rebecca's boss in hospital. 'Getting the job as a location manager. Picking Roseland for the movie. Coming here. None of that happened by chance, did it?'

Rebecca rolled her eyes. 'I refuse to make the same mistakes as my family. My mother and grandmother worked themselves into early graves. So did my useless father. Up to his knees in the revolting fish he caught at Polperro harbour.'

'Ah, right.' A penny dropped. 'I guess that's why you refuse to have fish in the house.'

'The smell of it makes me vomit.' Rebecca's mouth twisted, and she yanked at another bulrush, impatiently casting it away, before stalking further along the lakeside.

Once again, Cathy followed her, feeling like she was caught in an elegant game of cat and mouse, and as she walked, she pondered what Rebecca had said.

She'd picked up enough psychology from Chris to understand that such a powerful aversion most likely arose from an unconscious sensory association. Besides being poor, something very bad must have happened in Rebecca's childhood for the smell of fish to have left such a lasting impression. But this was the first time Rebecca had opened up, about anything. Cathy didn't want to scare her off by asking her directly what that trauma might be.

'So your dad worked in Polperro,' she said instead. 'I didn't realise you were born in Cornwall.'

Rebecca stopped walking and pointed across the lake. 'Less than a mile from here.'

Cathy stared at her in surprise. 'So close?'

'Almost in Roseland's shadow.'

'Wow.' Cathy let that sink in, for a moment, watching the emotions flickering over Rebecca's face. 'So you've been to Roseland before? I mean, before you came here for work.' It was impossible for anyone to have lived in this area and not be familiar with the estate.

'Correct.' Rebecca's brows arched, a hint of her earlier sarcasm returning.

Cathy didn't rise to it, now recognising her testiness as a defence mechanism. She didn't want to distract Rebecca by challenging her; she wanted to hear more. Not that she could forgive Rebecca's actions, necessarily, but she needed to understand them.

'I can't remember when the manor house was opened to the public,' she said, conversationally, and then frowned. 'Actually, I thought it wasn't until after Juliana signed it over to the National Trust. Did you ever get to go inside, back then? Or just in the gardens?'

'Oh, I had access all areas.' Rebecca smirked. 'On account of my grandmother having once worked here.'

'She did?' Cathy was astonished. That was the last thing she'd expected Rebecca to say, and she had an uncanny sense that there was an even deeper agenda at play in her coming to Roseland. A darker, premeditated intent, rather than the accidental encounter she had described so vividly at Jack's barbecue, when they'd first met. 'What did your grandma do?'

'Nothing important.' Rebecca shrugged. 'She was a seamstress. The lowest of the low.'

'But a skilled job,' Cathy pointed out. 'I realise the staff must have numbered in the hundreds, in those days. But I always understood a seamstress to be a valued position.'

'I suppose it depends on how popular you were. As it does now. In all jobs. My face doesn't fit at the company where I work. Hence the food poisoning.' A knowing arch of her eyebrows. 'Those who ask don't always get. And some get more than they want,' she added cryptically. 'But you can ask Juliana about that. Ask her about *Morwenna*.'

'Ask Juliana? She knew your grandmother, then?' She must have done, Cathy realised; they would have been around the same age, and Juliana was nothing if not mistress of her own home. But it was baffling that she'd never mentioned it — or, more specifically, any family connection with Rebecca. Quite the opposite, in fact; she'd been at pains to paint Jack's fiancée as a gold-digging stranger.

'Oh, she didn't just know her. She employed her.' Rebecca's mouth twisted. 'Although enslaved might be a better word.'

'Sorry?' That definitely didn't sound like Juliana. She could be snobbish, but she was kind and always generous. She paid Margaret a salary yet treated her like a sister, and Cathy knew of many local families that Juliana had personally helped. 'Are you suggesting —'

'I'm *saying*, my grandma worked her fingers to the bone, sewing dress after dress for *Lady Trelawney*. Filling those wardrobes with ridiculous finery for her to wear.'

Automatically, Cathy stared at the ballgown Rebecca was wearing. The exquisite silk and delicate stitchwork had been the handiwork of a London designer, not a local seamstress, but Rebecca's decision to wear it today suddenly seemed to take on new symbolism.

Cathy already suspected that Juliana might have had a hand in Violet tricking Rebecca into wearing the dress — in order to show her in a bad light to Jack. Now she wondered if Rebecca had disingenuously gone along with the scheme; if, indeed, she'd taken malicious delight in wearing it, for some darker reason other than reminding Jack of Eloise.

Rose had suggested that was the case, Cathy recalled, and she was beginning to think her clever goddaughter was right. She pictured the look on her face as she'd said: *It's her*. As though she'd just figured out something important — something she was keen to tell her grandma, Cathy remembered, reaching for a connection she couldn't quite grasp.

'You still don't get it, do you?' Rebecca smiled, almost pityingly.

'No,' Cathy said honestly. 'I mean, Juliana has never mentioned any Morwenna to me. She obviously doesn't remember you. Nor do I. Of course, you're a fair bit younger than I am. But I practically grew up at Roseland. If you spent time here, as you say . . .' She tensed. 'Oh my God. Did you ever meet *Eloise*?' The possibility was so shocking that, for a moment, Cathy felt breathless as she contemplated it.

The idea that Rebecca had secretly known Jack's first love — and had become engaged to him without ever disclosing that connection . . . That would be appalling. Cathy had already seen that Rebecca could be devious, but such secrecy would be deeply disturbed — perhaps even psychotic, she thought, and the tiniest knot of fear coiled in her stomach.

She thought of Juliana's insistence that Rebecca's beauty was a deadly mask, wishing now that she had pressed her more keenly on her dislike of the woman. Only, she'd dismissed it as irrational paranoia. Had she been naïve — about Juliana's agenda, as well as Rebecca's?

'No. I never met Eloise.' Rebecca's face flushed a mottled pink now. 'But I saw her. Only from afar, of course. Riding her pony across the estate. Dressed up in her fancy clothes. Living her charmed life. The Trelawneys' golden girl. But like I said, as far as they were concerned, my grandma was dirt. Which made me less than nothing. Irrelevant. *Invisible*.'

Cathy stared at Rebecca's striking face, thinking she had never met anyone less invisible, or more comfortable drawing attention to herself. Perhaps her childhood obscurity explained her adult ostentatiousness, she thought, beginning to feel a sliver of sympathy now.

Languishing in the shadows, watching this grand, aristocratic family from a distance, she could well understand how Rebecca might have been dying to step into the spotlight. She must have grown up bitter. Probably resentful. *Vengeful?*

'It sounds like you had a tough childhood,' Cathy said carefully. 'I can understand that you resented the Trelawney family. And I don't wish to make any excuses for their behaviour. Those were different times. If Juliana treated your grandma badly . . .'

Rebecca laughed, a shrill bark that sent a shiver through Cathy. 'And the rest. Poor old doddery Juliana Trelawney. The grieving, sainted matriarch. She's got you all fooled, hasn't she? She's pulled the wool over everyone's eyes. Except mine.'

52

'Fine,' Jack conceded, as Izzy continued to flick through Sir Charles Trelawney's ridiculous tome. 'Let's hear it, then. But just give us the edited highlights, OK?'

'Deal,' Izzy agreed. 'Then can we get the hell out of here? This place gives me the creeps.' She shuddered, then forced herself to concentrate on the diary. 'Right. Here we go.'

'Grandpa Charles was unfaithful to Grandma,' Violet blurted out, before Izzy could read a single word. 'He had an affair.'

Izzy frowned. 'Hang on. Are you sure it wasn't *Juliana* who had the affair?' She had already half made up her mind that it must be so.

'No, it was Grandpa,' Violet said impatiently. 'I can read, you know?'

'He wrote about it himself.' Rosie nodded at the book. 'I marked the page.'

'Jeez, what an idiot,' Izzy scoffed. 'What's the first rule of infidelity?' she said, thinking of her ex-husband. 'Destroy the evidence.' She pondered for a moment. 'In fact, come to think of it, Juliana was the one who gave you this diary, right? Why the heck would she want you to read about *that*?'

'Good point, Izzy.' Jack nodded at her. 'Sorry, girls, there must be some mistake,' he said to the twins. 'You know how proud your grandma is. She wouldn't want you to think —'

'Grandma wanted Rosie to know the *truth*,' Violet cut in, huffing impatiently again. 'She wanted us all to know what a monster her husband was.'

'Monster? That's a bit strong.' Thinking again about her theory that Juliana might have given up an illegitimate baby of her own, Izzy quickly revised it to wondering if that child had been her husband's . . . if, back in the dark days when rape within marriage wasn't yet a crime, he had abused her — and she had fought back, taking revenge by sending their baby away.

Perhaps giving the journal to Rosie was a pre-emptive strike: getting her story in first; revealing her husband's crimes as vindication, before anyone could accuse her of wrongdoing.

'People write all kinds of nonsense in diaries,' Jack said, matter-of-factly. 'Maybe Sir Charles was repressed. He could have been living out fantasies in his journal.'

'Does it say if they were married at the time?' Izzy asked, flicking through pages now. Words and phrases leaped out at her: 'irresistible'; 'cast a spell on me'; 'impossible situation'.

Rosie nodded. 'His mistress worked at Roseland. She was a seamstress. She actually made Grandma's wedding dress.'

Izzy rolled her eyes. 'Jeez. Nice.'

'Sir Charles was obsessed with her,' Rosie continued. 'He wrote poems to her in there.'

'Really?' Izzy flicked through more pages. 'Why didn't he send them to her?'

'Because she couldn't read. Morwenna was the most beautiful woman he'd ever seen, according to his diary. But she was very poor and uneducated.'

‘Morwenna.’ Izzy frowned. ‘So she was Cornish. A local woman. Is she still alive?’

Rosie shook her head. ‘She actually died a few months ago. But that’s not in the book.’

‘I googled it,’ Violet chipped in proudly.

‘Wow. This is incredible. I can’t wait to wave it in our dear grandma’s face.’ Although it wasn’t quite the strike against Juliana that Izzy had been hoping to find. In fact, she was beginning to feel reluctant sympathy for her. Izzy knew what infidelity felt like; she’d experienced it in her own marriage.

She was also disappointed that none of this explained her DNA match. If Juliana *hadn’t* secretly given away another child, meaning that wasn’t the person who had emailed her . . . who were they, and why had they warned her to back off?

Jack gave Izzy a serious look. ‘Perhaps it’s best not to tell Juliana. She’s been through a lot today. A shock like this might . . .’

Izzy arched an eyebrow. ‘Kill her?’

53

'When you say that Juliana behaved badly . . .' Cathy stared fearfully at Rebecca, praying she wasn't about to find out something terrible about the woman who had been like a second mother to her — who had been an honorary grandmother to her own children.

She knew how bitterly Izzy resented her, and that situation was complicated. *Adoptions* were complicated. But Eloise had been thirteen when she'd given birth; Juliana had faced the most difficult choice imaginable for a mother. As a child, Cathy hadn't understood it; as a mother herself now, she knew all too well that fierce protectiveness of her children.

'There's more than one way of being cruel,' Rebecca said softly. 'You don't have to physically hit someone to hurt them. Rejection and disdain can be just as painful.'

'I know Juliana can be snobbish,' Cathy acknowledged. 'But when you get to know her properly . . .'

'She never gave me the chance. Not now, and especially not back then. I suppose, in one way, I can't blame her. I mean, think of your own situation. If you found out that the woman your husband is shagging in Dubai had a kid, would you be nice to them?'

Cathy winced. The revelation of Chris's infidelity was still raw. She didn't know anything about the woman he claimed to have fallen in love with, but maybe Rebecca had a point. Perhaps she *would* find it hard to befriend anyone from that woman's family.

Not that she would be horrible to them, or blame them, but it was certainly a painful situation.

'I'm sorry,' she said quietly. 'I had no idea that your grandmother was —'

'Sir Charles Trelawney's whore?'

Cathy grimaced. 'I was going to say mistress.'

'Such a nice word, mistress, isn't it? Juliana was *mistress* of Roseland. My grandma was a slave.'

'I guess, sometimes, a woman might choose the arrangement? For their own reasons?'

'Well, my grandma didn't. She didn't choose to fall into that monster's bed. He forced her. Used her for his own gratification. Then, when he'd had enough, he simply cast her aside.'

Cathy felt sick. This wasn't the Trelawney family history as she knew it, and it was painful to hear. Fleetingly, she wondered if Rebecca was making it all up. She had no proof. It was her word against Juliana's. And what did she intend to do about it, anyway?

Was *this* Rebecca's true agenda? Cathy wondered. Not to sell Roseland in order to get rich, but rather to get even — to punish Juliana by taking what she valued most. Her reputation, as well as her home. Her good *name*. The Trelawney legacy that the old lady was so desperate to leave to her granddaughters.

'Surely, Juliana can't be blamed for her husband's actions?' she said, and once again she noticed a shift in Rebecca's expression, from fury to something that looked close to pain.

'Maybe not. But she didn't help. So much for female solidarity, hey? She turned her back on my grandmother. Her own maid. She banished her from Roseland. Cast her out onto the streets. Leaving her to fend for herself. Alone. Destitute.' A tear rolled down Rebecca's face now, and her voice finally broke as she rasped: 'Pregnant.'

54

Jack sighed. 'I think we can all agree that Sir Charles Trelawney wasn't a good man. It doesn't surprise me in the least that he was also a hypocrite. Laying down the law about other people's mistakes, and all the time he was an adulterer.'

'No wonder poor Grandma doesn't put flowers on his grave,' Rosie said sadly. 'Not like she does every week on Mum's.'

'Does she?' Izzy frowned. 'I didn't know that. How sad.'

'Maybe she doesn't leave flowers because she secretly bumped him off,' Violet said, eyes glinting. 'If I had a husband, and he cheated on me, I'd cut off his —'

'Now, now.' Jack tutted. 'Your grandma isn't a master criminal. She's a lonely old woman who's lost a lot. I probably haven't always been as understanding of her as I should. Only think how she must have felt reading that diary. It's one thing knowing her husband was unfaithful. If indeed she *did* know. It's quite another reading his love poems to another woman.'

Izzy rolled her eyes. 'She must have known. If not at the time, certainly after reading his journal. What I still don't get is why she gave it to *you*, Rosie.'

'She wanted to help. Like Letty said, she wanted me to know the truth.'

'Which is?' Izzy was still desperately hoping for something — anything — that would help slot the missing pieces of her own puzzle into place.

'Morwenna had a son,' Rosie told her eagerly. 'She called him Gryffyn. It means 'lord'. I looked it up.'

'So what happened to him?' Jack frowned. 'I've never heard of any son in the family. Eloise used to say how much her dad favoured boys and despised girls. Why has nobody mentioned this Gryffyn?'

'Because he was a *secret*,' Rose said. 'Obviously.' It was her turn to roll her eyes. 'No one knew he existed. And he never came to Roseland. Not once. Grandpa wrote about it in his diary. How he used to see Gryffyn in the village. *Oh, my boy, my poor sweet boy*,' she quoted sardonically, clasping a hand theatrically to her chest. 'But he never spoke to him. Then it was too late. Gryffyn was gone.'

Izzy huffed. 'Don't tell me Juliana banished him, too. She has a nasty habit of sweeping unwanted people under the carpet, doesn't she?'

'Actually, Grandma didn't know anything about Gryffyn. She had no idea why Morwenna left Roseland so suddenly, either.' Rose took the diary back off her sister and pointed to a paragraph she'd highlighted, reading aloud: '"The naivety of my new bride is shocking, yet most convenient, I find. She frets more over her garden than my presence. My body and heart cleave freely to Morwenna."

'Wow. So Juliana was made a fool of.' Izzy shook her head. 'That's shitty.'

'Grandpa did a lot of shitty things,' Rose said blithely. 'He was the stupid one, if you ask me. He was head over heels in love with Morwenna, but he sent her away. He was desperate for a son, but he refused to see Gryffyn. Because he was illegitimate. Charles was the last Trelawney baronet, you see? He didn't want to bring disgrace onto the family name.'

'What a man.' Jack glanced at the desk in the corner now, remembering Sir Charles sitting behind it, blustering about *decency* and *reputation*; spitting righteous indignation.

'You haven't told them the best bit yet, Rosie,' Violet chipped in excitedly.

Jack huffed. 'There's a *best* bit? Don't tell me, Gryffyn went on to be a self-made millionaire and lived happily ever after, despite his terrible childhood.'

'He died in his twenties,' Violet said bluntly. 'So did his wife. Smallpox.'

'Jeez.' Izzy rolled her eyes. 'Good job this isn't the movie they're making at Roseland, hey? *And they all died horribly*. Not quite the Hollywood ending everyone's hoping for. The Trelawneys don't have much luck, do they? Even the illegitimate ones. Wait, don't tell me they had kids, and they died, too?'

'Actually, they had a daughter.' Rosie's eyes glinted. 'And she's *definitely* alive.'

'Seriously?' Butterflies whirled in Izzy's stomach. 'Do you know where she lives?' *Surely, this had to be her mystery DNA match?*

'She was born near here, of course,' Rosie told her. 'In Polperro, where her dad was a fisherman. After her parents died, her grandma moved with her to Newquay. Morwenna worked as a cleaner there. Until she died as well. Last Christmas.'

'Of poverty and shame,' Violet chipped in, determined to take her part in telling the tale. 'Leaving her granddaughter all alone. Poor. Rejected. Bitter.'

'But *clever*.' Rosie frowned at Violet, irritated by her embellishments. She was always taking over, but she wasn't the one who had read the journal. 'And extremely ambitious. She went to university and studied media and law. Then she got a job in TV and moved to —'

'Bristol,' Izzy said, taking a wild stab as she thought of the mystery email address — the combination of letters and numbers that had to be a postcode. Almost immediately, tiny little pieces began to fall into place in her mind, and she felt as though the room had suddenly flipped upside down.

'Exactly.' Rosie looked at her in surprise. 'And then Talland Bay.'

Jack stared at her, and he too looked like he'd just been hit by a truck. 'Wait. Are you saying . . . Is Sir Charles Trelawney's granddaughter *Rebecca*?'

55

'Wait.' Cathy stared at Rebecca. 'You mean, your grandmother didn't already have a child when she came to work here. She had a baby . . . with *Sir Charles*?'

A sardonic twist of the mouth. 'I wouldn't put it quite that way. That makes it sound way more romantic than it was. But, yes. He made her pregnant. And she had a son. Who should by rights have been the heir to Roseland. Except Sir Charles ruthlessly disowned him. So he became a fisherman instead.'

'A fisherman . . . who worked in Polperro.'

'Exactly. Now you're beginning to get it.' Rebecca smiled, but her voice was flat; her eyes blank and joyless. 'Fortunately for Sir Charles, my father died young. Before my mother could convince him to change his mind about making a claim on Roseland. Then she died, too. But unfortunately for *Juliana*, my grandma didn't. She lived to tell me the whole sorry tale.'

'Which she did right before you came here,' Cathy surmised breathlessly.

'Well, a few months before. Plenty of scripts get optioned for production. Not all get made. It was touch and go for this one. But the location was never in doubt. Everyone loved Roseland from the moment I suggested it. I knew it would be perfect, and the producers agreed. Sadly, they didn't see me as quite so ideal. I was invisible, you see? Just like my grandma.'

Cathy let that pass. Clearly, Rebecca wasn't backwards in coming forwards; she'd made certain she got the job she wanted, in the most underhand way possible. She could hardly play the moral trump card, when she'd shown herself to be almost as ruthless as Sir Charles. She'd been scheming for weeks . . . perhaps months to get what she wanted. *Which was what, exactly?*

That was the only thing that still wasn't clear to Cathy. Why had Rebecca gone to so much trouble: engineering her job at Roseland; manipulating Jack into proposing? If it was recognition she wanted — or indeed Roseland — surely, all she would have needed to do was march up to its front door and introduce herself? 'Well, I'm no lawyer,' she said thoughtfully. 'But if Sir Charles *is* your grandfather, as you're suggesting, then —'

'You still doubt me?' Rebecca glared at her. 'Ah, I see. You need proof. My word isn't enough. Perhaps a DNA test will convince you. I've done one, you know? I registered with an ancestry website when I was living in Bristol. It's proved very interesting. I've even had a few anonymous email exchanges with . . .' She broke off, frowning. 'Anyway, I can give you —'

'I'm sure there's no need for a DNA test,' Cathy jumped in. Although she suspected Juliana would insist otherwise. 'It's just, there are always two sides to every story, aren't there? But if you're so confident about yours, I imagine you must have a strong legal claim on Sir Charles's estate. On *Roseland.* There was no need to go to such lengths. You didn't have to —'

'Humiliate everyone?' Rebecca let out a harsh, mirthless laugh. 'Oh, but you see, that was all part of the fun. My parents died destitute. Unnecessarily so. My grandma was treated like a pariah by the Trelawneys. I wanted to give them a taste of their own medicine.'

Cathy didn't bother to point out that Jack wasn't a Trelawney, guessing that Rebecca's engagement to him had been her smokescreen, allowing her to move freely amongst the family without attracting suspicion. She gave her a curious look, finally daring to ask the question that had been niggling at her. 'Do you think Juliana knows who you are?'

'Silly old woman. She's completely lost her marbles. Which, in one way, is extremely convenient. She's convinced Roseland is safe. But we all know she has dementia. My lawyer will rip that contract she signed with the Trust to shreds.' Rebecca's chin lifted. 'In fact, it's all in hand. I'm not stupid. I've done my homework.'

'Yes,' Cathy said sadly. 'Violet found it online.'

'That girl's so sharp, she'll cut herself one of these days. All credit to her, I guess. In fact, I'm actually pleased my victory hasn't gone completely unnoticed.'

'*Victory?*' Cathy couldn't think of a less appropriate word.

'Yes. You see, I fully intend to have the last laugh. Sir Charles got away with his crimes. Juliana won't. Sadly for her, she'll have to pay the price for both of them.'

Cathy stared at Rebecca in horror, and her fleeting pity for the journey she must have been on — her painful start in life, and the shocking discovery of her true identity at the eleventh hour, as her grandmother lay dying — evaporated once more.

She thought of Izzy, whose life had been equally derailed ten years ago by the revelation of her

Trelawney birthright. She recalled their conversation at the hotel, when Cathy collected her before the engagement party . . . her insistence that she'd never forgive Juliana.

Yes, Izzy was furious, too. But she made no secret of it. She wasn't scheming behind everyone's backs.

'You've been planning this a long time,' Cathy said quietly.

'My whole life.' A careless shrug. 'Only, I didn't know it. Back then, I thought Roseland was a palace. I used to watch Eloise swan around the place. Beautiful. Glamorous. Rich. Utterly privileged in a way I could only dream of.'

'Trust me, her life wasn't entirely a bed of roses,' Cathy said, still thinking of Izzy — and the painful separation from her baby girl that Eloise had written about in her diary.

'But it was the life I wanted. That I should have *had*.' For a moment, Rebecca looked wistful. Her cheeks flushed again, and she chewed her lip, looking much younger and softer. 'I suppose I dreamed of being her. Even before I knew she was my aunt.'

Aunt. Cathy could still hardly take it in. 'But what about Jack? And the twins? You really don't care about them? They were just a means to an end?'

Rebecca frowned, looking cross now. 'Don't try to make me feel sorry for them. They're part of this family, aren't they? They've grown up loved and cossetted. They have everything they could ever want. They don't need my pity. And as for Jack, he's a big boy. He can handle it. Besides, he'll have his consolation prize.' She gave Cathy a knowing look. 'You.'

'What?'

'Oh, don't bother to deny it. I know you were with

him last night.'

'Yes, but . . .' Cathy shook her head, recalling those tense, fearful hours at the hospital. 'That was a . . . a personal matter.'

'Sure,' Rebecca said tartly, but the look she gave Cathy was curious rather than cross.

'Anyway, we're here to talk about you. Your truth, not mine. So let's get to the point, shall we? Are you saying you haven't come here for Roseland . . . that it's revenge you want?'

'I prefer to call it justice. Vindication. Oh, I won't deny that I want Roseland. Seeing as we're speaking our *truth*.' Rebecca's eyes glittered now. 'But I suppose if I can't have it, I'll settle for Juliana losing it, too.'

56

'We did *try* to tell you she was no good, Dad.' Violet gave him a pitying look.

'She was never interested in me. It's Roseland she wants.' He wasn't so much hurt as disappointed: that anyone could be so ruthless and calculating. *Heartless.*

Jack always looked for the best in people, and perhaps, in other circumstances, he might have felt sorry for Rebecca. But she'd used his family; she had deceived his closest friends. He couldn't forgive that. He was also honest enough to admit that his pride had taken a battering.

'And when she gets it, she's going to sell it.' Violet held out her phone, showing him the same planning application that she'd shown Cathy.

Jack barely glanced at it. 'Impossible. Not even Juliana has a say in what happens to Roseland now.' As his wedding testified. Juliana had opposed everything about it, yet she hadn't been able to stop even the rehearsal.

Had she known all along who Rebecca was? Had that been Juliana's true objection to his fiancée? He recalled the insults the old lady had thrown at her; surely, had she known about Rebecca's illegitimacy, that would have been the first stone she'd have hurled?

It was bad enough that Rebecca physically resembled Juliana's daughter — a likeness that now made complete sense to Jack. But to allow the granddaughter of her husband's secret mistress even to set foot in

Roseland? No, Juliana couldn't possibly have known.

'I wouldn't be so sure about that,' Izzy said grimly. 'Rebecca definitely has a legal claim on Roseland. Illegitimate children, and grandchildren, still have a right of inheritance.'

'Really?' Jack was a doctor, not a lawyer. He'd also never had any reason to look too deeply into the terms of his children's trust funds. Apart from covering their school fees, they remained untouched; nest eggs for their futures.

He wanted nothing from them for himself, and although Rebecca had asked him who managed the twins' finances, and how they felt being heiresses to one of the grandest houses in the country, her interest had seemed casual, part of the getting-to-know-your-family phase of their relationship. *And the rest*, Jack thought, freely acknowledging that he'd well and truly been played for a fool. But as far as he was concerned, it was shame on her.

'I guess it's only fair,' Izzy said tightly. 'Just because parents aren't married, or grandparents object, why should a child be penalised?' She gave her dad a pointed look. 'That's what the lawyer told me, anyway. When I received my own trust fund from Eloise. Not that I've touched a penny of Trelawney money. All the same, I absolutely claim my right to it.'

'Of course. So you should,' Jack conceded immediately. 'But honesty and integrity matter. Rebecca could have come straight out and said what she wanted. Then I could have told her that the Trust controls Roseland. No one can get their hands on it. Not even you girls.'

'They control it. They don't *own* it,' Izzy pointed out. 'And Juliana's state of mind isn't exactly stable.

A good lawyer would rip that contract to shreds in a second. I'd stake my own inheritance on Rebecca knowing one.'

'So why did she want to marry you, Dad?' Violet asked bluntly. 'I mean, no offence, but she didn't have to. Not if it's Roseland she wants.'

'Or our money,' Rosie whispered. 'Like Ted. That's *really* why Rebecca took me on the boat, wasn't it? If I'd drowned, and she marries Dad . . .'

Jack crossed the room to pull the twins against his side. 'Don't say it. Don't even think it. I'd die before I let any harm come to you two.' He squeezed them both tighter. 'I'm sorry I didn't listen to you before. I knew you weren't keen on Rebecca. I guess I was deaf and blind to everything but what I wanted to see and hear. I was wrong. About everything.'

'I'm with Violet on this,' Izzy said thoughtfully. 'Whether Rebecca is after money, or Roseland, why marry you? I mean, sorry, no offence. I know you're a catch.' She raised her eyebrows. 'But Rebecca has her own right of inheritance. As you say, she didn't need to marry for money. Or Roseland. She can march right up to the bloody door and claim it for herself.'

Jack thought for a moment. 'You know, I have absolutely no idea.'

'Maybe she genuinely loved you.'

Jack threw Izzy a wry look. 'I'm under no illusions about that. I've been naïve, but I'm not vain. None of this happened by chance. Rebecca has obviously schemed very cleverly.'

'So you think it's *revenge* she wants?' Izzy's heart was thumping so loudly, she was convinced her dad must be able to hear it.

'Wouldn't you? That's a genuine question, by the

way.' Jack gazed intently at his eldest daughter. 'I know how much anger you've carried against this family yourself. Given everything, wouldn't you crave some kind of payback?'

'Well, I . . .' Izzy glanced at the door. 'You know, I really think we should leave now.'

Jack frowned. 'You keep saying that, Izzy. What's the hurry?'

'Nothing, just . . . What if Rebecca comes back?'

'Then we'll have a sensible conversation, like grown-ups.'

'Sure. OK.' Izzy chewed a thumbnail, still looking anxious. 'I'm not sure you'll be able to talk sense into her, though. After everything she's done, who knows what she's capable of?'

Jack looked around the library, taking what he hoped would be his last look at the place that already symbolised so much tragedy for him. Whatever Rebecca had planned next, he didn't want to be trapped inside a windowless room with his daughters when he found out. 'You're right. Come on. Let's get the hell out of here.'

Izzy nodded eagerly. 'About time. Lead on. We're right behind you.'

Striding to the door, Jack grabbed the brass handle, twisting it. 'Shit. I think it's stuck.' He tried again. Then again. Over and over, until the futility of his efforts finally sank in: the door was either jammed . . . or it had been locked from the outside.

'Dad? What's going on?'

Three sets of blue eyes appealed to him. Jack stared helplessly at them, then once more around the library, book-lined and oak-panelled, which offered no other means of escape. He heard Rosie cough;

then Violet. Then Izzy started coughing, too, and as Jack felt a tickle in his own throat, he felt a sudden draught and glanced down. Smoke was curling under the door.

'Fuck.' Yanking off his dinner jacket, he dropped to his knees. His first instinct was to block the gap and stop the smoke, buy himself time to think. But his thoughts were chaotic, tortured and full of guilty self-loathing for having put his girls in this position.

The twins had tried to warn him. *So had Cathy.* Fleetingly, he let himself picture her face — her warm eyes and kind smile. He wondered where she was. And Eve. Artie, too. Were they safe? Had Rebecca left? Or had she hung around to deliver one last, killer blow?

'Dad?' Izzy said again, and her face was as white as a sheet now.

Jack stared at her. This room was where he'd been forced to give Izzy up. He wouldn't lose her again, nor the twins. He wouldn't let Sir Charles win; he refused to allow Rebecca to finish whatever sick game she was playing.

'Stand back,' he ordered, and then almost had to laugh as, in unison, his three daughters ignored his instruction and moved immediately to his side.

They were nothing if not wilful, Jack thought, and, over the years, that had caused him more than one headache. Now, though, it might just be their saving grace.

'Right. So be it.' He gritted his teeth. 'On the count of three, brace yourselves. Let's barge this door down.'

57

'If you can't have it,' Cathy echoed nervously, watching Rebecca's expression shift again, this time to . . . satisfaction? *Triumph?* But she didn't reply, her attention riveted on something beyond them. As Cathy turned to look, she froze in shock. 'Oh my God.' Smoke was billowing above the manor house, but it wasn't emerging from the tall chimneys. 'Roseland's on fire.'

She didn't wait for Rebecca's response, or spare her a second glance. She ran as though her life depended on it — and, in truth, it did. Her family was the sole reason she got up every morning. Without them . . . without Jack . . .

Was he in that house? Were his daughters? Was Eve, and Arthur? Thank God Juliana had already left, she thought, even as the grim possibility occurred to her that Rebecca may not know that. 'Oh, God,' Cathy groaned, wondering if that accounted for the smug, knowing look on Rebecca's face . . . her glittering eyes. *If she can't have it, no one can.*

Stumbling to a standstill, Cathy turned to look back towards the lake. There was no sign of Rebecca; she seemed to have vanished into thin air. 'Did you do this? Is this your *justice*?' But there was no time to spare for further interrogation. The thought of her loved ones trapped inside a burning building overrode Cathy's concern about anyone and anything else.

Grabbing the skirt of her chiffon dress, she set

off again, almost immediately catching her heel in a divot. Beneath the springy grass, the earth was hard, starved of moisture by the recent heatwave. Feeling her ankle twist painfully, she kicked off her heels, limping onwards. It felt like for ever until she reached the gravel drive at the front of the house, but as soon as she did, the sight of the grand, ancient building once again stopped her in her tracks.

This close up, it seemed as though Roseland was being eaten alive by the fire. Its stone walls were already blackening, and flames curled out of the upstairs windows, like a great beast licking its lips. Cathy fumbled in her bag, but her trembling fingers found only silk. She cursed. Her phone must have fallen out down by the lake. 'Please let someone have called the fire brigade,' she pleaded loudly, half hoping to see a firefighter striding towards her, alerted by some internal alarm.

But there was no sign of anyone, and as Cathy limped up the wide stone steps towards the front door, wincing in pain, it felt as though she was entering an abandoned disaster zone. Smoke alarms beeped stridently, but there was no evidence of the sprinkler system. Then she remembered the drought warnings. Hosepipe bans had been in force throughout the summer heatwave. Had the estate manager been forced to economise on Roseland's water supply?

The foyer was so full of smoke, and fragments of floating ash, that she was forced to feel her way blindly across the tiled entrance, yelping as she stood on something sharp. Automatically, she crouched down, pulling a small shard of broken glass out of her bare foot.

Glancing frantically around now, she realised from

her new perspective close to the floor that she was better off staying low. The air was clearer, a draught swirling through the spacious vestibule, chasing the worst of the smoke towards the open front door. 'Where are you? Jack? Evie? Girls?' Desperately, she longed for some telepathic connection to guide her.

Still crouching low, she shuffled to the left, instinctively heading towards the great hall. Perhaps they were still there. Maybe their exit was blocked, and they needed help.

Making her way painfully slowly in that direction, Cathy felt a wave of despair at the damage already wrought by the fire. She could see valuable paintings blistered beyond repair, while antique furniture and artefacts that had entranced thousands of visitors were charred beyond recognition. Not even the fire brigade would be able to save Roseland, she feared. 'But someone has to save my family.'

Coughing and wheezing, Cathy finally reached the great hall. Sweeping pointlessly with her arms in an effort to forge a path through the smoke, she felt her eyes sting. 'Who would do this? Surely not Rebecca? She *wants* Roseland. Why destroy it? It must have been an accident. Or someone deliberately made it look like one . . .'

Shuffling onwards, she stared in horror at the once lavish, now singed curtains hanging in ragged shreds either side of the tall windows. The garlands of roses, so carefully staged for the wedding, had disintegrated. 'Whoever did it, I'll never forgive them.' The destruction was heart-breaking, and for a moment, Cathy felt rooted to the spot in grief.

A racking cough forced her to move. 'Keep going,' she ordered herself, but her lungs felt painfully tight as she headed by instinct rather than sight towards the rear of the room, knowing that behind the almost hidden door there, a corridor led deeper into the house. 'Did you go in there?' Maybe it had seemed a closer, easier escape route.

As her shin grazed something hard, she realised she was at the foot of the grand, sweeping staircase. 'The twins went up there. Rosie was going to show her sister something.' With all her heart, Cathy wished now that she'd simply taken them straight home, after the aborted rehearsal. 'Girls? Are you up there?'

She had to go and look, but she'd taken barely two steps when she spotted a burning pile in front of her. 'Oh, Ellie.' It was the portrait of Eloise. The one Rebecca had posed in front of only an hour or so before; it felt like days now.

Slowly picking her way towards it, taking care to avoid sparks from the smouldering ashes, Cathy sobbed at the sight of the beautiful gilt frame, now twisted and broken. The canvas itself was in tatters, little strips curled back, alight with flames. Where Eloise's stunning face had once gazed out at the world, there was now only a blackened void.

Once again, she thought of Rebecca, and how satisfied she would feel if she saw this. It felt like the ultimate insult. 'She's dead already. Can't you leave her to rest in peace?'

Fury drove her onwards, and Cathy dropped to her knees, crawling beneath the thickening layer of smoke, sticking to the middle of the stairs to avoid the flaming banisters. *Please, show me the way*, she begged, unsure whether she was appealing to God, or her friend's spirit.

'Evie? *Jack?*' she called out as, after what felt like

an age, she finally reached the top. Her breath was coming in laboured gasps now, and her head was spinning. It felt as though she was in a tiny box, and the sides were closing in . . . and then someone closed the lid.

58

'It's giving way. I can feel it. One more push, girls.' Jack put his back into his final charge, but he could feel his strength running out. So was the oxygen in the library.

If the door didn't give this time, he knew the chances of any of them making it out alive were next to none. The walls were too thick; their screams wouldn't be heard. Even if there was anyone on the other side to hear them. The thought fuelled his fury, and renewed his energy. If someone had deliberately locked them in this room . . .

'Oh my God. We did it!' Izzy could feel something wet trickling down her forehead, and she wasn't sure if it was sweat, or blood. But it was worth it: the door that had been upright only seconds before was now lying flat across the corridor, almost split in two.

'Is everyone OK?' Jack coughed, immediately feeling his throat fill up again with acrid smoke. 'Stay low. Keep moving. Follow me.' He half crawled, half dragged himself along the corridor, glancing back every other moment to check his daughters were behind him.

'It's getting thicker. We must be going towards the fire,' Izzy croaked.

'No, it's in the other direction,' Rosie insisted, continuing to move purposefully along the corridor, away from the great hall.

'I can see a door! It's open!' Impatiently, Violet

grabbed the hem of her white silk dress, hauling it up around her hips so that she could move faster. Lurching forwards, she almost dived towards the sliver of light visible at the end of the corridor.

'Wait!' Jack reached out to her, managing to grab the flouncy hem of her dress, pulling her back. 'We don't know what's on the other side of that door.'

'It's safe, Dad. Come *on*,' Rose insisted.

Jack hesitated, reluctant to put his daughters in danger again. But Rosie was strangely intuitive, and she seemed determined that this was the way to go. He looked over his shoulder, logic suggesting the fire would indeed most likely be raging through the more open reception rooms. Specifically, the great hall, lined with dozens of candles — that Rebecca had insisted on.

Ridiculous fire hazard, he recalled Juliana saying, as she'd imperiously surveyed the scene set for his wedding. In his gut, Jack knew this fire was no accident.

'It's fine, Dad.' Rose tugged on his arm. 'There's no fire this way, just smoke.'

Before he could stop her, she'd darted along the corridor and through the door that opened into what looked like one of the estate offices. Violet and Izzy followed close behind, and Jack was hot on their heels now. 'Jeez. Is this Dad's old office?' His mind flooded with memories, as he saw familiar filing cabinets and a desk. There was a phone on top.

'Do you think everyone got out?' Izzy worried, striding around.

'I don't know,' Jack answered honestly, growling in frustration as he tried the landline and discovered it was dead. The phone wires must be burnt out. 'But that's exactly what you three need to do. Right now.'

He looked around. 'There. That's a fire exit. It leads out onto a courtyard. Make your way to the front of the house. Stay clear of windows. Flying glass.'

Striding across the office, Jack's mind filled with yet more images of his dad, working in this room years ago as Roseland's estate manager, and as he braced his shoulder against the fire door, he caught sight of the cufflinks he'd chosen especially to wear today. 'Bring me luck, Dad,' he muttered, putting his full weight into an almighty shove, half expecting this door to be jammed, too — the ancient wood expanding in the heat, just as the library door had.

Or had it been locked? Grimly, Jack recalled Rebecca's moment of humiliation on the stairs. Was this her handiwork — her revenge? Not only towards him for inflicting public shame on her, but also the Trelawney family. *Juliana*. Who had rejected and despised his fiancée. *Former* fiancée, he thought determinedly.

The door gave way. 'Go. *Now*,' he ordered his daughters, before turning back into the office, heading towards the door they'd just come through.

'Dad, you can't go back there.' Rosie grabbed his arm.

'I need to check if anyone else is in the house. I didn't see where Eve and Artie went. Or Cathy.' She had been going to break the happy news to her daughter, Jack recalled. Perhaps they'd found a quiet room somewhere, to talk in peace. 'They might be upstairs.'

Rose shook her head. 'Me and Letty went up there. Right before we came to the library.'

'Oh?' Jack had thought they'd been with Izzy. So where had *she* gone?

'I went to get the *journal*.' Rose looked distraught now. 'I left it up there while we had the rehearsal.'

Sensing her growing panic, Jack grabbed hold of his daughter's shoulders, staring into her eyes. 'Rosie, you're not making any sense. What are you trying to tell me?'

She shook her head. 'Just that they weren't there. Cathy and Eve. *No one* was up there. Only us.' Her eyes filled with tears now. 'And we came down. To the library. To put the book back where Juliana said to leave it.'

'OK, love.' Jack gave her a hug, recognising that she was in shock, and possibly on the verge of hysteria. 'You go. Don't worry, I'll follow you out soon.'

A loud cracking noise made them both jump, and Jack spun around, staring in awe at the flames. He'd seen many bushfires in Australia, but this was different. Roseland was an enclosed space, and the corridor was filling with smoke, fast. It was also a very old building, made of ancient timber. *Firewood*, he thought fearfully. 'Girls. You have to get out. *Now!*'

'Not without you, Dad.' Once again, Rose tugged at his arm.

'Rosie, come.' It was Izzy, her usually tanned face deathly pale, eyes wide and fearful.

'Thanks, Izzy.'

'It's OK, Dad. Take care, won't you? And . . . I'm sorry.'

With that, she grabbed Rose's arm, pulling her away, and Jack's last sight of his daughters was three long blonde ponytails bobbing in sync as they sprinted across the courtyard. It was only as they disappeared around the corner, that he registered Izzy had called him 'Dad' instead of Jack.

'Huh. I guess it takes a fire to burn away some grudges.' He stared after them until he was sure they weren't coming back, all the while pondering Izzy's words. *I'm sorry.* He wondered what, exactly, she had been apologising for.

59

'Juliana?' Jack barely managed to call out her name, before he was forced to stop walking and release the choking cough that he could feel coagulating in his chest. '*Cathy?*' Picturing her face, he forced himself to move forward . . . to keep putting one foot in front of the other.

As he'd told his daughters, he had no idea if the two women were still inside the house — or Eve and Arthur — and he couldn't leave until he'd made absolutely certain. Rosie had seemed convinced there was no one upstairs, but as he reached the great hall and surveyed the catastrophic scene of destruction, something made him pause at the bottom of the staircase.

It wasn't only the sight of Eloise's portrait, now a smouldering heap. Something was pulling him up those stairs, even though he knew that once he'd gone up there, there might be no way back. The smoke looked even more dense at the higher level. Perhaps the fire had started up there, not on the ground floor.

Jack couldn't begin to figure out the most likely source; his brain had been trained to save lives, not destroy them. But if this had been a deliberate act of arson, as he feared, surely anyone with criminal intent would have executed it well away from the risk of public view?

The spitting inferno that lay beyond the half landing, where the stairs curved in a sweeping arc to the first floor, seemed to support the theory. It was also possible the fire had been smouldering for some time, Jack reasoned. Rebecca had already been here when he'd arrived, and he hadn't seen her since their confrontation.

Was she really capable of such a heinous act? Jack couldn't bear to think so, but he also recognised now how little he knew her. Everything he thought he'd known about Rebecca had turned out to be a lie — either directly or by omission . . . or putting a subtle spin on what little she'd told him.

Until today, it hadn't bothered him. Over the last month, Jack had happily kidded himself that there was plenty of time for them to get to know each other; now he realised that the air of mystery he'd once found so alluring had been entirely, manipulatively, intentional.

Rebecca had deliberately only told him the bare bones about herself, so as to keep her true identity — and agenda — a secret. Until she was ready to strike. 'I won't let others pay the price for my mistake,' Jack vowed fiercely.

Looking around for something to use as a mask, he stumbled towards the antique sideboard that Rebecca had staged as an altar. After the briefest pause to acknowledge the bitter irony that, right now, they should have been rehearsing their wedding vows, he grabbed the lace table runner. 'Till death do us part,' he muttered, pressing it to his face.

It wasn't much protection, but it would have to do. At least it might save him from the worst of the carbon monoxide; his legs were already starting to feel rubbery as he returned to the foot of the stairs. He made slow progress, battling heat more intense than he had ever known. His eyelids felt like they were on fire; his clothes were sticking to him. Every breath hurt.

'Cathy,' he murmured, dropping to his knees, pulling his way up the stairs, keeping his eyes down so as not to be intimidated by how many still lay before him. As he passed what he guessed to be the halfway point, he made the mistake of looking up, and, despite the intense heat, cold terror rushed through him.

Flames danced up the walls of the Long Gallery above, shimmying across valuable paintings and tapestries, and leaping between curtain poles. As one plummeted to the ground, Jack braced himself. 'Cathy?' he yelled, uncertain now whether he was trying to help her, or crying out for her to help him.

Pausing for a moment to rest, he closed his eyes. Immediately, he saw Cathy's face, and it was as though a curtain dropped in his mind, exposing everything he'd been hiding from himself — that Juliana had tried to tell him, but which he'd been too blind to admit.

Already, he'd realised that his love for Rebecca was bogus; a glittering but hollow imitation of genuine affection. Juliana had been right about that, too: where there was true love, there was need no need for spectacle. *All that glisters isn't gold*, he thought bitterly.

He'd been dazzled by Rebecca, his ego flattered by her attention. His unconscious mind had also gravitated to her familiarity . . . her resemblance to Eloise. There was no doubt that he'd enjoyed her company. Rebecca was vivacious, sensuous and stimulating; she never stopped talking and barely sat still. *Like a moving target*, Jack thought cynically.

From the moment of his proposal, she had scarcely given him time to draw breath, organising the wedding at Roseland with breathless speed. And Jack had been swept along, pushing aside all queries and objections from his family.

It was only seeing Cathy again that even a flicker of doubt had set in. She'd reminded him of his past, and for the first time a question mark had arisen in his mind about the future. He thought of her comforting Violet at the beach — her tenderness as she'd watched over Rosie. Her quiet, unintrusive concern for him, too, amidst all the drama.

Jack had known that Cathy wanted to blame Rebecca for the boat accident; foolishly, he'd defended his fiancée. But Cathy hadn't challenged him; she had trusted him, all the time continuing to keep a close eye on her goddaughters. Who needed her as much as Jack did.

Yes, it was constancy, honesty and pure unselfish kindness that would nourish and enrich him through his *autumn years*, he thought, just as Cathy had gently teased him. True love had crept up on him. Without any fanfare or overblown spectacle.

It had been hiding in plain sight, right under his nose, all this time. The woman his daughters trusted and clung to; the friend Eloise had relied on throughout her life, and death. *His* oldest friend; his deepest love. Cathy.

But Chris was his friend, too. And he was Cathy's husband. Jack had no right to expect more from her than the friendship she gave so generously. 'So be it.' He glanced up into the dark, smouldering void that lay beyond the top of the stairs, knowing that, no matter what, he would fight for her until his last breath.

Whatever life he had left, he wanted to spend it watching Cathy enjoy hers: becoming a grandmother again; being his friend, if nothing more. 'Hold on, my love. I'll find you. Wait for me. Please.' Slowly, fighting the crushing pain in his lungs, Jack dragged himself upwards.

60

Dizziness and nausea forced Cathy to rest for a moment, but as she urged herself to move forward again, her arms and legs felt as though they were made of cotton wool. Blinking, she realised that even without the smoke, her vision was blurry, and her hearing muffled.

'Cathy?'

Had she imagined the voice? Was it merely an echo of her wishful thoughts?

It came again. 'Cathy? Are you up here?'

Help! she screamed in her head, then immediately panicked that whoever was calling her might not have come to help, but to harm her.

There was something important she needed to remember, but she was struggling to hold on to consciousness now. Poisonous fumes clogged her lungs and confused her mind. Disoriented, she had no clear sense of where the voice had come from. She didn't even recognise it. All she knew was that if she stayed here, she would surely die.

Dragging herself painfully along the corridor — the Long Gallery, she realised — she pressed her body close against the wall, feeling her way by touch. 'Evie,' she slurred, almost drunkenly. 'You're going to live. You're going to be a lovely mummy.' She had to tell her. If only she could find her.

The wall came to an abrupt end, and, for a moment, Cathy's hands flailed in the air, until understanding dawned. She had reached a door. It was open.

'Rosie? Violet?' she croaked, suddenly remembering the girls scurrying upstairs. 'Are you in here? Girls?'

Something brushed against her hair. A hand? *The crow?* Terror filled Cathy's lungs, and the next thing she felt was her cheek smacking against the hard floor. After that, there was only the deep, silent darkness of nothing.

61

'We shouldn't have left Dad.' Izzy was distraught. Inconsolable.

'He told us to go,' Violet panted, as they continued to jog through what felt like a maze of interconnecting courtyards and narrow pathways, until, at last, they emerged onto the gravel drive that ran along the front of the manor house. 'Jesus. Look at it.'

Izzy shook her head. 'I can't. I can't bear it. We need to go back. Please, we need to help Dad. This is all my fault.'

'He'll be quicker without us. You heard what he said. He has to check the building. We'd only be in the way.' Violet paused now, gasping for air. Propping her hands on her hips, she turned to look at her big sister. 'Anyway, what do you mean, it's all your fault? And you said sorry to Dad. What for? What did you *do*?'

Izzy opened her mouth to reply, but no words came. Feeling hysterical, she almost laughed. She was *never* lost for a quick answer, or sarcastic comeback. Now her brain felt numb. 'Rosie?' she managed to gasp, catching sight of their sister ahead of them.

Frozen like a statue, Rose stood rigidly, arms like pokers outstretched before her, as though to fend off an invisible attacker. In the next moment, she began to tremble. With her long white dress quivering around her thin body, she looked like a delicate lily buffeted by a sudden storm. Then she let out a piercing scream. '*Grandma!*'

'What?' Violet whirled around, then immediately began running back towards the house, fearing that Rosie had spotted their grandma at a window. '*Where*, Rosie?'

All of the windows were lit up now, the rows of stained glass on each floor glowing like a cathedral at Christmas. Smoke seeped out of every crack, and for a moment all Violet could do was stand and stare. She had never, in her entire life, been so frightened. Not even her terror when Rose had climbed into that kayak with Rebecca compared to the horror of this.

That morning, Violet had put all her faith in their dad to save her sister. He had never, ever, let them down, and she'd felt certain that if anyone could rescue Rose, he would. He was a powerful swimmer, and he'd spent half his life on the ocean; he knew the riptides and currents, and how to anticipate, outwit and conquer them. But fire was an unknown enemy.

Many times, Violet had listened to her dad talk about bushfires in Australia, but her own experience was limited to Bonfire Night, once a year, when the Roseland estate hosted community events and put on a dramatic fireworks display. Violet adored it. She particularly loved the crush of the crowd, everyone huddled together in collective excitement, watching enthralled as a stuffed Guy Fawkes was hauled onto a towering wood pile to burn.

The thrill was in the danger; a tantalising sense that, at any moment, the flames might leap out of control. Children would dare each other to get closer to the bonfire; parents would anxiously pull them back, but never with any great urgency. They toyed with the beast; they had no concept of how terrifying it would be to see it truly unleashed, as it was now.

'They're all going to die.' Numbly, Violet stared at the blackening granite walls of the manor house. She prided herself on being logical, practical — not given to flights of fancy, like her twin — but as she heard the windows begin to splinter, and watched thick black plumes of smoke surge outwards, like angry bears charging out of their cave, she felt hope drain away. 'Mum, please, help them,' she prayed. 'If you're watching, please. *Do* something.'

'Violet, here! Come quickly!' It was Izzy.

'Sorry?' Violet spun around again, but smoke was pouring over the drive now. Her eyes were so blurred, she could barely see. She squeezed them shut, focusing on her inner sense of direction. In the distance, she thought she heard sirens. 'Oh, Mum. I *knew* you were listening.'

'Letty! We're here! In the rose garden!'

It was Rose, but her voice was growing fainter. Slowly at first, Violet began walking in the direction of the garden that had always been their grandma's pride and joy. Behind her, she could hear glass shattering, but she stopped herself turning to look. This wasn't Bonfire Night; there were no marshmallows to toast; no children running happily around, over-excited at the rare opportunity to step inside the grand home of the great Trelawney family.

Violet had so many happy memories here; she couldn't bear to watch Roseland burn. She was out of her mind with worry thinking of her dad still inside it. 'Rosie?' She dashed away her tears. She *never* cried; she was the strong twin. When there were problems, she fixed them. She led, while Rose followed. Now, suddenly, she felt lost.

'I'm right in front of you, Letty.' The voice was

calm, soothing. 'Keep going. I'm here.'

Only the tickle of grass on her ankles told Violet that she'd left the drive now. She could hardly see in front of her face, but she kept walking, faster and faster. Then she spotted it.

At first, it looked like a ragged bundle of clothes, discarded in a heap; as she moved closer, gradually, it began to take shape. There was a head, its face turned away from her. Thin legs and arms outstretched. 'Oh my God. Is she alive?'

'I don't know.' Rose sat with her head bowed, quietly sobbing.

'What the fuck has happened here?' Izzy's eyes looked wild.

The twins looked blankly at her, then back at the ground, frozen in shock as they began to register the full horror. 'Grandma?' they whispered in unison. But she didn't respond.

Eyes tightly closed, Juliana lay rigid and unmoving. Her arms were crossed over her chest, as though she'd been clutching the bunch of white roses when she fell. Petals were scattered everywhere, reminding Violet incongruously of the wedding aisle.

Fearfully, she picked up her grandma's hand, feeling for a pulse at her wrist. 'Oh my God,' she said again. Rose let out another scream.

62

One week later

'Is she breathing?'

'I think the machine's doing it for her.'

'She looks dead. She's whiter than the sheet.'

'The doctors are doing everything they can. We should let her rest now. We'll come back later and check on her. Why don't you two go and find the canteen?'

Cathy ushered the twins out of the room, deliberately holding on to her smile as she watched them walk down the corridor. They were good girls, and remarkably brave. Cathy was proud of them, and so thankful that they'd recovered fully, after the shocking experience they'd been through. But the twins were only fifteen; they needed her to be strong for them now.

Violet stared straight ahead, walking purposefully, urging her sister on, while Rosie glanced back anxiously. Cathy gave her a reassuring thumbs-up, but the moment the girls had disappeared around the corner, she reached for the chair by the door, sinking weakly onto it.

Her chest felt painfully tight, and she was still having blinding headaches. She should probably still be in hospital herself, but she'd been determined to get home as soon as possible.

'Cathy? Is that you?' The voice from the bed was

muffled, barely audible.

'Oh, Juliana! You're awake. I didn't want to disturb you.'

'Come closer, my dear. Just let me get rid of this wretched thing.' Impatiently, the old lady pushed the cumbersome oxygen mask off her face.

'OK. But I won't stay long.' Cathy hesitated for a moment, looking uneasily back towards the nurses' station outside the small private room. The doctors had instructed that all visits should be brief and as calm as possible.

'Shut the door, would you? There are too many nosy parkers in this hospital. It's so noisy here, too. Day and night. Chatter, chatter, chatter.'

Cathy smiled faintly, closing the door, before settling on the chair next to Juliana's bed. 'It's a busy hospital.' She didn't mention that, at first, the medics had wanted to airlift Juliana to one in central London that specialised in neurological care. It wouldn't help her to know that she very nearly hadn't made it even into the ambulance, so extreme was her dehydration by the time Izzy and the twins found her.

Thankfully, she'd sustained barely any smoke inhalation; that would certainly have been fatal, the doctors had said at the scene. Juliana had suffered a stroke; a bad one. They still weren't certain how much brain damage had been inflicted; they were monitoring her closely.

Cathy blamed herself. After the trauma of seeing Rebecca dressed up as her daughter, Juliana had disappeared. *She should have followed her*. She'd meant to, only Izzy had gone first to check on her grandma. Then Cathy had been caught up in her worries about Eve — and absorbed in that momentous conversation with Jack . . .

Jack. He hadn't been in a much better state than Juliana. From highly respected doctor, he'd become a patient in his own hospital. Cathy pictured his white face and bloodshot eyes as he'd somehow managed to carry her out of the room where she'd fainted. Eloise's old bedroom, as it turned out.

How he had found her, Cathy would never know — and Jack hadn't been able to explain. *Something must have guided me to you,* was all he'd managed to croak, before the paramedics had carried him, too, into a second ambulance.

Both were blue-lighted all the way to the hospital in Plymouth, while Cathy was driven separately by a first responder. After a rapid triage on Roseland's front lawn, she'd been assessed as being in a serious but stable condition, while Juliana and Jack were both deemed category-one casualties: in a critical, life-threatening state. But over the last few days, with Cathy almost constantly at his bedside, Jack had thankfully turned a clear corner.

'I owe Jack my life,' Cathy said softly. 'So do his girls. He saved us, Juliana.' She knew Jack would never take any credit for it; indeed, that he'd blame himself for them having been in such a terrible situation in the first place. 'And yours. Even though he was in such a bad way, he was still trying to give you CPR when the ambulances arrived.'

'Piffle,' Juliana dismissed. 'He should have let me die there. At Roseland.' Her green eyes turned watery. 'Is it very badly burned?'

'They're still assessing the damage,' Cathy said evasively. In truth, it would take a miracle — and millions of pounds — to repair Roseland. It looked like a ghost of its former self. Cathy had been in bits when she'd visited it two days ago with Eve, Artie, Izzy and the twins.

Eve had been more stoic, saying she was *glad to see it gone*. To begin with, her vehement insistence that the world was *better off without aristocratic privilege* had made Cathy suspicious; the cause of the fire had still been under investigation, at that point. They'd each had their theories, but none could be proven beyond reasonable doubt.

Only this morning had Cathy discovered the truth — which had been so shocking, so far removed from her own theory, that she was still struggling to process it. There was at least some relief in finally being able to stop speculating, and start looking forward to the future. But Cathy knew they had all been scarred by this experience, and not just physically.

Staring down at the light bandages on her wrists, she wondered if the burns on her arms would ever vanish completely. She was wearing a long-sleeved dress today, not because she was ashamed of her scars, but because the sight of them upset Eve, and Cathy was determined that her daughter should avoid any more stress, still being in the early weeks of pregnancy.

The thought brought a faint smile now, as she recalled the look of bewilderment on Artie's handsome, boyish face, after Eve broke the news to him. He'd alternated between anguish over her biopsy, joy that it had proved negative and exhilaration that they were to be parents — swiftly followed by terror at the prospect.

Arthur always wore his heart on his sleeve, Cathy thought fondly. But he was a good man, and he would be an amazing father — and husband. Although, as

Eve had drily commented, none of them were in the mood to think about weddings right now.

Izzy had surprised everyone — including herself — by sobbing as she'd stood looking up at the charred shell of Roseland. 'I hated it. But I loved it, too,' she'd said tearfully, admitting that although she had come to Cornwall hell-bent on revenge, she now realised that it wasn't vengeance she'd been craving, but acceptance.

After all these years spent trapped in resentment, feeling on the outside of her family, the fear of losing them had finally helped her understand that the fault lay partly with her. Wary of more heartache, she'd been pushing everyone away, before they could reject her again.

Rose had given her an enormous hug, while Violet had remained sceptical at first. Having got in the habit of playing detective, she was still trying to figure out who started the fire. Izzy had to work hard to reassure her that she'd had nothing to do with it — that her apology to their dad had purely been her way of recognising the hard time she'd given him.

Cathy hadn't intervened, despite having already pieced together her own interpretation of how the morning had played out. She sensed that Rebecca's name was hovering on everyone else's lips, too. But no one had wanted to speak it aloud — not then, and not since.

'At least it's cool in here,' Juliana said, after a little while, as they each sat turning over their own thoughts. 'It's a blessed relief to be out of that incessant heat.'

'You were lying in the rose garden for quite some time,' Cathy said gently.

'One moment I was there, gathering roses for Eloise. Then in the next . . .'

'Rest now,' Cathy said. 'As you say, it's lovely and cool in here. Actually, I think the heatwave has finally broken. Rosie says it might rain.' She smiled. 'She's very intuitive.'

'Of course she is. Just like her mother. And me. I *knew* we'd be visited by evil this summer. Such extraordinary weather. It's unnatural. It boded no good. All the signs were there. Bad ones. Bad *omens*.'

'Bad luck, you mean? That's certainly what the police have concluded,' Cathy said carefully. 'An antiquated hot water heater in a first-floor bathroom. A barely perceptible gas leak. The ignition switch unfortunately timed to come on during the wedding rehearsal.'

'That was very careless of someone, then.' Juliana paused for a moment, thinking, before continuing: 'But I expect the film crew were disappointed to miss all the drama. If the fire had happened a day later, during the wedding . . .'

'Indeed. Well, they've left now. I don't think anyone was sorry to see them go. Except perhaps Violet. She'd been hoping to learn more about the filming process. Media generally.'

'Oh, it's fine. Izzy is teaching her.'

'Sorry?' Cathy stared at Juliana in surprise. It was true that Izzy had decided to stay in Cornwall, working freelance, at least until Eve and Arthur had their baby. But Cathy had no idea how Juliana might know that — or indeed that Izzy had promised to give her younger sister a crash course in journalism.

'Izzy visited me here earlier,' Juliana revealed, smiling gently. 'We made our peace. Well, she made hers with me.'

Cathy smiled, too. 'And you'll be home soon enough. Then you can lie in bed and watch TV to your heart's content.' She chuckled, knowing Juliana despised television. 'It's just a shame the movie at Roseland had to be abandoned. The crew never did reveal what it was.'

Juliana huffed. 'Miserable lot. No doubt that was their retaliation for not being able to capture the *great fire of Roseland* on film. I expect the police were disappointed, too.'

'Oh?' Cathy felt a ripple of anxiety, wondering exactly what Juliana knew.

'If the cameras had been running, they might have caught the culprit on film.'

'Culprit?' Cathy's heart began to thump. 'But the police report blamed wear and tear.'

'And what does that remind you of? Rosie's kayak, that's what. Everyone insisted that was my fault. That I forgot to have it serviced. Only we both know who was *really* responsible, don't we? We know who's to blame for Roseland's destruction, too. Oh, she may not have lit the match. But in every other possible way, she started the fire.'

63

Cathy didn't respond. She stood up and paced to the window — not the one facing into the brightly lit hospital corridor, but to the other side of the room, looking out over the car park. It wasn't the best view; no doubt Juliana would complain about that, at some point. For herself, it was a relief to see people; life going on around her. There had been too much death.

'You're talking about Rebecca, of course,' she said at last. There was no putting it off any longer; it was time to bite the bullet.

'I speak as I find, my dear.'

Cathy came to sit on the bed now. 'I suppose it's no secret now. We all know why she really came to Roseland, don't we? For revenge.' She gave Juliana a shrewd look. 'Did you know who she was all along?' There was no reply, and, after a moment, Cathy said sadly: 'For all her wickedness, Rebecca was treated badly, too.'

'By my husband, yes. There was no need for her to wreak her vengeance upon my entire family. My *home*.' Juliana's eyes flashed now. 'If Roseland meant that much to her, she could have had it, and welcome.'

'You don't mean that.'

'Don't I? I spent a lifetime there. Trapped in a loveless marriage. With a man who spent more time with his mistress than his wife. When he wasn't drinking himself into a stupor.'

Even though Cathy had suspected that Juliana

must have known — that she'd given her husband's diary to Rosie so that *everyone* would find out how she'd suffered — her admission still shocked and saddened her. 'Just to be clear. You were fully aware who Rebecca was.'

A pause, then Juliana said quietly, 'The whore's granddaughter. Yes, I knew.'

Cathy winced. 'That's rather harsh on Morwenna.' As soon as she spoke the name, she noticed Juliana clutch her sheets, her bony fingers twisting the material into knots.

'Is it? I *remember* her. That tells you everything, doesn't it? After all these years. The hundreds of people who've worked at Roseland. But I remember *her*. Morwenna. With her big, soulful eyes and coy smile. Always waltzing around the place with that pathetic sewing basket on her hip. Sashaying up the corridors. Deliberately showing off her figure. But, of course, we know her real attraction for Charles.'

Cathy frowned. 'Which was?'

'*Fertility*. She promised my vain fool of a husband that she could give him a son. The heir he always wanted.' Another pause. 'And I guess she did.'

'Gryffyn.' Cathy sighed, remembering Rosie telling her the full story. 'Yes, I suppose she did. But then Charles disowned him. Allowed Morwenna to struggle in poverty. Her granddaughter, too. *Rebecca*.'

'Despicable woman. Like grandmother, like granddaughter.'

Cathy shook her head. 'Look, I'm not defending her. But there's another side to this. Historical abuse. That's what a lawyer would argue. From a modern legal standpoint, of course, but it still carries weight. Morwenna was an employee. Charles took advantage of her. And Rebecca bore the legacy of it. She grew up clueless about her real identity. The heritage that was hers by rights. She must have felt —'

'I had absolutely no idea about her,' Juliana cut in fiercely. 'You must believe that.'

She struggled to sit up, but Cathy gently encouraged her to lie back on the pillows, stroking her silver hair to calm her agitation. 'I want to believe you. But you just said —'

'I meant, I had no idea back *then*. About Morwenna. When I was still a young, naïve bride. I didn't know there was any child. A *grandchild*. I give you my utmost word on that.' She traced the sign of the cross on her chest. 'I didn't like Morwenna, but I would never have let her suffer, had I known. Please, it's extremely important. You must believe me.'

Cathy still wasn't entirely sure whether or not she did, but she was worried about how worked-up Juliana was becoming. She glanced at the monitors by the bed — heartrate; blood pressure; oxygen levels — becoming fixated on them, noticing the blinking numbers spinning higher. 'Perhaps we should leave all this for now. You should be resting.'

'*No*,' Juliana said urgently. 'We never know what time is granted us. You know that, too, don't you? Every bit as well as I do. Jack certainly does.'

'Yes. He does know it,' Cathy said huskily. 'All too well.'

'We've had our differences, but he's a good man. I will pray for his recovery. I, on the other hand, have long since outstayed my welcome. Thankfully, there is only one remaining thing for me to do before I shuffle off this mortal coil. I want to clear my name. My *conscience*.'

'Clear your name? What on earth do you mean? And you're not going to die, Juliana. Not here. Not for a long time.' Cathy felt a prickle of tears. As cantankerous as Juliana was, she'd known her since she was a little girl and was extremely fond of her. Her distress was hard to watch; her self-recrimination and obvious guilt was baffling and concerning.

'And if I do, thank God I'm not headed to the same place as my despicable husband. To spend half my life with him is one thing. To be trapped with him for all eternity . . .' Juliana turned her head slightly, staring straight into Cathy's eyes now. 'My one consolation is that Charles is burning in hell. And had I known all those years ago what I know now, I would have locked him in his study, and set fire to it myself.'

64

'Juliana.' Cathy heard her own gasp of shock. Her mind was whirling. Everything she thought she'd understood from Rose this morning now flew out of the window. 'I have to ask you. Did you read Charles's journal before you gave it to Rosie?'

'Of course I did.' A roll of her eyes. 'How else would I have discovered my husband's filthy secret? Yes, fine. I admit it all. I knew who Rebecca was from the moment Jack brought her uninvited into my home. And I guessed why she'd come to Roseland.'

That only confirmed what Cathy had suspected, but even so, she felt desolate at the realisation that the last few days might have played out very differently, if only Juliana had shared what she'd known about Rebecca, rather than sneakily letting Rosie discover it by reading her husband's diary. She'd pulled her granddaughter's strings — probably Violet's too, by planting the idea of Rebecca wearing Eloise's dress.

'Oh, you can give me those looks,' Juliana said defensively. 'Yes, I could have told Jack. I probably should have. But I was *angry* with him. At least, to begin with. I couldn't bear to see him with that fake, greedy woman on his arm. Not after my darling Eloise.'

'But you know how faithful Jack has been to Ellie's memory. Probably to his own detriment. He always puts everyone before himself. He deserves happiness, too, doesn't he?'

Juliana let out a long sigh. 'Yes, and you have my blessing, my dear. I have no doubt you'll be very happy together.' Her thin eyebrows arched. 'In his ridiculous glass house.'

'Sorry?' Cathy blushed, surprised that Juliana was aware of feelings that had only dawned on Cathy a few days ago — downstairs in this very hospital, as she'd watched Jack take care of Eve, and admitted to herself that she had turned to him before her own husband.

Those feelings had grown slowly, creeping up on her. They'd also come as a complete surprise to Jack. As Cathy had sat for hours at his hospital bedside over this last week, he'd spent every brief, waking moment telling Cathy how astonished he was that she'd fallen in love with him, too . . . how happy it made him to know that she was waiting for him.

It gave him the will to fight, he'd told her, his injuries preventing him from wiping away his tears. Cathy hadn't even bothered to wipe away her own, as she'd promised she would wait for him for ever. She had never known love so deep, nor trust so strong.

She couldn't wait for Jack to come home — and to join their lives together, wherever they might choose to spend their *autumn years*. Perhaps not at the cottage; Cathy had promised that to Eve and Arthur, who were going to stay there and work remotely until their baby was born. Izzy was planning to stay there, too, saying she never wanted her grandchild to know a second's doubt about how much they were loved and wanted.

'I told you, my dear. I see everything.' Juliana sighed. 'Although I will admit to a few blind spots. As I said, I was furious with Jack. But I realise now that it was actually *myself* I hated.' A solitary tear rolled down her thin cheek. 'Because I'd let him get away with it.'

Cathy frowned. 'Jack? Get away with what?'

'No, not Jack. *Charles*. My monster of a husband. I let him turn his back on Eloise. Send my darling Isabella halfway round the world. And when I read his diary, I knew he was the worst kind of hypocrite. I also realised I'd been a fool. *He* made a fool of me.'

'Oh, Juliana.' Cathy took hold of Juliana's hand.

'I should have stopped him. I've spent decades regretting it. Only it was too late. Isabella was gone. Then Eloise died.' Juliana fell silent, but her lips continued to move, her eyes fixed on a point in the corner of the room, as though she was carrying on the conversation with an invisible presence. 'But she came back to help me. She showed me the truth.'

'She . . . sorry?'

'The *journal*,' Juliana said urgently. 'I would never have found it, but for Eloise. She whispered in my ear, and I followed her instructions to the letter. I went to Roseland. To her father's library. I found his diary, hidden in his desk.'

'And gave it to Rosie.' Cathy groaned. 'Then told her to take it back there after the rehearsal. Which she did. Leaving it where the fire could destroy the evidence, yes?'

Juliana lifted a hand, giving a feeble wave. 'A futile, symbolic gesture, I know. The lawyers will still find a way to challenge ownership of Roseland.'

'But Rosie doesn't know that, does she?' Cathy said sternly. 'She blames herself. For the fire. You being in hospital. Her dad being at death's door.' For a moment, she thought about leaving Juliana alone to grapple with her own conscience. But the old lady was right: no one knew how much time they had left. 'Rosie truly believed she was doing the right thing. Stopping Rebecca from getting her hands on Roseland. She thought that's what you wanted.'

Juliana's pale cheeks flushed. 'But I never told her to —'

'To be honest, I don't think she meant any of it to happen,' Cathy cut in, eager to defend Rose and explain what the distraught, terrified teenager had confessed to her this morning. 'When she saw Rebecca dressed up as her mum, she knew instantly who she was. She'd been reading her grandpa's diary for days. She guessed exactly what Rebecca was after.'

Juliana gave a nod of satisfaction, wiping her eyes. 'My clever girl.'

'Her sister, too. Violet was the one who discovered Rebecca's plan to sell off Roseland.'

'She'll be a reporter, one day,' Juliana said proudly. 'Or a detective.'

Cathy ignored the interruption, seeing nothing good in what happened next, picturing Rose in bits back at home, worrying about the consequences of her actions. 'When Violet told Rosie about Roseland being sold off, I think she had a rush of blood to the head. She actually only went upstairs to get the diary. To show Violet. You see, she'd left it in Eloise's old bedroom, where they got changed. Just while we had the wedding rehearsal.'

Juliana smiled beatifically. 'They looked wonderful, didn't they?'

'But when she saw her mum's old things . . . her clothes and jewellery. Rosie couldn't bear the thought of Rebecca taking them. Taking *Roseland*. And she blamed her grandpa.'

'She set fire to the portrait of him in his upstairs study,' Juliana whispered, as though worried someone might overhear her. 'I don't blame her. Not for a heartbeat. I did tell her so, but I need to be sure she believes it. That she doesn't blame herself. You'll make sure she doesn't, won't you? You'll do that for me, Cathy?'

'Of course.' Realising now what Juliana had meant by clearing her conscience, Cathy took hold her hand, squeezing it, eager to give her what little comfort she could.

'I feel utterly wretched about it all. I was wrong to give Rosie the diary. I see that now. And Eloise's ball-gown . . . to Violet.'

Cathy sighed. 'So that *was* your idea.'

'Do the police know?' Juliana looked alarmed. 'About there being a second fire?'

Cathy shook her head. 'No. So many paintings were destroyed.' Tactfully, she didn't mention the one of Eloise. 'The detectives are satisfied that the faulty boiler was the principal cause.' She frowned. 'I'm not sure Jack is convinced, though. He still blames Rebecca.'

Cathy hadn't contradicted Jack when he'd grasped her hand, apologising for his former fiancée — for the actions that had put Cathy's life at risk. He wasn't well enough for her to share Rosie's confession with him. She hadn't yet decided if she ever would. So many lives had already been blighted by Sir Charles Trelawney; Cathy didn't want Rosie's to be, too.

Nor Jack's. She didn't want to put him in the position of having to choose between protecting his daughter and telling the police the truth. Knowing

Jack's sense of honour, he would instinctively shield his daughter by taking the blame on himself, confessing to a crime he hadn't committed. 'I think we should let the investigation take its course, don't you?'

'Thank you, my dear.' Juliana released a deep sigh. 'Let sleeping dogs lie.'

'Yes. Especially now Rebecca is gone.'

'With half my grandchildren's inheritance,' Juliana pointed out tartly.

'Ah. You heard that, too, did you? While you were asleep.' Cathy arched her eyebrows, wondering if Juliana hadn't been unconscious for quite as long as she'd made out. 'Yes. It was actually Izzy's idea. They each gave up a portion of their own trust funds. Rebecca was cruel and deceitful, for sure. But a share of the Trelawney fortune is rightfully hers.'

'Izzy was disappointed. Not to give up the money, but that Rebecca took it.'

'Yes.' Cathy was no longer surprised that Juliana knew the ins and outs of everyone's feelings. 'She actually felt a strong connection with Rebecca. They had a lot in common, I suppose. Both Trelawney grandchildren. Both growing up away from their families. I suspect Izzy also hoped . . . Well, she never had the chance to know her mum, did she? I guess she was hoping that getting to know Rebecca might fill some of the void inside her. After all, Rebecca was her mum's niece. She looks a lot like Eloise, too, doesn't she?'

Juliana huffed. 'Enough to have caught Jack's eye, I suppose. When she took it upon herself to go swanning around Roseland. Just like her grandmother.' Green eyes sparked. 'Oh, I feel sorry for Morwenna. I do. I'm sure Rebecca has told you quite the tale about her.'

'There are two sides to every story,' Cathy acknowledged.

'Three, if you count my cheating husband's. But the truth is, Morwenna was only ever after his money. Charles made a bad choice. My sole consolation is that he was the architect of his own downfall. He lost Morwenna. He lost his son. He lost *me*.'

'And everyone has lost Roseland.'

'Indeed.' Juliana frowned. 'You know, I'm with Jack on that. I *do* blame Rebecca.'

Cathy shook her head. 'I still can't help feeling sorry for her. Money is no substitute for a loving family. Rebecca's triumph is a hollow one, as far as I'm concerned.'

'Victory means different things to different people,' Juliana said cryptically.

'I suppose. And Rebecca did show a flash of conscience in the end. At least she had the good grace to call the emergency services. Jack said Roseland's phone lines were burnt out. And we'd both lost our mobiles in all the commotion.'

'Don't tell Violet, will you?' Juliana whispered. 'She thinks her mum summoned them.'

Cathy paused for a moment, fighting sudden tears. 'You know, it wouldn't surprise me in the least. Ellie loved her daughters beyond life. And I loved her dearly. I still do.'

'As she did you,' Juliana said gently, reaching for Cathy's hand. 'Which is why she entrusted her girls to your care. And, for what it's worth, I think she'd very much approve of you marrying Jack.' Once again, Juliana's gaze drifted towards the corner of the room.

A half-smile played over her mouth. 'In fact, I know she would. Because she told me so. Just now.'

65

As Cathy shut the door behind her, Juliana closed her eyes, blocking out this tiresome world, opening herself to the bliss awaiting her in the next. 'All is well, my darling. Your girls are safe once more. Jack is happy. He has found his heart. Roseland is gone. It is done.'

Only one thing irked her: that she had to depart this life with her mortal body trapped in this ugly metal hospital bed, rather than cocooned in the tranquillity of her beautiful rose garden, as she'd long wished . . . and as she had thought was finally to be the case.

After seeing Rebecca standing beneath Eloise's portrait, it had reignited Juliana's deep yearning to be with her daughter. Dear Maggie had come to her aid, as she always had. She was far more use and less trouble than any husband, Juliana thought, remembering her friend's gentleness as she'd urged her away from the great hall, helping her to her beloved rose garden.

She'd been huffing and out of breath, Juliana recalled, realising now that Margaret must have come straight from the upstairs bathroom. The faulty old boiler that the police had determined as the main cause of the fire hadn't been used for years. It was tucked away in the old servants' quarters. Only someone very familiar with the house would have known about it; only someone with good reason to wish destruction on Roseland would have tampered with it.

'Bless you, Maggie,' Juliana whispered. 'You wanted to punish Charles, too. My husband deceived you as well. You always believed he was a good man. You stood at my side as we mourned him. You scattered earth on his coffin. You shed tears for his loss. Then tears of rage at his betrayal.'

Once again, she heard Margaret's low voice as she'd read aloud snippets of Charles's journal. She recalled her friend's indignation and fury as she came across the first poem dedicated to Morwenna, and realised the enormity of his infidelity — and its consequences.

'Morwenna moved to Newquay?' Margaret had scorned. She couldn't imagine anyone choosing to live anywhere other than quiet, pretty Polperro. Although it had become so much busier during the heatwave, she'd added — later complaining of it to dearest Cathy, when she came for afternoon tea at the farmhouse.

Juliana chuckled at the memory. Maggie had almost given the game away then, her careless slip in danger of exposing that Juliana knew full well who Rebecca was, and that she was already scheming how best to get rid of her. She'd had no idea that Maggie had secretly been plotting something infinitely more dramatic than her own plan to expose Rebecca.

She forgave her old friend, though — far more readily than she did herself. Juliana's guilt over having manipulated her granddaughters into taking revenge for her had been eating away in her heart. She was truly grateful that Cathy had allowed her to clear her conscience just now.

If she could undo it all, she would. She hated to think of Rosie blaming herself for the fire. But Juliana had been pushed to her limit, seeing Rebecca crawling around her granddaughters. She'd been desperate for them to know *her* side of the story. The *truth*. Deep down, of course, she'd known the girls would try to do something about it. After all, they were their mother's daughters . . .

'They've done you proud, Ellie,' she whispered, just as she had when she'd gathered the most perfect roses she could find, intending to ask Bob to drive her over to the church, as usual. Only, it wasn't to be. 'Stroke, be damned,' Juliana muttered, glaring at the machines by her bed. 'It was simply my time. My work here is done.'

She remembered her last glimpse of Roseland — feeling again the dull thud of her heart when a loud noise like a firework had made her jump. Turning back to look, she'd seen smoke curling upwards, a dirty smudge on the bright blue sky.

Stress and shock had convulsed in Juliana's brain, sending a bolt of pain through her skull as she'd watched the windows of her former home explode outwards in a glittering, gem-like shower; a macabre parody of wedding confetti.

Briefly, fear and sadness had been replaced by satisfaction: that Rebecca would never get her hands on Roseland now; that her husband's pride and joy — the precious symbol of his Trelawney ancestry — was gone. Yes, Juliana had tasted the sweetness of victory. *She had won.*

She had no recollection of falling. All she remembered was lying on her back, clutching the roses she'd gathered most particularly. The last thing she saw was the crow that had visited so many times during this impossibly long, hot summer, alerting her to danger. 'My little messenger,' she had welcomed it. The last thing she heard was a sweet voice calling to her.

At first, she was convinced that she'd already crossed over — that it was her darling Eloise, come to greet her. Only it was Rosie, followed by Violet . . . then Isabella. Her three precious granddaughters, determined to pull her back from the edge, not realising she was ready to fly.

* * *

Her breath came slower now. Juliana felt her heart still, and she yielded willingly to a warm feeling of peace. It washed over her, like the gentle, rolling waves on Talland Beach. The twins had always adored playing there. *Five more minutes*, they would beg. She was so happy that they'd visited her this morning — dear, stubborn Isabella, too. Her first grandchild, and the most like her.

Juliana had shed no tears, nor said any goodbyes; she would see them again. On the beach, digging their toes into the silky sand. In her rose garden, as her girls gathered fresh blooms each June in remembrance . . . then at the churchyard, when they laid them by their mother's grave, and by hers at its side.

Jack and Cathy, too. Sweet Eve and her lovely Arthur, along with their new, precious baby. The next generation. Whenever and wherever they all looked for her, Juliana would be there.

Epilogue

Three weeks later

The roses smelled divine. Cathy removed the old ones, setting them carefully aside. Then she arranged fresh stems in the crystal urn, before reaching for a second bouquet.

'Sleep well, dear friends,' she whispered, reaching out to stroke each of the honey-coloured headstones in turn.

'Rest in peace, Juliana,' Jack said softly, kneeling at Cathy's side, head bowed. Then he turned towards the other grave, resting one hand on the headstone, saying nothing.

'I can leave you alone for a few minutes, if you like?'

Jack shook his head. 'No, please stay. I'm OK. I just haven't been here in so long. The twins come here, sometimes. And Izzy came this morning. But I . . .'

Cathy allowed the pause to stretch into comfortable silence, moving to sit on the bench to stare beyond the familiar tower of Talland Church towards the sea. It was calmer today; there was hardly a breath of wind, even this high up. But it was cooler, and after the intense heat of the last few weeks, the freshness was welcome.

Closing her eyes, she breathed in the sweet smell of lavender and thyme, savouring the delicate fragrance, letting her body relax.

'A penny for them,' Jack said, watching her.

Cathy smiled, then laughed as her stomach growled

hungrily. 'The twins are making dinner tonight, aren't they?'

Straightening up, Jack came to sit next to her. 'Arthur's giving them their very first cookery lesson. Evie's supervising.' He chuckled. 'From the sofa, with her feet up, I expect.'

'Good. I should hope so, too.'

'And no doubt Izzy will spend the evening laughing at them all.'

'I love her laugh. It reminds me very much of someone I used to know.'

They both turned to look at Eloise's headstone, almost covered in moss and ivy now, as though nature was slowly pulling a blanket over it. Straining all her senses, Cathy tried once again to tune in with her friend's thoughts. So intense was her concentration, she jumped as a crow flew down to settle on top of the grave.

'Oi! Shoo!'

'I know one magpie is said to be bad luck,' Jack said. 'But what's the deal with crows?'

'I don't believe in luck,' Cathy said firmly. 'Nor omens. Or talismans. Not anymore.'

Jack took hold of her hand. 'What *do* you believe in, then?'

Cathy thought for a moment. 'You. Me. Our kids. Our future.'

'Your book?' His eyebrows arched. 'You've been wanting to write one for ever. I know the kids have kept you busy, but —'

'As will our grandkids.'

'Yes, but the beauty of them is that we can hand them back.' Jack grinned, then said more seriously, 'This is *your* time now, darling. Enjoy it. Every moment.' He turned to stare across the churchyard, his handsome face softening, looking far younger than his almost sixty years in the mellow afternoon light. 'We never know how many more we're granted.'

Cathy linked her fingers through his, loving the slight roughness of his palms, from where he'd been gardening for hours each day — part of his recuperation after the fire. Goldeneye's clifftop grounds had never looked better; nor had her own cottage garden. Jack took care of them both. Even the potholes on Cathy's drive had been filled.

After discussion with her and the twins, Jack had decided to reduce his hospital hours to part time, saying he wanted to work less, and live more. The London house would be sold; Chris had remained in Dubai. It was to be an amicable divorce; her children hadn't even been surprised when Cathy had told them.

'You're right, Jack.' She sighed. 'We never know what's around the corner. We think we want one thing, then it turns out we wanted something quite different all along. As Juliana once said: happiness is a choice. And so is love. We can't wait for luck or fate to decide for us. We have to fight for what we want. Rebecca was right about that much, at least.'

Jack groaned. 'Please, never speak that woman's name again. But I couldn't agree with you more, my love. And I choose you. Today, tomorrow and for all the days yet to come.'

* * *

The church bells tolled, low and mournful. A sudden breeze picked up, rippling through the scrubby grass, and whispering through the tall yew trees guarding the graveyard. Startled, the crow squawked and took to the air. Flitting dartlike down the steep hill towards the cliff edge, it stayed low to the ground, disappearing at last over the craggy ridge, into the silver-blue of the bay beyond.

Acknowledgements

It's exactly ten years since my first novel, *Eloise*, was published — the date burned on my memory because it coincided with the birth of my first grandchild Ivy, who is now a beautiful little girl. *Eloise*, like *Roseland*, was set in Cornwall, the place which captured my heart twenty-five years ago, and still does. So my first acknowledgment is the debt I owe to this stunning land of legend and mystery, treasured so deeply by all lovers of Cornwall. And I want to thank the Duchy's people for the heroic efforts they've made to keep a welcome on the beaches and the cliff paths since Covid. The pandemic and its aftermath have been a difficult time, and Cornwall's suffered economically and spiritually; but it's still there, as ever offering its enchanting beauty to everyone who visits.

My thanks also to my agent, Luigi Bonomi, for his guidance, friendship and patience over the last decade. To my editor, Rosanna Forte, for her warm understanding, and to Cath Burke, who's looked after me from the beginning of my Cornish storytelling. Everyone at Sphere has been so enabling, and I'd like to thank Kirsteen Astor, who has made the necessary publicity a writer has to endure so easy and unthreatening. I'm grateful also to Sam Bulos for her talented support and thoughts.

Finally, thanks to you, dear readers, who've enjoyed reading about the Trelawney family, and discovering what happened to Eloise's loved ones. I so much hope you will enjoy *Roseland*.

Other titles published by Ulverscroft:

HAPPINESS

Danielle Steel

After an unhappy childhood and two failed marriages, bestselling thriller author Sabrina Brooks has finally found the life she's always craved. She's discovered that her writing, her close circle of friends, and her beautiful home in the Massachusetts Berkshire Mountains with her two beloved dogs are all that she needs to be happy and at peace.

Her perfect life is suddenly disrupted when she receives a mysterious letter informing her that she is now the sole heir to her recently deceased uncle's title and manor house in England. Determined to sell it, Sabrina is persuaded to cross the Atlantic and see the property for herself.

As she learns more about her family history, she starts to fall in love with the breathtaking beauty of the historic manor and its gardens — plus the devastatingly handsome lawyer who acts as her tour guide . . .